Special Deliveries

Her Gift,
His Baby

BEVERLY
LONG

CAROL
MARINELLI

BRENDA
HARLEN

Special
Deliveries
COLLECTION

August 2016

September 2016

October 2016

November 2016

December 2016

January 2017

Special Deliveries

Her Gift,
His Baby

BEVERLY
LONG

CAROL
MARINELLI

BRENDA
HARLEN

MILLS & BOON

First Published in Great Britain 2016
By Mills & Boon, an imprint of HarperCollins*Publishers*
1 London Bridge Street, London, SE1 9GF

HER GIFT, HIS BABY © 2016 Harlequin Books S.A.

Secrets of a Career Girl © 2013 Carol Marinelli
For the Baby's Sake © 2013 Beverly Long
A Very Special Delivery © 2013 Brenda Harlen

ISBN: **978-0-263-92717-7**

24-1116

Harlequin (UK) Limited's policy is to use papers that are natural, renewable and recyclable products and made from wood grown in sustainable forests. The logging and manufacturing processes conform to the legal environmental regulations of the country of origin.

Printed and bound in Spain
by CPI, Barcelona

SECRETS OF A
CAREER GIRL

CAROL MARINELLI

Carol Marinelli recently filled in a form asking for her job title. Thrilled to be able to put down her answer, she put 'writer'. Then it asked what Carol did for relaxation and she put down the truth—'writing'. The third question asked for her hobbies. Well, not wanting to look obsessed, she crossed her fingers and answered 'swimming'— but given that the chlorine in the pool does terrible things to her highlights, I'm sure you can guess the real answer!

PROLOGUE

THE PATIENTS LIKED her, though.

Emergency Consultant Ethan Lewis glanced up as an elderly lady in a wheelchair, with a younger woman pushing her, approached the nurses' station and asked if Penny Masters was working today. The lady in the wheelchair still had her wristband on and was holding a bag of discharge medications and a tin of chocolates.

'I think she's on her lunch break,' answered Lisa, the nurse unit manager. 'I'll just buzz around and find out.'

'No, don't disturb her. Mum just wanted to give her these to say thank you—she really was marvellous that day when Mum was brought in.'

'It's no problem,' Lisa said, picking up a phone. 'I think she's in her office.'

Yes, Ethan thought to himself. Unlike everybody else, who took their lunch in the staffroom, Penny would be holed away in her office, catching up with work. He'd been trying to have a word with her all day—a casual word, to ask a favour—but, as Ethan was starting to discover, there was no such thing as a casual word with Penny.

Ethan had been working in the emergency department of the Peninsula Hospital for more than three months now. It was a busy bayside hospital that serviced some of Melbourne's outer suburbs. The emergency department was, for the most part, a friendly one, which suited Ethan's laid-back ways.

For the most part.

He watched as Penny walked over. Immaculate as ever, petite and slender, her very straight blonde hair was tied back neatly and she was wearing a three-quarter-sleeve navy wraparound dress and smart low-heeled shoes. The female equivalent of a business suit perhaps, which was rather unusual in this place—most of the other staff, Ethan included, preferred the comfort and ease of wearing scrubs. Penny, though, dressed smartly at all times and gloved and gowned up for everything.

'Mrs Adams, how lovely to see you looking so well.' Ethan watched as she approached her ex-patient. Without being told, Penny knew her name. Though the greeting was friendly, it was a very professional smile that Penny gave and there was no tactile embrace. Penny stood there and enquired how Mrs Adams was doing with more than mere polite interest, because even though they had clearly just left the ward, the daughter had a few questions about her mother's medication and Penny went through the medication bag and easily answered all of them.

'Thank you so much for explaining,' Mrs Adams's daughter said. 'I didn't like to keep asking the nurse when I didn't understand.'

'You *must* keep asking.'

Yes, the patients loved Penny.

They didn't mind in the least that she was meticulous, thorough and incredibly inflexible in her treatment plans.

It was the staff that struggled—if Penny wanted observations every fifteen minutes, she accepted no excuses if they weren't done. If Penny ordered analgesia, it didn't matter to her that there might be a line-up at the drug trolley, or that there was no one available to check the dose, because her patient needed it now.

Penny walked Mrs Adams and her daughter to the exit, and stood talking for another couple of moments there. As she walked back through the department, Jasmine, a nurse who also happened to be Penny's sister, called her over to the nurses' station.

'What did you get?' Jasmine asked.

Penny glanced down at the tin she was holding. 'Chocolate macadamias,' she said, peeling off the Cellophane. 'I'll leave them here for everyone to help themselves.'

She wasn't even that friendly towards her sister, Ethan thought as Penny put down the chocolates on the bench and went to go. He would never have picked Penny and Jasmine as sisters—it had had to be pointed out to him.

Jasmine was dark and curvy, Penny blonde and very slim.

Jasmine smiled and was friendly, whereas Penny was much more guarded and standoffish. Ethan refused to play by her silent, stay-back rules and he called her as she went to head off. 'Can I have a quick word, Penny?'

'I'm actually at lunch,' Penny said.

The very slow burning Taurus within Ethan stirred a little then—his hazel eyes flashed and, had there been horns hidden under his thick black hair, Penny would now be seeing her first glimpse of them. It took a lot to rile Ethan, but Penny was starting to. Ethan had always known that there might be a problem when he had taken this job—two of the department's senior registrars had also applied for the consultant position.

Jasmine's new husband Jed was one of them.

Penny the other.

Knowing the stiff competition, Ethan had been somewhat taken aback when he had been offered the role. He had since learnt that Jed had taken a job in a city hospital, but Penny was still here and, yes, it was awkward. Ethan often reminded himself that her ego might be a touch fragile and that it might take a little while for her to accept him in the role that she had applied for.

Well, it was time that Penny did accept who was boss and, for the first time, Ethan pulled rank as she went to head back to her lunch.

'That's fine.' He looked into her cool blue eyes. 'But when you're finished, can you make sure that you come and find me? I need to speak with you.'

She hesitated for just a second before answering. 'Regarding what?'

No, there was no such thing as a casual word with Penny. 'I'm on call next weekend,' Ethan said. 'Is there any chance that you could cover me for a few hours on Sunday afternoon? I'm hoping to go to a football match with my cousin—' He was about to explain further, but before he could, Penny interrupted him.

'I've already got plans.'

She didn't add 'sorry'.

Penny never did.

As she turned to go Ethan's jaw clamped down and, rarely for him, his temper was rising. He was tempted to tap her on the shoulder and tell her that this was more than some idle request because his team was playing that weekend. His cousin was actually on the waiting list for a heart transplant.

No, he wouldn't waste the sympathy card on her and with good reason—Ethan actually smiled a twisted smile as Penny walked off.

'Did you use it?' Phil would ask when Ethan rang him tonight.

'*Nope*.'

'Good,' Phil would say. 'Save it for women you fancy.'

Yes, it was a black game, but one that got Phil through and gave them both a few laughs.

He certainly wouldn't be using the sympathy card on Penny.

'We're going to the airport to see Mum off on Sunday.' Jasmine had jumped down from her stool to help herself to the chocolate nuts and offered an explanation where her sister had offered none. She was trying to smooth things over, Ethan guessed, for her socially awkward sister. Except Penny wasn't awkward, Ethan decided—she simply wasn't the least bit sociable. 'It's been planned for ages.'

'It's not a problem.' Ethan got back to his notes as Jasmine, taking another handful of the chocolate nuts, headed off, but as he reached to take a handful himself Ethan realised that Penny hadn't even taken one.

She could use the sugar, Ethan thought darkly.

'You could try asking Gordon,' Lisa suggested when it was just the two of them, because Ethan had told her while chatting a few days ago about his cousin, and, no, he hadn't been using the sympathy card with Lisa!

'I'll see,' Ethan said. Gordon had three sons and another baby on the way. 'Though he probably needs his weekend with his family, as does Penny.' He couldn't keep the tart edge from his voice as he mentioned her name.

'You don't know, do you?' Lisa was trying to sort out the nursing roster but she too had seen the frosty exchange between Penny and Ethan, and though she could see both sides, Lisa understood both sides too. 'Jasmine and Penny's mum was brought in a few months ago in full cardiac arrest. They were both on duty at the time.'

Ethan grimaced. To anyone who worked in Emergency, dealing with someone you knew, especially a family member, was the worst-case scenario. 'Did you manage to keep it from them?'

'Hardly! Well, we kept it from Jasmine while the resuscitation was happening so at least she found out rather more kindly than Penny did.' Lisa put down her pen and told Ethan what had happened that day.

'Penny was just pulling on her gown when the paramedics wheeled her mother in,' Lisa said. 'You know how she gowns up all the time.' Lisa rolled her eyes.

'Penny takes up half of the laundry budget on gowns alone. Anyway, you know how she usually starts snapping out orders and things? Well, I knew that there was something wrong because she just stood there frozen. She asked for Jed—he was the other registrar on that day—but he was stuck with another patient. Penny told me that the patient was her mum and then just snapped out of it and got on with the resuscitation, just as if it were any other patient. And she kept going until we got Mr Dean here to take over. She did tell me not to let Jasmine in, though.'

Lisa gave a wry smile. 'I didn't even know, till that point, that Penny and Jasmine were sisters. Penny likes to keep her personal life well away from work.'

'I had noticed.'

'The cruise is a huge thing for their mother. Do you see now why Penny couldn't swap?'

'I do,' Ethan said, and got back to his notes. But that was the problem exactly—he'd never have heard it from Penny herself.

And then he stopped writing, took another handful of chocolate nuts as it dawned on him...

Like him, Penny had refused to play the sympathy card.

CHAPTER ONE

'HAVE YOU THOUGHT about letting a few people at work know what's going on?'

Penny closed her eyes at her sister's suggestion and didn't respond. The very last thing Penny wanted was the people at work to know that she was going through IVF.

Again.

It was bad enough for the intensely private Penny that her mum and sister knew but, given that Penny was seriously petrified of needles, she'd had no choice but to confide in Jasmine, who would be giving Penny her evening injections soon.

While she couldn't get through it without Jasmine's practical help, there were times when Penny wished that she had never let on that she was trying for a baby.

Yes, her family had been wonderfully supportive but sometimes Penny didn't want to talk about it. She didn't want to hear that they were keeping their fingers crossed for her, didn't always want to give the required permanent updates and, more than anything, she had hated the sympathy when it hadn't worked out the first time. Naturally they had tried to comfort her and understand what they could not—they had both had babies.

The two sisters were walking along the beach close to where they both lived. Penny lived in one of the smart townhouses that had gone up a couple of years ago and took in the glittering bay views. Jasmine lived a little further along the beach with her new husband Jed and her toddler son Simon, who was from Jasmine's first marriage. The newlyweds were busily house hunting and trying to find somewhere suitable between the city, where Jed now worked, and the Peninsula Hospital.

Now, though, the sisters lived close by and, having waved their mother off from Melbourne airport for her long-awaited overseas trip, they walked along the beach with Simon, enjoying the last hour of sunlight.

'It might be a good idea to let a couple of people in on what you're going through,' Jasmine pushed, because she wanted Penny to have the support Jasmine felt that she needed, especially as Penny was going through this all alone.

'Even my own friends don't really understand,' Penny said. 'Coral thinks I'm being selfish, and Bianca, though she says I should go for it if that's what I want…' Her voice trailed off. 'If I can't talk about it with my own friends, what's it going to be like at work?'

'Lisa especially would be really good.'

'Lisa is a nurse unit manager,' Penny broke in. 'I'm not a nurse.'

'She runs the place, though,' Jasmine said. 'She'd be able to look out for you a little bit.'

'I don't need looking out for.'

Jasmine wasn't so sure. She could see that the treatment was taking its toll on her sister, not that Penny would appreciate her observations.

Jasmine wanted so badly to help her sister. They had never really been close but Penny had always looked out for her—several years older, Penny had shielded her from the worst of their parents' rows and their mother's upset when their father had finally left. It had been the same when their mother had been brought into Emergency—Penny had made sure Jasmine hadn't found out about their mother in the same way that she had.

'I know this is all a bit new to you, Jasmine,' Penny said. 'But I've been living with this for years. I've known for ages that I had fertility problems.'

'How long did you and Vince try for?'

Penny heard the tentativeness in Jasmine's question. They were both working on their relationship, but there were still areas between them that were rarely, if ever, discussed.

'Two years,' Penny finally answered.

One year of serious trying and then a year of endless tests and consultations and a relationship that hadn't been able to take the strain. 'We didn't just break up over that, though,' Penny admitted. 'But it certainly didn't help. I can tell you this much.' She gave a tight smile. 'We'd never have survived IVF. It doesn't exactly bring out the best in you.'

'How are you feeling this time?' Jasmine asked.

'Terrible,' Penny admitted. 'I'm getting hot flashes.'

'Are you serious?'

'I'm completely serious. I'd forgotten that part—you

know, at the time you think that you will never forget, but you actually do.'

Jasmine opened her mouth to agree with her sister and then closed it again as Penny turned around.

Penny knew that Jasmine had been about to admit to the same thing, but for very different reasons—Jasmine's breasts were noticeably larger and she'd had nothing to eat at the airport and had then screwed up her nose when Penny had suggested they get some takeaway for dinner, choosing instead a slow walk on the beach.

Jasmine was pregnant.

Penny just knew.

'I don't need the whole department watching me for signs of a baby bump,' Penny said, though it was the opposite for Penny with her sister. She had been trying so hard to ignore the signs in Jasmine, but more and more it was becoming evident and Penny wished she would just come out and tell her now. 'Or gossiping,' Penny added.

'It wouldn't be like that.'

'Of course it would,' Penny snapped. 'And, of course, they'll all have an opinion on whether I should be doing this, given that I haven't got a partner.' She gave an exasperated sigh. It wasn't a decision she was taking lightly, not in the least. At thirty-four there was no sign of Mr Right on the horizon and with her fertility issues, even if he did come along, it was going to be a struggle to get pregnant.

After many long conversations with the fertility consultant, more and more Penny felt as if time was running out. 'If there's good news at the end of this, I'll tell people, but they don't need to know that I'm trying.'

'But the treatment is so intense. If people only knew...'

Penny didn't let her finish. 'You don't walk into the staffroom and tell them that you've come off the pill and had sex with Jed last night.' When Jasmine laughed, Penny carried on. 'No, you feed the sharks when you're good and ready.' Penny paused, waiting for her sister to open up to her, because even if Penny snapped and snarled a bit she wasn't a shark, but Jasmine changed the subject.

'I can't believe that Mum has finally made it to her cruise.' Jasmine smiled. 'Well, she's made it to her flight.'

'And she'll make it to her cruise.' Penny was firm.

'What if something happens while she's stuck in the middle of the ocean?'

'There's a medical team,' Penny said, but of course that didn't reassure her sister. 'Jasmine, are you going to spend the next month worrying about things that might happen and every imagined scenario while Mum is no doubt having the absolute time of her life?'

'I guess,' Jasmine conceded. 'Though I really did think we were going to lose her.'

'We didn't, though,' Penny broke in.

While Louise Masters's heart attack and emergency admission had been a most difficult time, from there good things had sprung—an urgent reminder for all concerned that you should live your life to the full.

Which was why their mother would soon be sailing

around the Mediterranean, why Jasmine had followed her heart and opened up to Penny's then fellow senior registrar Jed, and why Penny was, at this moment, walking along the beach with a face that was bright red and breaking out into a sweat as she experienced yet another wretched hot flash. Not that Jasmine noticed; her mind had moved on to other things.

'What do you think of Ethan?' Jasmine asked for Penny's thoughts on the new consultant, but Penny didn't answer; instead, she suggested a walk in the shallows, much to little Simon's delight. Both holding his hands, they lifted him up between them, swung him over the water, and finally Penny felt herself calm, the heat fading from her face, her racing heart slowing, and then Jasmine asked her again what she thought of Ethan.

'He thinks that he's God's gift.'

'So do a few other people,' Jasmine pointed out, because since Ethan had arrived, a couple of hearts had already been broken. 'He is funny, though.' Jasmine grinned.

'I don't think he's funny at all,' Penny said, but then again she didn't sit in the little huddles at the nurses' station, neither did she wait for the latest breaking news to be announced in the staffroom. Penny loathed gossip and refused to partake in it, though, given it was Jasmine, there was one thing she did divulge. 'He seems to think that he got the job over me.' Penny gave a little smirk. 'He has no idea that I declined to take it.'

'He doesn't know?'

'God, no!' Penny said. 'I would assume he knows that Jed turned it down to take the position at Melbourne

Central, but it would be a bit much for him to know that he was actually the third choice.'

'Wouldn't Mr Dean have told him?'

'Mr Dean wouldn't discuss the other applicants with him—you know what he's like.' Penny rolled her eyes. Mr Dean had put her through the wringer over the years—he was incredibly chauvinistic and had been reluctant to promote Penny to senior registrar. Penny was quite sure it was because she was a woman—she'd heard Mr Dean comment a few times how you trained women up only for them to get pregnant. Still, Penny had long since proven herself and, though Ethan might think otherwise, the consultant's position had been Penny's. She had chosen not to take it, deciding it would be too much on top of going through IVF, and more and more she was glad she had made that decision.

'Ethan's gorgeous.' Jasmine nudged her. 'He's so sexy.'

'Jasmine!'

'What? Just because I'm married I'm not supposed to notice just how stunning he is?'

Penny conceded with a shrug. Yes, Ethan Lewis was stunning. He had thick silky black hair that seemed always to be just a day away from needing a good cut and had unusual hazel eyes. He was very tall and broad shouldered and so naturally he stood out. He was also a bit chauvinistic, not that the women seemed to mind.

'The trouble with Ethan,' Penny said, 'is that he knows how gorgeous he is and he uses it unwisely. Someone should stamp "not the settling-down type" on his forehead. It might have helped warn the nurse in CCU who keeps coming down to the department to try and speak to him, and also that physiotherapist.'

Penny frowned as she tried to think of the young woman's name, but gave up. 'And that's just two that I've seen and heard about, and given that I'm the last person to know anything, I'm quite sure there must be a few more.'

'Well, at least he doesn't pretend he's interested in anything more serious,' Jasmine said. 'I was talking to him the other day and I apologised for going on too much about Simon and he just laughed and said he enjoyed hearing it, as it's the closest he'll ever get to having one of his own. He's lovely,' Jasmine sighed. 'You should have a fling with him.'

Jasmine would so love to see her very uptight sister unbend just a little. 'She should, shouldn't she, Simon?' Jasmine said as she picked up her little boy, who was finally starting to tire.

'Don't bring Simon into this.' Penny smiled fondly at her nephew. 'And don't you listen to your mother.'

Simon smiled back. He adored his aunt and he held out his hands for Penny to hold him, which she did. 'You're the cause of all this,' Penny teased, because seeing her sister pregnant and later as a mum had stirred already jumbled feelings in Penny and she desperately wanted a baby of her own.

'You tell Aunty Penny that she *should* listen to me and have some fun before she's ankle deep in nappies and exhausted from lack of sleep.' Jasmine smiled at her son and then turned to her sister. 'Just one last wild fling before you get pregnant!'

'I've never had a wild fling in my life and I'm certainly not about to start now. You've never had IVF, have you?' Penny's voice was wry. 'Believe me, Ethan Lewis and sex and wild flings are the very last thing on my mind right now.' Penny did suddenly laugh, though. 'Could you imagine if I did and then twelve weeks later announced that I'm pregnant?'

'Oh, I would just love to see that.' Jasmine was laughing too at the thought of the confirmed bachelor Ethan Lewis thinking for a moment that he was about to become a father. 'It would kill him!'

CHAPTER TWO

'WHERE THE HELL IS X-ray?' Penny snapped at Jasmine the next afternoon, just as she would to anyone—they weren't sisters here and no feelings were spared.

They were struggling to stabilise a patient in congestive heart failure who wasn't responding to the usual treatment regimes. John Douglas had presented to the department struggling to breathe, his heart beating dangerously fast and his lungs overloaded with fluid. It was a common emergency that Penny was more than used to dealing with, but what was compounding the problem was that John was also a renal patient and undergoing regular dialysis at a major city hospital so Penny was trying to sort out the far higher drug doses that were needed in his case.

'I'm just going to lean you forward, John,' Penny said, and listened again to her patient's chest. The oxygen saturation machine was bleeping its alarm. Vanessa, another nurse, returned with John's blood-gas results and it was confirmed to Penny that things were really grim. She had already paged the medics to come down urgently and was now considering putting out a crash call, because even though he hadn't gone into cardiac arrest he was very close.

'Give him another forty milligrams,' Penny called out to Jasmine, though she wasn't cross when Jasmine hesitated. 'He's a renal patient,' Penny explained, 'so he'll need massive doses of diuretics.'

Still, Penny was concerned about the amount of medication she was having to give and was carefully checking the drug guide, wishing the medics would hurry up and get there. She had just decided to put out a crash call when Ethan approached.

'Problem?' Ethan asked, and Penny quickly brought him up to speed.

'He's not responding,' Penny said. 'And neither are the medics to their fast page. I'm going to call the crash team.'

'Hold off for just a moment.' Ethan scanned the drug sheet to see what had been given. He had just come from working a rotation in the major renal unit in a city hospital, so he was familiar with the drug doses required in a case like this and he quickly examined the patient. 'He needs a large bolus.'

Ethan saw Penny's face go bright red as he took over the patient's care. 'Penny, where I worked before…' He didn't really have time to explain things and he wasn't about to compromise patient care by pandering to Penny's fragile ego—she was spitting with rage, Ethan could see it. In fact, he was tempted to lick his finger and put it onto her flaming cheek just so that he could hear the hiss.

'Go ahead,' came Penny's curt response, and she

thrust the patient notes into his hands and walked off quickly.

'Have we ordered a portable chest X-ray?' he asked Jasmine.

'It's supposed to be on its way,' Jasmine answered.

'You're going to be okay, sir.' Ethan listened to his chest and considered calling the crash team himself.

He could see Jasmine was blushing too at her sister's little outburst and was sorely tempted to ask Jasmine just what the hell her sister's problem was, though of course Ethan knew. Well, he wasn't just going to stand back, and if Penny didn't like it, she'd better start getting used to it. Penny Masters was an absolute… Ethan kept the word in his head as he saw the fluid start to gush into the catheter bag. The patient's oxygen saturations started to rise slowly. He was just ordering some more morphine when the radiographer arrived for the chest X-ray, along with a much calmer-looking Penny.

'Thanks for that,' she said, completely unable to look him in the eye. She had fled to her office, which had a small sink in it, and splashed her face with cold water and run her wrists under the tap. Penny would never have left the patient had Ethan not been there, but she had never had a hot flash so severe. She knew that Ethan was less than impressed, especially when, without a further word, he stalked off.

'Are you okay?' Jasmine checked as they waited outside while the patient was being X-rayed, Vanessa staying in with him.

'Of course I'm not.' Rarely for Penny, she was close

to tears. 'He thought I was cross at him for making suggestions and that I just walked off in a temper.'

He'd thought exactly that, Jasmine knew. She had seen the roll of his tongue in his cheek and the less than impressed rise of Ethan's brows. 'Penny, if people just knew—'

'What?' Penny interrupted. 'Do you really think that I'm going to explain to him that I just had a hot flash?'

Penny was mortified—absolutely and completely mortified. The down-regulation medication to stop her own cycle was in full effect, and she had a splitting headache as well, another of the side effects. The headache she could deal with, but for a woman who was usually so able to keep things in check, the rip of heat that had seared through her face and the rapid flutter of her heart in her chest had felt appalling. She had hardly been able to breathe in there but she had absolutely no intention of telling Ethan Lewis why. 'Do you really think that Neanderthal would be understanding?'

'Neanderthal?' Jasmine grinned in delight at her sister's choice of word.

'Just leave it,' Penny snapped.

Ethan didn't leave it, though.

Before heading for home, he passed her office, where Penny sat busily writing up her notes. She was sitting very straight, like some schoolmarm, Ethan thought as he knocked a couple of times on her open door.

In fact, it was rather like walking into the headmistress's office as those cold blue eyes lifted to his and gave him a very stern stare.

'What time are you on till?' Ethan asked.

'Midnight,' Penny answered—she knew that he hadn't just popped in for a chat.

'How is Mr Douglas doing now?'

'He's a lot better, but the medics are still stabilising him and then he'll be transferred so he can have his dialysis.' She wished he would just leave; she really didn't want to discuss what had taken place. 'Thank you for your help with him.'

'It didn't feel very welcome.' Ethan waited a moment, but Penny said nothing, just turned her attention back to her notes and, no, he would not just leave it. 'What the hell happened back there, Penny?'

'I don't know what you're talking about.'

'I think that you do,' came Ethan's swift retort. 'If there is an issue then it's time that we discussed it.'

'There is no issue.'

Ethan begged to differ. She was the most difficult woman that he had ever met and he'd met a lot of women! Yes, she was a fantastic doctor. Ethan had no qualms there, and in fact he was quietly surprised, having seen her work, that she hadn't been given the consultant's position. He could well understand how angry she must be, but somehow they had to work together and if she was going to storm off every time he stepped in on a consultation, something had to be said. 'We have to work together, Penny.'

'I'm aware of that.'

'Which means that at times we'll disagree.'

'I'm aware of that too.' Her face was starting to burn again, but from embarrassment this time. 'Look, thank you for stepping in with Mr Douglas, it was much appreciated. I'm not as familiar as I would like to be with renal patients so I'm very pleased that you were there. We do seem to have our wires crossed, though.' She gave tight smile. 'I wasn't cross or upset.' She saw his incredulous look.

'You walked off.'

Penny said nothing, just stared at this huge, very masculine man. She didn't know how to tell him and she didn't really want to try, except her silence invited him to continue speaking.

'I wasn't trying to take over. You seem to have formed an opinion that I'm—'

'Formed an opinion?' Penny stopped him right there. 'I'm actually a bit busy in my life right now. I haven't had time to think, let alone form an opinion of you.'

His lips twitched almost into a smile at her not-too-subtle putdown. 'Oh, but I think that you have,' Ethan said, and there and then he took the gloves off. He'd tried niceness, he'd tried politeness, he'd accepted that the situation might be a little difficult for her, but at the end of the day Penny needed to get over it and accept that he had been given the job. 'Do you know what, Penny? I'm starting to form an opinion of you, and your behaviour this afternoon is leading me to think it might be the right one.'

'Whatever!' Penny hadn't got this far in her career on charm. To do her job you needed to be tough and she certainly wasn't there to make friends. 'You carry right on forming your opinion of me and, while you do, I'll get back to my patients.' Penny stood. 'Or is there anything else you want to discuss?'

'Nothing that won't keep.'

She brushed past him and he was terribly tempted to catch her as she walked past, to turn her round and just have the row that was so clearly needed. Perhaps it was wiser to just let it go, Ethan thought, letting out a rare angry breath as he heard her heels clip down the corridor, but he turned at the sound of Lisa's voice. 'There he is.'

'Kate?' Ethan smiled when he saw that Lisa was with his sister, wondered, albeit briefly, what on earth she was doing at his workplace, and then properly read her face. 'One of the kids…'

'The kids are fine, Ethan.' She took a breath and he knew what was coming. 'It's Phil—we need to get to the hospital.' And still his brain tried to process things kindly. He waited for her to smile, to hold up crossed fingers and to say 'this is it,' that a heart had been found for their cousin, but she just looked at him. 'Carl's watching the kids. We need to hurry and get there.'

No, it would seem that Phil wasn't going to get that heart.

Ethan was glad that Kate hadn't told him by phone, realised that had he not stopped to talk to Penny he could have been sitting in his car, stuck on the packed Beach Road and finding out that Phil was about to die.

'I'll meet you there.' He was already heading to his office to grab his car keys but Kate shook her head. She knew how close Ethan and Phil were.

'I'll drive.'

It was just as well that she did, because the rush-hour traffic didn't care that there was somewhere they needed to be. Ethan could feel his temper building as they inched towards the hospital, could sense the mounting urgency, especially when his mother called to see how far away they were.

'A couple of minutes,' Ethan said.

'Get here,' came his mother's response.

They were pulling into Melbourne Central and again Ethan was very glad that Kate had been driving. He was grateful that there was no competition in the grief stakes between him and his twin—she knew that he and Phil were like brothers. Kate dropped him off at the main entrance and then went to find a place to park the car as Ethan ran through the hospital building, desperate to get to his cousin in time, still holding a small flame of hope that something could yet be done.

It was extinguished even before he got to Phil's room.

Because standing outside was Phil's ex-wife, Gina, and unless he was dying she'd never be there otherwise. She'd be sitting outside in the canteen as she usually did when she brought Justin in to visit. It had been a wretched divorce and Phil's parents hadn't exactly been kind in their summing up of Gina—and not just behind her back. There had been some terrible arguments too.

'Gina,' he said, but she just flashed him a look that said he was a part of the Lewis family and could he please just stay back.

'I'm here for Justin,' Gina said, and Ethan nodded and went in the room. His eyes didn't first go to Phil but to Justin. Ethan could see the bewilderment and fear on the little boy's face as Vera and Jack, Phil's parents, told him to be brave. Ethan felt his head tighten, wanted to tell them to stop, but then his eyes moved to the bed and to his cousin and there wasn't even time to say to Phil all he wanted to.

It was all over by the time Kate arrived.

CHAPTER THREE

PENNY PARKED HER car and took a couple of moments to sort out her make-up and hair. She wondered, not for the first time, how she was going to get through this. It was eight a.m. and she had just come from having a blood test and vaginal ultrasound. If the results were as expected, she would be starting her injections this evening.

She collected her handbag and the little cool bag holding the medication and told herself that lots of women worked while they went through this.

And she told herself something else, something she had decided last night—at the very first opportunity she would apologise properly to Ethan. Penny had come up with a plan. She wouldn't tell him everything, just explain to him that she was on some medication and that yesterday she hadn't felt very well. If he probed, she might hint that it was a feminine issue.

Her lips twitched into a smile as she pictured Ethan's reaction—that would soon silence him.

Walking towards Emergency, Penny saw a dark blue car pull up in the entrance bay, where the ambulances did, and she watched as a security guard walked towards it to warn the occupants that they couldn't park there.

Except the woman wasn't parking her car.

Instead, she was dropping Ethan Lewis off.

Penny tried not to look as they shared a brief embrace and then a thoroughly seedy-looking Ethan climbed out. He was unshaven and unkempt, dressed in yesterday's rumpled scrubs. She tried to turn her attention away from him, but her gaze went straight to the car he had just come from. And it was then that Penny felt it— the red-hot poker that jabbed into her stomach as she glanced at the woman, a red-hot poker that temporarily nudged aside her loudly ticking biological clock. And at six minutes past eight and a few months later than most women at Peninsula Hospital, Penny realised that Ethan Lewis really was an incredibly sexy man and it wasn't a hot flash that was causing her to blush as they walked into the department together.

'Ethan.' She tried to keep to the script she had planned. 'I was wondering if I could speak to you about yesterday. I realise that I—'

'Just leave it.' He completely dismissed her, so much so that he strode ahead of her and into the male changing rooms.

Charming!

Ethan ignored her all day and Penny decided that she wasn't about to try apologising again.

She took her lunch break in her office, waiting for the IVF nurse to ring, which she did right on time. Penny took a deep breath as she found out that, as expected, she was to start her injections that evening, which meant she needed to call Jasmine.

'I'm on till six,' Penny said. 'I don't think I'll be able to get away early.'

'Penny, when do you ever get away early? It's not a problem, I'll come and give it to you at work, but Jed won't be home so I'll have to bring Simon in.'

Penny grimaced. She did not want to make a fool of herself in front of her nephew as it would terrify him. Simon, like his mother, was very sensitive. Still, there was no choice.

There really wasn't time to worry about her upcoming jab. The department was busy enough to keep her mind off it and she smiled when she saw her next patient, an eight-week-old named Daniel.

'He's had a bit of a cold,' Laura, the mother, explained. 'I took him to my doctor yesterday and he said that he didn't have a temperature and his chest sounded fine. I've been putting drops up his nose to help with feeding,' Laura continued. 'But this afternoon I came in from putting out the washing and went to check on him and he was pale, really pale, and he'd been sick. I know he's fine now…'

He seemed fine and Penny examined Daniel thoroughly, but apart from a cold and a low-grade temperature there was nothing remarkable to find.

'Has he been coughing?'

'A bit,' Laura said, as Penny listened carefully to his chest, but apart from a couple of crackles it was clear.

Still, Penny was concerned and it did sound as if he

might have had an apnoeic episode so she decided to ring the paediatricians, who were very busy on the ward.

'They're going to be a while,' Penny explained to the mum. 'I'm going to take some bloods and do some swabs, so hopefully we'll have some results back by the time they get down here. And I'll order a chest X-ray.'

To show that she wasn't, in fact, too up herself to value Ethan's opinion, late in the afternoon when she was concerned about the baby and the paediatricians weren't anywhere around, instead of speaking with Mr Dean, Penny decided that she would ask Ethan.

He barely looked up from the form he was filling out when Penny asked if she could have a word.

'Sure.'

'I've got an eight-week-old I'm concerned about.' He glanced up. 'Mum found him very pale in his cot after his nap and he'd vomited, but he picked up well. He's had a cold, struggling to feed, he's a bit sniffly, just…' She moved her hand to show she was wavering. 'His chest is clear, and he's got a small cough, which is unremarkable. I've done some swabs and some bloods.'

'What did paeds say?' Ethan asked.

'They'll come down when they can, but they're busy and they're going to be ages,' Penny said. 'Mum just wants to take him home now that he's had the tests and wait to get the results, but I'm not sure.'

Ethan came and though he had been scowling at Penny, he was lovely with the mum. He carefully checked the infant, who was bright and alert and just hungry. Penny put some saline drops in his nose and they watched as the baby latched on and started to feed happily, but just as Ethan was about to go, Daniel spluttered and broke into a coughing fit. As he came off the breast Ethan took him and held him and Penny watched, the diagnosis becoming more and more evident as he broke into a prolonged paroxysmal cough and then struggled to inhale and then cough again. Ethan was holding him up and tapping his back as Penny turned on the suction, but thankfully it wasn't needed.

'He wasn't doing that.' Laura was beside herself, watching her son. 'He's just had a little cough.'

'That might have been what happened this afternoon,' Penny said, 'when you found him in his cot.' She had to explain to the mother that it would seem her baby had whooping cough.

'He's not making any noises, though.'

'People, especially babies, don't always, but he's struggling to get air in during the coughing attack,' Penny explained. 'It's not evident straight away but he's moved into the coughing stage now.' She looked at the baby Ethan was holding—he had stopped coughing and was again desperate to be fed. 'I'm going to call the paediatricians...'

'Can I feed him?'

'I'll watch him feed while you go and call Paeds,' Ethan said to Penny, handing the crying baby back to his mum. 'Wait one moment before you feed him.' He stepped out with Penny. 'He's to be transferred. I know he seems fine at the moment but, given his age, he needs to be somewhere with PICU.'

'I know.' Penny nodded.

'Can you get Lisa to come in and watch him feed? I'll stay in for now.'

Penny nodded. The coughing episodes were scary at best and someone calm and experienced needed to be in with the mum to help deal with them. 'I've never actually seen whooping cough,' Penny said to Lisa.

'I've had it,' Lisa said. 'Hundred-day cough they call it and I know why. Poor baby and poor mum having to watch him. I'll go and relieve Ethan.'

Penny spoke again to the paediatrician and started the baby on antibiotics, but really there was no treatment that could stop the coughing attacks and, as Ethan had said, given his tender age, he really did need to be somewhere with paediatric intensive care facilities in case he suddenly deteriorated.

'They're going to come down and see him just as soon as they can,' Penny said when Ethan came out. 'I'll go and let mum know.'

'She's in for a tough time,' Ethan said. 'Are you immunised?'

'All up to date,' Penny said, because though she was terrified of injections, before embarking on IVF she had *made* herself get all her immunisations up to date and poor Jasmine had been the one who'd had to do them. Still, it was worth it, Penny realised, for days such as this.

'Right.' Ethan glanced at his watch. 'I'm going home.'

'See you tomorrow,' Penny said, but Ethan shook his head.

'I'm on days off now.'

'Enjoy them.'

He didn't answer. In fact, since her attempt to apologise, unless it was about a patient, Ethan had said nothing at all to her and she felt like poking her tongue out at his back as he and his bad mood walked off together.

Maybe it was just as well he was on days off. Hopefully by the time he was back they could put yesterday's incident behind them and start again.

And she'd hopefully be finished with the hot flashes by then.

As predicted, there wasn't a hope of her getting away at six, but when it neared, Penny told Lisa she was taking a short break and, seeing Jasmine walking down the corridor with Simon in his stroller, the moment she had been silently dreading all day was finally here.

'I don't want Simon seeing me upset.' Penny was starting to panic. 'It could make him as terrified of needles as I am.'

'There'll be someone in the staffroom who can watch him for five minutes,' Jasmine said. 'You go on and get everything ready and I'll come in.' They both knew it wasn't a question of Penny being brave because her nephew was there—it was the one thing, apart from her fertility, that Penny couldn't control, and her response to injections was varied and unpredictable.

'Vanessa's watching him,' Jasmine said when she came into the office a few minutes later.

'I don't know if I can do this again,' Penny said. Her hand was shaking as she checked the doses the IVF nurse had given her.

'In a couple of moments you'll be one evening down.'

'With God knows how many more to go,' Penny said. She took a deep breath and undid her skirt. 'Just do it.'

She closed her eyes but could not stop shaking as Jasmine walked over. She had hoped so much that things would be different this time, but she was crying again, just as she had that morning at her blood test, and she was very glad that Simon wasn't there to see his aunt make an absolute fool of herself.

'It's done.' Jasmine massaged in the medication. 'You're done for the day.'

'It's ridiculous,' Penny whimpered. 'I've given so many injections today, I've taken blood from an eight-week-old…'

'Don't worry about it,' Jasmine said. 'You're actually better than you used to be.'

'Really?'

'A bit,' Jasmine lied. 'How are the hot flashes?'

'Only two today.'

'How's Ethan been?' Jasmine asked as Penny tucked herself in.

'Horrible,' Penny said. 'He's still sulking about yesterday. I tried to apologise but he wasn't having any of it. There's not much more that I can do.'

But even if she shrugged it off to her sister, Penny was rattled because, yes, she had wanted to put it behind them, had wanted to start again, and, no, she didn't want to but she felt the tiniest bit attracted to him.

CHAPTER FOUR

ETHAN HAD LONG known that his cousin might die but on the eve of the funeral he couldn't really acknowledge that Phil had.

Kate kept ringing and asking him to come over, except he didn't want to talk about it, not even with those closest to him. Ethan had been dreading the funeral, had found himself starting to tear up when he'd asked Gordon to cover for him for the day, though he had kept the details minimal. Then Gordon rang to tell Ethan that he was up in Maternity as his wife, Hilary, had gone into early labour so he wouldn't be able to cover Ethan's shift after all.

'Someone else should be able to cover you, though.'

'It's fine, Gordon,' Ethan said. 'I'll sort something out, you just do what you have to.' He wished him good luck and then looked at the roster. There were several doctors he could change with, he and Penny were on till six today, but tomorrow…

As she walked past he called over to her. Penny was perhaps not his first choice to ask, but it was a pretty straight swap.

'Can I ask a favour?'

Please, don't, Penny thought as she saw him looking at the roster because, in her impossible schedule, for the next couple of weeks there really was no room for manoeuvre, not that Ethan would know that.

'Tomorrow I'm on from nine till six and you're twelve till nine—is there any chance we can swap?' She just blinked. 'Though I might not get in till one.'

'I can't swap tomorrow, Ethan.' She couldn't. Not only did she have an ultrasound and blood test booked for tomorrow, she had a meeting with the specialist at nine.

'I've got to attend a funeral,' Ethan pushed, but didn't go into detail, didn't tell her that this was personal, he simply couldn't. 'Gordon was supposed to be covering for me, but his wife has gone into labour—premature labour,' he added.

Penny hesitated; she knew she couldn't say no.

Except she couldn't say yes either, she simply could not miss her blood test—it was as essential as that.

She'd ring the IVF nurse, Penny decided, see if she could fiddle around her appointment, but for now, till she had, she'd have to stand firm.

'Is there anybody else you can ask?'

'A few.'

'Well, see if they can help and if not, let me know.'

If she occasionally smiled, Ethan thought, she would actually be exceptionally attractive, but even then, with her terse attitude and unfeeling ways, Penny could never be considered beautiful. A black smile spread across his lips. She really was the limit and instead of leaving it there, Ethan found that he couldn't. 'What is your problem, Penny?'

'Problem?' Penny frowned. 'I don't have a problem. I simply can't come in early tomorrow, that's all.'

'It was the same when I asked you to come in for a few hours the other day.'

'So that you could go to a football match.' Penny stared back coolly, looking into his angry eyes and surprisingly tempted to tell him that she had a vaginal ultrasound and a blood test booked for ten past eight tomorrow, just so that she could watch him squirm. 'I'm sorry, Ethan, I have things on. I'm not able to simply change my schedule at a moment's notice. If you can check with the others…'

'Like it or not,' Ethan said, 'there has to be a senior staff member on at all times, and that sometimes means making last-minute changes to the roster.'

'I'm aware of that,' Penny responded.

'Yet you don't…' He watched two spots of colour rising on her cheeks, and then she turned abruptly to go, but Ethan refused to leave it there. 'You're going to have to be more flexible.'

Her back was to him and he watched as Penny stilled, her shoulders stiffened and she slowly turned around. 'Excuse me?'

'In the coming days you're going to have to be more flexible—Gordon will need some time after all.'

'If Gordon's wife having a baby leaves us short-staffed then it might be prudent to look at getting a locum because—and I am warning you now—I am not going to be dropping everything and coming into work and leaving here late and changing shifts at the last moment to accommodate Gordon, his wife and their baby.'

Penny was angry now and with good reason—part of her mandatory counselling before she'd commenced IVF had addressed problems such as this. Timing was important. These weeks were incredibly intense and to keep it from becoming a staffroom topic of conversation Penny had worked out her appointments very carefully around her work schedule. And now Hilary had gone into labour and she was supposed to juggle everything.

Well, Penny was doing this for *her* baby.

'You're such a team player,' Ethan said.

'Oh, but I'm not,' Penny responded. 'Ask anyone.'

'I don't need to ask, I'd say it's already common knowledge.' It was—Penny was the ice queen. He'd heard it from many and had seen it for himself, but she hadn't finished yet, pulling Ethan up on a very pertinent point.

'You're talking as if Hilary is about to deliver a micro-prem when, in fact, she's actually thirty-five weeks' gestation.' Ethan at that point actually had to suppress a smile, because she had well and truly caught him out. When he'd said premature labour he had been appealing or rather searching for the softer side to Penny, but he was fast realising that she simply didn't have one. 'I don't respond to bells and whistles, Ethan. Give me a real drama and I'll deal with it accordingly.' She walked off and Ethan watched.

She was absolutely immaculate. Her straight blonde hair was tied low at the back of her neck. Her sheer cream blouse looked as if it had come straight off a mannequin at an expensive boutique and her charcoal-grey skirt was perfectly cut to show a very trim figure. If she had been just a few inches taller she could be walking down a runway instead of the corridor of the emergency department.

'What do you respond to, Penny?' The words were out of Ethan's mouth before his brain had even processed them, and how he wished, the moment they were uttered, that he could take them back.

He was more than aware of the not-so-slight sexual undertone to them, and Ethan half expected her to turn on her low heels and march back to give him a sharp piece of her mind, or perhaps to head straight to Mr Dean's office, but what happened next came as a complete surprise.

Ethan watched as Penny threw her head back and laughed and then glanced over her shoulder at him. He saw not the glitter of ice in those cold blue eyes but something far more fetching. And her mouth was parted in a slightly mocking yet somehow mischievous smile as she answered him. 'That's for me to know!'

Ethan found himself smiling back, a proper smile this time. He almost called out that he was looking forward to finding out but then he checked himself, the smile fading, and he turned back to the roster he had been viewing before Penny had come along, and wondered what the hell had just happened. She had been completely immutable with the roster, thoroughly unfriendly and yet somehow it had ended in a smile.

A flirtatious one at that.

Ethan had no trouble with flirting—he was an expert

at it, in fact. He had just never expected to find himself going there with Penny, but more to the point, Ethan thought darkly, he still didn't have anyone to cover him for the funeral.

'Not now!' Penny said a few moments later when Jasmine knocked on her office door as she came in to start her late shift. Penny was seriously rattled by the small confrontation she'd had with Ethan and wanted a few moments alone to process things and to ring the IVF nurse to see if she could possibly swap. More unsettling than that, though, was the flutter in her throat and the blush on her cheeks at her response to him. Her face still burnt red even as she tried to put off her sister from coming in, but Jasmine wanted a quick word.

'It won't take a second—I'm just letting you know that Mum rang this morning from a satellite phone.'

'Where is she?' Penny smiled and it was genuine. She was thrilled to hear from her mum.

'Heading for Mykonos,' Jasmine said, and Penny groaned her envy.

'I'm sure that I don't need to ask if she's having a good time.'

'Completely loving it,' Jasmine said. 'She said that she should've done this years ago and…don't fall off your chair, but I think she might have met someone.'

'You mean a man?' Penny blinked in surprise. 'I don't know what to say…I don't know what to think.'

'I know.' Jasmine smiled. 'I can't imagine Mum with anyone.'

Louise Masters had been single since the day her

husband had left. A very volatile marriage had made Louise swear off men and instead she had focused heavily on her career and had done her best to instil the same very independent, somewhat bitter values into her daughters.

'Anyway,' Jasmine continued, 'we didn't talk for long. I've no idea how much it would have cost her to call. She just wanted to send her love and to find out how you were getting on. I told her that you were doing fine.' Jasmine hesitated. She'd heard a few whispers, knew that Penny was putting noses out of joint everywhere, which wasn't unusual. Penny was known for being tough, it was just a lot more concentrated at the moment. '*Are* you doing fine, though?'

'Not really,' Penny admitted. 'Actually, Jasmine, I think you're right, I might have to let a few people at work know. It's proving impossible. I've just had an argument with Ethan—he needs me to come in early tomorrow so that he can go to a funeral. God.' Penny buried her face in her hands. 'Imagine saying no to that—it's a funeral!'

'Penny, it was a football match a couple of weeks ago that Ethan asked you to cover him for.' Jasmine was indignant on her sister's behalf. 'And Mr Dean has a corporate golf day on Thursday and Rex is getting a divorce. The fact is that this place needs more doctors, but they still won't employ another one.'

'A funeral, though.' Penny groaned.

'Penny, you go to more funerals than anyone I know.' It was true. Of course they couldn't attend the funeral of every patient who died, but Penny's black outfits were taken for a trip to the dry cleaner's more than most. 'You *have* to keep the next few weeks clear.' Jasmine was firm. She knew how hard this was for Penny and just how hard her sister worked. 'And I do think you should let your colleagues know. Not everyone, but if you told Lisa…'

'How can Lisa help with the doctors' roster?'

'Well, just tell Ethan or Mr Dean…' Her voice trailed off.

'It's hopeless, isn't it?' Mr Dean wasn't going to be exactly thrilled to find out that his senior registrar was trying to get pregnant—it was the reason he had hesitated to promote her a few years ago—of that Penny was sure.

'Penny, you can't come in early tomorrow. You can't miss a blood test, it determines the whole day's treatment.'

'I know. I just really thought I could handle working and doing this. I thought that it might be easier the second time around, that I'd know more what to expect, that I'd at least be used to the needles.'

'Penny.' Jasmine sat on the edge of her sister's desk. 'I think you are going to have to face the fact that you are never going to get over your fear of needles.'

'I'm an emergency registrar!'

'With one weakness.' Jasmine gave a sympathetic smile. 'It's just a horrible weakness to have when you're going through IVF.'

'I made a right fool of myself this morning at my blood test.' Penny shuddered at the memory. 'It took two of them, one to hold me and one to take the blood. I was crying and carrying on like a two-year-old!'

'Then it's just as well that you're not having your IVF treatment here.'

Penny blanched at the very thought of that happening. Even if Peninsula Hospital offered IVF, which they didn't, Penny wouldn't take it. Oh, for the convenience, it would be wonderful to just pop upstairs for the endless blood tests, injections and scans that were part of the tumultuous ride she was on, but not so convenient would be to have your colleagues see you a shivering, terrified mess. She was bad enough at the best of times, but right now, tired and with her hormones all over the place, it was the worst of times.

'Do you have to work?' Jasmine asked gently.

'I took time off last time,' Penny said. 'And I had all that time off when Mum came out of hospital. I'd actually like to have some annual leave up my sleeve if I ever do get pregnant.'

'You will.' Jasmine slipped off the desk and gave her sister a hug, but it wasn't returned. Penny wasn't particularly touchy-feely. 'You're going to get your baby.'

'Easy for you to say.' Penny tried to keep the bitterness out of her voice. She loved Simon very much, but he had been an accident. Just one mistake had seen Jasmine pregnant. Yes, Jasmine had had a terrible time with a horrible husband and later as a single mum before she'd married Jed. But now, just a few months into her marriage, she was pregnant, although she hadn't told Penny.

Penny felt her sister's arms around her tense shoulders and it was time to face the white elephant in the room before it came between them.

'When are you going to tell me, Jasmine?' There was a long stretch of silence. 'You're pregnant, aren't you?'

'Penny, I…'

Penny heard the discomfort in her sister's voice and forced a smile before turning her face back to Jasmine. 'How many weeks?'

'Fourteen.' Jasmine flushed.

'Have you told Mum?'

'Not yet. We haven't said anything to anyone yet. I wanted to tell you first but I just didn't know how.' Jasmine's eyes were same blue as her sister's and they filled with tears. 'You were so upset when your last IVF attempt failed and then you've been building up for this one. I know how hard it is for you right now, and to find out my news right in the middle of an IVF treatment cycle, well, I know…'

Except Jasmine didn't know, Penny thought, though at least she tried to understand.

Penny took a deep breath. 'Even if it isn't happening easily for me, it doesn't mean that I can't be pleased for you.'

'You're sure?'

'Of course I am. I know I wasn't the best sister and aunt to Simon at first, but I've told you why. I was jealous when you were pregnant with Simon, but it's different now—I'm honestly pleased for you and Jed.' Penny gave a wry smile. 'And, of course, terribly, terribly jealous.'

'I know.' Jasmine smiled back. 'I'm so glad that we can be more honest with each other now.'

'We can be,' Penny said. 'Which means you won't be offended if I tell you I really need five minutes alone right now.'

'Sure.'

Penny waited till the door was closed and then put her head back in her hands.

Fourteen weeks.

She just sat there, a hormonal jumble of conflict.

She was pleased for her sister.

No, she wasn't!

She was jealous, jealous, jealous, and now she felt guilty for feeling so jealous, yet she was pleased for her sister too.

Oh, hell!

Penny really had forgotten just how awful the treatment made her feel. It was far worse than feeling pre-menstrual. The last time had been bad enough but she had gone through it at home, concentrating solely on her appointments.

Trying to work through it was unbearable.

And then she remembered her confrontation with Ethan—the reason she had come to the office in the first place—and reached for her phone and rang the IVF nurse to explain her problem. 'I'm booked in for ten past eight,' Penny said. 'I was wondering if I could come in on the early round. And also if, instead of my appointment, I could have a phone consultation with the specialist.' There was a bit of a tart pause, which Penny took as a warning. You had to be fully on board, she had been told this on many occasions, and she tried so hard to be.

Except she was also expected to be fully on board at work.

'There's a spot at six-twenty a.m.,' the nurse said, and an already exhausted Penny took it. She headed out of the office and back through to the department to catch up with Ethan and to show him what a *team player* she could be, but he was stuck with a baby who had suspicious injuries and later interviewing the parents. Oh, well, Penny thought, it would keep for later. He might already have someone else. Of course, Penny got caught up with work of her own and at the end of a very long shift, with a needle to look forward to, Penny wasn't in the happiest of moods when, just to cap it all off, Gordon came into the department with a huge smile on his face.

'It's a boy!'

'How lovely!' Penny offered her congratulations and Ethan came over and did the same, and they headed over to the nurses' station and stood while Gordon sat showing the many, many photos he had taken on his phone of his gorgeous new son.

'He's doing really well,' Gordon enthused. 'Though they will probably keep him in the nursery for a few days, given that he's a bit small, but we should get him home soon. Hilary's a paediatrician after all.' He gave a tired yawn. 'It's been a long day—do you want to join me in celebrating? Hilary is catching up on some sleep. I thought we could go and have a drink before I head back up there.'

'I'd love to,' Penny said as her phone alarm buzzed in her pocket to remind her that it was injection time. 'But I'm afraid that I can't right now.' She didn't dash straight off, though, and looked at a couple more photos. 'How is Hilary doing?'

'Really well,' Gordon said. 'She's a bit disappointed, of course, but she'll soon come round.'

'Disappointed?' Penny looked at an image of the tiny but, oh, so healthy baby.

'She really wanted a girl this time. Which I guess is understandable after three sons.'

'Didn't you find out what you were having?' Ethan asked Gordon, but Penny wasn't really listening. She could feel the incessant buzz from a phone in her pocket and she needed to go.

'Congratulations again!' Penny said to Gordon. 'But now you'll have to excuse me. Tell Hilary that I shall come up and visit her soon.'

A bit disappointed.

The words buzzed in Penny's ears as she walked around her office. She was being hypersensitive, Penny told herself. It was just that it seemed so easy for everyone else at the moment. Maybe if she had three sons she'd be disappointed too at not getting a girl, except she couldn't imagine it. Worse, she couldn't imagine having three babies—it was hard enough trying to get one.

And then she thought about the baby that Ethan had been looking after that afternoon and all the social workers and police that had been involved, and it just didn't seem fair that some people who had babies didn't even seem to want them.

'Hi, there.' Jasmine was waiting for Penny in her office. She had everything set up for the tiny injection that really should only take a minute, except Penny needed to be talked down from the ceiling each and every time. Penny hated the weakness. She'd had hypnosis and even counselling in a bid to overcome it, not that it changed a single thing. Every needle that went into her had her shaking with fear and this evening was no exception. If anything, this evening she was worse.

'I can't do this today,' Penny said as she closed the office door and let out a shaky breath. 'I'm honestly not just saying it this time, Jasmine. I'm really not up to it.'

'Penny.' Jasmine was very patient; she was more than used to this. 'You know that you can't miss one injection.'

'I don't think I want to do the treatment anymore.' Penny just said it. 'I can't keep going on like this. I'm snapping at everyone, I'm in tears all the time.'

'The same as you were last time,' Jasmine said.

'I was going to ring in sick tomorrow, or ask Mr Dean if I could take annual leave, but now with Gordon's wife having the baby…' Penny closed her eyes at the impossibility of it all. 'I don't want the injection.'

'You're *going* to finish this course.'

'And what if it doesn't work?'

'Then you'll have a proper break before you put yourself through this again,' Jasmine said firmly. 'It's no wonder that you're teary and exhausted. Let's just get this needle over and done with and then we'll talk.'

And she would have, except there was a sharp knock on Penny's door.

'Penny?' There was no mistaking Ethan's low voice, but Penny didn't answer. She'd forgotten to lock it and when he knocked again, it was so impatient that Penny wouldn't put it past him to simply walk in.

'What?' Penny asked angrily when she opened the door just a fraction.

'I was wondering if you could change your mind and come out for a drink with Gordon and I. There is no one else around to ask and Rex needs to stay here.'

'I can't,' Penny said. 'I've got the case review to prepare for.'

'One drink,' Ethan said. Surely she could manage one quick drink. 'Come on, Penny, I'm asking for some help here. I'm really not in the mood to go out celebrating tonight and I don't know how to do the baby talk thing.'

'Oh, and because I'm a woman, I do?'

'God, you just don't let up, do you?' Ethan snapped. 'I was just asking for some backup. It would be nice to do the right thing by the guy, the sociable thing. His wife's just had a baby, it's right to take him out.'

'It's right that the consultant takes him out!' Penny retorted sharply. 'I'm not a consultant, which means I get to go home and sign off from this place occasionally, and I'm signing off now. Good night, Ethan!'

Penny closed the door on him and promptly burst into tears. And because Jasmine knew her well, or rather better than anyone else knew Penny, she didn't try to comfort her at first. Instead, she undid her sister's skirt as Penny stood there and sobbed. Jasmine looked at her bruised stomach and, finding a suitable spot, swabbed her skin and then stuck in the needle. Penny continued to sob and then, having disposed of the needle, Jasmine went over and gave her sister a hug.

'It's done.'

'It's not just that,' Penny said.

'I know.'

'I made a right fool of myself just then. Ethan thinks that I'm jealous because I didn't get the job. I know that's what he's been thinking and I've just gone and proved it to him.'

'You're not jealous, though, Penny.' Jasmine tried to get her sister to see reason. 'He doesn't know what's going on. You turned down the job so that you could concentrate on your IVF.'

'No! I turned down the consultant's position so that I could have a baby.' Penny gulped. 'But the way things are going, I don't think that I'm going to get one.'

CHAPTER FIVE

ETHAN PAID THE taxi and let himself into his apartment.

A celebratory drink on an empty stomach, the way he was feeling right now, possibly hadn't been the best idea and it hadn't been just the one.

Given it had only been him with Gordon, he hadn't exactly been able to get up and leave after one, so instead he'd had to sit there and listen as Gordon had gone into spectacular detail about his day, or rather his wife's day.

Ethan had been hoping that now that the baby had been born, Gordon would come back to work.

He'd had no idea how it all worked.

As it turned out, Gordon was now on paternity leave and would be juggling toddler twins and a six-year-old's school run.

'Not a problem,' he had said to Gordon.

It was, though, a huge one.

Ethan had gone through everyone to cover for him in the morning and the only person who might possibly have been able to help had an *appointment*.

Well, Ethan had his cousin's funeral to attend.

He'd been dreading it, but he would far rather be there than not.

He would love to just ring in sick tomorrow, to let someone else sort it out, to just sign off on the place, as Penny had tonight.

Still, he had expected more from her.

She was senior too.

Ethan loaded some toast into the toaster and some tinned spaghetti into the microwave and tried not to think about Justin and how he'd be feeling tonight. Though, he consoled himself, Gina would surely be handling things better than his own mother had, given they had broken up a couple of years ago.

He couldn't not be there tomorrow and not just for appearances' sake—Ethan wanted to see for himself that Justin was okay.

Ethan thought about Phil and the black game they'd played and, sorry, mate, he said to his cousin, because even if he didn't fancy Penny, he was going to have to play the sympathy card.

He was scrolling through his phone to find her number when it rang.

'Ethan?' He didn't answer her straight away; instead, he frowned at the sound of her voice. 'It's Penny. Penny Masters from work.'

'Hi, Penny.'

'I'm sorry to call you so late. I meant to tell you before I left for home—it just slipped my mind. I changed my appointment. I can get into work by nine tomorrow, if you still need me to.'

'I do.' The words just jumped out of him. 'Thank

you.' Ethan closed his eyes in relief and it took a second to realise that she was still talking.

'I'd also like to apologise for my words before.' She sounded very prim and formal. 'I really wasn't in a position to go out tonight, but I didn't explain myself very well.'

Penny had explained things perfectly, Ethan thought privately, but he was so relieved that he would be able to get the funeral tomorrow that he let go the chance for a little barb, and instead he was nice. 'I don't blame you in the least for not wanting to come out tonight.' Relief, mixed with just a little bit too much champagne, had him speaking honestly. 'I really don't think that I'm going to be able to look Hilary in the eye when I go and visit her.'

'Too much detail?' He *heard* her smile.

'Far, far too much.'

'That's Gordon for you. He's very…' Penny really didn't know how to describe him.

'In tune?' Ethan suggested.

'Something like that.'

'I felt as if I was listening to him describe *his* labour,' Ethan said, and was rewarded by the sound of her laugh. 'Hold on a second.' The microwave was pinging and he pressed Stop on the microwave rather than ending the call, not that he thought about it. 'Look, thanks a lot for tomorrow. I hope it wasn't too much trouble.'

'It was!' Penny said, which had him frowning but sort of smiling too. 'Don't rush back.'

'I'll be back by one.' Ethan really didn't want to stand around chatting and drinking and talking about Phil in the past tense. He would be glad of the chance to slip away and just bury himself in work.

'Whose funeral is it?' Penny asked, and not gently, assuming, because he was fine to dash off from the funeral by one, that it was a patient from work and her mind was sort of scanning the admissions from the previous week as to who it might be, when his voice broke in.

'My cousin's.'

Penny closed her eyes, guilty and horrified too, because she'd been so upset tonight she had almost forgotten to ring him. 'You should have told me that! Ethan, I assumed it was a patient. You should have told me that it was personal.'

'I was just about to call you and do that,' Ethan admitted.

'Is that why you've been so…?' Penny's voice trailed off.

'That's fine, coming from you,' Ethan said, but it actually came out rather nicely and Penny found herself smiling into the phone as he continued. 'Yes, it's been a tough few days.'

'How old?'

'My age,' Ethan said. 'Thirty-six.'

'Was it expected?'

'Sort of,' Ethan said, and felt that sting at the back of his nose. 'Sort of not. He was on the waiting list for a heart transplant.'

There was silence for a moment. 'Was he the one you were going to go to the football with?' For the first time he heard her sound tentative.

'Penny…'

'Oh, God!' She was a mass of manufactured hormones, not that he knew, and this news came at the end of a very upsetting day. 'He missed the football match because of me.'

'It wasn't something at the top of his bucket list.' Ethan actually found himself smiling as he recalled the conversation he'd had with Phil when he'd told him that he couldn't get the time off, the one about the sympathy vote.

And, no, he didn't fancy Penny, he'd just had a bit too much to drink, he must have, because he was telling her that they'd often gone to watch football. 'He went anyway—with Justin, his son.' And he told Penny about the illness that had ravaged his cousin. 'He got a virus a couple of years ago.' And he could understand a bit better why the patients liked her, because she was very matter-of-fact and didn't gush out her sympathies, just asked pertinent questions and then asked how his son and wife were doing.

'Ex-wife,' Ethan said, and he found himself musing—only he was doing it out loud and to Penny. 'They broke up before he got ill, she had an affair and it was all just a mess. It must be hell for her too and she's coming tomorrow. She's bringing Justin.'

'How old is he?'

'Six,' Ethan said.

She asked how his aunt and uncle were.

'Not great,' he admitted. 'They're worried that they won't get to see Justin so much anymore. It's just a mess all round.'

And he told Penny the hell of watching someone so vital and full of life gradually getting weaker. How he hated that he had only just made it to the hospital in time. He let out more than he had to Kate, to anyone, and during that conversation Penny found out that it had been his sister who had dropped him off at work, but there was no room for relief or dousing of red-hot pokers, or anything really, as she could hear the heart-break in his voice.

'Thirty-six,' Ethan repeated, and was met by silence. He would never have known that her silence was because of tears. 'So, while I suppose we were expecting it, it still came as a shock.' He didn't really know how better to explain it. 'And it will be a shock for Justin too.'

'Poor kid,' Penny said.

'Anyway, thanks for swapping.'

He hung up the phone, poured his spaghetti on the toast and then frowned because it was cold. He'd surely only been on the phone for a moment and so back into the microwave it went.

They'd actually been talking for a full twenty minutes.

At five a.m. Penny stood, bleary-eyed, under the shower, trying to wake up. She got out and then dried her hair. At least she didn't have to worry about make-up yet, given that she would be crying it all off very soon.

And normally the terribly efficient Penny didn't have to worry about what to wear because her work wardrobe was on a fourteen-day rotation, except it wasn't so simple at the moment because her arms were bruised from all the blood tests and so her sleeveless grey top wasn't an option.

Even the simplest thing seemed complicated this morning.

A sheer neutral jumper worked well with her black skirt, except it meant that she had to change her underwear because it showed her black bra, and with all her appointments and tests the usually meticulous Penny's laundry wasn't up to date. Racing the clock, she grabbed coral silk underwear that she'd never usually consider wearing for work and then raced downstairs, so rushed and tired that by mistake she added orange juice instead of milk to her coffee and had to make her drink all over again.

Still, Penny thought, she was glad to have been able to help out Ethan, and there was just a flutter of something unfamiliar stirring. Penny hadn't fancied anyone for ages. Not since she and Vince had spilt up. Well, that wasn't strictly true—she'd had a slight crush on someone a while ago, but she certainly wasn't about to go there, even in her thoughts. She drove for what felt like ages until at last, at a quarter to seven, she lay with her knees up, loathing it despite being used to it, as she underwent the internal scan to find out how her ovaries were behaving. And if that wasn't bad enough, afterwards she headed for her blood test.

'Morning, Penny!'

They all knew her well.

Penny was determined not to make the scene she had yesterday. She was there willingly after all. But her resolve wavered as she sat on the seat and one of the nurses held her head as she cried while the other strapped down her arm—it was just an exercise in humiliation really.

'I'm not doing this again,' Penny said as she felt the needle go into her already-bruised vein.

But she'd said that the last time, yet here she was again, locked in the exhausting world of IVF.

Penny sorted out her make-up in the hospital car park and was, in fact, in the department well before nine.

'Morning, Penny.' Mr Dean was especially pleased to see her, because it meant that he could soon go home. 'I hope that you had a good night's sleep—the place is wild.'

Of course it was.

'Where's Penny?' was a frequent cry that she heard throughout the day and Penny didn't really stop for a break, just made do with coffee on the run, but by one o'clock she knew that she had to get something to eat, which she would, just as soon as Mrs Hunt's chest pain was sorted out.

'Cardiology knows that you're here,' Penny explained to her patient. 'They haven't forgotten you. They're just a bit busy up on CCU.' The medication patch wasn't working and Penny was just writing Mrs Hunt up for some morphine when the department was alerted that a severe head injury was on its way in.

'Can you sort out that medication, Vanessa?' Penny asked as she pulled on a fresh gown and gloves and her eye shield. 'Maybe you could give Cardiology another page, just remind them that she's here?' Penny said, because one look at her new patient and Penny knew she wouldn't be back in to see Mrs Hunt for a while.

'Fight at school,' a paramedic said as they lifted the young man over. 'Fell backwards…'

The teen was still in his school uniform and was, she was told, eighteen. Penny shut out the horror and focussed on her patient, feeling the mush of his skull beneath her gloved hands.

'CPR was started immediately and continued at the scene…' Penny listened to the paramedics' handover as she worked. He'd been intubated and they'd got his heart started again, but it wasn't looking good at all. She flashed a torch into his eyes but they were fixed and dilated. Still, he'd been given atropine, a medication that, amongst other things, dilated the pupils, which could account for that.

Hopefully.

'Has anyone seen Penny?' She heard Jasmine's voice.

'Curtain one, Resus,' Penny shouted. 'What?' she asked a moment later when Jasmine popped her head around.

'Nothing.' Jasmine saw the seriousness of the situation and came and helped Lisa with the young man. The trauma team arrived then as well, but despite their best efforts and equipment things were looking seriously grim.

'We'll get him round for a head CT.' The trauma consultant was speaking with Penny and she glanced up as Ethan came in. He was wearing a black suit and had taken off his tie. His face was a touch grey and he looked down at the young man on the resus bed and then at Penny. 'I'm just letting you know that I'm back. I'll get changed.'

'Before you do, could you just check in on curtain three?' Penny said. 'I had to leave her for this.'

Ethan never did get to change. Mrs Hunt's chest pain was increasing.

'Vanessa!' Penny was trying to concentrate on her patient but she could hear a commotion starting across the room. 'Did you give her that morphine?'

'I'm giving it now.'

It was a horrible afternoon.

Once the young patient was being dealt with by Trauma, Penny had an extremely tart word with Vanessa but she was just met with excuses.

'I was trying to get through to Cardiology and then I was waiting for someone to come and check the drug with me, but everyone was in with the trauma or at lunch…'

And Penny said nothing. She didn't have to, her look said it all.

'Two staff members have to check morphine.' Lisa stuck up for her nurse, of course. 'And nurses do have to eat!' Penny bit down on a brittle response, because she'd really love to have made it to lunch too. There was a gnawing of hunger in her stomach but more than that she was annoyed that Mrs Hunt had been in pain for a good fifteen minutes when the medication had been ordered well before that. 'We do our best, Penny,' Lisa said.

It just wasn't good enough for Penny, though she held on to those words.

The police came in and so to did the parents and as the trauma team had taken the young man from CT straight to Theatre, it was Penny who had to speak to them.

'Do you want me to come in with you?' Lisa offered, but Penny shook her head.

'I'll be fine.'

Ethan watched as she walked towards the interview room and thanked God that today it wasn't him about to break terrible news.

'Mr and Mrs Monroe.' Penny introduced herself and sat down. 'I was the doctor on duty when Heath was brought in.'

And she went through everything with them. They didn't need her tears, neither did they need false hope. She told them it was incredibly serious but that their son was in Theatre, and she watched as their lives fell apart. As she walked out of the interview room, Penny wondered if she could really bear to be a mum because the agony on their features, the sobbing that had come from Mrs Monroe was, Penny realised, from a kind of love she didn't yet know.

'How are they?' Ethan asked when she came back to the nurses' station.

'They're just having a nice cup of tea…' Penny bristled and then checked herself. She was aware she was terribly brittle at times. Jasmine had happily told her that on several occasions, but speaking with Heath's parents had been incredibly hard. 'Awful,' she admitted, then looked at his black suit and up into his hazel eyes and she could see they were a little bit bloodshot.

Normally Penny didn't ask questions, she liked to keep everything distanced, but she had seen his eyes shutter when he'd looked at the young patient, remembered the raw pain in his voice last night, and for once she crossed the line.

'How was the funeral?' Penny asked.

'It wasn't a funeral apparently, it was a celebration of life.' He turned back to his notes. 'It was a funeral to me.'

'How was the son?'

'Trying to be brave.' He let out a breath.

He looked beautiful in a suit; in fact, Penny couldn't believe that she'd never noticed until recently that he was a very good-looking man. Still, her mind had been in other places in recent weeks, but it was in an unfamiliar one now, because she wanted to say something more to him, wanted to somehow say the right thing. She just didn't know what.

'I need to get something to eat.' Penny, of course, said the wrong thing, but she was actually feeling sick she was so hungry. 'I'm sorry, Ethan, that sounded...'

'It's fine.' For the first time that day Ethan actually smiled. Penny really was socially awkward, Ethan realised. It just didn't offend him so much today.

'Can I have a word, please, Penny?' She turned at Jasmine's voice, remembered she had been looking for her earlier.

'Away from here.' Penny saw how pale her sister was and even before they had reached her office, Penny couldn't help but ask.

'Is it the baby?'

'No.' Jasmine swallowed before speaking. 'Jed's mum had a stroke this morning.'

'Oh! I'm sorry to hear that. How bad is it?'

'We're not sure yet. Jed's trying to get away from work and then he's going to fly over there.'

'You need to go with him.' Instantly, Penny understood her sister's dilemma—Jed's family were all in Sydney.

'I can't leave you now.' Jasmine's eyes were full of tears.

'Jasmine. Your husband's mum is ill, possibly seriously. How can you not go with him? You know how people had to just drop everything when Mum was sick.'

'You're mid-treatment and I promised you—'

'You made a bigger promise to your husband when you married him.' Penny was incredibly firm. 'I will be fine.' Jasmine gave her a very disbelieving look. After all, she was the one who gave Penny her injections and knew just how bad she was. 'I will be,' Penny insisted.

'You'll stop the treatment,' Jasmine said.

'I won't. I'll ring the clinic now and make an appointment or I'll go to my GP. Jasmine, you know that you have to go with Jed.'

She did.

There really wasn't a choice.

But what Penny didn't tell her was that there was little chance of her getting to the clinic by six and even if she did, tomorrow she was on midday till nine.

'Are you okay?' Ethan frowned as she joined him at the nurses' station.

'I just had some bad news,' Penny said. 'Jed's mother has had a stroke.'

'I'm sorry to hear that.' He saw tears starting to fill her very blue eyes and her nose starting to go red. 'Are you close?'

'No.' Penny shook her head. 'They live in Sydney, Jasmine is on her way there now.'

'I meant close,' Ethan said, as Penny seemed a little dazed, 'as in are you close to her?'

'Not really. I just met her once at the wedding.' Penny blinked. 'She seemed pretty nice, though. Ethan…' Penny took a deep breath '…could I ask…?' No, she couldn't ask him to cover for her now, because even if he said yes to tonight, what about tomorrow and the next day? 'It doesn't matter.'

She went to walk off to her office and Ethan sat there frowning. Really, all he did was frown any time he spoke to Penny. She really was the most confusing woman he had ever met.

Cold one minute and then incredibly empathetic the next.

Ethan looked up and qualified his thought.

Make that empathetic one minute and a soon-to-be blubbering mess the next. Her face had gone bright red and she had stopped in the corridor by a sink and was pulling paper towels out of the dispenser, and her shoulders were heaving.

He didn't know very much about Penny, she'd made sure of that, but from the little that he did know, Ethan was quite sure she would hate any of the staff seeing her like that. She was trying to dash off, but Lisa was calling out to her and he watched as the trauma registrar came into the department and caught a glimpse of her and, patient notes in hand, went to waylay her. Ethan stepped in.

'I need a quick word with you, please, Penny.' He took her by the elbow and sped her through the department into one of the patient interview rooms, and the second they were inside Penny broke down.

CHAPTER SIX

'PLEASE, GO, ETHAN.'

He just stood there.

'Ethan, please, just go.'

'I'm really sorry about your sister's mother-in-law.' He saw her forehead crinkle and then intermingled with sobs she let out a strange gurgle of laughter.

'It's not that.'

'Oh.'

'I'm not that nice.'

Ethan stood there awkwardly, not knowing what to do. He could handle tears from patients and their relatives but this felt more personal than that. She had a handful of paper towels so he couldn't even offer her a tissue.

Then she blurted it out.

'I'm having IVF.'

And any fledgling thoughts that possibly he might rather like Penny in *that* way were instantly doused. Still, at least, in this, he did know what to do. My God, he did, because he wrapped his arms around her and gave her a cuddle. As he did so he was filled with a sense of déjà vu, because his twin sister had been

through it so many times and had taught him what to
do. Often Kate had wept on him, on anyone who happened to be passing really.

Except there was no feeling of déjà vu when he actually held Penny in his arms. She was incredibly slim
and, he was quite sure from her little wriggle to escape,
that she wasn't someone who particularly liked to be
held. 'It must be horrible,' Ethan said, because Kate
had told him that that was a good thing to say when
he'd messed up a few times and said the completely
wrong thing.

'I'm a mess,' Penny mumbled.

'You're not a mess,' Ethan said. 'It's just that your
hormones are crazy at the moment.' He would ring Kate
tonight and thank her, Ethan thought as he felt Penny
relax in his arms. Then he ventured off the given script.
'So that's what's been going on?'

She nodded into his chest and Ethan realised then
that her on IVF was the only Penny he had ever known.
'It's my second go. That's why I was away when you
started here. I should have taken time off this time.'

He realised now why she'd been so inflexible with
the roster on other occasions, all the appointments she
would have been juggling would have made it impossible to change—and yet yesterday, at short notice, she
had. 'Why didn't you just say?'

'I didn't want anyone to know. But now I'm just
being a bitch to everyone.'

'You're not.'

'Everyone's saying it.'

'No,' Ethan lied, 'you just come across as a bit

tough.' He gave in then. 'I bet you're normally a really nice person.' He held his breath, worried that he had said the wrong thing, but he felt her laugh a little. 'I bet you're a sweet, warm, lovely thing really.'

'No,' Penny said. 'I *am* a bitch, but you've just met the exacerbated version.' And then she started to cry again. 'You missed going to the football with your cousin because of me. I'm a horribly selfish person.'

'Penny, stop it.'

Except she couldn't stop crying, just wished she could take back that day and he could have had that time with his cousin.

'Phil and I often went to football, it really wasn't a big deal, and remember Phil got to spend precious time with Justin that day.'

Finally she felt herself calming, embarrassed now at being held, and she pulled away.

'You need to go home,' Ethan said. 'Were you at the clinic this morning?'

Penny nodded.

'I can cover more for you now that I know. You come in to work a bit later some mornings, just text me.'

'It's not just because I'm tired that I'm crying.' She took a big breath and told him the embarrassing truth. 'I'm terrified of needles and Jasmine has been the one giving the injections to me. I'm due for one at six. I'm going to ring the clinic and see if they can give it to me, but I'm not sure what time they close, and then there's tomorrow...'

Ethan sat her down. 'Surely one of the nurses can give it to you?' Ethan suggested, but realised that, of course, she didn't want anyone to know she was on IVF. 'I can give you your injections.'

'God, no.' Penny shook her head. 'I'm not just a little bit scared of needles. I get in a right state sometimes—even worse than I am now.'

'Can't your partner come in?' Ethan asked, because Carl had given Kate hers. 'Surely he'd—'

'I don't have a partner. I'm doing this by myself.'

'You're doing this on your own?'

'Yes.'

'You mean you'd choose…' As Penny looked at him sharply, luckily Ethan had the good sense to stop talking. He just couldn't really believe someone would choose to be a parent, let alone a single one—babies really weren't his forte. But, whatever his thoughts on the subject were, they really weren't relevant here. Penny wasn't asking for his opinion, just some help with logistics. Instead, he asked where the clinic was and then looked at his watch.

'You really do need to get going if you're going to have a hope of making it there, but if the travelling gets too much, any time you need me to give you an injection, I'm more than happy to.'

'I don't think you realise how bad I am with needles.'

'There's a straitjacket in the lock-up room,' Ethan said. And he wasn't joking, there *was* a straitjacket in the lock-up room and he knew exactly how petrified some people were of needles. 'I do know how to give an injection to someone who doesn't want one, Penny. I tend to do it quite a lot.' He gave her a smile but she shook her head.

'I'll sort something out.'

'Go, then,' Ethan said. 'And thank you for today.'

Of course, it wasn't quite so straightforward as simply leaving the department and getting to her car. Three people stopped Penny on her way to her office, which she had to go to, because that's where her bag and keys were, and also her medication.

Penny dashed to her car and pulled out of the car park, ringing the IVF nurse as she did so and being put straight on hold.

Penny hit the beach road and it wasn't five in the morning, it was nearly five p.m., so the traffic was bumper to bumper. Ringing off, she turned the car round—it took fifteen minutes just to get back to work.

'I thought you'd be back.' Ethan smiled.

'Can I talk to you for a second?' She just had to let him know what he was getting into. 'I need these every night at six. I don't know how long Jasmine is going to be gone and we don't always work the same shifts.'

'I know I'm lousy at commitment, Penny,' Ethan said. 'But I think I can manage this. I can come into work if I'm not on, or you can come into me, or we can meet in a bar and go into a quiet corner.' He almost made her smile.

'From the noises I make they'd think you were attacking me!' Penny said. 'I'm not just a little bit scared of needles—I try not to, but sometimes I start crying. I just lose it.'

'It's fine.' He was annoyingly calm.

'I don't think you understand. You will not calm me

down and even if I say no, I don't want it, you have to ignore me. Just undo my skirt and stick it in.'

'I'm not even going to try to respond to that.' Ethan saw the flush spread on her cheeks and he met her eyes with a smile. 'Go and get something to eat and sit down for a while and then remind me closer to six.'

Penny tapped him on the shoulder at five to six.

'Could I have a word in my office, please, Ethan?'

'Of course.'

'I need you for a moment, Penny,' Lisa called as they walked past.

'It will have to keep.' Ethan's voice was gruff. 'Only buzz me if something urgent comes in. I need to speak with Penny.'

'It sounds as if I'm about to be told off.'

'Exactly,' Ethan said. 'So we shan't be disturbed.'

They walked into her office where Penny had things all set up and, she noted, he actually thought to lock the door. 'Is this what you were doing when I knocked for you to come for a drink with Gordon?'

Penny nodded.

'You really never know what goes on behind closed doors.' He gave her a smile and then, ever the doctor, he checked the vials and the use-by dates.

'I've already checked everything.'

'Good for you,' Ethan said, refusing to be rushed and taking the time to make sure, but it was all too much for Penny. It was bad enough that she was having a needle, but with Jasmine gone and everything it was just a whole lot worse. Seeing Ethan pick up the syringe,

Penny started to cry, and not as she had before. This was, Ethan realised, the sound of real fear.

'Okay.' He kept his voice practical, he was just going to go in and get this over and done with.

'No!' Penny shouted. She had worked herself up to try and stay calm. She could think of nothing worse then Ethan seeing her in such a terrible state and having to face him again, but her resolve had completely broken when she'd seen him pick up the injection. The last thing on Penny's mind was the result and the possibility of a baby; she just wanted to get out of there.

'No.' She said it again as he walked over with the kidney dish. 'Ethan, no, I've changed my mind.'

'Tough.'

Even as Penny said no, she was trying to undo her skirt and failing, and then when Ethan stepped in she tried to brush off his hands but failed at that too.

'Ethan, please!' Penny was doing her best not to sob and make a complete fool of herself. He put the kidney dish down on the desk behind her, his hands finding the side zip of her skirt. He pushed her against the desk and held her in place with one hip as he pulled her skirt down a little bit and reached for the alcohol swab on the desk behind him. Then Ethan turned her, resisting and crying, around and she felt the coldness of the alcohol on the top of her buttock. 'What the hell are you doing?' Penny shouted. 'It's sub-cut, you idiot…'

He turned her quickly to face him and before she even knew it, Ethan had swabbed her stomach and the needle was in.

'I know.' Ethan smiled, massaging the injection site

with one hand as he threw the needle into the kidney dish with the other. 'That's called a distraction technique, in case you were wondering.'

Only the distraction had been for him—the image of coral-coloured silk knickers and just a glimpse of the top of her bottom were branded in his mind. Now he was looking down at her lovely pale stomach as he massaged the injection in, and he saw the dots of bruises and his fingers wanted to wander there too. More than that he knew she was watching his fingers, knew he should stop now, or that she could take over, but they both just stood very close, looking down. And he actually wondered if it was wrong just how turned on he was now and, no, he did not want to fancy her.

It had been a hell of a day, a completely wretched day, and he blamed it on the funeral as he lingered a little too long. And Penny looked at his mouth and blamed it all on the hormones she was taking, because she was holding back from kissing him.

'Okay!' It was Ethan who took control, whose mind sort of jolted and alerted him to the fact that the woman he was very close to kissing, the woman he was hard for now, was very actively trying to get pregnant.

'You're done,' Ethan said. He picked up the kidney dish, turned his back and made a big deal about tipping the contents into the sharps dispenser.

She was a close colleague too, Ethan told himself. And an absolute cow to work with, he reminded himself a few times—except he knew why now.

No, he did not want to fancy Penny.

As Penny did up her zipper and smoothed down her

blouse she was not sure what, if anything, had happened just then. She was embarrassed at her tears, of course, but there was something else swirling in the room with them, an energy that must not be acknowledged.

'Thank you.'

'No problem,' Ethan clipped. 'Same time tomorrow, then?'

'Please,' Penny said. 'I mean, yes.'

CHAPTER SEVEN

ETHAN WAS ACTUALLY on a day off the next day.

He woke late, saw the black suit over the chair and tried not to think about yesterday.

Tried not to, because it had been a day of hellish emotion and it seemed impossible to think that Justin would be back at school today and the world was moving on, but not for some.

The transplant co-ordinator had been called up for the head injury patient, Heath, later in the evening, he had heard. Ethan had seen the boy's parents sobbing outside the ambulance bay on his way home.

Waking up to grief was a lot like waking up with a hangover, Ethan decided as he pieced together the previous day and braced himself to face the upcoming one. He lay there, eyes closed, trying to summon up the energy to move, to get on with his day. He should maybe ring his aunt and uncle, Ethan thought, see how they were, but he couldn't stomach it. Or ring his sister and find out how the rest of the wake had been.

Except he just wanted to be alone, just as he had wanted to be alone last night. He hadn't been able to face a bar. Even Kelly, a friend, who was more than a friend sometimes, had called, and knowing how tough the day would have been had suggested coming over.

He hadn't wanted that either.

He could go and do something, maybe a long drive down to the Ocean Road, just stay a night in Torquay or Lorne perhaps, watch the waves, get away, except, just as he thought he had a plan Ethan remembered he had to be at the hospital at six to give Penny her injection.

Penny.

Ethan blew out a breath as he recalled the near miss last night.

What the hell had he been thinking? Or rather, he hadn't been thinking in the least.

Still, he kept getting glimpses of coral underwear flashing before his eyes throughout the day.

He'd expected flesh coloured.

Not that he'd thought about it.

But *had* he thought about it, then flesh coloured it would be.

Sensible, seamless, Ethan decided as he drove to the hospital. Not that she'd need a bra.

Not that he'd noticed.

Ethan pulled into his parking spot and tried to go back, tried to rewind the clock to a few days ago, when he hadn't remotely thought of her in that way. When she had just been a sour-faced colleague who was difficult to work with, one who hadn't turned round and bewitched him with a smile.

'What are you doing here?' Rex asked as Ethan walked through the department, for once out of scrubs and dressed in black jeans and a black top.

'I need to take some work home. Is it just you on?' Ethan asked casually.

'Nope,' Rex said. 'Penny's on.' He pulled a poker face. 'She's just taking a break.'

Ethan knew that because he'd texted her to say that he was here, but he didn't want anyone getting even a hint so he stood and chatted with Rex a moment before heading to Penny's office.

'Sorry to mess up your day off.'

He checked the dose again, and she undid her zipper and just stared at the door as she lowered her skirt. Penny closed her eyes and hyperventilated but managed to stay much calmer, even if her knuckles were white as she clutched the desk behind her. In turn, Ethan was very gruff and businesslike and what they had both been silently nervous about happening was nowhere near repeated. In fact, it was all over and done with very quickly.

'Thanks for this.'

'No problem,' Ethan said.

'Will you carry on working?' Ethan asked, and Penny frowned as she tucked her shirt in. 'When you have the baby I mean.'

'If I have one,' Penny said. 'Did you ask Gordon the same question?'

'No.' He was so not into political correctness. 'But then again, Gordon isn't a single dad. And,' he added, 'despite his account of it, Gordon wasn't actually the one who got pregnant and gave birth.'

Penny laughed.

'Shall we go and see them?' Ethan said. 'It's quiet

out there at the moment and Rex is in. We could head up and just get it over with.'

'Get it over with?' Penny smiled. She had been thinking exactly the same thing. Gordon really could be the most crushing bore and she'd never really had a conversation with Hilary, a paediatrician, that hadn't revolved around baby poo.

'Sorry.' Ethan didn't know he was being teased. 'That was a bit…'

'Don't you like babies?' Penny asked as they headed towards the lifts that would take them to the maternity unit.

'Actually, no.' Ethan was honest. 'I don't actively dislike them or anything. My sister has had three now. I like the five-year-old, he makes me laugh sometimes.'

'How old is your sister?'

'Thirty-six,' Ethan said, and she remembered their phone conversation.

'You're a twin.' Penny smiled. 'On anyone else that would be cute.'

They stopped at the gift shop and bought flowers and balloons and Penny wrote a card but Ethan had forgotten to get one and asked if he could just add his name.

'You're giving me injections,' Penny said. 'Not sperm. Buy your own card.'

She was the most horrible person he had ever met, but she did make him grin, and Ethan was still smiling when they both walked into Hilary's room together.

'Penny!' Gordon seemed delighted to see them. 'Ethan!' He shook Ethan's hand. 'He's just woken up, we're just feeding.'

'Well, don't let us interrupt you. We just came in to give you these and say a quick hello.'

'Don't be daft,' Gordon said. 'Completely natural. What do you think? He's a good-looking little man, isn't he?'

Ethan peered down at the baby and to Penny's delight he was blushing. 'Congratulations,' he said to Hilary. 'He's very handsome.'

'He's gorgeous,' Penny said. 'He looks like you.'

'He looks like Gordon,' Hilary corrected her.

She could feel Ethan's exquisite discomfort beside her and to his credit he did attempt conversation, but she almost felt him fold in relief as his phone bleeped and he excused himself for a moment.

'I heard about Jed's mum,' Hilary said. 'Have you heard any news?'

'She's actually improving,' Penny said as Ethan came back in. 'They should be home in a couple of days.'

'I'm hoping to get him home soon.' Hilary looked down at her baby. 'He's a bit small, though, and the labour—'

Thankfully Penny's pager crackled into life, urgently summoning her down to Emergency.

'I'll come and see if they need me too,' Ethan offered.

'That was you.' Penny grinned as they fled out of Maternity.

'I'm sorry!' Ethan said. 'I just couldn't sit there while she fed the baby. I'm fine with patients, with women in cafés, but when I know someone…' He was honest. 'I was the same with my sister. I just break out in a sweat.

Please,' he said. 'I beg of you, when you have your baby, please don't feed it when I come to visit.'

'I promise I won't,' Penny assured him.

'I know that sounds terrible.'

'Absolutely not.' Penny could think of nothing worse than feeding a baby in front of Ethan. 'I don't even know if I want to feed it myself.'

'Stop!' Ethan said. He just didn't want to think about Penny and breasts and babies and the black panties she was wearing today.

Yes, he'd seen, even if he'd tried very hard not to.

'Sorry.' Even Penny couldn't believe she was discussing breastfeeding with him. 'You don't approve, do you?'

'Of bottle-feeding?'

She didn't smile at his joke. 'I meant you don't approve of me doing this on my own.'

'I can't really say the right thing here.'

'You can,' she offered, because she didn't mind people's *invited* opinions.

'No.' He was honest. 'I just can't imagine that someone would choose to be a single mum. My mum raised my sister and I on her own and it wasn't easy.'

'My mum got divorced,' Penny said, 'and, believe me, things got a whole lot better when Dad wasn't around.' Then she checked herself. 'Actually, things got a whole lot worse for a couple of years, but then they got better. And my sister was a single mum for a while.'

'By choice?'

'No,' Penny said. 'Well, yes, by choice, because she

had no choice but to leave Simon's dad. I really have thought things through.'

'Tell me?'

'I've got to work.'

'Dinner?' Ethan said, because he really was starting to like Penny, well, not fancy like, he told himself, but then he remembered the flash of her knickers and what had almost happened yesterday. Maybe he should recant that invitation to take her out for dinner, except he'd already asked.

'Why?'

Ethan shrugged. 'Well, I've been out with a new father and listened to his labour and if I add a woman going through IVF, I figure by the end of the week I could qualify as a sensitive new-age guy.'

Penny smiled and he had been right—she really was attractive when she did.

'Okay, then.' Her acceptance caught him just a little by surprise. He'd sort of been hoping, for safety's sake, that she might decline. 'Tomorrow,' she said. 'After you stab me.'

Penny was on a day off, so it was she who '*dropped in*' just as Ethan was finishing up.

She was wearing a dress that buttoned up at the front and her heels were a little higher. He caught the musky scent of her perfume as he followed her into the office and locked the door.

'I'll do it,' he said, taking her little cool bag.

She told him her doses and he heard the shake in her voice as she did so.

'I am so sorry about this.' He turned and she was trying to undo the little buttons on her dress. It really was a very genuine fear, made worse today because she'd had the whole drive here to think about it. Ethan actually saw her break out into a cold sweat as he approached and she was trying very hard not to cry.

'I need a bit more skin than that, Penny.' She'd only managed two buttons. 'Here.' He undid a couple more and felt the splash of a hot tear on the back of his hand. 'You must really want this baby.'

'I do.'

He could see tiny goose bumps rising on her stomach. He was really impressed with himself because he was completely matter-of-fact and, despite a glimpse of purple underwear and the heady scent of her, he was not a bit turned on. Two evenings in a row now!

He just kept reminding himself that there'd be a baby in there any time soon and that those small breasts would soon look like Hilary's.

'Done,' Ethan said.

'Thanks.'

'Where do you want to go and eat?'

Penny didn't care, so they ended up in the same pub near the hospital where he had been with Gordon, and they took a booth and sat opposite each other. He saw the dark smudges under her eyes and the paleness of her skin. The treatment must really be taking its toll by now.

'Jasmine's coming back the day after tomorrow,' Penny said. 'Well, as long as Jed's mother keeps improving, so tomorrow should be the last time you have to do it.'

'It's not an issue.'

'I am very grateful to you, though. Jasmine was worried that I'd just stop the treatment and I think she was right.'

'Have you told her I'm giving them?'

'Yes.' Penny nodded. 'She sends you her sympathies.'

He'd prefer self-restraint.

'When's your next blood test?'

'Seven a.m. tomorrow.'

'Do you want to change the next one?' Ethan asked. 'Go in a little bit later?'

Penny shook her head. 'Thanks, but it has to be done early.'

She ordered nachos smothered in sour cream and guacamole and cheese, and it surprised him because he'd thought she'd order a salad or something.

And usually she would but this was like PMS times a thousand so she just scooped up the cheesiest bit she could find and sank her teeth into it with such pleasure that Ethan wished he hadn't ordered the steak.

'Have some.' She saw his eyes linger on them.

'Who'd have thought?' Ethan said.

'I'm good at sharing.'

'I meant the two of us being out together. What a difference a week can make.'

Penny smiled and he rather wished she hadn't.

'How come you're so petrified of needles?'

'I'm not as bad as I used to be,' Penny said. 'I did hypnosis, counselling and everything, just to get to where I could let someone give me one.'

'So you think hypnosis works?'

She saw his sceptical frown. 'I don't know,' Penny admitted. 'I mean, I'm still scared of needles but the hypnotherapist did get me to remember the first time that I freaked out—I was at school and we were all lined up to get an injection and the girl in front of me passed out.'

'Mass hysteria?'

'Possibly.' Penny had thought about it practically. 'But my father had just left my mother a couple of weeks before, so apparently, according to the counsellor, it was my excuse to scream and cry.' She gave a very wicked smile. 'Load of rubbish really.' She took a sip of her drink. 'All I know is that the fear is there and I'm having to face it over and over and over. Sometimes it's terrible, sometimes it's not so bad. I was good at my blood test this morning.'

'You were good tonight.'

'Yep,' Penny said. 'And had Jasmine's mother-in-law not had a stroke, you'd never have known and we'd have been able to look each other in the eye.'

'I'm looking you in the eye now, Penny.'

She looked up and so he was. She saw that his eyes were more amber than hazel and there was a quickening to her pulse. How could she possibly be thinking such thoughts? She couldn't be attracted to Ethan. She had to stay focussed on her treatment—her plan to become a mother. Except thinking about babies had her thinking about making babies the old-fashioned way! With Ethan?

It was very warm in the bar; it must have been that causing this sear of heat between them, and Ethan wished he'd asked for his steak rare because it was taking for ever to come.

'Do you have any phobias?' she asked when thankfully his order had been delivered and normality was starting to return.

'I don't think so.'

'Flying?'

'Love it.' Ethan smiled.

'Heights?'

'They don't bother me in the least.'

She did, though, Ethan thought as he ate his steak and tried to tell himself he was out with a colleague, but Penny was starting to bother him a lot, only not in the way she once had. He was just in no position to say. To his absolute surprise where Penny was concerned, since that morning when she'd turned round and smiled, there had been a charge in the air.

One that to Ethan really didn't make sense, because he liked his women soft, curvy and cute, which was a terrible word and one he'd never admit to out loud, but that was what he liked.

And there was nothing soft about Penny and there wasn't a curve to be seen, and as for cute...

'What are you smiling at?' Penny frowned.

'Nothing.' He reminded himself of the reason they were actually out. 'So,' he asked, 'assuming this round of treatment is a success, how many embryos are you having put back?' He saw her blink at the rather personal question.

'Two.'

'I think I've just found my phobia.'

Penny grinned. He made no secret of the fact he had no desire to ever be a parent, so she asked him why.

'I'm not sure really,' Ethan admitted. 'It's the responsibility, I guess. I save it all for work. I've just never wanted to settle down, let alone have a baby.' He gave her a wide-eyed look. 'And certainly not two at the same time.'

'Twins would be lovely,' she said, 'then I'd never have to go through this again.'

'You should speak to my mum first,' Ethan said. 'I guarantee if you did you'd only put one back.'

'You said she was a single mum?'

'No,' he corrected her. 'I said that she raised us on her own. My father died when we were six.'

'I'm sorry.' She looked at him. 'Same age as Justin.'

He gave a small mirthless smile, her hit just a little too direct.

'How did you deal with it?'

Ethan gave a shrug. 'You just grow up overnight.' He never really talked about it with anyone. 'It's tough, though. I heard Vera, my aunt, telling Justin to be brave, and it was all the same stuff she told me. Then there was Jack, my uncle, he's my dad's brother, giving me lectures over the years about how I was the man of the house and I needed to be more responsible. I hope they don't say the same to Justin, it scared the life out of me.'

Maybe that was why he held on to his freedom so much, Penny mused, and she couldn't help asking more.

'And were you the man of the house?' Penny asked, and she gave a thin smile when he shrugged.

'I tried to be,' Ethan said. 'And resented every min-

ute of it. Then being a teenager sort of got in the way
of being sensible.'

'Did you miss having a dad?'

They were both being honest, and after all she had
asked, and he wasn't going to sugar coat his response
just because it was what she wanted to hear.

'Yes,' Ethan said. 'But I do accept that things are
very different now. Back then there weren't so many
women raising children alone. I used to feel the odd
one out. I'm sure that yours won't feel like that.' He
reminded himself to smile. 'Anyway, what would I
know?'

They ordered coffee and then chatted about work,
about her case review tomorrow, where once a week
the senior staff got together and reviewed a case. It was
Penny's turn and, no, she told him, she wasn't nervous.
'Just ill prepared,' Penny admitted. 'So I'd better get
home and rectify that.'

They walked out to their cars and there was a strange
moment because had she not been doing her level best
to get pregnant, had they just been out, Ethan would
have done his usual thing and kissed her. Right now
that would prove no problem at all, because as they
stood by her car, he actually forgot about needles and
ultrasounds and little people that made an awful lot of
noise and demanded to be fed a lot.

''Night, then,' she said, going into her bag for her
keys and then looking up at him.

''Night, Penny.'

He went to give her a kiss on the cheek, but changed
his mind midway. Except it was too late for that so he

went ahead, but there was an awkward moment because he missed his mark and his lips landed a little close to her mouth.

He felt the warmth of her blush on his lips and knew he should say good night and walk away. Except he wasn't holding a needle and she wasn't crying or asking him to stop and he could smell her hair and that musky perfume. He thought of the purple underwear he had glimpsed earlier.

It was all just a second, a very long second, and Penny was a guilty party in this too. Had been complicit as she'd carefully selected her underwear that morning, was as attracted as he was and, yes, she wanted his mouth. Now here it was, just the graze of his lips, and she felt as if a feather was stroking her from the inside. There was just a flare that lit between them and mouths that were a beat away from applying pressure, but neither did. Just two mouths mingling and deciding to linger, two minds racing and about to quiet and give in, but then they were literally saved by the bell, or rather by his pager.

'Did you arrange that one too?' Penny asked.

Ethan just grinned, because had he been thinking straight he might have arranged one for a few moments ago because he did not want to start anything with Penny.

Well, not Penny.

He didn't want to start anything with a soon-to-be-pregnant Penny, Ethan reminded himself as he telephoned work to find out what was happening.

'The place is steaming,' Ethan said when he came off the phone.

'Should I come in?'

'It's packed and they're not getting through them. I'll just go in for a couple of hours and help them clear the backlog. You go home.'

'You're sure?'

Ethan nodded, gave her a light kiss on the cheek that was definitely just a friendly one, a token effort to erase the one that had happened before, saw her into her car and then headed to his.

One more needle to get through, Ethan told himself.

He was almost as nervous about it as she was.

CHAPTER EIGHT

PENNY KNEW THE drill only too well.

After a very sleepless night, trying to prepare for her case presentation then later going over and over their near kiss, Penny was up at the crack of dawn and about to have her ultrasound. She went to hitch up her skirt, but she was wearing her wraparound dress and it was a bit too tight.

'Just open it up, Penny,' the sonographer said, and offered her a sheet, which she pulled over not just her stomach but her chest, because everything was exposed.

Damn.

She had been dressing for her presentation.

Or had she?

Penny honestly wasn't sure.

It *was* her presentation outfit, which had been sitting in its dry-cleaner bag for two weeks now, waiting for today. It was her grey wraparound and even though she didn't have a cleavage, it was a bit too low so underneath she wore a silver-grey cami with a bit of lace at the top, and because it was Penny she wore matching panties, which were rather more lace than silk.

And tonight she'd be getting her needle from Ethan.

It was too much, Penny decided. She'd just change into scrubs, except there was a part of her that wanted his eyes on her, a part of her that refused to be silenced, that wanted more than last night, and Penny was most unused to such strong feelings. Even now, walking to get her blood done, she was thinking of the near miss last night and what might have unfolded if they hadn't been interrupted by the pager. She blinked in astonishment at the depravity of her own thoughts.

'Morning, Penny.'

It took two attempts to get the blood this morning. She was stressed about her case presentation, worried about her choice of clothes, exhausted after a night of thinking and trying not to think about Ethan and a kiss that never happened and must never happen! This meant Penny sobbed like she never had as they took her blood.

'Finished.' The nurse smiled as she pressed down on the cotton swab. 'I think I left a bruise.'

'It's my own fault,' Penny said, because despite being held down her arm had jerked when the needle had gone in. As Penny blew her nose, instead of standing up and getting out of there as quickly as possible as she usually would, she asked a question. She was a typical doctor and had read up on things herself, but there was one bit now that was honestly confusing her. 'Can I ask a question?'

'Of course.'

'About…' She was going bright red but tried to sound matter-of-fact as she spoke. 'Increased libido?' Her voice came out as a croak and Penny cleared her throat, but the nurse was completely unfazed by her question.

'You're a walking cocktail of hormones at the moment, Penny,' the nurse said. 'Often women could think of nothing worse at this stage, but for some...'

'So it's normal?'

'Sure. Just make sure that you use protection,' the nurse said. 'It's only once we've done the embryo transfer that you need to refrain, and not just from sex, no orgasms either—which is unfortunate...' she smiled '...because an increase in libido is commonplace then.'

Penny blinked. She'd sort of skipped over all those parts, thinking that it would never really be a problem for her.

'You'll get a phone call later and we'll sort out your doses,' the nurse said. 'You'll be ready for your trigger injection any day soon. So just enjoy it for now.'

She certainly wouldn't be enjoying it! Penny just wanted these feelings to pass, wanted a neat explanation as to why she was nearly climbing the walls at the thought of Ethan. Did she fancy him or was it the medication?

And did it really matter?

Would it be so terrible to have sex with someone you really fancied even if it was going absolutely nowhere?

Stop it, she told herself as she drove to work.

Just stop it right there!

Of course the second she walked into work she saw Ethan. She tried to douse the fire in her cheeks, only it wasn't working—he was dressed in scrubs and very unshaven. He was scowling at the bed board and had clearly been up all night.

'Good sleep?' His voice was wry.

'Fantastic.' Hers was equally wry as she walked past, because she'd be lucky to have slept for more than a couple of hours, though she was glad now that she hadn't accepted the consultant's position. There was no way she could have juggled it all, she would not have coped if she'd been called in last night and had still been expected to work through the next day.

Penny got through the busy morning, doing her best to avoid him, and she had a feeling Ethan was trying to avoid her too. Both were trying to pretend that the near miss last night hadn't happened.

She headed to the lecture theatre and set up her computer, nodding a greeting as her colleagues filed in. She wasn't nervous as she was a very good public speaker, but her heart was fluttering as Ethan walked in. He'd been firing on coffee all morning but from his yawn as he took a seat in the lecture theatre for her presentation, she wouldn't be in the least surprised if he fell asleep midway through.

Penny had decided not to present about Heath, the young man with the head injury, and instead spoke about the renal patient who had come in with cardiac failure. She went through it all—the medication, the dosages, admitted to her own hesitation—suggesting a protocol sheet be implemented, and Ethan didn't fall asleep as she spoke. Instead, he watched her.

Watched her mouth move and speak, but hardly heard a word, his mind more on her pert bottom as she turned and pointed to the whiteboard. All he wanted to do was go home—why did he have to fancy Penny?

He knew that the extra jewellery and make-up and

heels were not for his benefit. It was the way Penny was and she was always going to make an extra effort for this type of thing. Except he could see the flash of lace on her cami and he wanted the effort to have been for him.

Then his eyes lingered on the tie of her dress and his mind wandered as to how he was going to get it off, or up, and it was then that she caught him looking. Her voice trailed off and they both just stared.

Really stared.

Ethan clamped his teeth together because he was incredibly tempted to silently mouth something *really* inappropriate to her, just to see those burning cheeks flame further.

'Penny?' Mr Dean asked when the silence dragged on. 'You said he was then given a bolus?'

'That's right.' She snapped back to her presentation and apart from that, apart from nearly jumping off the stage and straddling Ethan, Penny got through the rest of her speech really well. Attempting to be normal, Ethan congratulated her a little while later.

'Well done,' he said. 'I'm sorry if I offended you that day. I didn't mean to just walk in and take over.'

'But you didn't offend me.' Penny frowned and then remembered. 'I was having a hot flash, Ethan.' She watched his face break into a smile. 'It was the drugs— that was a glimpse of menopausal Penny.'

'Well, remind me, if we're both still working here then, that it's time for me to look for another job,' Ethan said laughingly.

'Are you heading off, Ethan?' Mr Dean walked past. 'You were here all night.'

'Soon,' Ethan said, then he looked at Penny. 'If I go home now I'm going to crash and I won't get back.'

'I'm so sorry.' He really did look exhausted.

'I'm going to go into the on-call room and sleep,' Ethan said. 'Get everything ready and then come and get me at five to six.'

'Thanks.'

She tried to ignore the on-call room, but every time she walked past, the thought of Ethan lying in there asleep flashed like a strobe light in her mind. If she was like this now, what the hell was she going to be like after the embryo transfer? She might be needing that straitjacket after all.

Penny set up her needle and swab and had it all laid out in her office and then, because she could at times be nice, she made Ethan a coffee before she knocked on the door of the on-call room. He was so zonked she could actually hear the low sounds of snoring.

'Ethan.' She knocked again and put her head around the door. 'Ethan, it's nearly six.' He sat up and sort of shook himself awake.

'Can you bring it in here?' He just wanted to get the injection over and done with and then go back to sleep but then he changed his mind and with good reason. 'I'll be out in a minute.'

'I brought you a coffee.'

She walked over in the darkness and he got a waft of her scent. He heard the slight rattle as she put his coffee down on the bedside table and it was right that her hand was shaking, Ethan thought, because she was seconds away from being pulled into his bed.

'Thanks,' Ethan said. 'I'll be there soon.'

He had to get himself under control—physically and mentally—before touching her.

Hurry home, Jasmine.

He'd never met Jed, let alone his mother, but he wished her the speediest, most uneventful of recoveries from her stroke. Ethan gulped his coffee and splashed his face in the sink and then walked to Penny's office.

'Ready?'

'Yes.' She was fiddling with the tie of her dress and he could hear her starting to cry, just sort of breathy sobs that she was trying to keep in.

'Okay, then.' He walked towards her, and she was a mess, a hot mess at that, Ethan thought as he looked at her eyes. They showed a mixture of fear and lust and if she said no to the injection this time, he would drop the needle.

He didn't want her to do this.

He wanted her to stop so that they could do what people who fancied each other did.

A lot.

He wanted to go out and have more dinners and have nachos himself next time and go far too far in a car park and then go even further back home.

'No.' She pushed at his hand as it reached for her dress tie, and he was breathing very hard now—tired, turned on, pissed off. He didn't want to do this either.

'What do you want, Penny?' He forgot he wasn't supposed to ask, he was supposed to go ahead and give her the needle. Her hands were on his arm and he tried to ignore the feel of her fingers on his skin. He tried to undo the tie for her as if he hadn't been thinking about doing just that all day.

She had on silver-grey knickers and a matching cami, and through the silk he could tell her chest was almost completely flat. He liked curves, Ethan told himself, except he wanted his mouth to lower to the thick nipples he could see rising out of the fabric, and as he swabbed her stomach he caught a glimpse of blonde hair above her panty line and he could see a bit through the lace too.

And he did *not* want to give her this needle. He could hear her gulping and soft whimpers and feel her breath on his cheek, and he did not want to do it.

But he'd signed up for the gig so he swabbed her skin and though he hesitated over her stomach, he finally stuck the needle in.

'There,' he said. 'You're done.'

Ethan rubbed her stomach and then she took over. His hand did not linger, he just wanted this over and done, wanted out and home. Maybe tonight he'd call Kelly, get this Penny fantasy out of his head once and for all.

Then he saw the lust in her eyes and her lips were moving towards his and he jerked his head backwards. 'Penny!' he warned.

She screwed her eyes closed at his rejection. She'd have to resign, it was all just so unlike her. 'I'm so sorry, Ethan. I think it's the drugs, it's like I'm on heat.'

He'd embarrassed her, Ethan knew that, which he'd

never wanted to do. She had no need to be embarrassed. He wanted her too, so he tried to soften things, except he was rock hard. 'I just don't want to start something with someone who's trying for a baby.'

'I know. I get that completely. I'm never like this...' She attempted her excuses again as he dropped the needle into the dish behind her. 'It's the drugs.'

'It's not the drugs, Penny,' Ethan said, because he wasn't taking any, but hormones were certainly raging and he stopped fighting it then, his mouth coming down on hers the way it had wanted to last night.

She almost came just at the pressure of his mouth as her stomach hollowed with lust. It wasn't a brief kiss, it wasn't unsure and whatever the opposite of tentative was should be called Ethan, because his tongue was deliciously crude, his unshaven jaw surely shredding her skin. Penny was no saint either. Her hands were in his hair, her scantily clad body pressing into him, feeling his fierce erection, and he pulled away just a little.

'Penny...'

'I know,' she said. 'I know this is going nowhere.'

'You understand?'

'Of course.' She was in her office, with her dress undone, and it was all so inappropriate, especially for someone like Penny, so much so that she fought an incredible urge to laugh. Then she stopped fighting and laughed a little bit. 'If you knew me, you'd know that it *is* the drugs. I'm going to be so embarrassed later.'

'Why?' He smiled down. 'It's just a kiss,' Ethan said, 'a one-off.'

'An anomaly,' Penny said. 'Never to be repeated or

mentioned again. As soon as you walk out the door we're done.'

'I'm not out the door yet.'

She was more than happy with the ground rules, just for the bliss of the return of his mouth.

It was just a kiss but it was a kiss with a secret. His fingers were working her nipples through the silk of her cami till she moaned in his mouth and then he slipped his hand up the cami so that skin could meet skin. He worked them a little more firmly. Normally she loathed that, hated the beat of disappointment when they found out that she really was quite flat-chested, but it just didn't matter right now. If anything he was even more turned on because he pressed his erection hard into her, and she almost came undone—a ball of hot tension in his arms.

And it was still just a kiss, but the secret was deepening, his hand now sliding into her panties, and they would both never repeat or mention it again, but in this too he knew what to do. He cupped her for a moment before he began to stroke her with precision, and he couldn't for a moment kiss and concentrate, so he let her mouth work his neck, and then he warned her to be careful because there must be no evidence, and as she removed her mouth, Penny lost her head.

She just gave in to the bliss and the scent of him, her hands around his neck to steady herself, her legs shaking as she fought the urge for him to lift her, to wrap her legs around his waist, yet she stood as she forgot how to breathe.

Ethan felt the rip of tension and her quiver and her

thighs clasp around his hand and he stroked through her pulses as frantic need left her and leached into him, and he got back to kissing her, but with urgency. Pressing himself hard into her, Ethan's hands moved to lift her, a fierce need to be inside her, but then sense reared its head and moved into his and he released her hips, because if he didn't, he would have her over that desk.

And, no, Ethan told himself, that he did not want.

Except he did.

No wonder he didn't like being responsible, Ethan thought, peeling them apart. 'And now I'm handing you back to Jasmine.' He looked down and smiled and she looked up and nodded, and there was that awkward bit, because she had come and he hadn't, and she wanted more too, yet he was releasing her, about to head out there to where this had never happened.

'Ethan…' She wanted more of him, wanted more than a corner of chocolate before it was wrapped and returned to the fridge, and she didn't care if they were in her office; right now, she simply didn't care.

'Penny.' He gave her a small kiss to interrupt her invitation, and then he made it very clear where they were. 'You go and concentrate on getting that baby.'

CHAPTER NINE

IT WAS ALL happening.

It was like a train she had boarded and she so badly wanted the baby at the end, but she'd lost something along the way. Ethan was a bit aloof and she was back to being frosty but she missed the Ethan she had glimpsed and, in turn, he wanted more of Penny, just not *that* much more.

Because Ethan knew what was happening now. He didn't turn a hair when she asked if they could swap their days off at short notice.

'Sure,' was all he said.

He asked no questions, though he did look things up on the internet, knew that when she came back after her couple of days off, there was a high chance she would be as horny as hell.

But no orgasms allowed, Ethan thought with a black smile as he knocked on her office door to update her on one of her patients.

'I feel like a delivery boy,' he said, holding a card and chocolates.

She wished she had a delivery boy who looked like Ethan—she'd be ringing for pizza every night, Penny thought as he handed his wares over. 'Heath's parents asked me to give these to you.'

'You should have buzzed me.' Immediately Penny stood, but Ethan shook his head.

'I went to, but they were getting upset so they asked if I could just hand these to you. I think they were a bit overwhelmed being back in Emergency.'

Penny nodded and sat back down.

'I spoke to them for a bit,' Ethan told her.

'How were they?' Penny asked as she read the letter.

'Just struggling through. They said they knew that one day they'd be pleased with the decision they had made for Heath to be a donor, but not yet.' And Penny nodded because the letter said much the same—thanking her for her care that day and for gently preparing them for what was to come a few hours later. She showed the letter to Ethan and as he read it he forgot to be aloof, forgot he didn't really want to be talking with Penny at the moment.

'I couldn't have dealt with it that day,' he admitted.

'I'm not surprised.'

'Phil used to feel guilty about that. He said he was lying there basically hoping someone would die.'

'You can't think like that.'

'But you *do* think like that,' Ethan admitted. 'Because even I was thinking that if Phil had lasted for just a few more days...'

'There are a lot of people waiting for hearts.' Penny said, practical with the facts. 'And a lot of hearts are wasted. How's Justin dealing with it all?'

'I don't know,' Ethan admitted, and saw the rise of

her eyebrows. 'It's all a bit of a mess. Gina wants nothing to do with Phil's side of the family and I can't say I blame her. She wasn't exactly treated well by my uncle and aunt.' He gave a tired shrug. 'Anyway, there's nothing I can do.' He went to ask how she was doing, but changed his mind—he really didn't want a conversation about egg retrieval and a five-day wait before embryo transfer. 'I'd better get back out there.'

'Sure,' Penny said, but there was an impossible tension between them.

And so they muddled through and it was a bit easier to be aloof than he'd thought it might be, because he was a bit fed up too, not just with Penny but with himself. He didn't particularly like the superficial Ethan who, a couple of weeks later, had this guilty image of Penny's test results being negative and asking her for a night out in the city to cheer her up and then taking her back to his apartment to make love, not babies.

And, yes, he was glad it was a long weekend coming up and that in one hour from now he'd be out of there.

Hopefully without seeing Penny, because she was about to start a stint of nights and was off today.

Then, just when he thought he'd got through it, in Penny walked. She had Jasmine's toddler son with her—must be picking him up from crèche to help Jasmine out. He saw Jasmine give her a brief, excited hug, saw Penny warn her to hush, and even without that, Ethan knew that she was pregnant, he just knew from the timing, because he'd been back on the IVF site again.

And, no, there was no avoiding her and no avoiding

the fact he was crazy about a woman who was pregnant, and not with his child.

'Hi, there.' Jasmine had taken Simon to the vending machine and he came over when she caught his eye. 'Ready for nights?' he asked.

'As I'll ever be.'

'So?' he asked, because even if he didn't want to know, he knew. 'How are you?'

'Good,' Penny said, and her back teeth clamped down because she wanted to tell him her news but it was far too early. But more than that she wanted to flirt, she wanted him and he was just out of bounds. She wanted dates and dinners and laughter and fun, yet she badly wanted the baby inside her too. 'What are you doing for the long weekend? Anything nice?'

'Yep.' Ethan nodded. It had been a long day and now, with the unspoken news hanging between them, more than ever he just wanted to get away. 'I've got the long weekend and then two days off, I'm not back here till Thursday. I'm going out on a boat and hopefully we'll all be eating too much, drinking too much and talking too much.'

'With friends?' She thought her face would crack from smiling.

'Family,' Ethan said. 'We do it every year.'

'Sounds great,' Penny said. 'Kate will have her hands full.' Penny could imagine nothing worse than being at sea with toddlers—she'd have a nervous breakdown.

'God, no.' Ethan pulled a face. 'Once a year my mum has them all for her so she can get away. Kate says it keeps her sane. It would never happen otherwise.'

'I don't blame her,' Penny said. 'She'd be worried sick trying to keep tabs on them on a boat.'

'I meant I wouldn't be going if she brought them.' He hesitated, tried to turn it into a joke and then stopped, but he'd said it all, really—he was Mr R&R, heading off, kicking back and just so removed from the world she was about to join.

'It sounds lovely,' Penny said, because a few nights out at sea with Ethan, well, there was not a lot she could think of that sounded nicer than that.

He looked at her for a very long time, wished she could come along, could almost see her in a sarong with sunburnt shoulders, and he couldn't help but regret all the things they could have done, all the dates they could have been on and he was, for a ridiculous moment, tempted to ask her to see if she could swap her nights with someone and come with him, but he stopped himself, because even if the impossible could be achieved, he soon saw the real picture.

No wine, because she wasn't drinking.

No seafood either.

And throwing up on the hour every hour as Kate had done one year.

'Have a good break,' Penny said.

Oh, he fully intended to!

Only it wasn't that great.

Given what had had happened in recent weeks, it was a far more sombre affair, of course.

'You're quiet,' Kate commented on the Saturday

morning. It was a glorious day, the sky blue, the wind crisp and the sun hot.

'I think we're all quiet,' Ethan said.

'I rang Gina.' Ethan looked over, hoping there had been some progress, but Kate shook her head. 'I said maybe we could get the kids together, but she said no. Surely she can't keep Justin from his grandparents?'

'I guess she can,' Ethan said. 'Or she can make it as difficult as possible for them to see him, which she is.' He shook his head. 'I'm staying out of it.'

'Ethan, you can't do nothing.'

'I can,' he interrupted, 'because if I say what I really think about the situation, it's going to be a few very long days at sea.'

'Say it to me,' Kate pushed.

'Are you sure?' He looked at his sister, who nodded. 'Phil should have sorted this.' He watched her jaw tighten and Kate struggled for a moment before she could respond.

'He didn't know this was going to happen.'

'Yes, he did,' Ethan interrupted. 'I told him to sort this. I told him he had to work things out between his parents and Gina. Phil knew full well the mess he'd be leaving behind if he didn't sort something out. I know he did, because I told him. Frankly, I don't blame Gina for wanting to have nothing to do with us. Maybe Jack and Vera should have thought about the future before they opened their mouths when Gina had the audacity to break up with their son.'

'No one knew then how sick Phil was going to get.'

'No one ever knows what the future holds.' Ethan

refused to turn Phil into a saint and even if his aunt and uncle were grieving, it didn't suddenly make them infallible. 'I love Jack and Vera and I loved Phil, but the fact is that some of this mess is of their own making,' Ethan said. 'See now why I'm staying out of it?'

Kate nodded and looked at her rarely angry brother and was positive something else was eating him. 'Is there anything else going on?'

They were close, they were twins and they spoke a lot, but Ethan had only once before said what he was about to. 'I like someone.'

Kate saw his grim face. 'Married?' she groaned.

'No.'

'How long have you known her?'

'Since I started my new job, well, just after. She was having a couple of weeks off.'

'What's she like?'

'Moody, angry, funny, single…'

'Kids?' Kate checked, because there had to be a 'but'.

'Pregnant.' He looked at his sister. 'Only just.'

'Ethan!' Kate couldn't keep the excitement from her voice, but she didn't get carried away when she saw his face. 'I know you said it's not for you, but—'

'The baby's not mine!' Ethan quickly interrupted. 'Penny's on IVF. She's determined to be a single mum, she'd already started her treatment when we met.'

'Oh, Ethan.'

'I was giving her the shots.'

'Why?'

'Because she's petrified of needles and I didn't fancy her then, or maybe I did.' He shook his head. 'Kate, I don't even think I want kids, you know it broke Caitlin and I up. But even if I could somehow wrap my head around that, I mean even if I'd met Penny and she already had a child...' He pulled a face. 'I don't know, Kate. I can't walk around watching her get bigger with someone else's child.'

'Ethan,' Kate said. 'You know Carl and I were both having problems.' She was very careful not to say too much, but he knew that they had both been having problems, that all three of their children were Carl's in everything but genes.

'I get that,' Ethan said. 'But I bet Carl took a bit of time to get his head around it, and I bet he said a few things while he did that he wished he could take back now.'

And Kate stayed silent, because her brother was right—it had taken a lot of talking and a lot of soul searching before Carl had come round. 'And that was with two people who both desperately wanted kids and I don't even know that I do. I just walked in on the end of Penny's decision and I'm supposed to be fine with it? Well, I'm not and I'll tell you this much. I can't even...' He shut his mouth. He wasn't going to discuss *everything* with his sister and he couldn't explain properly, even to himself, the strange possessiveness that had gripped him when he'd almost slept with Penny.

'What do *you* want, Ethan?'

'Penny,' Ethan said. 'But I want time with Penny. I want to get to know her some more, it's still early days. I don't want to start something with someone who has a baby on board and be the one holding the sick back when I didn't cause it.' He looked at his sister. 'Selfish?'

'Honest.'

'And I'm angry too.'

'Why?'

'It doesn't matter.'

'Ethan?'

'It really doesn't matter,' Ethan said, even though he hated it when others did that. 'Because it's not relevant now.'

They couldn't carry on talking as they were being called for. The engines were still and he stood there as Phil's ashes were scattered. He looked at his aunt and uncle, who had been so strong at the funeral, celebrating his life, weep as the wind carried away the last thing they could do for him.

Only it wasn't just Phil that Ethan was thinking about as they stood in silence on deck. He wanted Penny to be happy, he was pleased for her, just terribly disappointed for them. Maybe he could do it, maybe he would wrap his head around it in a few months' time, but he felt as if there were a gun to it now and he looked at the ashes sinking into the waves and he was crying.

Not a lot and he didn't stand out, there wasn't a dry eye on board. He had every reason to be choked up, but he was, Kate knew, shedding a tear for other reasons too.

Penny didn't mind working nights, and she was actually glad that Ethan was on leave because she just wanted a pause to sort out how she felt about him. She wanted the hormones to calm down so she could look at things a bit more objectively. Not that she'd had even a moment to think about Ethan tonight; the place had been busy from the start of her shift and she was trying to put an NG tube down a very restless patient.

'Come on, Mia, swallow,' Penny said. 'You need this.'

'I don't want the tube.'

'Then you have to drink the charcoal.'

Mia had taken an overdose and to stop the tablets from being absorbed further, she had to be given a large drink of activated charcoal. It looked terrible, it was black and chalky, but as Penny and Vanessa had told the patient over and over, it actually didn't taste too bad. It was all to no avail, though—despite a lot of coaxing they'd only managed to get half the liquid into Mia.

'If you can let me put this tube down your nose and into your stomach, we can put the rest of it down and you won't have to taste it,' Penny said, 'and then you can have a rest, but it's imperative that you have the charcoal.'

'I can't.' The poor girl was upset already—after a huge row at her boyfriend Rory's house she'd stupidly swallowed some pills and when she'd got home her parents had thought she'd been drinking. When Mia had finally admitted what she had done, before calling the ambulance, there had been another row for Mia with her parents shouting at her, even as the paramedics arrived.

They'd started shouting again when Rory had arrived at the hospital, when most of all Mia needed calm, and

Penny was doing her best to ensure that Mia got it, but first she *had* to get the charcoal in.

'Do you want Rory to come in?' Penny suggested. 'He offered before.'

Mia nodded and Penny called the young man in. At eighteen Rory was very mature and he held both Mia's hands as Penny got ready to have another go at putting the tube down.

'Big breath,' Penny said, 'and then start to swallow when the tube hits the back of your throat.'

Except she didn't swallow. Instead, Mia vomited all over Penny's gown, so much so that it soaked through to her clothing.

'It doesn't matter,' Penny said soothingly as Mia started sobbing her apology. 'Let's give it another go.'

The cubicle looked as if someone had been playing with a black paintball and the staff and patients didn't look much better either, but finally the tube was in. Penny checked its position, relieved that the tube was in the right spot.

'Right, let's get the charcoal in and then you can have a rest.' The medication was poured down and Penny had a word with the intern, Raj, before she headed to the changing rooms. She was incredibly tired and couldn't wait for the couple of hours till the end of her shift.

Penny kept a spare set of clothes at work, but it was five a.m. and she was past caring so, rarely for her, she pulled some scrubs off the trolley, filled the sink with water to try and soak her shirt, and it was as she did so that Penny felt it—a cold feeling down below. She wanted to be imagining things, wanted to be wrong, so she dashed to the loo, but as she pulled down her panties it was confirmed that, no, she wasn't imagining things.

'Please, no,' Penny begged as she sat with her head in her hands, trying to tell herself it was normal, just some spotting, that it wasn't her period she was getting.

Penny couldn't stand to call it a baby; it was the only way she had been able to get through it last time. So she told herself that it was just a period, said over and over to herself that most women wouldn't have even have known that they were pregnant at this stage.

Except Penny knew that she fleetingly had been.

'Penny!' She heard Vanessa come into the changing room.

'Can I have two minutes?'

'Mia's not well.'

'I'm on my way,' Penny said through gritted teeth.

'She's seizing,' Vanessa went on.

'Then what are you doing in here, talking to me?' Penny shouted. 'Put out an urgent page for the medics.'

As Vanessa fled, with shaking hands Penny had to find change to buy a pad and then pulled on scrubs and dashed back to Mia. Raj was there and had given Mia diazepam; she had stopped seizing but was clearly very unwell.

'She's taken something else,' Penny said, because the medications Mia had admitted to taking would not have caused this.

'I've just spoken to the family.' Vanessa's voice was shaky. 'The boyfriend's ringing his mum to go through all the bins and things as they were at his house when she took them.'

'Good.'

Penny was tough, she *had* to be tough, she just didn't let herself think about personal things; instead she focussed on saving a sixteen-year-old girl who had made a stupid mistake that might now cost her her life. As soon as Rory came off the phone she spoke to the distressed boyfriend to try and get more clues as to what Mia might have taken.

'Mum's on anti-depressants.' Rory looked bewildered. 'I didn't even know that she was, but she's had a look and one of the packets is missing. She thinks—'

'Okay, what are they called?'

He told her and Penny kept her expression from reacting—she didn't want to scare the young man any more than he already was, but tricyclic antidepressants were very serious in overdose and could cause not just seizures but cardiac arrhythmias.

Leaving Rory, Penny told the medics what the young girl had taken and then dealt with the parents, who were still blaming the boyfriend.

'He has been very helpful,' Penny said. 'If it wasn't for Rory, we wouldn't have known what Mia had taken, and he also helped us to get the tube down. Mia's actually had the right treatment—the charcoal will stop any further absorption, but she'll need to go to Intensive Care for observation.'

'When can we see her?' the father asked.

'I can take you in there now,' Penny offered, because Mia was awake now, though very drowsy, but first she just wanted to clarify something with the parents. 'I know you're very upset at the moment, but it has to be put aside for now. Mia needs calm, she is not to be distressed.' Penny looked up as Rory walked in.

'What the hell did you say to upset her enough to take all those pills?' the father flared. 'You caused this.'

'I'm sorry!' Penny stood. She'd heard enough. 'Until you calm down, you're not coming in to see Mia.'

'You can't stop me from seeing her.'

'Absolutely I can.' Penny stood firm. 'Mia is to be kept as calm as possible. We're trying to prevent further arrhythmias or seizures, not actively bring them on.'

She walked off and started writing up her notes, and finally a rather more contrite father asked if he could go in and see his daughter now, assuring Penny he would not cause her any further distress.

'Of course.'

She stepped behind the curtain to have a quick word with Vanessa before letting them in.

'Mia's parents want to come in,' Penny said. 'Don't take any nonsense from the dad if he starts getting angry. Just ask him to leave.'

'I don't take nonsense from the patients and their relatives,' Vanessa said, and as Penny turned to go she heard the nurse mutter, 'I've got no choice with the staff, though…'

Penny didn't have the time, let alone the emotional capacity, to respond to Vanessa, or even to dwell on it. She had no alternative other than to drag herself through the last part of her shift, then she got into her car and finally she was home.

Penny took off her scrubs. Her stomach was black

from the charcoal and she showered quickly then put on a nightdress and picked up the phone.

'I'm bleeding.'

The IVF nurse was very practical and calm and, yes, a bit of spotting was normal, but this was more than a bit of spotting and they went through the medications, but Penny could feel herself cramping.

'Should I rest?' She wanted to ring in sick but she knew deep down that it wouldn't make any real difference.

But she rang in sick anyway.

Work was less than impressed, because it was the long weekend and one consultant was out on a boat and Mr Dean was on a golf weekend, but whether or not it would make a difference to the outcome, Penny couldn't have gone into work anyway—she just lay in bed, trying to hold on to something she was sure she'd already lost.

'I'm sorry, Penny.' It was Tuesday night. She'd actually stopped bleeding but didn't dare hope, yet there was a tiny flicker there when she took the call, only to hear that her HCG levels were tumbling down.

All that for twenty-four hours of being pregnant.

Jasmine's periods were later than that sometimes.

'Oh, Penny, I'm so sorry!' Jasmine, who the second she'd heard that Penny had called in sick, had been in and out of her home all over the weekend. She was there too when the nurse called with her blood results and Jasmine wrapped her in a hug when Penny put down the phone after the news. But Penny could feel Jasmine's belly soft and round and pressing into her stupid empty flat one and Penny said some horrible things.

Horrible things.

Like, no, actually, Jasmine didn't understand.

And that it was all right for Jasmine to stand there and be so compassionate and understanding when she didn't actually have a clue how it felt to not even be able to get pregnant. Except it was a bit worse than that because Penny used the F word and then asked her sister to get out.

'Penny, please!'

'No!'

She was back to being a bitch.

CHAPTER TEN

THERE WERE DISADVANTAGES to being a consultant, as Ethan was finding out, because when he came back from his long-awaited days off, which had actually turned into more of an extended wake, half his colleagues were sulking because he'd been out of range and they'd been called in to work.

'Penny's sick?' Ethan frowned when Lisa told him.

That Penny might be ill wasn't the problem apparently, though it was the problem for Ethan. 'We had a locum for two nights and Mr Dean came in, but he wasn't too pleased.' Lisa brought him up to speed.

'But if she's sick, she can't help it,' Ethan pointed out as a knot tightened in his stomach. 'When did she ring in?'

'Saturday morning.' Lisa sighed. 'At the beginning of a long weekend. It's been a bit grim here, to say the least.'

But it wasn't just Penny they were annoyed at.

'Did you have a good break?' Mr Dean gave a tight, mirthless smile as he walked past, but Ethan just rolled his eyes. He didn't give a damn about things like that—he worked hard when he was here and was entitled to his days off. The only person Ethan was worried about now was Penny.

Except when he tried to call her, she didn't pick up her phone.

'How's Penny?' Ethan asked a worried-looking Jasmine when she arrived for her late shift.

Jasmine's cheeks flushed and she just gave a brief shake of her head.

'Did she lose it?'

Ethan grimaced when Jasmine gave a reluctant nod.

Ethan headed to his office and rang Kate and told her the little he knew.

'Don't call it *it*,' Kate suggested.

'I didn't mean it like that.'

'I know,' Kate said. 'Poor thing.'

'I don't know what to do.' Ethan didn't even know how he felt. He was gutted for Penny as he thought of all she had been through.

But there was guilt there as well.

'I don't know what you can do either,' Kate admitted, because Carl had been as invested in the procedures as she had and had been right there beside her when on many occasions the news hadn't been good. But though she utterly understood where her brother was coming from, he wasn't going to react as Carl had.

'Do I just not mention it? I mean…'

'No,' Kate said, but then halted. 'I don't know. You said she hadn't told you she was pregnant?'

'I can't just ignore it,' Ethan said. 'She won't pick up the phone.'

'You really like her?'

'Yes.'

'Then I think you ought to go over there and just be ready.'

'For what?'

'For anything.'

Even as he rang the bell, Ethan had absolutely no idea if he was doing the right thing.

It just couldn't go past without being noted.

That was all he knew.

She opened the door in her dressing gown, except it was undone and underneath she had on a short night-dress. Ethan hadn't known many woman who wore silky nightdresses and matching dressing gowns, but this was Penny, he reminded himself, and even if she was a bit washed out, she still looked stunning.

'I'm so sorry, Penny.'

She looked at him, all brown and healthy and brim-ming with energy from nearly a week off, and she felt drab and pale in comparison. 'How do you know?' Penny asked. 'Did Jasmine say something?'

Ethan hadn't even made it through the door and he'd already put his foot in it. 'No,' Ethan said. 'I asked her when I heard you'd called in sick.'

'She shouldn't have said anything.'

'She didn't say a word,' Ethan said. 'I asked if you'd…' He breathed out. 'Penny, I knew before you went away that you were pregnant.'

'How?'

How? Because she was buried so deep in his skull, he'd been on IVF sites and working out dates and watching her unseen, constantly tuned in to her, though she didn't need to hear that. 'I just knew,' Ethan said. 'Jasmine didn't say a word.'

Penny opened the door further and let him in.

'I didn't know what to bring.' He was very honest with his discomfort and it helped that he didn't try to hide it. It helped that he had come too.

'Wine would have been nice.'

'I can go out and get some.'

'I've got some open.' Penny looked at him warily. 'I'm not very good company.'

'I'm not here for a party.'

'Well, you won't get one. I'm boring even me now in my quest for a baby, so I'd run for the beach now if I were you. I know it's not your thing. I'll be back to normal soon.'

'Come here,' he said, and he gave her a cuddle. She wriggled a bit as she had the first day he'd held her and then she gave in; it felt really nice to be held by him.

'Do you want me to go out and get a bottle?'

'No. I'm drinking alone. Well, not alone, I've got my cat.'

And an ugly cat it was too, Ethan thought as feline eyes narrowed in suspicion at a big male stomping through the room. He followed Penny to where she was retrieving her glass and bottle from her bedside table and hovered at the door.

'I'm a cliché,' Penny said. 'I'll be the mad aunt, if Jasmine ever lets me see them again.' She closed her eyes. 'I had a terrible argument with her when I found out. I'm a horrible sister.'

'I'm sure you're not.'

'I am.' Penny sniffed. 'We've never been that close, but for the last few months we've both really tried, and now I've gone and ruined it. I told her that she had no idea how I felt.'

'She doesn't,' Ethan said.

'But she tries so hard to. It's not her fault, I just…' She was embarrassed to admit just how bad she'd been, but was too guilt ridden to gloss over it. 'She gave me a cuddle and I could feel her stomach and I told her that, no, she didn't know, but I said it more nastily than that.' Worried blue eyes lifted to him and a dark blush spread on her cheeks. 'It wasn't just that she's pregnant, though.' She stopped. She certainly wasn't about to share her shameful truth. 'It doesn't matter.'

'Tell me.'

'I can't.'

'You can.'

'I really can't.'

'I hate that,' Ethan said. 'I hate it when people go, oh, it doesn't matter, when clearly it does, and then they say they can't tell you, and you know that it's something relevant, except you're not allowed to know.'

She actually smiled a little when she responded to him. 'You're *not* allowed.'

'Fine.' Ethan sulked.

'If I told you and you ever said anything, I'd have to kill you.'

Ethan couldn't help but smile but more than that they were sitting down on the sofa together and Penny was, Ethan realised, actually going to reveal. 'When my mum was bought in in cardiac arrest, it was awful. I mean, just awful. Jasmine was on duty but I managed to keep it from her...'

'While you worked on your mum?'

'And I was upset. I mean, really upset.'

'I would imagine so.'

'And Jed gave me a cuddle, nothing more. What I didn't know then was that Jasmine was seeing Jed. Confused?'

'Not yet.'

'But Jasmine saw us together, before she knew about Mum, I mean...'

'And thought you two were together?' Ethan checked, and Penny nodded. 'And were you?'

'Never.'

'Not a little bit?' Ethan checked.

'Not a smudge,' Penny confirmed. 'But...' She just couldn't bring herself to say it.

'You liked him?'

'A bit.' She was just this ball of guilt. 'I wasn't having dirty dreams or anything.' She went red as she looked at Ethan, because she was having the rudest ones about him. 'But, yes, I sort of liked him. I don't remotely in that way now, I mean that, but at the time...'

'It hurt to find out they were together.'

'Yes,' Penny admitted.

'And now she's got the baby.'

'Two.'

'Penny.' Ethan was honest too. 'Can I tell you something?' He took her hands. 'I think it's completely normal to like someone, to fancy them. I like and fancy people all the time, it's not an issue, even if the two of you…'

'Nothing happened.'

'Which makes things a whole lot easier. But…' he didn't really see the issue '…suppose,' Ethan said, 'just suppose Jasmine was single, and given all we've done is had one kiss, well, a bit more than that…'

And Penny felt the heat of breath in her nostrils, and it burnt a whole lot more than it had with Jed, except she couldn't really tell him that when he was trying to prove a point about how inconsequential it was.

'Okay, bad example.' Ethan scrambled for other scenarios. 'Suppose—'

'I get your point.' She did. In one fell swoop he'd made her realise just how teeny her feelings for her— unknown at the time—future brother-in-law had been. She thought of Jasmine walking alongside her on the beach, admitting how gorgeous Ethan was, and what a tiny deal it had been then.

'You've done nothing wrong,' Ethan said. 'Are you not supposed to like anyone, just in case your sister might?'

'I guess.' Penny couldn't believe how easily a simple conversation had dispersed the complicated into nothing. 'I don't want Jed, and I am pleased she's pregnant.' She looked at Ethan. 'It was just all too much that day. Do you ever feel jealous that Kate has a family?'

'No.' He was honest. 'I just can't imagine ever being settled like that, just one person for the rest of your life. And…' he gave a shrug '…I think we've found another phobia of mine.' He took a deep breath; there was one thing he needed to know. 'Will you try again?'

'I don't know,' Penny said. 'Probably. But they like you to wait a couple of months.'

'You're thirty-four, Penny,' Ethan said.

'Thirty-five,' Penny said. 'It's my birthday.'

He didn't know what to say.

And clearly neither did Jasmine, because the phone rang then and Penny took it into her bedroom. It was a very short, terse phone call and when it was over Penny looked up at him in the doorway, only this time he came in.

'Do you ever fight with your sister?' she asked as he sat with her on the bed and put his arm around her.

'Not really,' Ethan said.

'With anyone?'

'No.' He gave her a smile. 'You.'

But it wasn't enough for Penny. She wanted him to have done something as terrible as she had, and so he thought for a moment, searched his brain for someone he'd had a huge stand-up row with, just to make her feel better.

'With Phil.'

'When?' Penny frowned.

'Last year. There was stuff that needed dealing with and Phil wasn't dealing with it. And I told him so and pretty loudly too.' Ethan gave her a nudge. 'So if you feel bad, imagine having a shouting match with someone who has a heart like a balloon about to burst.'

'But it didn't.'

'No, it didn't. Well, not for another year.' Ethan shook his head; he wasn't going to go there.

'You really loved him, didn't you?'

'Yep.' Ethan nodded. 'But I'm here about you.'

They were lying on the bed now, more two friends chatting than this being about anything sexual, even as the conversation turned to sex. 'Have you ever thought about going about it the old-fashioned way?' Ethan asked. 'Meet someone, fall in love, live the fairy-tale.'

'Been there, done that. Well, I thought it was love and we were frantically trying for a baby for a very long time.'

He'd been doing really well, Kate would have been proud of him, but he grimaced a bit then and she noticed.

'What?'

'Nothing.' Ethan shrugged. He just didn't like the image of her *frantically* trying with someone else.

'I'm not very fertile—I'm sub-fertile. Isn't that the most horrible word? It put a terrible strain on our relationship. It wasn't just that, though, he was…' She was about to say it didn't matter, but Ethan hated it when she did that. 'Vince was all for the modern working woman, or so he said, yet I was the one who was going to be the stay-home mum.' Ethan looked at her. 'I earned more than him, yet it was just assumed that I'd be the one to stop work.' She saw him frown. 'What?' Penny asked again.

'Why, if you're doing all you can to have a baby, would you want to work?'

'I love my work, I'd go crazy without it, but I would

certainly slow things down. It wasn't just that, though, there were other things.'

'Like what?'

'Like I was starting to resent that it was always me stopping at the supermarket on the way home from work and getting dinner. Aside from the fact that I can't have babies, I don't think I'd make a very good wife.'

'What's for dinner, Penny?'

He made her smile.

'What about you?'

'I have no idea,' he said, and turned and smiled at her now-frowning face on the pillow beside him. 'I've never had my fertility checked.'

'You think you're funny, don't you?'

'I know I am,' Ethan said, 'because you're trying really hard not to smile.'

'I meant, have you been in a serious relationship?'

'Apparently,' Ethan said. 'Though I didn't know it at the time.' He sighed at the memory. 'I thought it was great, she wanted to move in…'

'Oh.'

'Or look for somewhere to live, or get engaged and then married and make lots of babies one day.'

'What was her name?'

'Caitlin. I led her on apparently, but I didn't know that I was, I just thought we were having a good time. I didn't realise it had to be leading somewhere—so now I make things a little more clear from the start.' He waited, his eyes checking that he had.

'I get it, Ethan.' She gave him a smile and then she

told him. 'Jasmine said I should have a wild fling with you before I got pregnant.'

'I'm that much of a sure thing, am I?'

'Apparently,' Penny said. 'She thought I should forget about making babies and just enjoy myself for once.'

'Have you ever had sex for the sake of it?' He screwed up his face. 'I mean, how long since you've had sex without trying for a baby?'

'A very long time.' She looked at him. 'There was one time that I would have, but he declined.'

'Well, maybe he was just being all male and territorial and couldn't quite get his head around...' He screwed up his face again, tried to spare the details. 'You know in a few days' time you...'

'Might have been pregnant?'

'No, not just that.'

Penny frowned and then got it. 'With someone else's baby!' She actually laughed. 'You *are* a caveman!'

'Nope, just a normal man.' Ethan grinned, glad to see her smile. 'And the only one I want you *frantically* describing is me.'

And he was getting his words wrong, because he meant that he didn't want to sit here and listen about her ex and her in bed, or did he mean that he wanted to give her something to frantically describe?

That wasn't what he'd come here for.

'I'm going to go.'

He pulled up on his elbow and gave her a kiss, though it was a bit pointless to pretend it was a friendly one, given what they'd been like, and that they were lying on the bed, but Ethan did kiss her with no intention other than to say goodbye.

Except he'd forgotten just how much he liked kissing her till he was back there, and Penny was remembering all over again too. It was so nice to be lying down being kissed by him, nicer too when a little while later his hands crept to her breasts that clearly didn't disappoint because she could feel him harden against her thigh as he stroked.

Only this time he did what he had wanted to that time, his mouth moving down, slipping down the fabric and licking around the areola and then taking her in his mouth.

She was on her back, his expert mouth suckling her hard, and Penny was gasping, wanting to turn to get to him, to explore him too, but loath to end the bliss of his mouth.

He turned her to him, gave her other breast the same attention. Ethan, who loved breasts, actually loved that she hardly had any. Penny was grappling to pull out his top, desperate to feel his skin as his mouth sucking her breast drove her to higher pleasures.

But Ethan moved her hands away, his intention to take his time, but as his hand slid down the jut of her hips, her nightdress had ridden up and he found his hand cupping her bare bottom. 'Hell, Penny,' he moaned, 'have you been walking around all this time with no knickers on?' He blew out a breath, remembered then the reason he was there, and when Kate had said to be ready for anything, he was quite sure she hadn't meant that. 'Sorry.'

'For what?'

'Taking things too far.'

'You've never taken things too far,' Penny said. 'You haven't taken things far enough.'

They were at each other again, a knot of arms and legs and deep kisses, her hands going to his buckle, but he halted her.

'Penny.' He took her face in his hands and he wrestled with indecision, not sure if it was Hot Mess Penny he was talking to, whom he completely adored and could deal with, or Baby Making Mode Penny, who terrified him, and she got that much.

'I'm not asking you to get me pregnant.'

'Isn't it too soon?' Ethan checked.

'Nope.' And she thought of sex for the sake of it, and how lovely he had been and how badly she wanted the rest of that chocolate bar out of the fridge now. And so too did Ethan. They were back to kissing, only pausing to strip the other off and pray for condoms in his wallet, which, hurrah, there were.

She buried her head in his chest and smelt and felt close-up and naked Ethan. He was stunning, muscled but not too much with a smooth tanned chest and flat brown nipples that shifted from view as his mouth slid down again, only this time not to her breasts. He licked down to her stomach and he did what he had wanted to do that first day he had given her her injection, and he kissed her till she was writhing.

Penny had felt like a pincushion these past weeks, a failed baby-making machine at times, but his mouth was slowly turning her back into a woman as he lingered at each step. Penny closed her eyes in bliss as his mouth moved lower still and with each measured stroke she lost a little more control but gained mounting pleasure. Her hands pulled tight on his hair as Ethan revelled in the taste of her. The scent that had been alluring him for weeks was now his to savour and he carried on kissing her deeply there as she throbbed to his mouth and he returned her to herself.

A new self.

'Ethan.' Penny lay catching her breath, went to say something, she didn't know what. She wanted to sit up and face him, wanted to go down on him. It took a moment to realise it wasn't her decision to make. He was over her, sheathed and poised at her entrance.

'Love-thirty,' he said, sexy and smiling and not a moment too soon for Penny, through with being patient.

She moaned as he filled her. Ethan folded his arms behind her head so that her face was right up to him, and she had forgotten how lovely sex could be. Or rather, Penny amended as he moved deep inside her, she'd never really known just how lovely sex could be. Then, as Ethan shifted tempo she made one final amendment before she lost rational thought. She'd never known sex could be so hot.

She didn't get poor-Penny sex; she got the full bull in Ethan. A surprise birthday present that had her as wild as him. One of his arms moved down to her hips and he practically lifted her off the bed each time he thrust into her. Had Penny ever had any doubt as to all those times she'd thought him aroused, they were gone, because every missed opportunity, every subdued thought

Ethan had had seemed to be being banished now over and over deep in her centre.

His want, his desire, the absence of tentativeness had Penny flooded in warmth, her legs wrapping around him, her skin scalding, grinding into him as she tipped into climax.

'Penny…' Ethan was trying to hold on, but feeling her shatter, feeling her jolt as if she'd been stunned, by the time he felt her strong, rapid clenches Ethan was on the way to meeting them.

Almost dizzy, he collapsed on top of her and then moved to the side, pulling her with him, more than a bit bewildered about what had happened, because Ethan loved sex but had never had sex like that, and while going down on her his intention had been to be gentle.

'Did we land on the beach?' Ethan asked.

'I'm not sure,' Penny admitted. 'I can't actually see.' She felt a gurgle of laughter swirl inside her, only it wasn't laughter, she realised, just this glimpse of being free. 'And it's actually thirty-fifteen now,' Penny said. 'You forfeited the last game if I remember rightly.'

He'd had no idea what to expect when he'd arrived tonight at her door, but felt as if, in that small conversation, he'd met the real Penny, the one that he'd sometimes glimpsed. Or was it more that it was a different him? Usually Ethan was snoring his head off right about now, but instead it was Penny dozing as he went and dimmed the lights before climbing into bed beside her.

'Happy birthday, Penny.'

And as she lay there, feeling his big body beside her, she thought that it really shouldn't have been a happy birthday; it had had every ingredient for it not to be, except it had just turned into her most memorable, possibly favourite one.

'Thank you,' Penny said, and then turned over to him. 'You were right—it wasn't the drugs.'

CHAPTER ELEVEN

'IT'S MY MUM.'

Unfortunately Penny hadn't come into the bathroom to join him in the shower later the next morning. They were up to deuce after a much more tender lovemaking session and Penny was fixing some breakfast while Ethan showered when the intercom buzzed. 'I know this sounds like I'm eighteen…'

'You want me to hide?' Ethan grinned as she pulled on her nightdress and then her dressing gown.

'Not hide, just don't come out of the bedroom,' Penny said. 'She'll tell Jasmine and, honestly, by the time we get back to work they'll all have us engaged or something.'

'Mum!' Penny opened the door and stood as her mum gave her a cuddle.

'I'm so sorry, Penny, I wish I'd been here. I told you not to try till after my trip.'

And there were so many things she could have said to that, but Penny buttoned her lip and forced a smile.

'How was the cruise?'

'It was amazing!' It must have been because Louise *looked* amazing! She was suntanned and relaxed-looking and wearing new clothes and jewellery, and her hair was a fabulous caramel colour and very well cut. 'I had the best time, Penny. You'd love it!'

'I think I might,' Penny said, because till her mother had set off, she'd never even considered one, but she was seeing the benefits now.

'All you do is eat and be pampered—I've got so much to tell you!'

And Ethan lay on the bed, reading magazines, listening as Penny did her best to limit his exposure to her mother's love life, because Penny kept asking her to describe islands, but her mum just kept talking about a man she had met. 'I go all the way to Greece and Bradley's from Melbourne and he's so romantic. One night—'

'Hold on a minute, Mum,' Penny interrupted. 'I'm just going to get changed.'

She brought Ethan in a coffee, which she would pretend she'd left in her room, not that her mother would notice. She was way too busy discussing Bradley and comparing the differences with Penny's father.

'I'm so sorry.'

'It's interesting.'

It was, and it became more so because Penny could not stop her mother from talking, and Ethan heard how useless her father had been and that maybe Louise had been a bit harsh in her summing up of *all* men to her daughters, because Bradley was nothing like that at all.

They were serious, in fact, he heard her tell Penny.

'It's a month, Mum.'

'And I'm old enough to know what I like and that this is right.'

'Well, why not just see how it goes now you're back?' He could hear Penny's wariness and then her mother's exasperation.

'Can't you just be happy for me, Penny?'

'Of course I am.'

But they all knew it was qualified and then the strain was back in Penny's voice, especially when her mother asked how she felt about losing the baby.

'It wasn't a baby, Mum! I got my period.' Ethan closed his eyes. Kate had been right—it was different for everyone, because Kate had had photos and named every embryo. 'It just didn't work.'

'Okay, Penny.'

They chatted some more and then with Penny promising to go round tomorrow she finally got her mother out of the door. Ethan looked up at Penny's strained features as she came through the bedroom door.

'Sorry about that.'

'No need to say sorry.'

'She just goes too far.' Penny let out an angry breath. 'I can't think of it as a baby.' Ethan was terribly aware suddenly that he was lying not in a bed but a minefield. 'I'd go mad otherwise, if I thought like that.'

'I know.'

'I bet she didn't ask Jasmine to hold off trying to conceive till she got back.' Ethan swallowed, thought it best not to say a thing, though was tempted to fire a quick SOS to his sister just in case he said the wrong thing. 'Well, she can go over there now and hear Jasmine's latest happy news.' Penny joined him on the bed. 'She's met the love of her life, apparently.'

'Bradley,' Ethan said, and she gave a little laugh.

She turned to him. 'I'm supposed to be happy for her.'

'Aren't you?'

Penny looked back at him. 'From past experience I really don't trust my mother's taste in men so no, I'm not going to clap hands and get all excited. He's the first person she's seriously dated since my father left.'

'Do you ever see him?'

'Never,' Penny said. 'And I've never wanted to. I see enough of his sort at work and I've stitched up enough of his sort's handiwork too.' She didn't want to talk about her father. 'What did you do while we were talking?' Penny asked.

'Read,' Ethan said. 'Had a little walk around the bed, worked out that you rotate your wardrobe...'

'Of course I do,' Penny said. 'I haven't got time to think what to wear each day.' She climbed off the bed. 'I'm going to have a shower.'

'Good,' Ethan said. 'And I'll find you something to wear.'

'I can choose my own clothes, thank you.'

'You don't know where we're going.'

'Ethan, I don't want to go out.'

'Which is exactly why you should.'

Penny chose her own clothes, thank you very much. A pair of shorts and a T-shirt and wedge sandals and Ethan watched in amusement as she applied factor thirty to every exposed piece of skin. When they walked out of her smart townhouse and didn't head straight for his car, Penny actually felt a bit shaky.

'I've been inside too long.'

'I know you have.'

Really, since her walk on the beach with Jasmine it had been work and appointments and stopping at the supermarket on the way home, she told Ethan as they walked down to the beach.

'I'm a terrible wife even to myself,' Penny said, taking off her sandals and holding them as they walked down the path to the beach. 'I try to remember to make lots of meals and then freeze them and I always mean to make healthy lunches and take them in.'

'Same,' Ethan said.

'And I do it for one day, sometimes two.'

'That's why there's a canteen, Penny.' Ethan smiled. 'For all the people who have rotting vegetables in the drawer at the bottom of their fridge and didn't have time to make a sandwich, and if they did they don't have any super-healthy grain bread.'

Penny smiled. It was actually really nice to be out. It was a very clear day, the bay as blue and still as the sky, and the beach pretty empty. It was just nice to feel the sand beneath her feet and she thought of the last time she had been here with Jasmine and Simon, having hot flashes and carrying petrified hope and talking about wild flings with Ethan.

Penny glanced over at him, glad and surprised that the one thing she hadn't wanted that day had transpired.

'How come you ended up at Peninsula?' Penny asked.

'I wanted a change.' Ethan's voice was wry. 'I thought a nice bayside hospital would mean a nice laid-back lifestyle—I mean, given we don't have PICU and things.' He gave a shrug. 'I didn't count on catchments and that we'd get everything for miles around and then end up transferring them out.'

'You don't like it?'

'I love it,' Ethan mused. 'It just wasn't what I was expecting it to be—and I know that I don't do this sort of thing enough.' Ethan thought about it all for a long moment as they walked—thought about the wall of silence he had been met with because he hadn't been able to suddenly come back when Penny was sick. Thought about all that was silently expected of them. Ethan wasn't a rebel, just knew that there had to be more than work, and he told her that.

'You go out,' Penny said, because she'd heard that Ethan liked to party hard.

'I do,' Ethan said, 'but…' Just not lately. Ethan had once thought of days off counted in parties and bars and women and how much he could cram in. But since Phil's death it had all halted. Right now, just pausing on the beach on his one day off, Ethan actually felt like he'd escaped.

'I'm going to join a gym.' Penny broke into his thoughts.

'So you can feel guilty about not going?'

He made her smile because, yes, over the years she'd joined the hospital gym and the one near home many times.

'Why don't you just walk here more often?' Ethan suggested.

'Why don't you?'

They took the path off the beach that led into town and ordered brunch—smoked salmon and poached eggs on a very unhealthy white bread, washed down with coffee and fruit juice, and it was nice to sit outside and watch the world passing. Ethan was right, it was so good to be out, but being out meant exposure and after half an hour sitting at a pavement café she heard a woman call his name.

'Ethan.'

Penny looked up and it was the woman who had dropped him off that time, except she was pushing a stroller with a three-year-old and a very young baby.

'Kate.' Ethan smiled and looked down at his niece and nephew and gave them a wave then remembered to make the introductions. 'This is Penny from work and, Penny, this is my sister, Kate.'

'Of course you should join us,' Penny said when Kate insisted she didn't want to interrupt. She sat but when there wasn't a waiter to be found Ethan headed inside to order coffee and a milkshake for the three-year-old.

It was horribly awkward for Penny, because she and Kate were just so different; both lived close by yet both moved in completely different circles.

Both had a bit of what the other wanted.

'Days off?' Kate asked.

'Yes,' Penny answered. 'Well, I've been off sick, but I'm back tomorrow.'

'I'm sorry to hear that,' Kate said, aching at the defensiveness in Penny's voice, because she knew so much more.

'Ethan said you had three children?'

'Yes, the eldest is at school,' Kate said, nodding towards the school over the street. 'You work in Emergency with Ethan?' she checked, as if she didn't already know. 'I think I saw you when I dropped Ethan off one morning.'

'That's right.' Penny did her best not to blush, because it had been the morning she had actually realised just how gorgeous Ethan was.

Yes, it was awkward because Penny just said as she always did, as little as possible about herself. If she'd only open up, Ethan thought when he returned, then Kate would tell her all about the hell she had gone through to get her three, but instead they talked about work and weather and things that didn't matter, till Kate had to go. 'I'll catch up with you soon, Ethan.' She gave her brother a friendly kiss on the cheek. 'It was lovely to meet you, Penny.'

'And you.'

'She seems nice,' Penny said.

'She is,' Ethan said, but if she'd just spoken properly to her, then Penny would know that Kate didn't just *seem* nice, she actually *was*.

Penny, Penny, Ethan sighed in his head. What to do?

'Shall we go to the movies?'

'The movies?' Penny frowned. 'I haven't been to the movies since...' She thought for a moment. 'I can't remember when.'

At her insistence, Penny bought the tickets and he

went and got the popcorn and drinks and things, but as she walked over she saw him talking to a woman and a young boy and stopped walking.

The woman was being polite, but her face was a frozen mask. The young boy beside her was smiling up at Ethan and she just knew then that it was Justin. He looked like Ethan.

She was shaking a bit inside, her mind racing. She'd got it wrong with his sister; she couldn't keep jumping to the conclusion that every woman he spoke to he'd slept with. Penny made a great deal about putting the tickets into her purse, pretending to jump in surprise as Ethan came over.

'Okay?' Penny checked.

'Sure.'

She could tell he wasn't.

Still, the movie was a good one and it was so nice to sit in the darkness—so nice not to have to think. They sat at the back in a practically empty cinema and ate popcorn and just checked out of the world for a little while, which for Penny was bliss. It was nice too for Ethan to not go over and over the terse conversation with Gina. To just accept that Gina didn't want her ex-husband's cousin involved in her son's life.

He turned in the darkness to Penny about the same time she turned to him. There was the rustle of popcorn falling to the floor as they acted more like teenagers than a responsible couple in their thirties. After the movie Ethan wished he had brought the car as they walked quickly along the beach, almost running, not just to be together but away from problems each needed to face.

It felt so good to fall through the door, to lift her arms as he slid her out of her top, to undo the zipper of her shorts, as she did the same to him.

'Why did we leave it so long?' He was kissing her, not thinking of anything else but her mouth and her body and all the times they had missed, and how much better the boat would have been if he'd had Penny there with him.

'You know why.'

Ethan's head was in two places as he remembered what had kept them apart, but that problem had gone now and he just wasn't thinking, or rather he was thinking out loud, but before he had time to stop himself suddenly the words were out.

'Maybe it's for the best.'

CHAPTER TWELVE

'YOU DIDN'T SAY that?' Kate grimaced. 'God, Ethan.'

'I can't believe I said it.' The once laid-back Ethan had his head in his hands as Kate grilled him further.

'What did she do?'

His look said it all because Penny had said the F word again, quite a few times, as she'd kicked him out.

'I'm not saying you have to tiptoe around her, but honestly, Ethan, it is the most awful time. Carl and I never row, but we have every time I've been on IVF, and if he'd said that...' Kate let out a long, angry sigh that told Ethan her reaction would have perhaps been as volatile as Penny's.

'I can understand you'd be upset if Carl said it, but I didn't mean it like that,' Ethan said. 'I meant...' He stopped talking then.

'What?' his sister pushed.

'That I can barely get my head around a long-term relationship and having kids of my own, let alone going out with someone who was pregnant with someone else's child. When I said it was for the best I just meant that at least now we had a chance.'

'You need to tell her that.'

'You've met her,' Ethan told his twin. 'She's the most difficult, complicated…' And there it was, she was everything he wanted, the one woman who could possibly hold his attention. And she was still holding it fully on her first day back at work.

Penny was wearing a grey skirt with her cream sleeveless blouse but she'd lost weight around her hips and maybe he *was* a bit of a caveman because he wanted to insist she take some proper time off and haul her to his bed, and feed her and have sex with her and then watch late-night shows in his dark bedroom while she slept, while she healed. He wanted to take care of her. Instead, he had to stand and watch as she nitpicked her way through the department, upsetting everyone. Any minute soon he was going to have to step in.

'Why hasn't his blood pressure been done?' Her voice carried over the resuscitation room. Penny was checking the obs chart on her patient. She had ordered observations to be taken every fifteen minutes and when she saw that they hadn't been done for half an hour she called out to Vanessa.

'It has been done,' Vanessa said, taking the chart. 'Sorry, Penny, I just didn't write it down. It was one-eighty over ninety.'

'Which means nothing if it isn't written down.' Penny held her breath and told herself to calm down, but she'd told Vanessa about this a few times. 'You *have* to document.'

'I know.'

'Then why don't you do it?' Penny said, and as she walked off, she was aware that Ethan was behind her. He tapped her smartly on the shoulder but she ignored him.

'Stop taking it out on the nurses.'

'I'm not,' Penny said. 'What's the point of Vanessa knowing the patient is hypertensive and not telling me or even writing it down? If he strokes out—'

'Penny.' He knew all that, knew that she was right, but he could see the dark shadows under her eyes and could feel her tense and too thin under his hand on her shoulder. 'I'm sorry for what I said.'

'I don't want to discuss that.'

'Tough.' She had marched to her office and Ethan had followed and stood with his back to the door. 'I said the wrong thing. I say the wrong thing a lot apparently.'

'You said how you felt.'

'How could I have when I don't even know how I feel?' Ethan couldn't contain it any longer and to hell with lousy timing, it had been lousy timing for him as well. 'I'm sorry that I didn't arrive in your life with a fully packed nappy bag, ready to be a father to another man's child.' Penny closed her eyes. 'Instead, I walked in on the end of a huge life decision you'd made.'

'I didn't make it lightly.'

'But I was supposed to,' Ethan said. 'I was supposed to be fine with it, delighted that you were pregnant, and for you I was, just not for us!'

And she was just so bruised and raw and angry and lost she didn't know how to respond anymore.

'Just leave it.'

'How can I leave it?' Ethan demanded. 'Because I'm

trying to sort the two of us out and you're talking about going for it again.'

'No, I'm not.'

Today, Ethan wanted to add, but just stood there, trying to hold on to his temper, because only a low-life would have a row with a woman going through this. 'Okay, let's just leave it,' Ethan said, 'but I will not have you taking it out on the nurses. You've upset Vanessa.'

'Vanessa knows me.' Guilt prickled down her spine. 'I've worked with Vanessa for years.'

'Hey,' Ethan snapped. 'Do you remember that guy I stitched who'd just had a remote control bounce off his skull?'

She had no idea what he was talking about. 'Well, maybe you weren't working that day, but he said the same. "She's never moaned, we've been married for years."' His eyes flashed at Penny. 'People will put up with so much, Penny, but not for ever.'

'I get that!' Penny screwed her eyes closed on tears. 'I've always been strict with observations, I've always been tough.'

'There's another word to describe you that's doing the rounds right now, Penny.'

'I know that. It's just been so intense.'

'I know that,' Ethan said, 'but the staff don't. I'm not going to stand back and let you take it out on them, Penny. Please.' He was trying to pull her up, trying to talk her down; he just wanted to take her home, but she didn't want him to and as he tried to take her in his arms Penny was backing off.

'I know it's been hell for you,' Ethan said.

'Well, it's over.' Penny swallowed down her pain. 'I just want to get back to my life, back to my career. I can't believe that I turned down a prom...' She stopped herself.

'Say it.'

Penny looked at him.

'It doesn't matter.'

'You know how I really hate that.' And so he waited.

'I turned down a promotion so that I could concentrate on IVF.'

'You mean you turned down my job?' Ethan checked, and she gave a tight shrug. Then he was on side with the masses—Penny could be such a bitch at times. 'Thanks a lot, Penny.'

She wanted to call him back, except he walked out, and if that wasn't enough to be dealing with, a moment later there was a knock at her door.

'Hi, Lisa.' Penny gave a tight smile. 'It's not really a good time.'

'No, it isn't a good time,' Lisa said. 'My nurses work hard, Penny, and they put up with a lot and they do many extra things to help you that you probably don't even notice.' Penny swallowed as Lisa continued. 'But you might start to notice just how much extra they did for you when they stop.'

'It will be okay,' Jasmine said.

Penny had left work early, to Mr Dean's obvious displeasure, and the second she had got home she had rung her sister and said sorry, and Jasmine had come round. They'd had a cuddle when Jasmine had arrived at her door and, this time, when Penny had felt the swell in her sister's stomach, while it had hurt, overriding that Penny was happy for her sister and just so pleased to see her that she told Jasmine about work.

'I've upset all the nurses.'

'Penny!' Jasmine flailed between divided loyalties. 'You haven't been that bad. Lisa can be a cow at times— and Vanessa's always forgetting to write things down, but if you were more friendly, if people knew more what was going on in your life…'

'I don't know how to tell people.'

And Jasmine got that, because since she had been a little girl it had been Penny who had taken care of things, who had let her little sister open up to her about all the scary stuff going on with their parents and had said nothing about her own fears.

'You told Ethan.'

'Because I had to.'

'So how did the Neanderthal do?' Jasmine asked.

'He was great,' Penny said, and she let out a sigh as she remembered that day, how he'd stepped in when she'd broken down, how he'd actually said all the right things. 'Not just with the injections.'

'You like him?'

Penny nodded. 'And I just hurt him,' she said. 'I let it slip about the promotion.'

'You didn't just let it slip,' Jasmine said. 'You did what you always do whenever anyone gets close.'

'Probably,' Penny admitted.

'Try talking to him,' Jasmine said.

'I don't want to talk to him about this, though,' Penny

said. 'It's all we talk about and I'm tired of it. I wish I'd met him without this damn IVF hanging over me. I want us to have a chance at normal.'

'Tell him, then,' Jasmine urged.

'I can't yet,' Penny admitted. 'I need to sort out myself first, work out how I feel about other things.' Penny took a deep breath. 'I've just been going round in circles and I can't anymore and I'm not going to dump on Ethan. I need to think of myself.'

When Jasmine had gone she rang Mr Dean.

Told him she was struggling with some personal issues and that she was taking some time off.

Just let him put a word wrong now, Penny thought.

'That's fine, Penny.' Mr Dean must have heard the unvoiced warning in her tone, because he told her to take the two weeks of annual leave she had left and more if she needed it, and even though he could be very insensitive, for once he was incredibly careful not to say the wrong thing.

Unlike a certain someone, Penny thought as she stripped off her work clothes and headed for the shower.

Unlike Ethan.

Penny's eyes filled with tears then because part of what she liked about Ethan was that he did say the wrong thing and wasn't always careful at times, wasn't tentative and constantly wearing kid gloves around her, which she hated.

He'd never deliberately hurt her, he'd just been trying to say how he felt about her losing… Penny screwed her eyes closed, tried to block the pain, but she couldn't do it anymore. There wasn't a needle in sight but she let it all out then, folded up on the shower floor, crying and sobbing as she mourned. Because it wasn't just a failed IVF, she hadn't just got her period that horrible time. For a little while there she had thought she'd got her baby.

While she might feel better after a really good cry, Penny thought, she certainly didn't look better.

Huddled on the sofa in her nightdress, watching but not watching the news, Penny surveyed the damage. Yes, IVF was expensive, and she wasn't just talking dollars.

Penny rang her mum and had a nice talk with her, a really nice talk, because her mum told Bradley she was taking the call upstairs and they spoke for a good hour. Louise offered to come over but Penny didn't want her to.

Next.

Unable to say it, she fired off Ethan a text saying she was sorry for being such a bitch about his job.

And then he sent her a text with a photo attached— a big bear with a tiny dart in it.

Just a bruised ego—all mended now.

Which made her smile, and when a little while later her doorbell rang she wasn't sure if it was Ethan or her mum, but as she opened it, Penny knew her response would be the same.

'I really want to be on my own.'

'Why?' Ethan said. He'd come straight from work and was in his scrubs and looking far too gorgeous for someone feeling as drained as Penny did.

'Because I'm such good company.' She didn't need

to tell him she was being sarcastic. He looked at her swollen eyes and lips and the little dark red dots on her eyelids and he couldn't let her close the door.

'I need to talk to you, Penny,' Ethan said. 'I lied to you.'

'That's fine.'

'You don't even want to know when I lied?'

'No,' Penny said. 'I want to think about me.' But she did let him in. Ethan pulled her into his arms for a cuddle but he felt her resistance and just wanted to erase it, wanted to take some of her hurt, but she simply wouldn't let him. 'I wish you'd spoken to my sister. Kate's been through it many, many times. I wish you'd let people in.'

'I wish I would too,' Penny said.

'Then why don't you?' He could see the confusion swirling in her eyes, guessed she was trying to answer that by herself. He was going to make her talk, was determined to sort things out, and he led her to the couch and sat down beside her. 'You don't have to keep it all in. It's not good for you. You said you didn't get upset when your dad left and then a few days later—'

'Oh, don't start.'

'I have started,' Ethan said.

'Of course I was upset when he left,' Penny said.

'You just couldn't show it.'

'No!' Penny said. 'Because Jasmine was sobbing herself to sleep, Mum was doing the same on the couch, and someone had to do the dishes and make Jasmine her lunch and…' She swallowed the hot choking fear she had felt then. 'How would falling apart have helped?'

'It might have stopped you falling apart now,' Ethan suggested. 'It might have meant your mother would have stepped up. It might have meant someone stepping in.'

'I'm not falling apart,' Penny said, and she meant it. 'I did that a couple of hours ago.'

He looked at her swollen face. 'I could have been there for you.'

'Oh, no,' Penny said. 'I'm so glad that you weren't.' She gave him a smile, a real one, because there were things she simply didn't want another person to see, and she actually felt better for her mammoth cry and was ready now to face another truth.

'So when did you lie?'

'I *was* serious about Caitlin.' The smile slid from her face when she didn't get the answer she was expecting. 'Not quite walking-up-the-aisle serious, but serious. And then Phil got sick and the thought of being married, having kids, leaving them behind?' He was honest. 'It just freaked me out.'

'I do understand. It is scary to think of being responsible for another person,' she admitted.

'But you want it,' Ethan said. 'You're brave enough to do it your own.'

'Not on my own,' Penny said, 'because even if we fight I do have my sister and mum, and if something happened to me, they'd be there.' She looked at him. 'I thought you were about to tell me you had a son.'

He gave her a barking-mad look.

'I saw you at the cinema.'

'That was Justin.'

'He looks like you,' Penny said, smiling now at her own paranoia.

'Phil looked like me,' Ethan said, then changed the subject because she was getting too close to a place that hurt. 'You do too much on your own.'

'Better than not doing it at all.' She smiled and nudged him, except Ethan didn't smile, and to her horror she watched him swallow, watched him struggle to get a grip, saw him pinch his nose and it was her arm around him now.

'Ethan?'

'Sorry.' He let out a slightly incredulous laugh, shocked how much was there just beneath the surface, how much he had just refused to let out.

'Is it Phil?'

He shook his head and again he got how the patients liked her because she sort of went straight to the really painful bit rather than tiptoeing around it. 'Justin?'

'If you get famous and they name a perfume after you, it won't be called Subtle, Penny.'

'No, it will be called Pertinent,' Penny said. 'You *need* to be there for him, Ethan.' And he nodded, rested his head in his hands, and Penny felt the tension in his shoulders, heard him struggle to keep his voice even as he gave a ragged apology. 'This was supposed to be about you.'

'How selfish of you.' Penny smiled.

'I don't know what to do—I've been trying to stay out of it but I can't. And it's not just the family stuff and that Gina's keeping him from his grandparents. The thing is, I know how he feels. It's like I'm looking at a mini-me. I saw him at the hospital, heard my aunt saying the same things she did to me when my father died—to be brave, be strong. It's not what he needs to hear right now.'

'You can be there for him.'

'I don't want to go rushing in and make promises I might not keep,' Ethan admitted. 'I've never been able to commit myself to anything except work. Penny, I don't want to let him down.'

'You won't.' She saw him blink at the certainty in her voice. 'I know you won't let him down, precisely because you haven't rushed in. Just take your time and you'll work something out.'

'I don't know what, though.' He looked to where she was sitting and pulled her onto his lap, and this time she didn't resist when he pulled her in for a cuddle. 'So much for cheering you up.'

'You have, though.' Penny smiled and he smiled too. 'Thank you for everything,' Penny said. 'Not just the injections but…' she looked at the man who was still there despite all that had gone on these past weeks '…thank you for being my friend through this.'

'A bit more than a friend.' And to confirm it gave her a kiss. A kiss that seemed at odds with the way she was feeling, because there was this well of happiness filling her at what should have been the saddest of times.

'Are you wearing no knickers again?' Ethan smiled again and he had possibly the nicest mouth a man could have, and she was looking into his hazel eyes and it hadn't just been manufactured hormones that had been raging that time. Penny could fully see it now. It had been lust, all the flush of a new romance, the big one, because right now for Penny it was looking like something a lot bigger than lust.

Something she'd never really felt before—an L word that would probably be as shocking to Ethan as the F word had been to Jasmine, and if that mouth returned to hers now, she might be tempted later to say so, and again it was just too much and too soon.

'You need to go,' Penny said.

'Do I?'

'Yes,' Penny said, 'because I want to go to bed and have sex with you and I want to get up tomorrow and do it again, and then I want you to take me out tomorrow night, but I think I need to think about things properly. I need to work some stuff out.'

'And you can't do that with me?'

Penny looked at him and, no, she didn't want to try to do this with Ethan—her fertility issues were conversations that should be had far later along in a relationship, dark places a couple might visit later that had instead been thrust on them at the beginning.

'It's a girl thing,' Penny said, because with or without Ethan in her future she needed to properly know how she felt. And as to the other issue, the L one—well, she didn't need him by her side to work that out.

Penny already knew.

So much for a wild fling—of all the times to go and fall in love with someone.

'I could make love to you on the sofa and then leave,' Ethan said, cupping her naked bottom and making her laugh.

'I suppose that might be a compromise.'

He kissed her again, pulled her around on his lap so she was facing him, and his hands were everywhere and so too were hers. 'I'm crazy about you, Penny.'

'I know,' she said, kissing him back and trying to hold on to a word he might not be ready to hear. 'I'm crazy about you too.'

Her hand went to his back pocket, which gave him lovely access to her neck. She could feel his tongue, his mouth most definitely leaving evidence that hers hadn't been about to, but it was bliss and she had a whole two weeks off, so she let him carry on, working her neck and his hands stroked her breasts as she slid the condom on him.

'You'll call me if you need me,' Ethan said as she sank herself down onto him.

'You'll call me too,' Penny said, locked in an erotic embrace, hardly able to breathe. 'But not for this.'

'Penny.' He was lifting his hips and thrusting into her, protesting her impossible rules.

'I mean it,' Penny panted, because she could bury herself in Ethan and stay there forever, just as he was burying himself deep in her now.

Yes, a good cry and a good orgasm and Penny felt a whole lot better as she kissed him goodbye at her door. Still stuck on deuce but with play suspended.

Penny *was* going to sort herself out.

And so too would Ethan.

CHAPTER THIRTEEN

'PENNY!' KATE SMILED as she walked past the café and ignored Penny's burning cheeks.

'Oh, hi,' Penny said, as if she just happened to be sitting there at a quarter to nine in the morning, as if she hadn't been looking up school times on the internet, as if she hadn't spent forty minutes trying to cover the marks on her neck and her puffy eyes. 'How are you?'

'Good.' Kate smiled. 'Though I could do with one of them.' She nodded to Penny's coffee and, yes, she'd love to join her and, yes, Penny thought, it was another woman she needed for this and this link was thanks to Ethan.

'How's work?' Kate asked, taking a seat.

'I'm taking some time off.' She told her why and Penny realised that Kate probably already knew.

'Did Ethan tell you?'

'Do I have to answer that?'

'No.' Penny shook her head.

'Then I won't.'

Kate had been there and knew, though she couldn't have a second coffee, not at the café anyway because the baby needed feeding. In truth, she shouldn't really have stopped for the first, but she'd been where Penny was.

'We could take a coffee back to mine,' Kate suggested, 'and talk there.'

It *was* another woman Penny needed, one who'd been there and knew—who knew it so well that she took phone calls for a support group.

'Everyone was pregnant when I started trying,' Kate said, making up bottles for Dillon a little while later as Penny sat at the kitchen table.

It *was* so nice to talk and to hold someone else's baby and not feel guilty for shedding tears. She'd always tried to smile with Jasmine and friends, and say, no, no, she was fine. It was nice to hold one and have a little weep.

'I think I've gone a bit mad,' Penny admitted.

'It's par for the course.'

Penny looked at Dillon and though she'd never be disappointed with a boy, Penny admitted to herself that deep down she would have loved a girl too. Oh, a boy would be fantastic, but she'd have loved a mini-Penny. A little girl who she could do everything right by and fix the world for, who she could unashamedly show all the love that bubbled and fizzed inside.

But she could do it for herself too, Penny realised.

'I've just had a text,' Kate said a little while later. 'My brother's coming around.'

'I'll go, then.'

She thanked Kate for the morning and they had a hug and she handed back little Dillon. It wasn't that she didn't want to see Ethan, it was more there was something she was ready to face and she wanted to face it alone. Penny headed to the beach and walked for a while, adding up all the months, all the years, all the time she'd lost trying. She was ready to stop and so she said it out loud—but to herself first.

'I'm not going to be a mum.' She actually didn't cry as she said it, just felt relief almost as she let go of something she had never had, anger shifting towards acceptance; sadness a constant ache but one she could now more readily wear.

Yes, times alone were needed for both of them, yet Kate was the strange conduit that linked them.

'She's been here.' He could just tell, when about ten minutes after Penny left he was at his sister's door and Kate was blushing and flustered when she answered.

'Why do you say that?'

'Because I can smell her perfume,' Ethan said.

'You really have got it bad,' Kate said. 'What did you do to her neck?'

Ethan wasn't going to answer that one, so he asked a question instead. 'What was she talking about?'

'Not about you,' Kate said, then added, 'She's really nice.'

Not *seems*, Ethan noted—finally, it would appear, Penny was letting people in.

'She is.'

'Well, I hate to chuck you out so soon, but I've got nothing done today and I'm on fruit duty at playgroup.' Kate was putting sandals onto her daughter's feet. The baby was asleep and instead of letting her wake him, as usually Ethan would, he offered to watch him instead.

'Are you sure?' Kate checked. 'There's a bottle in the fridge if he wakes up.'

'Go.'

And later he sat with Dillon on his lap and stared at a very little man who would, God willing, grow up.

And, Ethan realised, taking out his phone, it was time for him to as well.

Just not yet.

He made every decision alone—it was simply the way he was, but instead of ringing who he meant to, he dialled Penny.

She probably wouldn't pick up.

'Hi.'

'Hi, Penny,' he said. 'What are you doing?'

'Sitting on the beach. What about you?'

'Watching my nephew. Kate's at playgroup.' He took a deep breath. 'I'm going to ring Gina.'

'That's good.'

'I think I need to say sorry first, for how the family has been.' He was really just thinking out loud.

'Maybe,' Penny said, 'but are you ringing on behalf of the family?'

'No.'

'You could just keep it more about you,' Penny said, and they chatted for a while about what he might say till the baby on his lap decided that a bottle might be a good idea, and Penny could hear his little whimpers in the background.

'You'd better go,' Penny said. 'It sounds like the baby needs feeding.'

As he hung up the phone he sat for a moment, wondering if he'd upset her with the baby crying and everything, but she'd seemed fine. It had been their first full conversation without a mention of babies.

'Apart from you,' he said to Dillon as he headed to the fridge.

Ethan offered the baby his bottle but he spat out the cold milk so Ethan warmed it up. 'It was worth a try.' He grinned at his new friend and they settled back down on the sofa. There was no putting it off any longer and Ethan again picked up his phone.

'Gina…' He took a deep breath. 'It's Ethan.' He was met with a very long silence. 'I'm really sorry for all that the family has put you through.'

'You didn't.'

'No,' he said. 'But I do know what happened and I know too what Jack and Vera can be like.' He took a long breath. 'But I'm not ringing about them, I'm ringing about Justin. I lost my dad around the same age.'

'I know.'

They chatted for a bit and it was awkward at first and there was a long stretch of silence when he made his suggestion. 'I was thinking, if it's okay with you, I could get Justin his football membership. I can't take him every week, it depends on the roster, but…' He thought of Penny, because he so often did and, yes, she'd swap now and then and so too would the others.

This he could do.

Would do.

'I would be able to take Justin to most games.'

'He'd love that,' Gina said. 'But…' She hesitated for a moment.

'I'm not starting something I won't see through,' Ethan said. 'I'm not saying I'm never going to move, but I will be there for him. I wouldn't be offering otherwise.'

Only that wasn't what Gina was hesitating about. 'Maybe you could take him to his grandparents' after the match, but not every week. Maybe he could stay over?' Gina let out a sigh. 'But I can't face picking him up.'

'I can do that,' Ethan said. 'We can work out times.'

'Would you talk to Vera and Jack first?' Gina said. 'I don't want Justin going there and being told what a terrible person I am.'

'I'll talk to them,' Ethan said. 'And if it's not working out, I'll talk to them again, but whatever happens there, I'll be around for Justin.'

They chatted some more and it was agreed he would ring Justin and tell him the good news that night. When Ethan hung up the phone he looked into the solemn eyes of his nephew.

'How did I do?'

He got no answer.

'When you're a bit bigger I might take you to the football too.' He got a smile for that and again his mind tripped back to Penny. 'I'll be the mad uncle.'

And so the weekend came around and he picked up a six-year-old with a pinched, angry face. He knew that look only too well and sat where they always had, only this time without Phil.

And they shouted at the opposition and the umpire and let off a bit of a steam, but instead of talking about the game on the way to Justin's grandparents' they spoke about what mattered.

'Well, if he wanted to live so much then he should have tried harder,' Justin said, because he was tired of hearing that his dad had tried so hard to be there for him. And he got to be six and very angry instead of being told to be brave and strong. And maybe Penny has sprayed Ethan with some Pertinence before he left because instead of being subtle, instead of dropping him off at his Vera and Jack's and hoping for the best, Ethan warned him how things might be.

'They're upset,' Ethan said, 'and you remind them of your dad, and it's just so hard on everyone.' He blew out a breath because there was just so much hurt all around, but so much love too.

'They hate my mum.'

'They don't,' Ethan said, and then corrected himself, because it was Justin who was dealing with this. 'Well, if they do, you shouldn't have to hear it. You tell me if they say anything that hurts. And if they are less than nice about her, it's because they don't know your mum,' Ethan said. 'She's great.'

He saw the smile lift the edge of Justin's lips as finally someone in the Lewis family said something nice about his mum.

Yes, Ethan decided, having dropped Justin off—this he could do.

CHAPTER FOURTEEN

'MORNING, ETHAN.' VANESSA was just coming on duty and smiled when she saw him, but then pulled a face. 'I'm guessing, from the state of you, that you're going off duty?'

Finishing up a week of nights, Ethan was aware that he probably wasn't looking his best. He had meant to shave before he'd come on last night, and had also meant to shave the night before that too. 'So, if you're going off duty…' Vanessa said, looking at the board that Lisa was filling in—it showed all the on-take doctors and who was on duty today. 'Oh, no!' Vanessa said as she watched Lisa write 'Penny Masters' in red. 'She's back.'

'She will be soon,' Lisa teased the nurses. 'Party's over for you lot.'

'Tell me about it. Who knows what her problem is,' Vanessa groaned, and Ethan wanted to tell them to give her a break, that the two of them had no idea what Penny was going through.

But Penny would hate that.

She was just this tough little thing choosing to go it alone, and for the last couple of weeks he'd had to force himself to respect that while trying to sort out how he felt about IVF and babies and things. Ethan still didn't know. He couldn't work out how he felt about dating someone who wanted a baby, oh, say, about nine months from now.

He'd bought flowers for the first time in his unromantic life and they were waiting in her office, along with an invitation for dinner. Maybe they could just take it slowly, start at the beginning without those blasted needles hanging over them.

Though he'd rather liked giving them!

Play was resuming, Ethan thought with a smile.

He heard the bell from Triage and Lisa stopped writing on the board and sped off with Ethan following. They got outside to find nurses trying to get an unconscious woman from the back seat of a car onto a trolley as her panicked husband shouted for them to hurry up. Security was nowhere to be seen.

'What happened?' Ethan asked the man.

'I just came home from work and I couldn't wake her...' The man was barefoot and jumping up and down on the spot. As his wife was placed on the trolley Ethan tried to get some more information, but apart from a urine infection there was nothing wrong with her, the agitated husband said.

'You're going to have to move your car,' Lisa told him as they started to move the patient inside, but he ignored her, instead running alongside his wife.

'You need to move your car,' Ethan said, because even if it sounded a minor detail, it wasn't if there was an ambulance on its way in with another sick patient.

'Just sort my wife out!' the man roared at Ethan.

'Stop worrying about the car.' There was a minor scuffle; the man fronted up to Ethan, fear and adrenaline and panic igniting. Ethan blocked the man's fist, but Ethan was angry too.

'Man up!' Ethan said. 'You want me to stand here fighting, or do you want me to sort out your wife? Go and move your car.'

He did so, but as they sped the woman through, the usually laid-back Ethan, who let things like that go, glared over at Lisa.

'Where the hell was Security?'

Lisa didn't answer.

'I want that reported.'

'He's just scared.'

'Yeah, well, we're all scared at times.'

They were now at the doors to Resus and Ethan was dealing with the patient, who was responding to pain and her pupils were reacting. He could smell what was wrong—there was the familiar smell of ketones on her breath. Lisa was attaching her to monitors as Ethan quickly found a vein and took bloods. 'Add a pregnancy test,' Ethan said, because she was of childbearing age and a diabetic crisis could be dangerous for any foetus. By the time the husband returned from parking his car there was saline up and Lisa was giving the patient her first dose of insulin. His anger was fading, but still it churned.

'Are you all right, Ethan?' Lisa checked.

'Sure.'

'I'll do an incident form after...'

'Forget it.' He gave a small smile that said he had overreacted.

'Touched a nerve, did it?' Lisa smiled back.

'Must have,' Ethan said.

He thought of his own fear as he'd raced to get to his cousin, yet it wouldn't have entered his head to front up to anyone, and he thought of Kate, who had done the right thing and not just left the car, even though she must so badly have wanted to. 'I want to know where Security was, though,'. Ethan said, and then got back to the patient. The medics were on their way down but for now Ethan went in to speak with the husband.

'I'll come in with you,' Lisa said.

'No need,' Ethan said.

'I wasn't offering.' Lisa had worked there a very long time and gave him a smile that told him there was no way she was leaving the two of them in the same room.

'Come on, then.'

They walked in and the man was sitting in there, his head in his hands.

'Mr Edmunds.' Ethan looked at the patient sheet that had been handed to him.

'Mark.' He looked up. 'Sorry about before.'

Ethan would deal with that later. He was actually glad Lisa had insisted on coming in as there was still this strange surliness writhing inside Ethan and he looked down at the patient card again for a moment before talking.

'Your wife, Anna, did you know she was diabetic?' Mark shook his head. 'No…she's been fine, well, tired, but like I said, she thought she had a urine infection.'

Ethan nodded. 'One of the signs is passing urine a lot but we're checking for any infection.' He explained things as simply as he could to the very confused and very scared man—that his wife had type one diabetes and she was in ketoacidosis—her glucose was far too high and would be slowly brought down. But it affected everything and she would be very closely watched, and while she was very sick, he expected her to soon be well.

'She'll still be diabetic?'

'Yes.' Ethan nodded. 'But she'll be taught to manage it and this will hopefully be the worst it ever is.' Ethan took a breath. 'Is there any chance that your wife might be pregnant?'

'We're trying.'

'Okay,' Ethan said.

'Would it damage the baby?'

'Let's just wait for results and then we'll see what we're dealing with. Do you want to come in and see your wife?'

Mark nodded and then said it again. 'I am sorry about earlier.'

'And I accept your apology,' Ethan said. 'But there is no place for that sort of carry-on here.'

'I was just—'

'Not an excuse,' Ethan broke in. 'There were two women there and your fist wasn't looking where it was going. We've got doctors here who are barely five foot…'

Yes, there was his problem—everything went back to Penny.

But, hell, Ethan thought, it could have been Penny on duty and she could have been pregnant, and he stood up and walked out and took a deep breath.

'Where was Security?' Ethan asked Lisa.

'Over in the car park,' Lisa said. 'Someone was trying to break into a car. They can't be everywhere, Ethan.'

He knew that, but he wanted them everywhere, wanted two burly guards and an Alsatian walking alongside Penny at all times.

Maybe he was a caveman after all.

CHAPTER FIFTEEN

YES, SHE HAD always rotated her clothes, mixing and matching her outfits with precision, changing them with the seasons. Not anymore. Today she had *chosen* a floral dress that buttoned at the front. Instead of low, flat heels, she wore sandals, and because she hadn't been meticulous with her factor thirty, Penny's legs were sun-kissed and she wore her hair loose.

She smiled as she walked into work and Ethan, tired after his night shift, chatting to the medics, noticed the glow in her and had a feeling her decision had been made and that there were embryos about to be taken out of storage in the very near future.

'Morning, Vanessa,' Penny said as she walked past.

'Er, morning, Penny.'

'Hi, Lisa.'

'Penny.'

Penny swallowed. 'Lisa, can I have a word with you, please?'

It was the hardest word and Lisa gave her a smile as they moved into an empty cubicle, and Penny said it. 'I've been going through some things and I should never have brought it to work. It was just…' And she did what Jasmine had advised all along and what Penny had thought she would never do—let Lisa know what had been going on.

'Well, you can't really leave your hormones at home.' Lisa smiled. 'You could have said.'

'I know.'

'I am discreet.'

'I know that too,' Penny said. 'I'll have a word with Vanessa and apologise. Anyone else?' And then Penny gave a guilty smile. 'Should I just call a staff meeting?'

Yes, it really was the hardest, hardest word because sometimes when you had to say it, it meant that you'd really hurt someone.

'I'm so sorry, Vanessa.' Penny saw the red cheeks and the flash of tears in her colleague's eyes and it wasn't actually the blood pressure she hadn't written down or the delays in medication that were the problem. There was another morning Penny hadn't properly apologised for, and though she didn't want to play the sympathy card, Penny did want Vanessa to know that her outburst hadn't been aimed at her.

Penny took her into an interview room.

'You were right to come and get me that morning and let me know what was happening. I know you'd never leave a patient and that Raj was there. I wasn't angry at you—I was just upset. When you came to find me I'd just got my period,' Penny said. 'I'd been trying for a baby and I thought I was finally pregnant.' And, no, she didn't tell her that for twenty-four hours she had been pregnant, neither did she say anything about the IVF, but it was enough for Vanessa to put her arms around her. Penny gave a little self-conscious wriggle, but then found out that it was nice sometimes to have a friend and be held.

Ethan watched them walking out of the interview room, smiling and chatting, and he excused himself and walked over.

'Morning, Penny.'

'Morning.'

'Nice break?'

'Very.'

'What did you get up to?'

'Not much.' How lovely it was to say that.

'Glad to be back?'

'Not yet.' Penny took a deep breath. 'I'm sorry I've been such a cow to work with.' Even though he knew why, she still felt she ought to say it here in the workplace and not just to Ethan. 'I should have recorded my apology before I came back to work. You're the third and I haven't even got halfway down the corridor.'

'Maybe you could ask the receptionist to play it over the loudspeaker?' Ethan grinned.

She walked off to her office and turned and flashed that smile but he didn't follow at first.

He just stood there thinking, because he knew how he felt now, and he checked with himself for a moment and the answer was still the same so he headed to her office to tell her.

'I would have loved your baby.' Ethan stood at the door and whether it was the wrong or right thing to say, he told her what he now knew.

'Ethan…'

'I'm not just saying that.' He wasn't and he told her why. 'I know you're going to go for it again,' Ethan said, 'I could see it when you walked in. I'll tell you this, if you were pregnant now, if it had worked out for you, well, I might have taken a while to come around but I would have, because it wouldn't change the way I feel. It's just taken a bit of a time for me to understand that.'

'I'm not going for it again.' She saw him frown. 'This is Tranquil Penny.'

'Oh.' He came over and took her in his arms and introduced himself. 'Pleased to meet you.' Then he frowned. 'What do you mean, you're not going to try again?'

'I can't have children.' She'd practised saying it, not just to Ethan but at other times in her future. 'I know I might want to try again someday, but now I just want a break from it—I want lots of sex for sex's sake, preferably with you.' She reached into her bag and took out a packet of pills and waved them. 'It's probably over-kill—left to their own devices my ovaries squeeze out two, maybe three eggs a year—but I'm taking the pressure off.'

She gave him a smile. 'Yes, please, to dinner.' He kissed her and he had never been so pleased to kiss a woman, just relieved to find her mouth and what had been missing in every other mouth he had kissed.

Here it was, the love he hadn't been looking for.

'I'm going home to sleep,' Ethan said.

'Not yet,' Penny grumbled.

'I am, and then I'm going to set my alarm so I've time

to tidy up in case I end up bringing my date back.' He gave her a smile. 'You've never seen my home.'

Penny blushed. Yes, there was a lot to get to know and lots of fun to be had before a guy like Ethan might settle down. And it might never happen, but she wanted him in a way she never had. There was a love inside Penny so much bigger than this kiss. A love that crowded out so many other things, and she just had to hold on to her feelings a bit, not terrify him with them by jumping in too soon.

'Or maybe...' Ethan said, and he undid a couple of buttons and had a peek and she was in coral, his favourite '...we could skip the restaurant and eat at my place?'

'What's for dinner, Ethan?'

They had the tiniest of histories, but it was enough to make the other smile.

'That all depends on what you pick up at the supermarket on your way home from work,' Ethan said.

And he glimpsed then a future and there would be no remote-control flinging because they would look out for each other, argue and tease each other, and then kiss and make up and not let things fester.

'Do you want to go to the football on Sunday?'

'No!' Penny pulled a face; she could think of nothing worse, but then it clicked. 'Are you going with Justin?'

'It will be our second week,' Ethan said.

'Gina agreed?'

'More than that. Afterwards I'm taking him to my aunt and uncle's and he's staying the night, and then in the morning I'll go and collect him and take him back to his mum's. We'll be doing that a couple of times a month and it's working out well.'

'That's some commitment.' Penny smiled at her commitment-phobe.

'I'm getting good at them.'

Yes, there was still a lot she didn't know about Ethan, because as he stood there looking at her he was doing the maths. She was thirty-five and at a rate of two to three eggs a year there weren't a whole lot of chances, but he was prepared to take them now. Ethan picked up the pill pack she was still holding and, just as Penny had with the needles to get what she wanted, he faced his fears over and over, twenty-eight times, in fact.

He punched each pill into the sink, even the sugar-coated ones, and then turned on the tap and watched them swirl in the water. Then he broke out in a sweat because it was *him* now talking about making babies when he'd never thought he might.

'I've got more at home.'

'I want whatever happens,' Ethan said. 'And I don't want to take away even one of your chances.'

'And I don't want to ruin this,' Penny said. They were chasing the same dream from different directions, both terrified to miss or even to clash and blow them apart. Penny was standing at the silver lining of acceptance that there might never be babies, and Ethan was just starting to accept that there might be. 'I don't want you to find out you do want babies after all and then be disappointed.'

And he was the most honest, sexiest, funniest man

she had ever met, even as he voiced her unspoken fears. 'And then go off with someone years younger...'

'Ha, ha,' Penny said, because they could talk about things, tell each other things and, yes, they could tease each other too. 'Someone soft and curvy and cute.'

'Did I really used to go for cute?' Ethan smiled. And he looked at her and he knew where his heart was. 'Actually,' Ethan said as he faced another of his fears, 'for one hot mess you'd make a very cute bride.'

She blinked at him.

'I want to see Menopausal Penny and I want you to see Midlife Crisis Ethan.'

'So do I.' She was kissing him again. 'Going out in your sports car and joining a gym and things.'

'And if there are no babies, we'll be the mad aunt and uncle who spoil all their nieces and nephews but make their parents jealous as we go off on cruises and travel around the world. But,' Ethan said, 'if we're really clucky, we'll move to America and adopt little twin monkeys.'

'And dress them in tutus.'

'No,' Ethan said, because it was his future they were planning too. 'Not the boy one.'

EPILOGUE

'IT'S CALLED A spontaneous pregnancy,' her GP explained as Penny sat there, stunned. 'Some women do get pregnant naturally after IVF.'

It would seem so.

Penny honestly didn't know how she felt.

She'd imagined hearing she was pregnant so many times, but now that it was here, she actually didn't know how to deal with the news.

They had just returned from their honeymoon—Louise had given them the cruise bug and they had sailed around the Mediterranean, getting brown and being spoiled. Penny closed her eyes at the thought of the champagne and the things she had eaten, though now, when she thought about it, she hadn't really indulged that much.

'We nearly didn't go,' Penny admitted as she chatted to the doctor. She'd thought they'd have to call it off because Mr Dean had told them that they couldn't both take annual leave at the same time.

'We're hardly going to go on separate honeymoons,' Ethan had said—that was how they had announced their news—and given Ethan didn't actually have any annual leave and would be taking it unpaid, they could afford a locum to cover him.

'Be glad that you had your cruise.' Her GP smiled. 'Because you won't be doing that sort of thing for a while.'

And Penny was glad that they had, so glad, because they'd had nearly a year of just them and it had been amazing—dating for all of a week before Penny had put her house on the market and she and the cat had moved in with him, then just getting to know each other and learning how to laugh and to love.

Penny drove home. She was supposed to be getting her hair done as it was her mother's wedding in a few hours' time, but instead she'd have to make do with heated rollers.

She just had to see Ethan, had to find out how he would take the news.

'Your hair's nice,' Ethan said when she got back. He was in the bathroom, shaving, the cat sitting by the sink watching him.

'I didn't get my hair done.' Penny had to laugh.

'Oh,' Ethan said. 'Well, it still looks nice. Where did you go?' He saw her hesitate and he pretty much guessed she'd been to her GP.

Penny had been fantastic and absolutely adored Jasmine's little baby girl, Amelia, and they'd just found out that Kate was going to try for a fourth. There were so many friends and relations getting pregnant that Ethan was noticing and he was starting to feel little pinpricks of disappointment when Penny's period rarely came.

And not just for Penny.

He liked the time spent with Justin, and Penny was good with him too. He wanted now what Penny had wanted—a baby—though he couldn't really tell her that. No doubt soon they'd be off to America to look at little monkeys, but first…

'You'll be all right at the wedding?' He rinsed his face and then turned round. 'You're all right with your mum and Bradley?'

'Apart from his name,' Penny said. 'And do they have to be so affectionate in public?'

She was the oddest person he had ever met and he loved her all the more for it. And maybe the timing wasn't right, maybe he should bring it up after the wedding because he didn't want to upset her beforehand, but right or wrong he said what was on his mind.

'If you want to go again…'

'Go again?'

'On IVF,' Ethan said. 'I'd be fine with that.'

'You're sure?' Penny's eyes narrowed. 'That doesn't sound very enthusiastic.'

'Okay.' He tried again. 'Why don't *we* go on IVF?' He thought for a moment. 'That makes me sound like Gordon.' And then he was serious. 'If you want to then so do I.'

'What do you want, Ethan?'

'I can't believe I'm saying this,' Ethan admitted. 'But I'd like to try for a baby…' He rushed into his 'but if it doesn't work then I won't be disappointed' speech, but she halted him. There was no need for that. She loved it that he wanted this too, that it wasn't something she was foisting on them too soon.

'We don't need to try,' Penny said. 'I've just come from the doctor's.'

He was scared to get too excited, just in case it was like last time, only it was nothing like last time.

'I'm thirteen weeks,' Penny said, and she watched his reaction as it sank in that while they'd been busy with weddings and football matches and honeymoons and juggling work and falling deeper and deeper in love, she'd been pregnant.

'Can we tell people?' Ethan asked.

'I guess,' Penny said, because they were out of the first trimester. 'But not just yet. It's Mum's day today.'

And it was just as well she didn't get her hair done because it would have been messed up anyway as they were soon off to bed to celebrate. Ethan had the good sense to set the alarm just in case they got a bit carried away.

'Can't be late for your mum's wedding,' he said as a very tanned Penny stripped off.

They were on two sets to one, with Ethan winning, and each game spent an awful lot of time at deuce.

Record times!

'Hey, I bet when you were fantasising about having your wild fling with me,' Ethan said as he dropped his towel, 'you never imagined it ending up like this.'

'No,' Penny said, because the best she had been able to imagine then had been a shocked reaction and a baby that wasn't his.

The truth was so much better.

* * * * *

For Mary, Linda, Karen and David.
Family and friends, too. We're lucky!

Beverly Long enjoys the opportunity to write her own stories. She has both a bachelor's and a master's degree in business and more than twenty years of experience as a human resources director. She considers her books to be a great success if they compel the reader to stay up way past their bedtime. Beverly loves to hear from readers. Visit beverlylong.com, or like her at Facebook.com/beverlylong.romance.

Chapter One

Liz Mayfield had kicked off her shoes long before lunch, and now, with her bare feet tucked under her butt, she simply ignored the sweat that trickled down her spine. It had to be ninety in the shade. At least ninety-five in her small, lower-level office.

It was the kind of day for pool parties and frosty drinks in pretty glasses. Not the kind of day for sorting through mail and dealing with confused teenagers.

But she'd traded one in for the other years ago when she'd left her six-figure income and five weeks of vacation to take the job at Options for Caring Mothers—OCM.

It had been three years, and there were still people scratching their heads over her choice.

She picked the top envelope off the stack on the corner of her desk. Her name was scrawled across the plain white front in blue ink. The sender had spelled her last name wrong, mixing up the order of the *i* and the *e*. She slid her thumb under the flap, pulled out the single sheet of lined notebook paper and read.

And her head started to buzz.

You stupid BITCH. You going to be very sorry if you don't stop messing in stuff thats not your busines.

The egg-salad sandwich she'd had for lunch rumbled in her stomach. Still holding the notebook paper with one hand, she cupped her other hand over her mouth. She swallowed hard twice, and once she thought she might have it under control, she unfolded her legs and stretched them far enough that she could slip both feet into her sandals. And for some crazy reason, she felt better once she had shoes on, as if she was more prepared.

She braced the heels of her hands against the edge of her scratched metal desk and pushed. Her old chair squeaked as it rolled two feet and then came to a jarring stop when a wheel jammed against a big crack in the tile floor.

Who would have sent her something like that? What did they mean that she was going to be *very sorry?* And when the heck was her heart going to stop pounding?

She stood and walked around her desk, making a very deliberate circle. On her third trip around, she worked up enough nerve to look more closely at the envelope. It had a stamp and a postmark from three days earlier but no return address. With just the nail on her pinkie finger, she flipped the envelope over. There was nothing on the back.

Her mail had been gathering dust for days. She'd had a packed schedule, and it probably would have sat another day if her one o'clock hadn't canceled. That made her feel marginally better. If nothing had happened yet to make her *very sorry,* it was probably just some idiot trying to freak her out.

That, however, didn't stop her from dropping to the floor like a sack of potatoes when she heard a noise outside her small window. On her hands and knees, she peered around the edge of her desk and felt like a fool when she looked through the open ground-level window and saw it was only Mary Thorton arriving for her two-o'clock appointment. She could see the girl's thin white legs with the terribly annoying skull tattoo just above her right knee.

Liz got up and brushed her dusty hands off on her denim shorts. The door opened and Mary, her ponytail, freckles and still-thin arms all strangely at odds with her round stomach, walked in. She picked up an OCM brochure that Liz kept on a rack by the door and started fanning herself. "I am never working in a basement when I get older," she said.

"I hope you don't have to," Liz said, grateful that her voice sounded normal. She sat in her chair and pulled it up to the desk. Using her pinkie again, she flipped the notebook paper over so that the blank side faced up.

Mary had already taken a seat on one of the two chairs in front of the desk. Pieces of strawberry blond hair clung to her neck, and her mascara was smudged around her pale blue eyes. She slouched in the chair, with her arms resting on her stomach.

"How do you feel?" Liz asked. The girl looked tired.

"Fat. And I'm sweating like a pig," Mary replied.

Liz, careful not to touch or look at the notebook paper, reached for the open manila folder that she'd pulled from her drawer earlier that morning. She scanned her notes from Mary's last visit. "How's your job at the drugstore?"

"I quit."

Mary had taken the job less than three weeks earlier. It had been the last in a string of jobs since becoming Liz's client four months ago. Most had lasted only a few days or a week at best at the others. The bosses were stupid, the hours were too many or too few, the location too far. The list went on and on—countless reasons not to keep a job.

"Why, Mary?"

She shrugged her narrow shoulders. "I gave a few friends a little discount on their makeup. Stupid boss made a big deal out of it."

"Imagine that. Now what do you plan to do?"

"I've been thinking about killing myself."

It was the one thing Mary could have said that made Liz grasp for words. "How would you do it, Mary?" she asked, sounding calmer than she felt.

"I don't know. Nothing bloody. Maybe pills. Or I might just walk off the end of Navy Pier. They say drowning is pretty peaceful."

No plan. That was good. Was it just shock talk, something destined to get Mary the attention that she seemed to crave?

"Sometimes it seems like the only answer," Mary said. She stared at her round stomach. "You know what I mean?"

Liz did know, better than most. She leaned back in her chair and looked up at the open street-level window. Three years ago, it had been a day not all that different from today. Maybe not as hot but there'd been a similar stillness in the air.

There'd been no breeze to carry the scent of death. Nothing that had prepared her for walking into that house and seeing sweet Jenny, with the deadly razor blade just inches from her limp hand, lying in the red pool of death.

Yeah, Liz knew. She just wished she didn't.

"No one would probably even notice," Mary said, her lower lip trembling.

Liz got up, walked around the desk and sat in the chair next to the teen. The vinyl covering on the seat, cracked in places, scratched her bare legs. She clasped Mary's hand and held it tight. "I would notice."

With her free hand, Mary played with the hem of her maternity shorts. "Some days," she said, "I want this baby so much, and there are other days that I can't stand it. It's like this weird little bug has gotten into my stomach, and it keeps growing and growing until it's going to explode, and there will be bug pieces everywhere."

Liz rubbed her thumb across the top of Mary's hand.

"Mary, it's okay. You're very close to your due date. It's natural to be scared."

"I'm not scared."

Of course not. "Have you thought any more about whether you intend to keep the baby or give it up for adoption?"

"It's not a baby. It's a bug. You got some bug parents lined up?" Mary rolled her eyes.

"I can speak with our attorney," Liz said, determined to stay on topic. "Mr. Fraypish has an excellent record of locating wonderful parents."

Mary stared at Liz, her eyes wide open. She didn't look happy or sad. Interested or bored. Just empty.

Liz stood up and stretched, determined that Mary wouldn't see her frustration. The teen had danced around the adoption issue for months, sometimes embracing it and other times flatly rejecting it. But she needed to make a decision. Soon.

Liz debated whether she should push. Mary continued to stare, her eyes focused somewhere around Liz's chin. Neither of them said a word.

Outside her window, a car stopped with a sudden squeal of brakes. Liz looked up just as the first bullet hit the far wall.

Noise thundered as more bullets spewed through the open window, sending chunks of plaster flying. Liz grabbed for Mary, pulling the pregnant girl to the floor. She covered the teen's body with her own, doing her best to keep her weight off the girl's stomach.

It stopped as suddenly as it had started. She heard the car speed off, the noise fading fast.

Liz jerked away from Mary. "Are you okay?"

The teen stared at her stomach. "I think so," she said.

Liz could see the girl reach for her familiar indifference, but it had been too quick, too frightening, too close. Tears welled up in the teen's eyes, and they rolled down her smooth, freckled cheeks. With both hands, she hugged her middle. "I didn't mean it. I don't want to die. I don't want my baby to die."

Liz had seen Mary angry, defensive, even openly hostile. But she'd never seen her cry. "I know, sweetie. I know." She reached to hug her but stopped when she heard the front door of OCM slam open and the thunder of footsteps on the wooden stairs.

Her heart rate sped up, and she hurriedly got to her feet, moving in front of Mary. The closed office door swung open. She saw the gun, and for a crazy minute, she thought the man holding it had come back to finish what he'd started. She'd been an idiot not to take the threat seriously. Some kind of strange noise squeaked out of her throat.

"It's all right," the man said. "I'm Detective Sawyer Montgomery with Chicago Police, ma'am. Are either of you hurt?"

It took her a second or two to process that this man wasn't going to hurt her. Once it registered, it seemed as if her bones turned to dust, and she could barely keep her body upright. He must have sensed that she was just about to go down for the count because he shoved his gun back into his shoulder holster and grabbed her waist to steady her.

"Take a breath," he said. "Nice and easy."

She closed her eyes and focused on sucking air in through her nose and blowing it out her mouth. All she could think about was that he didn't sound like a Chicago cop. He sounded Southern, like the cool, sweet tea she'd enjoyed on hot summer evenings a lifetime ago. Smooth.

After four or five breaths, she opened her eyes. He looked at her, saw that she was back among the living and let go of her waist. He backed up a step. "Are you hurt?" he repeated.

"We're okay," she said, focusing on him. He wore gray dress pants, a wrinkled white shirt and a red tie that was loose at the collar. He had a police radio clipped to his belt, and though it was turned low, she could hear the background noise of Chicago's finest at work.

He reached into his shirt pocket, pulled out a badge, flipped it open and held it steady, giving her a chance to read.

"Thank you, Detective Montgomery," she said.

He nodded and pivoted to show it to Mary. Once she nodded, he flipped it shut and returned it to his pocket. Then he extended a hand to help Mary up off the floor.

Mary hesitated, then took it. Once up, she moved several feet away. Detective Montgomery didn't react. Instead he pulled his radio from his belt. "Squad, this is 5162. I'm inside at 229 Logan Street. No injuries to report. Backup is still requested to secure the exterior."

Liz stared at the cop. He had the darkest brown eyes—almost, but not quite, black. His hair was brown and thick and looked as if it had recently been trimmed. His skin was tanned, and his lips had a very nice shape.

Best-looking cop she'd seen in some time.

In fact, only cop she'd seen in some time. Logan Street wasn't in a great neighborhood but was quiet in comparison to the streets that ran a couple blocks to the south. As such, it didn't get much attention from the police.

And yet, Detective Montgomery had been inside OCM less than a minute after the shooting. That didn't make sense. She stepped forward, putting herself between the detective and Mary.

"How did you get here so quickly?" she asked.

He hesitated for just a second. "I was parked outside."

"That was coincidental," she said. "I'm not generally big on coincidences."

He shrugged and pulled a notebook out of his pocket. "May I have your name, please?"

His look and his attitude were all business. His voice was pure pleasure. The difference in the two caught her off balance, making her almost forgive that he was being deliberately evasive. There was a reason he'd been parked outside, but he wasn't ready to cough it up. She was going to have to play the game his way.

"Liz Mayfield," she said. "I'm one of three counselors here at OCM. Options for Caring Mothers," she added. "This is Mary Thorton."

The introduction wasn't necessary. The girl had been keeping him up at nights. Sawyer knew her name, her social security number, her address. Hell, he knew her favorite breakfast cereal. Three empty boxes of Fruit Loops in her garbage had been pretty hard to miss. "Miss Thorton," he said, nodding at the teen before turning back to the counselor. "Is there anybody else in the building?"

The woman shook her head. "Carmen was here earlier, but she left to take her brother to the orthodontist. Cynthia, she's the third counselor, just works in the mornings. We have a part-time receptionist, too, but she's not here today. Oh, and Jamison is getting ready for a fund-raiser. He's working off-site."

"Who's Jamison?"

"He's the boss."

"Okay. Why don't the two of you—"

Sawyer stopped when he heard his partner let loose their call numbers. He turned the volume up on his radio.

"Squad, this is 5162, following a gray Lexus, license Adam, John, David, 7, 4, 9. I lost him, somewhere around Halsted and 35th. Repeat, lost him. Keep an eye out, guys."

Sawyer wasn't surprised. He and Robert had been parked a block down the street. Sawyer had jumped out, and Robert had given chase, but the shooter had at least a two-block advantage. In a crowded city, filled with alleys and side streets, that was a lot. Every cop on the street in that general vicinity would be on the watch now, but Sawyer doubted it would do any good. Mirandez's boys would have dumped the car by now. He turned the volume on his radio back down.

"Why don't you two have a seat?" he said, trying hard to maintain a hold on his emotions. They hadn't gotten the shooter, but maybe—just maybe—he had Mary Thorton in a position where she'd want to talk.

The counselor sat. Mary continued to stand until Liz Mayfield patted the chair next to her.

Facing both women, he said, "I'd like to ask you a few questions. Are you feeling up to that?"

"You okay?" Liz Mayfield asked Mary.

The girl shrugged. "I suppose."

The woman nodded at Sawyer. "Shoot," she said.

Mary snorted, and the pretty counselor's cheeks turned pink. "Sorry," she mumbled. "We're ready. Proceed. Begin."

Wow. She was a Beach Boys song—a regular California girl—with her smooth skin and thick, blond hair that hung down to the middle of her back. She wore a sleeveless white cotton shirt and denim shorts, and her toenails were the brightest pink he'd ever seen.

What the hell was she doing in a basement on the south side of Chicago?

He knew what he was doing there. He was two minutes and two hundred yards behind Dantel Mirandez. Like he had been for the past eighteen months.

And the son of a bitch had slipped away again.

Sawyer crossed his legs at the ankles and leaned back against the desk, resting his butt on the corner. He focused his attention on the teenager. She sat slouched in her chair, staring at the floor. "Ms. Thorton, any ideas about who is responsible for this shooting?"

Out of the corner of his eye, he saw Liz Mayfield sit up straighter in her chair. "I—"

He held up his hand, stopping her. "If you don't mind, I'd like to give Ms. Thorton a chance to answer first."

"I don't know anything, Cop," the teen said, her voice hard with irritation.

Damn. "You're sure?"

Mary raised her chin. "Yeah. What kind of cop are you? Haven't you heard about people in cars with guns? They shoot things. Duh. That's why they call them drive-by shooters."

It looked as if she planned to stick to the same old story. He walked over to the window and looked out. Two squad cars had arrived. He knew the officers would systematically work their way through the crowd that had gathered, trying to find out if anybody had seen anything that would be helpful. He didn't hold out much hope. In this neighborhood, even if somebody saw something, they wouldn't be that likely to talk. He heard a noise behind him and turned.

"I'm out of here." Mary pushed on the arms of her chair and started to get up. "I've got things to do."

He wasn't letting her off the hook that easy. "Sit down," he instructed. "We're not done."

"You can't tell me what to do," Mary shouted.

You can't tell me what to do. The words bounced off the walls, sharp, quick blows, taking Sawyer back seventeen years. Just a kid himself, he'd alternated between begging, demanding, bribing, whatever he'd thought would work. But that angry teenage girl hadn't listened to him, either. She'd continued to pump heroin into her veins, and his son, his precious infant son, had paid the ultimate price.

Sawyer bit the inside of his lip. "Sit," he said.

Liz Mayfield stood. "Detective, may I talk to you privately?"

He gave her a quick glance. "In a minute." He turned his

attention back to Mary. "I'm going to ask you one more time. What do you know about this shooting?"

"What I know is that you talk funny."

He heard Liz Mayfield's quick intake of breath, but the woman remained silent.

"Is that right?" Sawyer rubbed his chin, debating how much he should share. "Maybe I do. Where I come from, everybody talks like this. Where I come from, two drive-by shootings in one week is something worthy of note."

Mary lowered her chin. Liz Mayfield, who had remained standing, cocked her head to the side and studied Mary. "Two?" she asked.

Sawyer didn't wait for Mary. "While Ms. Thorton shopped in a convenience store just three days ago, the front windows got shot out," he said.

"Mary?"

Was it surprise or hurt that he heard in the counselor's voice?

The teen didn't answer. The silence stretched for another full minute before Liz tried again. "What's going on here?" she asked.

"There ain't nothing going on here," Mary said. "Besides me getting bored out of my mind, that is."

"Somebody's going to get killed one of these days." Sawyer paced in front of the two women, stopping in front of Mary. "How would you like it if Ms. Mayfield had gotten a bullet in the back of her head?"

"I got rights," Mary yelled.

"Be quiet," he said. "Use some of that energy and tell me about Mirandez."

"Who?" the counselor asked.

Sawyer didn't respond, his attention focused on Mary. He saw her hand grip the wooden arm of the chair.

"Well?" Sawyer prompted. "Are you going to pretend you don't know who I'm talking about?"

"Stupid cops," Mary said, shaking her head.

He'd been called worse. Twice already today. "Come on, Mary," he said. "Before somebody dies."

Mary leaned close to her counselor. "I don't know what he's talking about. Honest, I don't. You've got to believe me." A tear slid down the girl's pale face, dripping onto her round stomach. He looked away. He didn't want to think about her baby.

"If I can go home now," Mary said, looking up at Liz Mayfield, "I'll come back tomorrow. We can talk about the adoption."

The woman stared at the teen for a long minute before turning to him. "Mary says she doesn't know anything about the shooting. I'm not sure what else we can tell you."

Sawyer settled back against the desk and contemplated his next words. "That's it? That's all either of you has to say?"

Liz Mayfield shrugged. "I'd still like a minute of your time," she said, "but if you don't have any other questions for Mary, can she go home?" She brushed her hair back from her face. "It has been a rather unpleasant day."

Maybe he needed to describe in graphic detail exactly what unpleasant looked like.

"Please," she said.

She looked tired and pale, and he remembered that she'd already about passed out once. "Fine," he said. "She can go."

Liz Mayfield extended her hand to Mary, helping the girl out of the chair. She wrapped her arm around Mary's freckled shoulder, and they left the room.

He had his back toward the door, his face turned toward the open window, scanning the street, when she came back. "I'm just curious," he said without turning around. "You saw her when I said his name. She knows something. You know it, and I know it. How come you let her walk away?"

"Who's Mirandez?" she asked.

He turned around. He wanted to see her face. "Dantel Mirandez is scum. The worst kind of scum. He's the guy who makes it possible for third graders to buy a joint at recess. And for their older brothers and sisters to be heroin addicts by the time they're twelve. And for their parents to spend their grocery money on—"

"I think I get it, Detective."

"Yeah, well, get this. Mirandez isn't just your neighborhood dealer. He runs a big operation. Maybe as much as ten percent of all the illegal drug traffic in Chicago. Millions of dollars pass through his organization. He employs hundreds. Not bad for a twenty-six-year-old punk."

"How do you know Mary is involved with him?"

"It's my job to know. She's been his main squeeze for the past six months—at least."

"It doesn't make sense. Why would he try to hurt her?"

"We don't think he's trying to hurt her. It's more like he's trying to get her attention, to make sure she remembers that he's the boss. To make sure that she remembers that he can get to her at any time, at any place."

"I don't understand."

"Three weeks ago, during one of his transactions, he killed a man. Little doubt that it wasn't the first time. But word on the street is that this time, your little Miss Mary was with him. She saw it."

"Oh, my God. I had no idea."

She looked as if she might faint again. He pushed a chair in her direction. She didn't even look at it. He watched her, relaxing when a bit of color returned to her face.

"I'm sure you didn't," he said. "The tip came in about a week ago that Mary saw the hit. And then the convenience store got shot up. She got questioned at the scene, but she didn't offer anything up about Mirandez. I've been following her ever since. It wasn't a coincidence that my partner and I were parked a block away. We saw a car come around the corner, slow down. Before we could do anything, they had a gun stuck out the window, blowing this place up. We called it in, and I jumped out to come inside. My partner went after them. As you may have heard," he said, motioning to his radio, "they got away."

"It sounded like you got a license plate."

"Not that it will do us any good. It's a pretty safe bet that the car was hot. Stolen," he added.

"Do you know for sure that it was Mirandez who shot out my window? Did you actually see him?"

"I'm sure it wasn't him pulling the trigger. He rarely does his own dirty work. It was likely someone further down the food chain."

She swallowed hard. "You may be right, Detective. And I'm willing to try to talk to Mary, to try to convince her to cooperate with the police. You have to understand that my first priority is her. She doesn't have anyone else."

"She has Mirandez."

"She's never said a word about him."

"I assume he's the father of the baby," he said. "That fact is probably the only thing that's keeping her alive right now. Otherwise, I think she'd be expendable. Everybody is to this guy."

Liz shook her head. "He's not the father of her baby."

"How do you know?"

She hesitated. "Because I've met the father. He's a business major at Loyola."

"That doesn't make sense. Why isn't he tending to his own business? What kind of man lets his girlfriend and his unborn child get mixed up with people like Mirandez? He knows about the baby?"

"Yes. But he's not interested."

"He said that?"

"Mary is considering adoption. When the paternity of a baby is known, we require the father's consent as well as the mother's."

"I guess they're not teaching responsibility in college anymore." Sawyer flexed his hand, wishing he had about three minutes with college boy.

"Can't download it," she answered.

Sawyer laughed, his anger dissipating a bit. "And where does Mirandez fit into this?" he asked. "You saw her face when I said his name. She knows him all right. The question is, what else does she know?"

"It's hard to say. She's not an easy person to read."

"How old is she?"

"She turned eighteen last month. Legally an adult but still very young, if you know what I mean."

"Yeah, well, she's gonna be young, foolish and dead if she doesn't get away from Mirandez. It's only a matter of time." He wanted Liz to understand the severity. "Otherwise, if I can prove she was at that murder scene, then she's an accessory and that baby is gonna be born in jail."

"Well, that's clear enough." She turned her head to look at her desk. She took a deep breath. "It may not have anything to do with Mary."

He lowered his chin and studied her. "Why do you say that?"

She walked over to the desk and flipped over a piece of notebook paper. She pointed at it and then the envelope next to it. "They go together. I opened it about a half hour ago."

He looked down and read it quickly. When he jerked his

head up, she stood there, looking calmer than he felt. "Any idea who sent this?"

She shook her head. "So maybe this has nothing to do with Mary. Maybe, just maybe, you were busting her chops for nothing."

For some odd reason, her slightly sarcastic tone made him smile. "I wasn't busting her chops," he said. "That was me making polite conversation. First time you ever get something like this?"

"Yes."

"Anybody really pissed off at you?"

"I work with pregnant teenagers and when possible with the fathers, too. Most of them are irritated with me at one time or another. It's my job to make them deal with things they'd sometimes rather ignore."

He supposed it was possible that the shooting wasn't Mirandez's work, but the similarities between it and the shooting at the convenience store were too strong to be ignored. "I imagine you touched this?"

She nodded.

"Anybody else have access to your mail?"

"Our receptionist. She sorts it."

"Okay. I'll need both your prints so that we can rule them out."

She blew out a breath. "Fine. I've got her home number. By the way, they spelled my name wrong," she said. "That doesn't necessarily mean it's not someone who knows me. Given that *business* is also spelled wrong and the grammar isn't all that great, I'd say we're not dealing with a genius."

"They still got their point across."

She smiled at him, and he noticed not for the first time that Liz Mayfield was one damn fine-looking woman. "That they did," she said. "Loud and clear."

"Why don't you have a seat? I'll get an evidence tech out

here to take your prints. That will take a few minutes. In the meantime, I've got a few questions."

She rolled her eyes. "I'll just bet you do," she said before she dutifully sat down.

Chapter Two

"Hey, Montgomery, you owe me ten bucks. I told you the Cubs would lose to St. Louis. When are you going to learn?"

Sawyer fished two fives out of his pocket. He hadn't expected his boys to win. But he'd been a fan since coming to Chicago two years earlier and going to his first Cubs game at Wrigley Field. He wasn't sentimental enough to believe it was because of the ivy growing on the walls that it somehow reminded him of home. He liked to think it was because the Cubs, no matter if they were winning or losing, were always the underdog. Sort of like cops.

He folded the bills and tossed them at his partner. "Here. Now shut up. Why does the lieutenant want to see us?"

"I don't know. I got the same page you did." Robert Hanson pulled a thick telephone book out of his desk drawer. "It's a damn shame. Veronica spent the night, and she's really at her best in the morning. Very enthusiastic."

"Which one is Veronica?"

"Blonde. Blue eyes. Nice rack."

That described most of the women Robert dated. Sawyer heard the door and looked up. Lieutenant Fischer walked in.

"Gentlemen," their boss greeted them, dropping a thick green file on the wood desk. "We've got a problem."

Robert sat up straighter in his chair. Sawyer stared at his

boss. The man looked every one of his fifty years. "What's up?" Sawyer asked.

"We've got another dead body. Looks like the guy was beat up pretty good before somebody shot him in the head."

"Mirandez?" Sawyer hissed.

"Probably. Our guys ID'd the deceased. Bobbie Morage."

Sawyer looked at Robert. "Morage was tight with Mirandez until recently."

Robert nodded. "Rumor has it that Morage was skimming off the top. Taking product home in his pockets."

Lieutenant Fischer closed his eyes and leaned his head back. "No honor among thieves or killers."

"Any witnesses?" Sawyer asked.

His boss opened his eyes. "None. Got one hysterical maid at the Rotayne Hotel. She found him on her way to the Dumpster. Look, we've got to get this guy. This makes three in the past two months. Eight in the past year."

Sawyer could do the math. He wanted Mirandez more than he'd wanted anybody in fifteen years of wearing a badge.

"Are you sure you can't get Mary Thorton to talk?" The lieutenant stood in front of Sawyer, his arms folded across his chest.

"I don't know. Like I told you yesterday, she's either in it up to her eyeballs, or she's just a dumb young kid with a smart mouth who doesn't know anything. I'm not sure which."

"What about her counselor? What was her name?"

"Liz. Elizabeth, I guess. Last name is Mayfield."

"Can she help us?"

"I don't know." Sawyer shook his head. "If anyone can get to Mary, I think she's the one. She said she'd try."

"We need the girlfriend. Push the counselor if you need to."

Sawyer understood Lieutenant Fischer's anxiety. People

were dying. "She does have her own issues," he said, feeling the need to defend the woman.

Lieutenant Fischer rubbed a hand across his face. "I know. You get any prints off the note she got?"

"Nothing that we couldn't match up to her or the receptionist. We got a couple partials, and we're tracking down the mail carrier to rule him or her out. I don't know. It could be coincidence that she got this and then Mirandez went after Mary Thorton again."

"I don't believe in coincidence," Lieutenant Fischer said, his voice hard.

Sawyer didn't much, either. "I'll go see her now."

"I'll go with you," Robert offered, clearly resigned that Veronica was an opportunity lost.

Blonde. Blue eyes. Nice rack. Liz Mayfield had green eyes, but other than that, she was just Robert's type. "No," Sawyer said, not even looking at Robert.

"Hey, it's no problem. I like to watch you try to use that old-fashioned Southern charm."

"I don't need any help." Sawyer looked at his lieutenant and got the nod of approval he needed.

"Fine," Robert said. "Go ahead and drag your sorry ass over there again. I'll just stay here. In the air-conditioning."

Lieutenant Fischer shook his head. "No, you don't. You're going to the hotel to interview the maid again. She doesn't speak much English."

"Doesn't anybody else speak Spanish?" Robert moaned.

"Not like you do. I've got officers who grew up in Mexico that don't speak it as well."

Robert grinned broadly. "It's hell to be brilliant." He ducked out the door right before the telephone book hit it.

A HALF HOUR LATER, Sawyer parked his car in front of the brick two-story. He walked past a couple brown-eyed, brown-skinned children, carefully stepping around the pictures they'd created on the sidewalk with colored chalk.

Sawyer nodded at the two old men sitting on the steps. When he'd left OCM the day before, he'd taken the time to speak to them personally, hoping they'd seen the shooter. From his vehicle, just minutes before the arrival of what he still believed was Mirandez's band of dirty men, he'd seen them in the same spot, chatting.

They'd seen the shooter. It didn't help much. He'd worn a face mask.

He took the steps of OCM two at a time. He just needed to get inside, talk to Liz Mayfield and get the hell out of there. Before he did something stupid like touch her. He'd thought of her skin for most of the night. Her soft, silky skin. With legs that went on forever.

Sawyer glanced down at the street-level window. Plywood covered the opening, keeping both the sun and unwanted visitors out. He didn't stop to wonder how unwelcome he might be. He walked through the deserted hallway and down the steps. He knocked once on the closed door and then again when no one answered. He tried the knob, but it wouldn't turn.

"She left early."

Sawyer whirled around. He'd been so focused on the task that he hadn't heard the woman come up behind him.

"Sorry." She laughed at him. "Didn't mean to scare you."

Looking at her could scare almost anybody. She had bright red hair, blue eyeliner, black lips, and she wore a little bit of a skirt and shirt, showing more skin than material. She couldn't have been much older than eighteen. If she had been his daughter, he'd have locked her in the house until she found some clothes and washed the god-awful makeup off.

His son would have been just about her age. "What's your name?" he asked.

"Nicole." She held up the palm of her hand and wriggled her fingers. "Don't you recognize me?"

She was the part-time receptionist who had gotten her prints taken. An evidence tech had taken care of it for him. He'd been busy filling out case reports—one for the shooting, a separate one for Liz Mayfield's threat. "Sorry. Thanks for doing that, by the way."

"I'd do almost anything for Liz. Like I said, though, she's not here. She left early. Maybe to get ready for the dance."

Sawyer tried to concentrate. "A dance?"

"OCM is having a dance. A fund-raiser. Jamison says we're going to have to shut the doors if donations don't pick up."

Sawyer had finally had the opportunity to talk on the telephone with Jamison Curtiss, the executive director of OCM, late the evening before. The man had flitted between outrage at both the shooting and the note Liz Mayfield had received, to worry about the bad press for OCM, to despair about the neighborhood all in a matter of minutes.

Sawyer had told himself, several times while he was shaving this morning, that it had been that conversation that had spurred dreams of Liz Mayfield. Otherwise, there'd have been no reason to take his work home, to take it literally to bed with him.

Dreaming about a woman was something Robert would do.

"Dinner is two hundred bucks a plate," the girl continued. "Can you believe that? Like, I'd cook 'em dinner for half that."

"Where?"

"Like, at my house."

Sawyer shook his head. "No, where's the dinner?"

"At the Rotayne Hotel. Pretty fancy, huh?"

"As fancy as they get." *As long as they keep the dead bodies hidden in the alley.* "What time does it start?"

"Dinner's at seven. My grandmother wanted me to go. Thought I might meet a nice young man there." She wrinkled her nose.

"Not interested?" he asked.

She shook her head. "Last one I met got me knocked up. Guess Grandma kind of forgot about that. I don't know what I would have done if Liz hadn't helped me find a family for my baby. Now she's living in the suburbs. Like, with a mom and dad and two cats." The girl's eyes filled with tears.

"Uh…" He was so far out of his league here.

"Anyway," she said, sniffing loudly. She tossed her hair back. "She's the best. Some lawyer guy helps her. He talks fast, drinks too much and wears ugly ties. Easy to spot."

"What's his name?" Sawyer asked.

"Howard Fraypish. Liz went to the dance with him."

Sawyer pulled his notebook out of his suit coat pocket and made a note of the name. Yesterday, after they'd gotten Liz Mayfield's prints, he'd asked her whether she was seeing anybody. It was a legitimate question, he'd told himself at the time.

She hadn't even blinked. Said that she hadn't dated anyone for over a year.

Going to a dance with somebody sounded like a date.

"I think she just feels sorry for him," the girl added.

So, she and lawyer guy weren't close. Maybe there was someone else. He had a right to ask. Maybe the connection wasn't Mary or Mirandez. Maybe the shooter's target had been the pretty counselor. It wouldn't be the first time a spurned love interest had crossed the line. "She seeing anybody else?"

"Not that I'm aware of."

He was glad that Liz hadn't lied to him. But it still surprised him. A woman who looked like Liz Mayfield shouldn't have trouble getting a date. She had the kind of face and body that made a man stupid.

He'd made that mistake once in his life. He wouldn't make it again.

HE TRIED TO REMEMBER THAT, two hours later, when he watched her glide around the room. She had on a long, dark blue dress. It flowed from her narrow waist, falling just shy of her ankles. It puffed out when she turned.

She'd pulled her hair up, leaving just a few strands down. Sawyer rubbed his fingers together, imagining the feel of the silky texture. The dress had a high collar and sleeves ending just below the elbow. She barely showed any skin at all, and she was the sexiest woman there.

Classy. It was the only word he could think of.

Determined to get it over with, Sawyer strode across the dance floor, ignoring the startled whispers or shocked glances in his wake. He felt as out of place as he knew he looked with his faded blue jeans and his beat-up leather jacket. He'd shed his suit earlier that evening before suddenly deciding that he needed to see Liz Mayfield tonight. She'd had her twenty-four hours. It wasn't his fault that she was a party girl and wanted to dance.

He met her eyes over the shoulder of her date. Her full lips parted ever so slightly, and her face lost its color. He shrugged in return and tapped the man between them on the shoulder.

The guy, early forties and balding, turned his head slightly, frowned at Sawyer and kept dancing.

Sawyer tapped again. "I need a few minutes with Ms. Mayfield."

They stopped. When the guy made no move to let go of her, Sawyer held out his hand. She stared at it for several seconds then stepped away from her date. Suddenly she was in his arms, and they were dancing.

He wanted to say something. But his stupid mind wouldn't work. He couldn't think, couldn't talk, couldn't reason.

She smelled good—like the jasmine flowers that had grown outside his mother's kitchen window.

He wanted to pull her close and taste her. The realization hit him hard, as if someone had punched him. He wanted his tongue in her mouth, her breasts in his hands and her thighs wrapped around him. He wanted her naked under him.

Sawyer jerked back, stumbling a bit. He dropped his hands to his sides. The two of them stood still in the middle of the dance floor like two statues.

Why didn't she say something? Hell, why didn't she blink? She just kept her pretty green eyes focused on his face. Sawyer kept his breaths shallow, unwilling to let any more temptation into his lungs. "Any more letters?" he asked. He kept his voice low, not wanting others to hear.

She shook her head. "Our mail doesn't usually arrive until after lunch. I left before it got there."

"So, no news is good news?"

"For tonight."

He understood avoidance. At one point in his life, he'd perfected it. He felt silly standing in the middle of the floor. He stepped closer to Liz Mayfield, and she slipped back into his arms as if it was the most natural thing in the world.

Which didn't make sense at all because it had to have been ten years since he'd danced with a woman. It felt good. She felt good.

He really needed to remember that he wasn't here to dance. "What did your little friend have to say?" he asked.

Her body jerked, and he realized he'd been more stern than necessary. "I'm sorry," he said.

"That's fine," she said. "It's just that I…I didn't see Mary today."

"She didn't show, did she?"

Liz shook her head and jumped in with both feet. "I had to cancel most of my appointments. I didn't feel well." That much at least was true. She'd been sick after hearing Mary's voice mail. *I'm not coming today. I'll see you tomorrow at the regular time.*

Liz had tried to call her a dozen times before giving up. Dreading that Detective Montgomery would find her before she had the chance to locate Mary, she'd left the office. She'd worried that a frustrated Detective Montgomery might take matters in his own hands and track Mary down.

Liz had never expected he'd show up at the fund-raiser. But she should have known better. Detective Montgomery didn't seem like the kind of guy who gave up easily. In fact, he seemed downright tenacious. Like a dog after a bone.

She tried to hold that against him. But couldn't. While it made for an uncomfortable evening, she couldn't help appreciating the fact that he'd held her to her twenty-four hours. He took his work seriously. She could relate to that.

"Are you okay now?" he asked, sounding concerned.

She nodded, not willing to verbalize any more half-truths. From across the room, she caught Carmen's eye. She was standing behind the punch table, pouring cups for thirsty dancers. Liz could read the concern on her pretty face. She'd had that same look since Liz had told her about the letter.

Liz shook her head slightly, reassuring her. Carmen was little, but she could be a spitfire. If she thought Liz needed help, she'd come running.

"Who's that?" Detective Montgomery asked.

"Carmen Jimenez. She's a counselor, too. I think I mentioned her yesterday."

"I remember. Did you tell her about your letter?"

"Yes."

"She hasn't gotten anything similar?"

Liz shook her head.

"I've got some bad news," Detective Montgomery said. "We found another dead body this morning. Right outside of this very hotel. He'd been shot. Up until a few weeks ago, he'd been a cook for Mirandez."

"Mirandez has a cook?"

He leaned his mouth closer to her ear, and she felt the shiver run down the length of her spine. "Not like Oprah has a cook. A cook is the guy who boils down the cocaine into crack."

"Oh. My."

"People keep dying," he said. "It's my job to make it stop. If Mary knows something, it's her job to help me."

She'd been wrong. He wasn't like a dog after a bone. He wanted fresh meat. She pulled away from him, forcing the dancing to stop. She couldn't think when he had his arms around her, let alone when his mouth was that close. "If you had enough to arrest her," she protested, "you'd have done it yesterday. You don't have anything but a wild guess."

He had more than that. The tip had come from one of their own. It had taken Fluentes two years to work his way inside. Sawyer didn't intend to sacrifice him now.

Push the counselor. He could hear Lieutenant Fischer's words almost as clearly as if the man stood behind him. "She was there. And you need to convince her to tell us what she saw. She needs to tell us everything. Then we'll protect her."

"You'll protect her?"

"Yeah." For some reason Liz's disbelieving tone set Sawyer's teeth on edge. "That's what we do. We're cops."

"She's eight months pregnant."

"I'm aware of that. We would arrange for both her and her baby to have the medical care that they need."

"And then what?" she asked, her tone demanding.

Sawyer threw up his hands. "I don't know. I guess the baby grows up, and in twenty years, Mary's a grandmother." Sawyer rubbed the bridge of his nose. His head pounded, and the damn drums weren't helping. "Look, can we go outside?" he mumbled.

She seemed to hesitate. Sawyer let out a breath when she nodded and took off, weaving in and out of the dancers, not stopping until she reached the exit. They walked outside the hotel, and he led her far enough away that the doorman couldn't hear the conversation.

She spoke before he had the chance to question her. "I'll talk to her. She's supposed to come to OCM at eight tomorrow morning. It's her regular appointment."

"And you'll convince her to talk to us?"

"I'll talk—"

"Liz, Liz. Back here. What are you doing outside?"

Sawyer turned back toward the hotel door. Her date stood next to the doorman, wildly waving his arm. The man started walking toward them, his long legs eating up the distance.

"He doesn't know about my letter," Liz said, her voice almost a whisper. "I'd like to keep it that way."

When the man reached Liz's side, he wrapped a skinny arm around her and tugged her toward his body. For some crazy reason, Sawyer wanted to break the man's arm. In two, maybe three, places. Then maybe a kneecap next.

"You had me worried when I couldn't find you," he said.

She stepped out of the man's grasp. "Detective Montgomery is the detective assigned to the shooting at OCM." She turned back to Sawyer. "Detective Montgomery, Howard Fraypish," she said, finishing the introduction.

The guy stuck his arm out, and Sawyer returned the shake. "I'm OCM's attorney," Fraypish said.

The man's hot-pink bow tie matched his cummerbund.

"I better get going," Sawyer said. "Thanks for the information, Ms. Mayfield."

"I certainly hope you arrest the men responsible for the attack at OCM," Fraypish said. "Where were the city's finest when this happened? At the local doughnut shop?"

Was that the best the guy could do? "I don't like doughnuts," Sawyer said.

"Are you sure you're a cop?"

Liz Mayfield frowned at her date. The idiot held up both hands in mock surrender. "Just a little joke. I thought we could use some humor."

Sawyer thought a quick left followed by a sharp right would be kind of funny.

"I should have called you, Detective. Then you wouldn't have had to make a trip here," she apologized.

"Forget it." His only regret was the blue dress. He knew how good she looked in it. He wondered how long before he stopped thinking about how good she'd look without it.

Liz woke up at four in the morning. Her body needed rest, but her mind refused to cooperate. She'd left the hotel shortly after midnight. She'd been in her apartment and in bed less than ten minutes later. She'd dreamed about Mary. Sweet Mary and her baby. Sweet Mary and the faceless Dantel Mirandez. Jenny had been there, too. With her crooked smile, her flyaway blond hair blowing around her as she threw a handful of pennies into the fountain at Grant Park. Just the way she'd been the last day Liz had seen her alive. Then out of nowhere, there'd been more letters, more threats. So many that when she'd fallen down and they'd piled on top of her, they'd covered her. And she hadn't been able to breathe.

Waking up had been a relief.

She showered, put on white capri pants and a blue shirt

and caught the five-o'clock bus. Thirty minutes later, it dropped her off a block from OCM. The morning air was heavy with humidity. It had the makings of another ninety-degree day.

She entered the security code, unlocked the front door, entered and then reset the code. She didn't bother to go downstairs to her office, heading instead to the small kitchen at the rear of the first floor. She started a pot of coffee, pouring a cup before the pot was even half-full. She took a sip, burned her tongue and swallowed anyway. She needed caffeine.

While she waited for her bagel to toast, she thought about Detective Montgomery. When he'd walked away, in the wake of Howard's insults, she'd wanted to run after him, to apologize, to make him understand that she'd do what she could to help him.

As long as it didn't put Mary in any danger.

But she hadn't. When Howard had hustled her back inside the hotel, she'd gone without protest. Jamison had made it abundantly clear. Attendees had coughed up two hundred bucks a plate. If they wanted to dance, you danced. If they needed a drink, you fetched it. If they wanted conversation, you talked.

Liz had danced, fetched, talked and smiled through it all. Even after her toes had been stepped on for the eighteenth time. No politician could have done better. She'd done it on autopilot. It hadn't helped when Carmen had come up, fanning herself, and said, "Who was that?"

"Detective Montgomery," Liz had explained.

"I suspect I don't have to state the obvious," Carmen had said, "but the man is hot."

Liz had almost laughed. Carmen hadn't even heard the man talk. Or felt the man's chest muscles when he'd held her close—not too close but close enough. She hadn't smelled his clean, fresh scent.

Detective Montgomery wasn't just hot; he was *smoking* hot.

Her bagel popped just as she heard the front door open. She relaxed when she didn't hear the alarm. Who else, she wondered, was crazy enough to come to work at five-thirty in the morning?

When she heard Jamison's office door open, she almost dropped her bagel. He probably hadn't gotten home much before two.

She spread cream cheese evenly on both sides and started a second pot of coffee. Jamison was perhaps the only person on earth who loved coffee more than she did. She had her cup and her bagel balanced in one hand and had just slung her purse over her shoulder when she heard the front door close again.

She eased the kitchen door open and glanced down the narrow hallway. Empty. All the office doors remained closed. "Hello?"

No answer. She walked down the hallway, knocked on Jamison's door and then tried the handle. It didn't turn.

She walked down the steps to the lower level. Her office door and all the others were shut. "Good morning?" she sang out, a bit louder this time.

The only sound she heard was her own breathing.

Liz ran up the stairs, swearing softly when the hot coffee splashed out of the cup and burned her hand. She checked the front door. Locked. Alarm set.

She relaxed. It had to have been Jamison. What would have possessed him to come in so early and leave so quickly? She hoped nothing was wrong. She walked back downstairs and unlocked her office. It was darker than usual because no light spilled through the boarded-up window.

She had to admit that the wood made her feel better.

Maybe she'd ask Jamison to leave it that way for a while. At least until she got her nerves under control.

Rationally, she didn't put much stock in the letter. It wasn't out of the realm of possibility that one of her clients or their partners had decided to jerk her chain a little. It didn't make her feel any better, however, to think that the shooter had been aiming for Mary.

She intended to somehow make the girl open up to her, to tell her if there was any connection between her and Dantel Mirandez. But in the meantime, she needed to get busy. She sat down behind her desk and opened the top file. Mary was not the only client who was close to delivery. Just two days before, Melissa Stroud had been in Liz's office. They'd reviewed the information on Mike and Mindy Partridge, and Melissa had agreed to let the couple adopt her soon-to-be-born child. Liz needed to get the necessary information to Howard so that he could get the paperwork done.

At twenty minutes to eight, she heard the front door open again. Heavy footsteps pounded down the stairs, and within seconds, her boss stuck his head through the open doorway.

"Hey, Liz. Nice window."

She shook her head. "Morning, Jamison. How are you?"

"Exhausted. It ended up being a late night. We didn't leave the hotel until they pushed us out the door. Then Reneé and I and a couple others went out for breakfast. I didn't want to say no to any potential donors. I've got a heck of a headache, though. It was probably that last vodka tonic."

"Jamison, you know better." Liz smiled at her boss. "Had you been to bed yet when you stopped by here this morning?"

"This morning? What are you talking about?"

"You stopped in about six. I had coffee made, but you left before I could catch you."

"Liz, how many glasses of wine did you have last night?"

Liz dismissed his concern with a wave of her hand. "Two. That's my limit."

"Well, you may want to cut back to one. Reneé had set the alarm for seven, and we slept through that. I barely had time for a two-minute shower just to get here by now."

Liz shook her head, trying to make sense out of what Jamison said. "I heard the door. The alarm didn't go off. I'm sure I heard your office door open. But when I came out, there was nobody around."

"It must have been a car door."

"No, it wasn't," Liz protested.

"Then it was Cynthia or Carmen or one of the other staff. Although I can't imagine why anybody would have gotten up early after last night. What were you doing here?"

"Mary Thorton is coming at eight. I wanted to get some stuff done first." No need to tell Jamison that she'd been running from her dreams. He already thought she was losing her mind.

"Have you talked to her since the shooting? Poor kid. She must be pretty shook up."

"I'm sure she was. Detective Montgomery thinks she knows more than she's letting on."

"Is that why he came to the dance last night?"

Liz was surprised. Jamison rarely noticed anything that didn't directly concern him. But then again, Detective Montgomery had a way about him that commanded attention.

"Yes."

"At least he wasn't in uniform. That wouldn't have been good for donations. How do you think the party went?" Jamison asked, sitting down on one of Liz's chairs.

"People seemed to have a good time," Liz hedged. When his eyes lit up, her guilt vanished. He could be a bit self-centered and pushy, but Liz knew he'd do almost anything for OCM. She would, too.

Even spend an evening with Howard Fraypish, who had been Jamison's college roommate. After college, Jamison had taken a job in social services and married Reneé. Howard had gone to law school, graduated at the top of his class, married his corporate job and produced billable hours. Lots of them, evidently. The man had a huge apartment with a view of Lake Michigan, and he'd opened his own law office at least five years ago.

The two men had stayed connected over the years, and when Jamison had been hired as the executive director of OCM, he'd hired Howard's firm to handle the adoptions.

"Want a warm-up?" Jamison asked, nodding at Liz's empty cup.

"Sure."

They walked upstairs to the kitchen. Liz had poured her cup and handed the glass pot to Jamison when his cell phone rang. Liz started to walk away, stopping suddenly when she heard the glass pot hit the tile floor.

She whirled around. Jamison stood still, his phone in one hand and his other empty. Shards of glass and spilled coffee surrounded him.

"Jamison?" She started back toward her boss.

"There's a bomb in my office." He spoke without emotion. "It's set to go off in fifteen minutes."

Chapter Three

Detective Sawyer Montgomery arrived just minutes after the bomb squad had disarmed, dismantled and disconnected—she wasn't sure of the technical term—the bomb that had been left in the middle of Jamison's desk. It had taken them eleven minutes to arrive. The longest eleven minutes of Liz's life.

Beat cops had been on the scene within minutes of the 911 call that Liz had made from Jamison's phone after she'd pulled him, his phone and herself from the building. They'd blocked off streets and rousted people from their apartments. OCM's neighbors, many still in their pajamas, had poured from the nearby buildings. Mothers with small children in their arms, old people barely able to maneuver the steps, all were hustled behind a hastily tacked-up stretch of yellow police tape.

Liz had wondered if Detective Montgomery would come. She hated to admit it, but she'd considered calling him. In those first frantic moments before help had arrived, she'd desperately hoped for someone capable. And Detective Montgomery absolutely screamed capable. She doubted the man ever encountered anything he couldn't handle.

But now that he'd arrived, Liz wanted to run. She couldn't decide if she wanted to run to him to seek shelter in his embrace or run far from him to protect herself from his intensity, his questions, his knowing looks.

Liz watched him get out of the car and scan the crowd. He said something to the man who rode with him. Liz knew the exact moment he spotted her. It didn't matter that three hundred yards separated them. Liz felt the shiver run up her arm just as if he'd touched her.

"What the hell happened?" he asked when he reached her.

Liz swallowed, trying very hard not to cry. How ridiculous would that be? No one had been hurt. No one injured. And she hadn't even thought about crying until Detective Montgomery had approached.

"Bomb threat," she said. "Actually, more than a threat, I guess. The bomb squad removed it just a few minutes ago."

"Where was it?"

"In the middle of my boss's desk. In a brown sack." The tears that she'd dreaded sprang to her eyes.

"Hey." Detective Montgomery reached out and touched her arm. "Are you okay?"

He sounded so concerned. That almost made the dam break. "I'm fine, really. Everyone's just been great."

Detective Montgomery frowned at her, but he didn't let go. The most delicious heat spread up her arm.

"Come over here." He guided her toward the curb.

"Okay." Whatever he wanted. As long as she didn't have to think. Because then she'd think about it, the bomb and the look on Jamison's face. She'd remember the pure panic she'd felt as they'd run from the building.

He pulled his hand away, and Liz felt the immediate loss of heat all the way to her stomach, which was odd since his hand had been nowhere near her stomach. He unbuttoned his suit coat, took it off and folded it. He placed it on the cement curb. "Why don't you sit down?" he suggested, pointing at his coat.

"I can sit on cement," she protested.

"Not and keep those…short pants clean," he said. His face turned red. "I know there's a word for them, but I can't think of it right now."

He was smokin' hot when he was serious and damn cute when he was embarrassed. It was a heck of a combination. "They're called capri pants."

He smiled. "It might have come to me."

Oh, boy. She sat down. She knew she needed to before she swooned. "I'm sure it would have, Detective Montgomery."

"Sawyer," Detective Montgomery said. "Just Sawyer is fine."

Liz nodded. The man was just being polite. After all, in a span of less than forty-eight hours, their paths had crossed three times. They weren't strangers any longer. She was sitting on his coat. "Liz is fine, too," she mumbled.

"Liz," he repeated.

She liked the way the *z* rolled off his tongue. She liked the way all the consonants and the vowels, too, for that matter, rolled off his tongue. It was a molten chocolate center bubbling out of a freshly baked cake. Smooth. Enticing.

Maybe he could read her the dictionary for the next week.

"I need to ask you some questions," he said.

She wasn't going to get a week. "Sure." Why the heck not? Together they sat on the faded gray cement, hips close, thighs almost touching. Liz wanted to lean her head against his broad shoulder but knew that would startle the hell out of him.

She settled for closing her eyes. It seemed like a lifetime ago that she'd crawled out of bed and caught the five-o'clock bus.

"Sawyer?"

Liz opened her eyes. The man who had been with Sawyer when he'd arrived now stood in front of the two of them.

He was an inch taller and probably ten pounds heavier than Sawyer. He had the bluest eyes she'd ever seen.

Was the sky raining gorgeous men?

"What did you find out?" Sawyer spoke to the man.

"Bomb, all right. Big enough that it would have done some damage. Quick to shut down. Looks like they wanted to make it easy for us."

Sawyer didn't say anything.

"Who are you?" Liz asked.

The man's face lit up with a broad smile showing perfect teeth. "I'm Detective Robert Hanson. My partner has no manners. Otherwise, he'd have introduced us."

"I'm Liz Mayfield."

"I guessed that. It's a pleasure to meet you. I—"

"What else?" Sawyer interrupted his partner.

Detective Hanson shrugged. "We'll get the lab reports back this afternoon. Don't expect much. Guys thought it looked like a professional job."

"Professional?" Sawyer shook his head. "Half the kids in high school know how to build a bomb."

"True." Detective Hanson stared at Sawyer. "Did you get her statement?"

"Not yet," Sawyer said, pulling a notebook and pen from his pocket.

Detective Hanson frowned at both of them. Then he turned toward Liz. "Who got in first this morning?"

"I did," she said. "I got here about five-thirty."

Sawyer looked up from his notebook. "Short night?"

Liz shrugged, not feeling the need to explain.

"Door locked when you got here, Ms. Mayfield?" Detective Hanson asked.

"Yes. After I came in, I locked it again and reset the alarm."

"You sure?"

"I'm usually the first person in. I know the routine."

"Did you see anything unusual once you got inside?"

"No. I went to the kitchen and started a pot of coffee."

"Then what?"

"I heard the front door, and then I thought I heard Jamison's door open. It appears I was right."

"You didn't see anybody?" Detective Hanson continued.

"No. When I left the kitchen, I looked around."

"Then what—"

"You looked around?" Sawyer interrupted his partner.

"Yes."

"You should have called the police."

She frowned at him. His tone had an edge to it. "I can't call the police every time I hear a door."

"You got a threat mailed to your office, and then shots were fired through your window," Sawyer said. "Maybe you should have given that some thought before you decided to investigate."

"Maybe we should keep going." Detective Hanson spoke to Sawyer. "You're taking notes, right?"

Sawyer didn't respond.

"After I *looked around*—" she emphasized the words "—I went down to my office and started working. After Jamison arrived, we came upstairs for coffee."

"What time was that?"

"Almost eight. Jamison's cell phone rang and then…we called 911. That's about it."

"It sounds like you stayed pretty calm. That takes a lot of guts." Detective Hanson smiled at her again.

She smiled back this time. "Thank you."

Sawyer grabbed Robert's arm. "Come on. Let's go. I want to talk to the boss."

Liz stood—so quickly that her head started to spin. She

picked up Sawyer's suit coat, shook it and thrust it out to him. "Don't forget this," she said.

He reached for it, and their fingers brushed. The fine hairs on her arm reacted with a mind of their own. What the heck was going on? She'd never ever had this kind of physical reaction to a man. Especially not one who acted as if he might think she was an idiot.

Sawyer jerked his own arm back. "I'll...uh...talk to you later," he said. Great. She had him tripping over his own tongue.

Sawyer got twenty feet before Robert managed to catch him. "Hang on," he said. "What the hell is wrong with you?"

Sawyer shook his head. "Just forget it."

"You act like an idiot and think I'm going to forget it?"

"Maybe you've forgotten this. We're here to investigate a crime. We've got a lot of people to talk to. I didn't think it made sense to spend any more time with Liz."

"Liz," Robert repeated.

"Yeah, Liz." Sawyer did his best to sound nonchalant. "She told me I could call her Liz."

"Since when do you hang all over witnesses?"

"I wasn't hanging all over her. She seemed upset. I offered her some comfort. Perhaps you've heard of it. It's called compassion." Sawyer started to walk away.

Robert kept pace. "That wasn't compassion I saw. That was a mating call. What's going on here, partner?"

Sawyer didn't know. Didn't have a clue why he started to unravel every time he got within three feet of Liz. "Liz Mayfield is a material witness to a crime. We had questioned her. I figured we needed to move on."

"That's it?"

"What else could it be?"

Robert looked him in the eye and nodded. "Your timing

sucks. I could have had little Lizzy's phone number in another two minutes."

"Lizzy," Sawyer repeated.

"She's my type."

Sawyer clamped down on the impulse to punch his partner, his best friend for the past two years. "She is *nothing* like your type."

Robert cocked his head. "Really?"

"Yeah. Really."

"I'll be damned." Robert laughed, his face transformed by his smile. "You like her."

"You don't know what you're talking about." Sawyer walked away from his partner.

Robert ran to catch up with him. "You're interested in a witness. Mr. Professional, Mr. I-always-use-my-Southern-manners. This has got to be killing you."

"Liz Mayfield is going to help me get Mirandez. That's my only interest," Sawyer said.

Robert slapped him on the back. "You just keep telling yourself that, Sawyer. Let's go talk to the boss."

When Sawyer and Robert reached Liz's boss, the man held up a finger, motioning them to wait while he finished his telephone call. From the one side of the conversation that Sawyer could hear, it sounded as if the guy was making arrangements to refer his clients on to other sources. After several minutes, the man ended the call and put his smartphone in his pocket.

"Detective Montgomery." The man greeted Sawyer, giving him a lopsided smile. "I have to admit I was hoping there wouldn't be any reason for us to talk again."

Sawyer felt sorry for him. He looked as if he'd just lost his best friend. "This is my partner, Detective Robert Hanson."

"Nice to meet you, Detective Hanson. I'm Jamison Curtiss, the executive director of OCM."

Sawyer watched Robert shake the man's hand, knowing Robert was rapidly cataloging almost everything there was to know about Jamison.

"I understand you got the call this morning, warning you of the bomb," Sawyer said.

"Yes. I'd just gotten to work. It was probably about ten minutes before eight."

"What happened then?"

"Liz and I left the building."

"Then what?" Sawyer prompted the man, reaching into his pocket for his notebook.

"Then I got a second call."

"What?" Sawyer stopped taking notes.

"The second call came in just after they'd found the bomb. Same guy who called the first time. Congratulated me on following directions. Then he told me that unless I closed the doors of OCM, there would be another bomb. I wouldn't know when or where, but there would be one."

"Liz Mayfield didn't say anything about a second call." Sawyer couldn't believe that she'd withheld information like that.

"She doesn't know. I'm not looking forward to telling her."

"Anybody else hear this call?" Not that Sawyer didn't believe the guy. The man looked shaken.

"No. It lasted about ten seconds. Then the guy hung up."

"What are you going to do?" Sawyer asked, keeping one eye on Jamison and casting a quick glance back at Liz. His heart skipped a beat when he didn't see her right away. Then he spied her. She had her back toward him. It took him all of three seconds to realize he was staring at her butt and another five to tear his glance away.

Robert laughed at him. He was quiet about it—just loud

enough to make sure Sawyer heard him. Jamison Curtiss looked confused. Sawyer nodded at the man to continue.

"In the past forty-eight hours," Jamison said, "one of my employees received an anonymous threat. On top of that, my business has been shot at and almost blown up. Who-ever is trying to get my attention has it. Unless you can tell me that you know who's responsible, I don't think I have a lot of options."

"We don't know—" Robert spoke up "—but we will. Who has a key to OCM?"

"All the counselors. And our receptionist. Everyone has a slightly different schedule."

"And everybody knows the code to turn off the alarm?" Robert asked.

"Of course."

"Keys to the office doors all the same?"

"Yes."

"Same as to the front door?"

"Yes."

Sawyer and Robert exchanged a look. One key and a code. Child's play for somebody like Mirandez.

"You already gave us a list of employees with their home addresses. I'd like their personnel files, too," Robert said.

Jamison wrinkled his nose. "Is that really necessary?" he asked.

"Yes." Sawyer answered in a manner that made sure Jamison knew it wasn't an option.

"Fine. I'll have them to you by this afternoon."

"Anybody else have a key? A cleaning service, perhaps?"

"We all know how to run a vacuum. We can't afford to pay someone to clean."

"Anybody really new on your staff?"

"No, we've all been working together for years. Liz and Carmen came at about the same time."

"Carmen?" Robert asked.

"Lucky for her, her brother wasn't feeling well this morning. She came to work late." Jamison pointed to the group of counselors gathered across the street. "Carmen Jimenez is the dark-haired woman standing next to Liz."

"My God, she's beautiful," Robert said, then looked surprised that the comment had slipped out. "Sorry," he added.

Jamison shrugged. "That's the reaction most men have. Many of our clients are Spanish-speaking. She's a big asset."

Sawyer studied the two women who stood close together, deep in conversation. Carmen stood half a head shorter, her black hair and darker skin a stark contrast to Liz's blond hair and fair complexion. "Liz and Carmen close?"

"Best friends. We're all like family." Frustration crossed Jamison's face. "I've got to talk to them," he muttered. "They deserve to know what's going on."

Sawyer watched him walk across the street, joining Liz, Carmen and one other woman, who looked about ten years older. He assumed it was Cynthia, the counselor who just worked mornings. He couldn't hear what Jamison told them, but by the looks on their faces, they were shocked, scared and, he thought somewhat ironically, Liz and Carmen looked downright mad.

It took another ten minutes before the group broke up. Jamison walked back to Sawyer and Robert. "Well, they know. I told them that I've already started making arrangements for our current clients to be referred to other agencies. We have a responsibility to these young girls."

Sawyer understood responsibility. After all, he'd made it his responsibility to bring in Mirandez. "I'm going to go talk to Liz," Sawyer said to Robert.

Robert gave Liz and Carmen another look. "I'll go with you," he said.

When Sawyer reached Liz, he realized that Mary Thorton sat on the bench directly behind her. The young girl looked up when Sawyer and Robert approached. She didn't smile, frown or show any emotion at all. She just stared at the two of them.

Sawyer couldn't help staring back. The girl had on a green shirt and a too-tight orange knit jumper over it. With her big stomach, she looked like a pumpkin. Then the dress moved in ripples.

Sawyer remembered the first time he'd felt his baby move. It had rocked his world. He'd first put his hand on his girl-friend's stomach, then his cheek. It had taken another hour for the baby to roll over again, but the wait had been worth it.

Sawyer stuck his hand out toward Carmen Jimenez. "Ms. Jimenez," he said. "I'm Detective Montgomery."

"Good morning," she said.

"This is my partner, Detective Hanson."

Robert reached out his own hand. "It's a pleasure, Ms. Jimenez." Robert smiled at the woman. It was the same smile Sawyer had seen work very well for Robert in the past.

Carmen Jimenez didn't have the reaction that most women had. She nodded politely and shook Robert's hand so briefly that Sawyer wasn't sure that flesh actually touched.

Sawyer turned his attention to Mary, keeping his eyes trained on her face. He didn't want to make the mistake of looking at her baby again. "Mary." He spoke quietly. "Where were you at six o'clock this morning?"

"Sleeping."

"Alone?"

Mary gave him a big smile. "I don't like to sleep alone."

"So, I guess whoever you were sleeping with could verify that you were in bed this morning?"

"I don't know. Maybe."

"Come on, Mary. Surely he or she would know if you'd slipped out of bed."

"Trust me on this, Cop. It wouldn't be a she."

"Didn't think so," Sawyer said. "What's his name?"

"I can't tell you."

The girl's eyes had widened, and Sawyer thought her lower lip trembled just a bit. Liz must have seen it, too, because she sat down next to Mary and wrapped her arm around the girl's shoulders.

Sawyer deliberately softened his voice. He needed Mary. Hated to admit it but he did. "Mary, we can help you. But we need to know what's going on. You need to tell us."

"I don't know anything. You'd need to talk to him."

"Mirandez?"

Mary shook her head and frowned at Sawyer.

"No."

"Who, Mary? Come on, it's important."

She hesitated then seemed to decide. "Well, okay. His name is Pooh."

"Pooh?"

"Yeah. Pooh Bear. He's been sleeping with me since I was six."

He heard a laugh. Sawyer whirled around, and Robert suddenly coughed into his hand. Carmen, her dark eyes round with surprise, had her fingers pressed up against her lips. Sawyer looked at Liz. She stared at her shoes.

Damn. He could taste the bitter metal of the hook. The girl had baited her pole, cast it into the water and reeled him in. It was all he could do not to flop around on the sidewalk.

"Funny," he said. "Hope you're still laughing when you're sitting behind bars, waiting for a trial."

Liz stood up and jerked her head toward the right. "May I speak to you in private, Detective?"

Sawyer nodded and walked across the street. When he stopped suddenly, Liz almost bumped into him. She was close enough that he could smell her scent. It was a warm, sticky day already, but she smelled fresh and cool, like a walk through the garden on a spring night.

"Don't threaten her," Liz warned. "If you're going to charge her with something, do it. Otherwise, leave her alone. This can't be good for her or the baby."

Sawyer took a breath and sucked her into his lungs. As crazy as it seemed, it calmed him. "She's a little fool."

"She's a challenge," Liz admitted.

Sawyer laughed despite himself. "Paper-training a new puppy is a challenge."

Liz smiled at him, and he thought the world tilted just a bit.

"I'll talk to her," Liz said.

"How? Isn't she being referred on?"

Liz glanced over her shoulder, as if making sure no one was close by. "I'm going to keep seeing her. She needs me."

"Your boss is closing shop."

"I know. Carmen and I already discussed it. We'll see clients at my apartment."

Calm disappeared. "Are you nuts?"

She lifted her chin in the air.

He pointed a finger at her. "You received a threat. Which may or may not have anything to do with the shooting. Which may or may not have anything to do with today's bomb. Which may or may not have anything to do with Mirandez or Mary or the man in the moon. What the hell are you thinking?"

"I have to take the chance."

She'd spoken so quietly that Sawyer had to lean forward to hear her. "Why?" The woman had a damn death wish.

"I just have to," she said.

Was it desperation or determination that he heard in her tone? All he knew for sure was that nothing he could say was going to change her mind. "When? When are you starting this?" he asked.

"Mary's coming to see me tomorrow."

Great. That gave him twenty-four hours to figure out how to save them both.

Chapter Four

Liz's small apartment seemed smaller than usual after she set up shop at the kitchen table and Carmen took the desk in the extra bedroom. Girls came and went, and while the surroundings were different, the conversations were much the same as if they had occurred in a basement on the South Side.

It was late afternoon when Carmen made her way to the kitchen. "I thought Detective Montgomery might have a stroke yesterday." She took a swig from her water bottle. "He looked like he wanted to wring your neck."

Liz laughed and reached for her coffee cup. She took one sip and dumped the rest down the drain. No coffee was better than cold coffee. "He thinks we're idiots."

"He might be right." She hesitated. "What time was Mary's appointment?" she asked softly.

Liz looked at the clock. "Three hours ago."

"Did you call her?"

"Four times."

Carmen didn't say anything. Finally, she sighed. "There's something very wrong here."

"I know. I just don't know what it is." She ran a hand through her hair. "Are you done for the day?"

"I am. I could stay with you."

"Don't you dare. Your brother is still sick. Go home. Pick up some chicken-noodle soup for him on the way."

"You're sure?"

Liz nodded.

"Okay. I'll call you tomorrow."

Liz watched her friend leave. She waited fifteen minutes before trying Mary's cell phone again. It rang and rang, not even going to voice mail. She tried her three more times in the evening before finally giving up and going to bed.

She woke up the next day, tried Mary, didn't get an answer and finally admitted to herself that she needed help. Carmen was right. Something was very wrong.

Liz called Sawyer. He answered on the second ring.

"This is Liz Mayfield. Mary had an appointment yesterday, but she didn't show or call. I'm worried about her."

She wasn't sure, but she thought she heard him sigh.

"Can't the police do anything?" she asked. "She's just a kid."

"I'll put the word out to my contacts. If anybody sees her, they'll call."

"What about a missing-person report? Should I do one of those?"

"You can." Sawyer didn't think it would hurt but he doubted it would help much. Every day there were lots of teenagers reported missing. Most showed up a few days later safe and sound, sure that they'd taught their parents a thing or two. The true runaways usually called home a couple weeks later, once their money had run out. The smart ones anyway. The dumb ones slipped into a life of prostitution that killed them. Even those who were still technically breathing, working the streets each day, were as good as dead.

Fluentes had made contact late the night before. He had heard that Mirandez had slipped out of town but didn't have specifics. Sawyer thought it likely that Mary had gone with him. For all he knew, the two of them were hiding out in some fancy hotel somewhere, living off room service, enjoying all the benefits that drug money could buy.

"Do you think we should check the hospitals?" Liz asked.

"Probably a good idea. Hell, maybe she had her baby."

"I doubt it. Mary's scared to death of labor. I think she'd call me."

If she could. But maybe Mirandez had put the screws to that. "Are you this tight with all your clients?" Sawyer asked.

"No. But Mary really doesn't have anybody else."

"She has Mirandez," Sawyer said.

"He must have opted out. Maybe he's afraid of blood?"

"Only of seeing his own," Sawyer said. "What about her family? Anybody around here that she'd stay with?"

"Her mother died several years ago. I've met her father. He kicked her out when he found out about the pregnancy. I tried to reason with him, but it was no use. Something along the lines of she's made her bed, now let her lie in it."

His parents had been furious when he'd come home and confessed that he'd gotten his girlfriend pregnant. His mom had cried. His dad had left the house for four hours. But then he'd come home, quietly conferred with his wife, then the two of them sat Sawyer down so that they could discuss what he intended to do about the situation.

He'd wanted to marry Terrie. He found out it didn't much matter what he wanted. Terrie's parents refused to even consider the idea. He'd been the poor kid from the wrong side of the tracks. They'd wanted more for their daughter.

Sawyer had been standing at his son's freshly dug grave when Terrie's father had confessed that not allowing his daughter to marry Sawyer had been a mistake. Sawyer hadn't even responded. Sawyer knew the man thought he could have pulled Terrie back from the drugs that crushed both her body and mind.

Sawyer knew better. He hadn't been able to help Terrie. A marriage license wouldn't have helped him wrestle her away from the cruel grip of addiction. He'd believed Terrie when she'd promised to quit the drugs. In doing so, he'd failed her. That haunted him. He'd failed his helpless son. That had rocked his soul, causing it to crack and bleed.

"She have any friends?" Sawyer asked.

"She talked about a couple girlfriends. But I never met them."

"Okay. Then I guess we wait. See if something comes up."

"There is one place we might check," Liz said. "Mary mentioned a children's bookstore that she liked. Said she spent a lot of time there, looking through books."

"Got a name?"

"I've got an address. I wrote it down. I had planned on finding it and picking out a baby gift." She opened her purse, pulled out the slip of paper and read it to him.

He whistled softly. "Are you sure that's right?"

"Yes. Mary raved about this store. She said Marvis, the owner, was really cool. It's not an area I'm familiar with."

"I'd hope not," Sawyer mocked. "I don't think there're a lot of bookstores in that neighborhood. There are, however, a lot of really great crack houses. I'll go check it out and let you know."

"You're kidding, right?"

He didn't answer.

"Look, Sawyer. You need Mary. I'm the best link you have to her. But if you cut me out—if you even think about leaving me behind—that's the last information I'll share with you."

Sawyer counted to ten. "To interfere with a police investigation is a crime. To willfully withhold evidence is a crime."

"You'd have to prove it first."

Sawyer almost laughed. He'd used his best I'm-a-hard-ass-cop voice. The one that made pimps and pushers shake. But she didn't even sound concerned. "What about your clients?"

"I'll call Carmen. We both had a light day today, so she should be able to cover my clients. She can meet them at a coffee shop near OCM."

"Fine. Be ready in twenty minutes."

Sawyer hung up the phone. He ran his fingers across the stack of manila folders that had been delivered late last night, hot out of the filing cabinets of OCM. Personnel files. Liz Mayfield's file.

He sifted through the pile. When he found hers, he flipped it open. Copies of tax forms. Single with zero exemptions. Direct-deposit form. Emergency-contact form. Harold and Patrice Mayfield, her parents. They had a suburban area code.

He set those papers aside. Next was her résumé. With plenty of detail.

He scanned the two-page document. The label Ph.D. jumped out at him. Liz had a doctorate degree in psychology from Yale University. Up until a few years ago, she'd worked for Mathers and Froit. The name meant nothing to him. He read on. She'd been a partner, responsible for billing out over a half million a year. That was clear enough. She'd been in the big time.

But she'd left that all behind for OCM. Why? With a sigh, Sawyer closed the file. He stood up and snatched his keys off the desk. He almost wished he'd never looked. Even as a kid, he'd been intrigued by puzzles.

He opened his car door just as Robert pulled his own vehicle into the lot. He waited while his friend parked.

"I've got a lead on Mary Thorton," he said when Robert approached.

"Need me to go with?"

"No. It's probably nothing. The personnel files are on my

desk. Spend your time on them. Maybe the connection to OCM isn't Mary. Maybe it's something else."

WHEN SAWYER AND LIZ pulled up to the address, Sawyer started to laugh. A dry chuckle.

Liz looked at the slip of paper and then checked the numbers hanging crooked on the side of the old brick building. There was no mistake. Mary's bookstore was the Pleasure Palace. Brown shipping paper covered the front windows. "What do you think?" she asked.

"I think it's not a Barnes & Noble," he said, smiling at her.

"Let's get this over with," she said, opening her car door.

Sawyer caught up with her fast. "Stay behind me," he instructed. "It's too early for the drug dealers or the prostitutes to be doing business, but there's no telling what else lurks around here."

Liz slowed her pace and let him take the lead. He pushed the door open with his foot. "Also, no telling where people's hands have been that turned that handle," he said almost under his breath.

There were magazines everywhere. Women, their bodies slick with oil, in every pose imaginable. Men with women, women with women, women with dogs. Where the magazines ended, the ropes, chains and harnesses took up.

"I don't believe this." Sawyer let out a soft whistle and pointed.

There, surrounded by DVDs, handcuffs, and plastic and rubber appliances in all shapes and sizes, was a table piled high with kids' books. They were used but in good shape.

Sawyer picked one off the pile. It was the familiar Dr. Seuss book. "I hate green eggs and ham," he said, "Sawyer, I am."

"You think this is funny, don't you?" Liz hissed.

"It's hilarious. It's worth the price of admission."

"There was no admission."

"Trust me on this. There's always a price. We just don't know what it is yet."

"Hello." A voice sang out from the corner.

"But we're just about to find out," Sawyer whispered.

A woman, almost as tall as Sawyer and pleasantly plump, wearing a flowing purple pantsuit floated toward them. She had big hair and bright red lipstick. "Welcome to the Pleasure Palace. I'm Marvis. May I help you find something? A nice DVD perhaps? Or we have some brand-new battery-operated—"

"We're trying to find a book for our friend," Sawyer interrupted. He nodded at the table.

"A children's book?"

"Yeah."

"Well, you've come to the right place. Everything is half-off the cover price. All of these belonged to my grandchildren. They are in good shape. The books, that is." Marvis laughed at her own joke, her double chin bouncing. "Not that my sweet babies aren't fit as a fiddle, too. They can run circles around me."

It would be a fair amount of exercise just getting around Grandma Marvis. Liz caught Sawyer's eye and knew he was thinking the same thing.

"There are over two hundred books here. Every one of my eight grandkids could read before they were five."

"Our friend comes here all the time. She's about five-three, fair skin, freckles, blondish-red hair and pregnant." Sawyer pretended to browse through the pile, all the while keeping an eye on the door.

"Let me think." The woman tapped her polished pink fingernail against her lips.

Sawyer walked over to the counter. He picked the top

DVD off the rack. He looked at the price and pulled a fifty out of his pocket.

"Oh, now I remember. Mary, right?" The woman's doubled chin tucked under when she smiled.

"That's the one."

"Wonderful girl. Loves her books. Always takes one of the classics." She waved her hand toward the end of the table. "Last time she was here, she got *Little Women.* Said she hoped that if she had a daughter she'd be as pretty as Winona Ryder."

"When was she in last?" Sawyer asked.

"It had to have been at least a week ago. I was telling Herbert, he's my man friend, just yesterday that I bet she had her baby. What did she have? She was carrying it so low, I couldn't help but think it was a boy."

"No baby yet. In fact," Sawyer said as he pulled a book off the children's table and threw another twenty at the woman, "if she happens to stop by, would you tell her to call Liz?"

"I'll do that. You all have a nice day. Are you sure I can't interest you in something? We've got a whole new line of condoms. Cartoon characters."

"No thanks." Sawyer literally pulled Liz out of the store and back to the car. He unlocked her side, threw the merchandise in the backseat and got in on the driver's side. He started to drive away without another word.

"I wonder if they come in an assorted box," Liz said.

Sawyer almost ran the car into a light pole.

Not that he needed to worry about causing an unexpected pregnancy. A quick trip to his physician ten years ago had taken care of that. But there were other good reasons to wear protection. With a woman like Liz Mayfield in his bed, he'd probably be hard-pressed to remember that. He'd want her, all of her, without anything to separate the two of them. He'd want—

"Hey, are you all right?" she asked. "You look a little pale."

Sawyer whipped his eyes back to the road. In another minute, she'd start to analyze him. If she found out what he was thinking, she'd probably jump out of the car. "I'm fine," he said.

"So, now where?" she asked.

"I'm taking you home."

"We can't just give up."

"I'm not giving up. But until a clue turns up, we wait. Maybe Mary will get smart and call you."

"You're determined to think the worst of her, aren't you?"

"She's up close and personal with a drug dealer. It's hard to think of her as Mother Teresa."

"Why don't you try thinking of her as a mixed-up, scared, lonely kid?"

"I can't do that." He risked a quick glance at her.

Liz folded her arms across her chest and stared straight ahead. When she spoke, he had to strain to hear her.

"You need to try harder," she said.

He tried. Every damn day he tried. Tried to rid the streets of scum. Tried to arrest just one more of the human garbage that preyed on young bodies and souls. She had no idea how hard he tried. Just like she had no idea that he wanted her more than he'd wanted a woman in years. Maybe ever. And that, quite frankly, scared the hell out of him.

Yeah, he needed to try harder. He needed to keep his distance, needed to remember that getting Mirandez was the goal. Not getting into Liz Mayfield's pants or letting her get into his head.

LIZ WASHED HER DISHES, cleaned her bathroom, sorted some old photographs and even managed to force down a peanut-butter sandwich. She went through all the motions of a regular life. But what she really did was wait for Mary's call.

When the phone finally rang at seven o'clock, she jumped off her couch, ran to the kitchen and managed to stub her toe on the way.

She tried to keep the disappointment out of her voice when Jamison greeted her. "Liz, I talked to Carmen late this afternoon," he said. "I understand that Mary was a no-call, no-show yesterday."

Jamison would understand her worry. She knew she could confide in him. But she couldn't bring herself to utter the words. To somehow give credence to the fact that Mary might be in trouble. That Mary might be, at this very moment, crying out for help, but there would be no one around to hear. If she said it, it could be true.

"You know how these kids are. I'm sure I'll hear from her soon."

"I hope you're right," he said. "I don't know how much help this is, but I did get a lead on Mary that you can pass on to Detective Montgomery."

"What?"

"I reviewed some case files today, and I saw a note that one of my girls had heard about OCM from Mary Thorton. They met at a club."

"What's the name of it?"

"Jumpin' Jack Flash. I guess they have a dance contest every Tuesday night. The women don't pay a cover, and all the drinks are two bucks. It's somewhere on the South Side, on Deyston Street."

Liz knew just where it was. She and Sawyer had passed it this morning on their way to the bookstore. And today was Tuesday.

"He might want to check it out. From what I understood

from my client, it's a real hangout for the young crowd. I had thought about trying to put a few brochures there."

His business, her life.

"Thanks for the tip, Jamison."

"You'll tell Detective Montgomery?"

"I will. Thanks, Jamison." Liz hung up and dialed Sawyer. After four rings, his voice mail came on. "Hi, Sawyer," she said. "I've got a tip on Mary. It's a dance club on Deyston. Call me, okay?"

She waited an hour. She'd tried his line again. When voice mail picked up again, she pressed zero. A woman answered. Detective Montgomery was not in. Was it an emergency? Did she want to page him?

She almost said yes but realized he could be in the middle of trouble. The man had a dangerous job. He didn't need to be interrupted.

She'd just go there by herself, look around and ask a few questions. She'd only stay a short while. Then she could report back to Sawyer. It would probably be better if he wasn't there anyway. He'd do his tough-guy cop routine and scare away any of the girls who might know Mary.

Liz had learned a lot about teenage girls in the past three years. When they got scared, they clammed up. She didn't want the girls circling the proverbial wagons and making it impossible to find Mary.

Liz ran back to her closet and started sorting through her clothes. Business suits or jeans. Old life, new life. She didn't have much in the middle. But tonight, she needed a young, nonestablishment look. It took her twenty minutes to find something that might work. She pulled the short, tight black skirt on, hoping like heck that she wouldn't have to sneeze. The zipper would surely break. Then she put on a black bra and topped if off with a sheer white shirt that had come with one of her swimsuits. She left her legs bare and stuck her feet into high-heeled, open-toed black sandals.

She teased and sprayed her hair, put on three times the amount of makeup she normally wore and walked her body through a mist of perfume. For the finishing touch, she applied two temporary tattoos, one on her breast, just peeking over the edge of her bra, and the other on the inside of her thigh, low enough that it would show when she crossed her legs. She'd remembered them at the last minute. They'd come in a box of cereal. One was a snake and the other a flag. Not exactly what she'd have chosen but better than nothing. Every girl she met had some kind of tattoo or body piercing.

When she got finished and looked in the mirror, she wasn't too dissatisfied with the effort. She didn't look eighteen, but she thought she could pass for her mid-twenties. At least they might not guess she was thirty-two—so far into adulthood, from their perspective, that she couldn't possibly even remember what it was like to be young.

She grabbed a small black purse, stuck her cell phone in it as well as two hundred bucks. She remembered Sawyer's advice from earlier in the day. Everything had a price. She needed to be prepared to pay for information.

She waved down a cab and ignored the guy's look when she told him the address. Thirty minutes later, when he pulled up to the curb, she sat still for a minute, for the first time wondering if she had made a big mistake.

Music poured out of the small, old building. Ten or fifteen teens gathered around the door, lounging against the cement walls. Everybody had a cigarette and a can of beer. More boys than girls. And the few girls who were there were clearly taken. One straddled a boy who sat on a wooden chair. He had his hand up her shirt. Another girl, plastered from lips to toes to her boy, his hands possessively curled around her butt, almost blocked the doorway.

"You getting out, lady?" The cab driver raised one eyebrow at her. "I don't like sitting still in this neighborhood."

Liz swallowed. This morning, the neighborhood had looked gray. Gray buildings, gray sidewalk. The sky had even seemed a little gray, as if it were a reflection of the street below. But tonight, the street seemed black and purple and red. Violent and passionate, the colors of sex and sin. Firecrackers popped, music blasted, the air almost sizzled.

"Yes, I'm getting out." Liz threw a twenty at the driver and stepped from the car.

Chapter Five

"Oh, baby, I do like blondes." The voice came from her far left. Liz couldn't see him until he stepped away from the corner of the building. He looked older than the other teens, probably in his early twenties. He cocked a finger at her. "Come here. Let's see if they really do have more fun."

A couple of the other teens pushed each other around, laughing, but nobody else said anything. Liz ignored them all and walked into the club.

If it had been loud outside, it was mind-blowing inside. It made her head hurt. She managed to make her way through the crowd and got up to the bar. She stood next to a group of girls, most of them looking about Mary's age. Where the hell were the police? These kids couldn't be old enough to drink. Liz wanted them all busted but just not until she got the information that she wanted.

"I was talking to you outside, baby."

Liz felt heat crawl up her neck. She turned around. It was Creepy Guy from outside. She knew immediately that ignoring him wasn't going to work.

"I heard you." She smiled at him. "But I got to find my friend before I can have my own fun."

He stared at her breasts. Liz resisted the urge to slap him and tell him to get cleaned up and get a job. "I'll help you, baby. Who you looking for? I know everybody here."

She debated for all of three seconds. "Annie Smith. She likes to dance here."

"Don't know her." The man grabbed her arm and pulled her close. He smelled like cigarettes and cheap rum. "Let's you and me dance."

He stood five inches taller, probably eighty pounds heavier and had wrists twice as big as hers. Liz felt the fear spread from her toes to her head. It didn't matter that he was ten years younger. Age and experience didn't give her an advantage. Brute strength would win every time.

She took her free hand and stroked him under the chin with the back of her fingers. "I'd like that," she said. When he took his free hand and cupped her butt, she forced the smile to stay on her face. "You stay here," she said. "I'm gonna be right over there with those girls. You'll be able to see me." She opened her purse and pulled out a twenty. "Buy me a drink, sugar. Buy yourself one, too."

Then she pulled away from him and edged over to the group of girls that were still gathered just feet away. Several of them turned and stared at her when she joined the group. Then they started talking again as if she wasn't there.

Lord, it was just like high school.

She couldn't wait for them to warm up to her. She had only minutes before the creep at the bar got tired of waiting. She moved around the group, stopping when she stood next to a girl she guessed to be about five months pregnant.

"What do you want?" The girl took another drag off her cigarette.

Liz wanted to rip it away. Didn't she know what that was doing to her baby's lungs?

"I'm looking for Mary Thorton."

The girl looked over both shoulders then started to move away. "Stop, please," Liz pleaded, keeping her voice low.

"My name is Liz, and I think she's in trouble. I want to help her."

"Liz who?"

"Liz Mayfield. I work at Options for Caring Mothers on Logan Street."

Liz saw the flicker of recognition in the young girl's eyes. "You'll get in trouble asking about Mary," the girl advised, her voice low. "She ain't around anyway. She and Dantel went to Wisconsin. She said they were going fishing. Up by Wisconsin Dells."

"Are you sure?" Liz asked, aware that the man from the bar, a drink in each hand, walked toward her.

"That's what she told me. I don't think she wanted to go, but I don't think her boyfriend likes the word *no*."

Liz wanted to hug the young woman. Instead, she winked at her, took a step backward and loudly said, "Hey, if you don't know Annie Smith, you don't need to be such a bitch about it. I just asked a freakin' question."

She turned toward the door, but the guy with the drinks intercepted her before she got five feet. *Damn.* "Oh, thanks," she said and reached for the drink that she had absolutely no intention of sipping. She might be thirty-two and well past the bar scene, but she knew all about date-rape drugs.

Creepy Guy looked her up and down. Then he put his nearly empty glass and her full glass down on the nearest table, grabbed her hand and yanked her out into the sea of bodies. "Let's dance, baby. You can drink later."

The smell of sweat and cheap liquor almost overwhelmed Liz. When the man pulled her close and she could feel his erection, her mind almost stopped working. He had his hands on her butt and his mouth close to her ear.

She thought she might throw up.

Suddenly, the crowd parted and girls started screaming. Twenty feet away, two men were fighting. One had picked up a chair, and the other had a knife. Liz watched as yet another man, holding a beer bottle like a club, stepped into the mix.

Creepy Guy let go of her.

"I gotta pee," Liz said and ran for the bathroom.

There was no damn window in the bathroom. She moved into one of the stalls and grabbed her phone out of her purse. She dialed Sawyer's number. It rang and rang.

"Hey, don't take all day. The rest of us got to pee, too." An angry fist pounded on the door.

"Just a minute," Liz said. Sawyer's voice mail kicked on. Liz flushed the toilet so that she could talk. "Sawyer, I need help. I'm at 1882 Deyston." She disconnected that call and had just started to dial 911 when the door to the stall was kicked open.

"Everybody out," a female cop yelled at her. "Put your hands in the air and walk to the door."

Liz wanted to put her arms around the woman and hug her. But the gun pointed at her told her that wouldn't be appreciated.

Liz walked out into the club area. Some of the grayness from the daytime had eased back in. The lights had been turned on, and the music had been turned off. There were at least ten cops, with more pouring through the open door. Within minutes, the cops paired off, breaking the group into smaller groups. Everybody had to empty their pockets, their purses. A female officer patted Liz down, looking for weapons. She didn't care.

Liz didn't even care when she had to sit on the dirty floor, her hands on top of her head. Anything was better than dancing with that man, his erection pressed up against her, his hands grabbing at her butt. Thank God he hadn't tried to kiss her. Even now, the thought of it made her gag.

She sat quietly. The girl next to her cried; the boy on the other side screamed obscenities at the cops who stood around the perimeter of the room. Liz scanned the area for the pregnant girl who'd given her the info, but she was nowhere to be seen. Somehow, she'd managed to slip out.

Liz tried to remember every cop show she'd ever watched. When did people get fingerprinted? When was the mug shot taken? Would she get to make a phone call before or after all that?

Who the heck would she call? Sawyer hadn't been at his desk. She couldn't ask Carmen to come down to the police station at eleven o'clock on a Tuesday night. The only person she could call was Jamison. He'd have a cow, but then he'd come.

A minute later, when Sawyer, with his partner Robert on his heels, came through the doors, she realized that Jamison wasn't the only one likely to have a cow.

Sawyer literally skidded to a stop. He didn't say a word. He couldn't.

"Damn," Robert said.

"Hi," Liz said.

"What the hell are you doing here?" Sawyer demanded. God, he'd been scared. When he'd gotten her messages, he'd driven like a crazy person to the bar, calling Robert on the way. They'd gotten there almost at the same time. When he'd seen more than a dozen squads outside, all kinds of crazy thoughts had entered his head.

Now that he was sure she wasn't hurt, he wanted to wring her little neck. "You came here, looking like *that?*" he said.

She put her chin in the air. "I had to fit in. I couldn't wear my jeans."

"Did you have to dress like a damned hooker?"

He regretted it the minute he said it. But he was scared. He hadn't been there to protect her. What if she'd gotten hurt? Raped? Killed?

"I didn't think a three-piece suit would fit in," she said.

"You didn't think. Period."

If anything, she put her nose a bit higher in the air. "I called you. I tried to reach you."

"You left a stupid message. Page me. That's why I leave the number."

"I didn't want to bother you," she said.

"Bother me?" This woman drove him crazy. "All you've been is a bother since the day I met you."

"Look, Sawyer," Robert interjected. "There's no harm done. She's fine. We're all fine. Don't be an idiot about this."

Sawyer rubbed a hand across his face. He could see the pain in Liz's pretty green eyes. It was hurt he'd caused.

He took a deep breath. When he spoke, he raised his voice just enough that Liz could hear but that the rest of the people in the room would have to make up their own story. "I'm sorry, Liz. I'm more sorry than you can imagine. I was worried and…and I'm not handling this well." His voice cracked at the end.

"I want to go home," Liz said. "Will you take me?"

He felt the weight of the world lift off his shoulders. "Yeah, I'd be glad to." He looked at Robert and nodded his head at the officer who seemed to be in charge. "Can you…"

"No problem. I'll give our boys the CliffsNotes version so that they understand why she's making a quick exit. Get going."

Sawyer nodded, wrapped an arm around her and walked her out of the bar.

He wished he had a coat, something that he could throw over her, cover up some skin. What in the hell had she been thinking?

Once inside his car, Sawyer kept his hands firmly wrapped around the steering wheel, afraid that he might just reach out and shake her. Of course, once he touched her, he'd be toast. It would all be over for him. He'd end up kissing and touching her and maybe more if she didn't have the good sense to stop him.

It would be wrong. She deserved better than what he had to offer. Which was nothing. Liz Mayfield was young, pretty and someday would make some man a fine wife. They'd have pretty babies, and God willing, she and her husband would see them grow up, go to their first baseball game, drive a car, go to college, have a life.

He'd thought he'd had it. Then he'd lost it. His baby's precious body had grown cold in his arms. The nurses, the professionals who were used to saying the words *baby* and *death* in the same sentence, let him be. They walked around his rocking chair, careful to keep their voices down, their eyes never quite meeting his.

Much wiser now, he knew what he had. He had his work, his career. He made important arrests that got scum off the streets. He made a difference every day. That was more than some people had in a lifetime. It had to be enough for him.

He'd been half out of his mind with worry when he'd gotten the two voice mails from her. He'd listened to the first and realized that she intended to go to Deyston Street and then the second; when he'd heard the panic in her voice and knew she was scared and possibly hurt, his heart had almost stopped.

It had been a huge relief when he saw her. And then he'd turned stupid. The worry eating at his soul had burst from his mouth, and he'd hurt her. He regretted that. But she needed to understand how big of a mistake she'd made. For her own sake. She didn't understand how violent, how cruel, how humiliating the street—and those who called the street their home—could be.

He would take her back to her apartment, and they would talk. He wouldn't yell, and he wouldn't accuse. It would be a civil conversation, one adult to another. He'd make her understand that she needed to let the police look for Mary. That she needed to stop seeing OCM's clients at her apartment. Then he'd leave.

Sawyer found a spot near the front of Liz's apartment building. "I'd like to come in," he said. He was proud that he sounded so calm, so reasonable. See, he could do this.

"I'm not sure that's a good idea."

"We should talk. I'd be more comfortable talking in your apartment." Wow. *He* should be the shrink.

He waited until she nodded before he quickly got out of the car. Yep, everything would be fine. They'd have a nice quiet conversation, and he could leave, knowing that she'd be safe.

He walked around the car and opened Liz's door. Oh, hell. From this angle, her legs went on forever. She had them crossed, one sexy, small foot, with painted red toenails, dangling over the other. Tanned legs, absolutely silky smooth. Round knees, firm thighs and a...a snake. No way! It couldn't be! He squatted down next to the open door, and with his index finger, he tapped against the tattoo.

"What the hell is this? Are you nuts?"

"Sawyer, it's just..."

"It's not just a tattoo," he yelled. "You have the most beautiful, incredibly sexy legs." He pulled his hand back and rubbed his temple, as if he suddenly had a very bad headache. "How could you even think about getting a tattoo? And a snake. Were you drunk on your butt or what?"

"Stop yelling. My neighbors will call the cops. I'm not dealing with that again tonight."

She unbuttoned the top three buttons on her shirt. "It's a rub-on. See? Just like this one."

He did not intend to look. There was really no need. But he couldn't stop himself. And when she stuck two slim fingers in her mouth, wet them with her tongue and then rubbed her breast, blending the stars and stripes of the American flag, his knees almost gave out.

Chapter Six

"You need to stop doing that," he warned.

"But…" She looked up at him, confusion clear in her green eyes. "I just wanted you to see—"

"I see. I don't need to see another thing. Let's go." He turned away, not looking as she maneuvered those long legs out of the car.

"They came out of a cereal box," she said.

He'd never be able to eat his Cheerios again. "Fine. Let's not talk about tattoos anymore, okay?" He motioned for her keys, and she handed them to him. He unlocked the apartment door. He held up his palm, stopping her. He went inside, took a quick look around the apartment, and when he came back, he pulled her inside and shut the door.

"You and I are going to talk. But first, go take a shower. I'll make coffee."

"I don't really drink coffee at night. I'd prefer some tea. Something herbal. It's in the cupboard."

Herbal. He needed strong, get-a-grip caffeine and she wanted herbal. "Fine. Whatever. Just get that stuff off your face and get rid of those tattoos."

He made the stupid tea and tried not to think about how she'd look in the shower, the water sliding over her slim, firm body. The woman truly had an incredible shape. He'd appreciated it before, but now that he'd seen a bit more of it, he might have moved into the worship stage.

He had already finished one cup of tea when she came back to the kitchen. Her long hair, looking a bit darker when wet, was pulled back in a loose braid. She had on a T-shirt, a pair of jogging shorts and white socks. No makeup. Not a speck. She looked about sixteen. He felt better. He wouldn't be tempted to stick his hands up her shirt if she didn't look legal.

"Here's your tea."

"Thanks."

She sat on the stool next to the kitchen counter and took dainty little sips. Neither of them said a word for a few minutes. When she did speak, she surprised him.

"I did a stupid thing tonight," she said.

Yeah, that was exactly what he'd intended to tell her.

"Something bad could have happened, and it would have been my own fault."

Right. That about summed it up. Why didn't it give him more pleasure to hear her say it? To have her admit that she was out of her league?

"I didn't want to miss meeting Mary's friends. I didn't stop to think about all the other people who would be there."

He hated—absolutely hated—seeing her this beaten. "Just forget it," he said. "It's over."

And then she started to cry. She might sip daintily, but she cried loud and rough. Her nose got red, big tears slid down her cheeks, her shoulders shook and she made choking sounds. Knowing it was stupid, knowing he'd probably regret it, he walked around the counter and wrapped his arms around her.

"Now, now." He tried to comfort her. "You had a tough night. Everything will be better in the morning."

"I hate being a girl. I hate being smaller, shorter, weaker. I hate being afraid."

The muscles in his stomach tightened.

"Did somebody threaten you?" He pulled back just enough so that he could look her in the eye.

"No. It's nothing. I'm just tired."

She was lying. "Did somebody touch you tonight?" He felt a burn. It started in the pit of his stomach, then exploded into his arms and legs, making him shake. He was going to kill the bastard.

She shrugged her shoulders, trying to dismiss him. He stopped her. "I told you once. Don't lie to me. Don't ever lie to me."

She gave one last sniff and lifted her chin in the air. "When I got out of the cab, there were a bunch of teenagers outside of the building. One of them said something. He looked a bit older than the rest, maybe twenty or so. I just ignored him. But when I got inside, I couldn't shake him."

"What did he do?" He didn't want to know. He didn't want to hear it.

"He wanted to dance."

"Okay."

"I tried to get out of it. He was too strong. I couldn't get away without making a scene. I'd gotten the information I needed. All I wanted to do was get out of there without a bunch of people wondering who I was and why I was there. I think he might have been high on something. He seemed just on the edge of being out of control."

She'd gotten information about Mary. He didn't care. "What did he do to you?"

"He pulled me close and I could feel…him." She blushed but recovered quickly. "I could feel him poking into me and I got scared. I was in a strange place, I didn't know a soul and he outweighed me by at least eighty pounds." She blinked her eyes, where tears still clung to her thick lashes. "Then there was a fight. I guess that's why the cops came. Anyway, I told him I had to pee and I ran to the bathroom. When the cops came, I almost hugged them."

He pulled her close, held her next to his heart and bent his mouth very close to her ear. "I'm sorry that happened to you. I'm sorry he touched you. I'm sorry he scared you. But you need to forget it. You're never going to see him again."

She moved even closer, and her curves suddenly filled his hands. Her heat warmed him. She kissed the side of his neck.

Let it be enough, he prayed. *Let it be enough.* But he knew it wouldn't. He wanted her mouth, he wanted her hands, he wanted her legs spread apart. He wanted to make love with her for about a day. That might be enough.

"I'm very grateful," she said, making him feel like a lecherous old man. She looked sixteen, and she'd just given him a shy, sweet little kiss and a gracious thank-you. And all he could do was think about pushing her backward, getting her legs hooked over his arms and coming inside of her until one of them passed out.

Then she wrapped her arms around his back and hugged him. He could feel the whole length of her body. It pressed up against him, tempting him. She smelled so good. Sweet and fresh. He bent his head over her wet hair, breathing in the scent of her shampoo. He moved his hands across her back, fingering the bottom of her T-shirt. God help him, he needed to touch her.

He put one hand under her shirt, lightly rubbing her bare back. He moved his fingers over her warm skin, loving the silky feel of her. He moved his hand a bit higher, finding only skin. The woman hadn't put a bra on. Was she crazy? Didn't she have a clue what that did to him, to feel her warm skin, to know that he was just inches away from holding her breast in his hand?

And when she lifted her face and her lips were just inches from his, he went down for the count. He kissed her. Long and slow. And when he slid his tongue into her mouth and she suckled lightly on it, he got instantly hard.

Never taking his mouth away from hers, he moved his hand across her ribs and cupped one breast, loving the feel of the heavy weight, loving the softness, the warmth. He brushed his fingers across her nipple, groaning when she arched her back and pressed her breast more fully into his open hand. He shifted, pressing his hardness against her softness.

She jerked her head back, her eyes wide open.

Her soft, liquid warmth had turned into a hard, solid block of ice.

He was an idiot. A senseless, selfish idiot. She'd already had one man tonight poking into her, causing her to be scared. And now he was doing the same thing. With grim resolution, he pulled away from her, putting a good foot between their bodies.

"I'm sorry," he said. "I can't believe I did that. I…I should be shot."

She laughed. A bit shaky perhaps but it gave him a little hope. "I think that's extreme," she said.

"I'm not so sure. I'm attracted to you," he said. "But you don't have to worry. It would be unprofessional for me to pursue a relationship with you."

She stared at him.

"I'm a cop," he said, reminding both of them. "I'm investigating a murder. I can't do anything to compromise that investigation."

He could tell that she was starting to get it.

"Never mind," Sawyer said, thinking he'd rather be just about anywhere else than explaining to her why he couldn't even think about sleeping with her. "I think I'd better go." He grabbed his keys off the counter.

Liz's braid had flipped over one shoulder, and she played with the wet ends. "Don't you even want to know what I learned about Mary?" she asked, her voice subdued.

Yes. No. Hell, he'd been so far gone that he'd forgotten all about Mary. He moved behind the counter, needing the physical barrier. "What?"

She took a sip of tea. "Mary and Dantel Mirandez are fishing in Wisconsin."

He laughed, glad that he still could. "Sure they are."

Her cheeks turned pink. "I talked to one of Mary's friends tonight. At first, she wouldn't tell me anything. But then I think she decided that I might be able to help Mary."

"Did she say Mary needed help?"

"No, but she acted nervous, like she didn't want to be caught talking about Mirandez or Mary."

"Smart girl. Liz, I can't see Mirandez with a fishing pole. Not unless he'd diced somebody up and was using them for bait."

"You said Mirandez was smart. If he wanted to disappear, doesn't it make sense that he'd go somewhere you'd never think to look?"

"Yeah, but fishing? And anyway, even if I believed it, there has to be at least a thousand lakes in Wisconsin. We'd never find him."

"It's someplace near Wisconsin Dells."

Near Wisconsin Dells. Or The Dells, as all the vacationers called it. One of the detectives he worked with had just taken his family there. He'd called it Little Disney. There were lots of water parks, miniature golf courses and restaurants. Home of the Tommy Bartlett ski show and the boats shaped like ducks that cruised up and down the Wisconsin River.

He couldn't for the life of him see Mirandez at a place

like that. "It just sounds too bizarre," he said, absolutely hating to see the look of disappointment on her face. "Even if he's there, we wouldn't have a clue where to start looking."

"Yes, we do. He's at a cabin. We just have to check out the cabins in the area."

"It's Wisconsin. The state is full of cabins and campgrounds. Even if we know it's around The Dells, it's a big area to search."

She didn't look convinced. "I have to try," she said.

He got a bad feeling in the bottom of his stomach. "You're not trying anything. Wasn't tonight enough of a lesson?"

She swallowed hard, and he felt bad about throwing it in her face. But if that was what it took to keep her safe at home, he didn't feel that bad.

"Yes, tonight sucked. I got hit on by a kid and spent a half hour sitting on a dirty floor. But it's nothing in the grand scheme of things. I have to find Mary."

"The police will find Mirandez. And Mary will be there. We've got a huge amount of manpower out on the street. It's only a matter of time."

"Not if he's fishing."

"Gang leaders do not fish." Sawyer pounded his fist against the kitchen counter.

"You can't be sure of that." Liz started to pace around her apartment. "I don't know what's going on here. I've thought about it for days, and nothing seems to make sense. Well, maybe one thing. That first day we met, after the shooting, you said that it seemed like Mirandez wanted Mary's attention. That he wasn't actually trying to hurt her."

"Right. She's his girlfriend. Maybe he's partial to sleeping in the same bed every night."

"No. It's more than that. I think Mirandez thinks it's his baby."

"You told me it belonged to a student at Loyola."

"Yes. But I think Mary told Mirandez something different."

"Why?"

"Because she's young and alone and probably desperately wanted someone to want both her and the baby."

"Then the Loyola kid was just convenient."

"Perhaps. But he didn't deny that he'd slept with Mary."

"Who knows how many men she slept with?" He hated to be quite so blunt, but Liz needed to stop looking at Mary with rose-colored glasses. She surprised him when she didn't look offended.

"You're right. We don't know. And maybe Mirandez doesn't, either. You said that Mary had been his girlfriend for the past six months. She's eight months pregnant."

Sawyer sat down on one of the counter stools, tapping two fingers against his lips, deep in thought. "So, she's two months along before she ever sleeps with Mirandez. But he doesn't know it."

"Maybe she didn't even know it. But she probably figured it out fast enough. By that time, Mirandez was taking care of her, giving her money, making her feel important."

"So, she doesn't want to walk away from a good thing." Sawyer didn't bother to try to hide his disgust.

"Or she was afraid to try to walk away. Especially once she saw the murder. Maybe that's why Mirandez tried to frighten her. To let her know that he wasn't going to let her walk away."

"Because he loves her?" Sawyer shook his head. "It's possible, I suppose."

"Maybe he wants the baby?" Liz raised an eyebrow.

Sawyer shook his head. "He's a killer. Why would a gang leader, a professional drug dealer, want a baby? And what's so special about this baby? Who knows how many kids he already has running around the city?"

"I don't know. But if I'm right and he does want the baby, then Mary's life isn't worth the price of bubblegum once she gives birth."

Sawyer didn't say anything for a few minutes. "Or maybe she and Mirandez are playing house somewhere, and she doesn't want to be found. She might not be in any danger at all."

"I can't take that chance. Mirandez might be holding her against her will. She's the one person who can send him to jail. Once she has that baby, she's a loose end that he can tie up."

"She should be safe enough for a couple weeks. Didn't you say that the baby wasn't due until September?"

"Babies are known to come early."

"We'll alert every hospital in the state. In Wisconsin, too. Hell, in the whole damn country. If someone comes in matching Mary's description, we'll have her."

"But what if he won't let her go to the hospital?"

"He's a drug dealer, not a doctor." Even Mirandez wouldn't be stupid enough to try to deliver a baby.

"Blood probably doesn't bother him."

Yeah, but delivering a baby? Sawyer had watched the obligatory films in the academy. But in all his years on the police force, he'd never had to deliver a baby. Even before that, when his son had been born, his girlfriend hadn't called until it was all over. He'd raced to the hospital to see his four-hour-old son. He'd barely left the hospital for the next thirteen days. He'd slept and eaten only when he'd been on the verge of falling down. He'd stayed there until they'd taken the body of his son from his arms, leaving him forever alone.

"I gave her a chance to come forward. If she was scared of Mirandez, why didn't she say something?" Sawyer asked.

"I don't know. Maybe she thought that Mirandez would

kill her, too. Maybe she thought Mirandez would rest easy once he found out that she didn't intend to turn him in."

"I don't think he's the type to forget. They don't teach you to turn the other cheek in the hood."

"I don't think she has lots of experience with men like Mirandez."

"No one does. They all die first."

Liz shrugged. "That's why I'm going after her."

No way. Evil surrounded Mirandez. He wouldn't risk letting that evil leak out and touch Liz. "That's not possible. It's a police matter."

"But you said the police are searching in Chicago. They aren't going to find Mirandez or Mary."

"We know Mirandez has dropped out of sight. But we don't have any reason to believe that Mirandez is in Wisconsin. I told you that we have people on the inside. There's been no talk about fishing. He would have told somebody in his organization. And our guys would know."

"I think the girl at Jumpin' Jack Flash told me the truth."

"What was her name?"

Liz blushed. "I didn't ask. I didn't want to scare her. She had dark hair, about shoulder length, with olive-colored skin. Late teens. I'd estimate she was five or six months pregnant."

"Of course."

Liz raised an eyebrow when she heard the bitterness in his voice. "Are you automatically discounting everything she said because she's young and pregnant?"

Young pregnant women lied. His girlfriend had lied to him. Mary had lied. Why wouldn't this one lie? "No. But I don't accept it as gospel."

Liz shook her head, clearly disgusted with him. "I'm going to Wisconsin. She needs me."

"You don't even know where to begin," he protested.

"I'll get a map. I've got some recent photos of Mary. I'll

show them around, and somebody will have seen her. Someone will know where I can find her."

If it was that easy, they wouldn't have a stack of missing-person reports. "It's too dangerous. I can't let you do it." When she opened her mouth to protest, he held up a hand. "I'll ask Lieutenant Fischer to send a few guys north. We'll expand the search. We'll notify both local and state authorities in Wisconsin." It was the best he could do. Probably better than the half-baked lead deserved.

"Thank you. But I'm still going. I have to."

She wasn't going to let him keep her safe. "Mary doesn't deserve this kind of loyalty. She lied to you. She told you that she didn't even know Mirandez. You know that she's been living with him for the past six months. Don't you even care that she looked you in the eye and lied to you?"

"Mary's in a fragile state right now. I'm not sure she's able to make good decisions."

"*You're* not making good decisions," he accused. When she shrugged in return, he knew continued arguing would get them nowhere.

"You should probably go," she said. "I want to get an early start."

"I hope to hell she's worth it," he said as he pulled the door shut behind him.

Chapter Seven

Sawyer called Lieutenant Fischer from his car, knowing he had a responsibility to give the man any information that might lead to Mirandez's capture. The older man listened, asked a couple questions and agreed it was a long shot. That said, he'd assign a few resources to Wisconsin. They couldn't afford to ignore any lead, no matter how preposterous.

"There's one other thing, Lieutenant," Sawyer said. Now that he'd had a minute to think about Liz going to Wisconsin, he realized that there was one good thing about it. If whoever had sent the threat was serious about it, it got her out of harm's way here.

"Yes."

"Liz Mayfield intends to search, as well. Would you… Could you get the word out? I don't want her getting caught in any cross fire."

Lieutenant Fischer didn't answer right away. When he did, he surprised Sawyer. "We should use Liz Mayfield."

The department didn't use civilians. They weren't trained. They could botch up almost any action, putting officers at risk. "I don't understand, sir."

"You think that Mary Thorton willingly went with Mirandez?"

"I think there's a high probability of that," Sawyer answered. "She's been living with him for months. She didn't turn on him when she had the chance."

"If that's true, she's going to run if she thinks the cops are closing in. Or she's going to tell Mirandez and they'll both run, or there's going to be a bloody battle between Mirandez and us. But if Liz gets close, she may be able to talk to the girl. You said yourself that there seemed to be a really strong bond between the two of them. That if anyone could get to Mary, it would be her."

Sawyer regretted ever having said those words. "Sir, you *cannot* send her after Mirandez. He's a monster. He wouldn't think twice about killing her."

"That's why I'm sending you with her. It's your job to keep her safe. If she gets hurt, I'm going to have the mayor and her boss and God knows who else wanting my head. Stick to her like glue."

There was no damn way. "No."

"Why not?"

He couldn't tell his lieutenant about what had happened in Liz's kitchen, that he'd almost exploded from wanting her. "She's not going to like having me as her shadow."

"Too bad. She doesn't have a choice. Some things just can't be negotiated."

He was a doomed man. "Will you let Robert know where I am?"

"Sure. By the way, I talked to him just a little while ago. He told me that the two of you had sprung Liz from Jumpin' Jack Flash."

Good call on Robert's part. Better to tell the boss rather than let him hear it through the grapevine. "Seemed like the right thing to do," Sawyer said.

"It's fine," his boss said.

Sawyer understood. Lieutenant Fischer wasn't going to worry about the small stuff when he was close to snagging Mirandez.

LIZ FROZE WHEN SHE HEARD the knocking on her front door. In the mirror, she could see the reflection of the digital alarm clock. Eight minutes after four. No one knocked on her door at that time of the morning.

Mary. She spit out the toothpaste, took a gulp of water and grabbed a towel. She wiped her mouth on the way to the door. "Just a minute," she yelled. She wanted to yank the door open but took the extra second to check the peephole. She looked, pulled back, blinked a couple times and looked again.

Sawyer. She twisted the bolt lock to the right, pulled the chain back and opened the door.

"What happened?" she said.

"Can I come in?"

She opened the door wider. "It's Mary, isn't it? Oh, God, is she all right?"

"Liz, calm down. I don't know anything more than I knew last night when I left here."

"Oh." She felt the relief flow through her body. No news wasn't necessarily good news, but it wasn't bad news, either. Swiftly on the heels of the relief came annoyance. "What are you doing here?"

She thought he looked a bit unsure. But that must be her imagination. *Capable* Detective Montgomery didn't do unsure.

"You said you were leaving early." Sawyer gave her a slight smile. "I know you sometimes get up at the crack of dawn. I didn't want to miss you."

"It's four o'clock," she said.

He shrugged his broad shoulders. "I didn't wake you."

No, he hadn't. She'd already showered, dried her hair and packed her bag. In another ten minutes, she'd have been gone.

"Why are you here?" she asked again.

"I'm going with you. To look for Mary."

She backed up a few steps and shook her head. Her tired mind must be playing tricks on her.

"Do you have any coffee made?" Sawyer asked.

"No." She didn't intend to offer him coffee. First of all, the man had kissed her like crazy and then stopped. It was the stopping she was mad about. Then he had compounded his errors by dismissing the notion that she might have gotten a viable lead on Mary. Now he acted as if he had every right to come to her house at four in the morning for conversation and coffee.

He crinkled his nose and pretended to sniff the air. "Funny. That smells like coffee."

She'd been done in by hazelnut beans. "I've got a timer. It must have turned on."

"Great. I could use a cup."

He could pour his own. She intended to go finish packing, and then they would go their separate ways.

"Fine. Cups are on the counter. I've got things to do."

He nodded and pointed at the corner of her mouth. "You've got just a speck of toothpaste there."

Oh, the nerve of this guy. "I was saving it for later," Liz said, her voice dripping with sweetness.

Sawyer laughed. "Good one. You're funny in the morning."

He'd think funny when she left him standing on the curb.

Ten minutes later, Liz walked into the kitchen. Sawyer stood at the counter, drinking out of her favorite cup and eating a piece of toast. "I made you some," he said. "I didn't know if you liked jelly."

"Sawyer." Liz smiled, purposefully patronizing. She felt

calmer now that she'd had a few moments to herself. "This is bizarre. You can't come to my house at four in the morning and have breakfast."

"I packed enough to last a week. I suggest you do the same."

A week? He expected her to spend a week with him?

Liz grabbed for the piece of toast he held out to her. She needed food. She surely had low blood sugar. He couldn't have said *a week*. It would all be better once she'd eaten.

"I did an internet search last night," Sawyer continued, as if he had every right. "I've identified the most likely places."

Likely places? "Sawyer, stop. You're giving me a headache. First of all, when did you have time to do an internet search? You left here just hours ago. Did you sleep at all? And more important, why are you doing this? Last night you didn't seem to think that my information had much value."

"Any lead is better than no lead."

"Well, you can't go with me." She couldn't spend a week with him. Heck, she couldn't spend an hour with him without itching to touch him. Mr. Can't-compromise-the-investigation had no idea that given another two minutes last night, she'd have been all over him. The man had no idea just how much at risk he'd been. The desire had been swift, hot, almost painful.

Throughout the very short night, she'd relived the scene over and over again. By morning, she'd been almost willing to admit that he'd probably done the right thing. There was no need for the little spark between the two of them to grow into a really big flame. With air, a little encouragement and fresh sheets, it could be spontaneous combustion.

They'd both be burned, hurt worse than they could imagine.

Which was ridiculous. Absolutely not necessary. They both wanted Mary. He wanted to use the girl. She wanted to save her. Same goal, different objectives. No common values or mission statement. There was no need to share strategy. Certainly no need to share a car.

"I want to go by myself," she stated.

"No."

Who had died and put him in charge? "You can't stop me."

"I can," he said, suddenly sounding very serious, more like he had the night before. "I'm the lead detective on the case. If you don't cooperate with me, I'll have you arrested for interfering with a police investigation."

"You wouldn't do that," she accused. He just stood there, not blinking, not moving.

"I'll do what I have to do."

"You...you..." she sputtered, unable to find the word that captured her anger. "You cop." It was the best she could do at four in the morning.

He shrugged. "I want Mirandez. Mary's my ticket. She testifies against Mirandez and we get to throw away the key. I haven't made any bones about what I'm trying to do. You think they're in Wisconsin. That's as good a guess as any right now. Are you ready to go?"

She wasn't going anywhere with him. "I'm packed. I'm leaving. Solo. Alone. You can follow me if you want, but we aren't going together."

"That's a waste of gas if we're both going the same way."

He didn't *really* care about wasting gas. "You're afraid that I'm going to warn Mary. You don't trust me."

He looked a little offended. "I trust you. About as much as you trust me."

She didn't trust him one bit. He'd steal her heart and never give it back. She'd be the Tin Man looking for the Wizard.

"I want Mirandez to pay for his crimes," Liz said. "If you're right and Mary can testify against him, I'll do everything I can to persuade her to do so."

"You still refuse to accept that she might be part of this."

"She's not."

"Fine. I'll be the first to say I'm wrong. But if I'm right, I'm going to arrest both of them. Maybe it would be in Mary's best interests if you were with me when I find them."

Mary wouldn't talk to Sawyer. Liz knew that. He was everything she despised. She'd clam up, or worse yet, she'd spout off and probably irritate the hell out of him. She didn't think Sawyer would arrest her out of spite. He wasn't that type of cop or man. No, Sawyer wasn't the wild card. But Mary was. She needed to be there when the two of them met up again.

"All right," she said. "We'll go together. But you'd better not slow me down."

"Don't worry. We'll be there in three hours. Then we start working the river."

"Working the river?"

"Yes. In that area, most of the major campgrounds and resort areas are close to the Wisconsin River. We'll pick a point and then work both sides of the river, north and south. The girl at Jumpin' Jack Flash said he was fishing. He's got to be staying in the area. Could be a tent, a cabin or a damn resort. We'll check them all. If we're going to do this, we do it right."

That seemed like a whole lot of *we*. "Fine." Did she just say *fine?* What was she thinking? "Let's go."

"We can take your car or I'd be happy to drive."

"Oh, no," she said. "Let's take my car."

"Then follow me over to the police station. I'll drop my wheels there."

How had this happened? She was drawn to Sawyer like some cheap magnet to a refrigerator. He could see the attraction, yet he had some crazy ethical, moral or puritanical code—she wasn't sure which—that prevented him from acting on it.

So, however much she tried to avoid it, she'd be squirming in her seat for days, and he'd be determined to withstand it. To prevail.

It made her furious. With herself and with him. "I'll get my bag," she said. "While you're waiting, find a thermos. I think there's one in those cupboards. I'm gonna want coffee."

SAWYER PULLED INTO a truck stop shortly after seven. They'd beaten the rush-hour traffic, scooting out of the Chicago-land area before lots of commuters hit the road. It had been a straight shot north up I-94, and now they were headed west, just twenty minutes shy of Madison.

Liz hadn't said a word to him since they'd left his car at the station and he'd climbed into hers. Not even when he'd ask her if he could drive. She'd just looked at him and dropped the keys to her Toyota into his open hand. He'd pushed the seat back and tried to get comfortable. She'd sat on her side of the car, drank coffee, fiddled with the radio stations and generally ignored him.

He didn't care. A little dislike between him and Liz could go a long way. He hoped it went far enough that it kept him from wanting her, from taking her into his arms, from pulling her under his body.

He didn't think he'd be satisfied with less. He knew he didn't have a right to ask for more. He needed to keep his hands on the wheel and let her be pissed off at him. It was safer and ultimately easier and better for the both of them.

"I'm hungry," he said.

"Fine." She barely spared him a look before she turned her face to the window.

"We need gas, too."

"Fine," she repeated. She reached down between her feet, opened her purse and pulled out a twenty.

"I'll buy gas," Sawyer told her. "This is police business."

"Your boss knows you're going?"

"Of course. He thinks it's probably a wild-goose chase. But since Mirandez has had us chasing our tails for over a year, he's pulling out all the stops."

"When we find Mary, I'd appreciate it if you'd let me talk to her first. She'll be scared."

She had no idea she was playing into Lieutenant Fischer's hands. That was exactly what the man had hoped for. The lieutenant wanted Liz to draw Mary in, to get her to testify against Mirandez. Lord, he hated using Liz like this. "I'll do my best." Sawyer heard the stiffness in his voice. He ignored the quick look Liz shot in his direction and pulled the keys out of the ignition. "Let's go."

Sawyer took the lead, but no one even glanced up when they walked through the door. Not until Liz walked past the two men who were sitting in the middle booth drinking coffee. Sawyer heard the soft whistle first, then "Wouldn't mind having those wrapped around my waist."

Sawyer stopped in his tracks. He balled up his fist and turned.

Chapter Eight

"Sawyer, please," she said. "Let it go."

It was the look in her eyes that stopped him. She didn't want a scene. Sawyer gave the men a look, and they had the good sense to take an interest in their eggs. He turned, walked another ten feet and slid into the empty booth at the end of the row. He faced the door. "They're stupid," he said.

"Agreed," she answered.

"You should wear pants," he lectured her. "No," he said, shaking his head. "That's not fair."

She waved a hand. "Nor practical. It's going to be a hundred degrees today." She picked up the plastic-covered listing of the day's specials.

"I imagine women get tired of men acting like idiots."

She sighed. Loudly. "Yes. Especially when they have dirty hair, food on their faces and bellies that hang over their pants."

It didn't take much for him to remember how he'd ogled those same legs last night. Yeah, his face and hair had been clean and his stomach still fairly flat, but that didn't make him much better than those creeps.

"How much farther?" she asked.

"We're twenty minutes east of Madison. Then it's another hour or so north to Wisconsin Dells. Our first stop is Clover Corners."

She shook her head, apparently not recognizing the name. "Why there?"

"Like I said earlier, we look everywhere. But there are a few places that seem more logical than others, so we start there."

"I'm not sure I understand the logic."

"I know Mirandez. He's a low-profile kind of guy. That's what has kept him alive so long."

"I thought you said he was twenty-six."

"You meet very few middle-aged gang leaders."

"I suppose. What kind of fishing would a low-profile type of guy do?"

"He'd look for a place where he could stay, eat and buy his bait without ever having to venture out. Especially because he probably can't go anywhere without dragging Mary with him. People notice pregnant women."

Liz nodded in agreement. "Last week when I went shopping with her, four people stopped to pat her stomach. Four complete strangers."

He didn't want to talk about Mary's pregnancy.

"It's like her stomach has become community property," Liz continued. "I told her she should get a sign for around her neck."

Despite himself, he wanted to know. "What would it say?"

"Something along the lines of Beware of Teeth. Then they wouldn't be able to sue her when she bit their hand."

There'd been a couple times that Mary had looked as if she wanted to bite him. Maybe a quick couple of nips out of his rear.

"But the really sick part is that I—"

"Two coffees here?" A waitress on her way past their booth stopped suddenly. She dropped a couple menus down on the corner of the table.

"Just water, please," Liz replied.

"Coffee would be fine," Sawyer said. Liz hadn't shared in the car. She'd been too busy being mad at him.

The waitress walked away. "What's the really sick part?" Sawyer asked.

Liz leaned forward. "Sometimes, I just can't help myself. I just have to touch their stomachs. I always thought that a pregnant woman's stomach would be soft, like a baby is soft. But it's this hard volleyball. It's so cool."

It had been cool. Cool and magical. His girlfriend had been thin. She hadn't actually showed for the better part of four months. And then one day, her flat little stomach had just popped out. And suddenly the baby had been real. He'd had no trouble at all suddenly visualizing what his son or daughter would look like, how he or she would run around the backyard at his parents' house, how he or she would hold his hand on the first day of school.

Even though he was just a kid himself, becoming a dad hadn't scared him.

He'd been too damn stupid to be scared.

He hadn't even considered that his child would be born weak, suffering, too small to take on the world.

He'd learned the hard way. Babies weren't tough at all.

The waitress came back with their drinks. "What can I get you this morning?"

"A bagel and cream cheese, please," Liz said.

"That's it?" Sawyer frowned at her.

She nodded.

Well, hell. He couldn't force her to eat. "Ham, eggs, hash-brown potatoes, and a side of biscuits and gravy," Sawyer said. The waitress wrote it down and left.

"Work up an appetite driving?" Liz asked.

Yeah, but not for food. But he wasn't going there. He'd managed to pull back last night. It had cost him. He'd spent most of the night mentally kicking his own butt. It hadn't helped that he knew he'd done the right thing. No, he'd been wound too tight, been too close to the edge. He'd wanted her badly.

But he couldn't sleep with Liz. Not with the possibility that he was going to have to arrest Mary. He knew that once he slept with Liz, once he let her into his soul, he'd be hard-pressed to be objective about Mary. And he couldn't afford to let up on the pursuit of Mirandez now. Not when they were so close.

"You may be sorry," he said. "We're not stopping again until lunch."

"It'll be okay. If I get hungry, I'll gnaw off a couple fingers."

"Mine or yours?" The minute he said it, he was sorry. He didn't need to be thinking about her mouth on any part of his body. "Just remember," he said, working hard to keep his voice from cracking, "the per diem reimbursement rate is $50 a person per day. They actually expect us to eat."

"Last of the big spenders, huh?"

"Big spender? The city? No. They barely buy us office supplies."

She put her elbows on the table and rested her chin on her hands. "Did you always want to be a cop, Sawyer? Was that your dream?"

His dream had been to raise his child. "No."

"How did you end up wearing a badge?"

It had seemed like the only thing to do. "I didn't go on to college right out of high school. I worked for a while." He'd worked like a dog when he'd found out Terrie was pregnant. He'd been determined to provide for her and his child. It was afterward, when he faced the truth that Terrie had continued to use drugs during the pregnancy, that he thought he'd worked too much. He'd been so focused on providing for his child that he'd neglected to protect him.

"But then…things happened, and I decided I wasn't going to get anywhere without an education. I started at the junior college and then went on for a bachelor's degree. I've been a cop for fifteen years. I don't know how to do much else."

"You haven't been in Chicago for fifteen years."

"How do you know?"

She looked over both shoulders and leaned forward in the booth. "Like Mary said," she whispered, "you talk funny."

"I do not. You people in the north talk funny."

"I wouldn't say that too loudly. A body can go missing in the woods for a long time before somebody stumbles upon it."

"Duly noted."

"Why Chicago?"

"Why not?" He took a drink of coffee. That was probably all he needed to say, but suddenly he wanted to tell her more. "My father died two years ago. My mom had passed the year before. With both of them gone, there was no reason to stay in Baton Rouge."

"Aha. Baton Rouge. I had guessed New Orleans."

"I spent some time there."

She settled back in her booth. "Drinking Hurricanes at Pat O'Brien's? Eating beignets at Café du Monde? Brunch at the Court of Two Sisters?"

He'd been working undercover, mostly setting up drug buys with the underbelly of society. "Sounds like you know the place."

"I did an internship there when I was working on my doctorate. I loved everything about it. The food especially. After I left, I dreamed of gumbo."

"I can do a crawfish boil better than most."

She sighed. "Don't tease me. You don't really know how to cook, do you?"

His mother had believed that cooking was everybody's

work. In the South, family meant food. Hell, maybe when this was all over, he'd have Liz over for dinner.

Maybe they'd eat in bed. He'd feed her shrimp creole and drizzle the sauce across her naked body.

Lord help him. He reached for his water and knocked his silverware on the floor.

She scooted out of the booth and reached over to the next table to grab him a fresh set. He saw the smooth, tanned skin of her back when her shirt pulled up.

He did a quick look to make sure the two goons in the middle booth weren't copping a look.

Nope. It was just him.

"No other family there?" she asked.

"What?" He shook his head, trying to clear it.

She slid the silverware toward him. "Do you have other family in Baton Rouge?"

He'd brought Jake with him. That had taken some doing, but there'd been no other option. "No." She was getting too close. He needed to change the subject.

"How about you?" he asked. "Did you always want to be a social worker at OCM?"

"No, I worked in private practice for several years. Sort of chasing the American dream. You know, a fancy house, a new car, trips to Europe, three-hundred-dollar suits."

He knew that much. He wanted to know why she'd left it all behind. "Doesn't sound all that bad."

"It's not bad. Just not enough."

He let her words hang. When she didn't continue, he jumped in, not wanting the conversation to die. "Just decided you'd had enough of living in the lap of luxury?"

She smiled, a sad sort of half smile. "You got it. Decided I couldn't take any more caviar and champagne."

He thought about pushing. Over the course of his career, he'd persuaded street-smart drug dealers, high-priced hookers and numbers-running bookies to talk. Some had been easier than others. But he rarely failed.

But he didn't want to pry or coerce Liz into offering up information. Maybe it was as simple as she made it sound. Maybe she just got tired of the fast lane. If so, no doubt it would lure her back, sooner or later. She'd get tired of slugging her way through the day at OCM, the hours filled with fights with belligerent teens.

If she didn't want to talk, okay with him. He didn't care what had driven her to OCM.

Right. He wanted to know. Wanted to know everything about her. Might have asked, too, if the waitress hadn't picked that moment to slam down their breakfasts in front of them. He picked up his fork, dug into his eggs, grateful for the diversion.

They didn't speak again until they were both finished eating. "I've got a picture of Mirandez in the car," Sawyer said. "It's a good shot, shows his face really well. When we get to each place, you can go into the office and show Mary's picture as well as Mirandez's."

"And if they haven't seen them?"

"We move on. But leave a card. Put my cell-phone number on the back." He reached out, tore off a corner of the paper place mat and wrote down the number. "Oh, by the way—" he tried for nonchalant "—when I was doing my internet searches, I got us a place to stay."

Liz was glad she had finished breakfast. Otherwise, she might have choked on her bagel. He made it sound so married-like. As if they were on vacation and he'd taken care of the reservations: *Hey, honey. We're going to the Days Inn.*

Problem was, they weren't married and this was no vacation.

"Where?" she managed to ask.

"Lake Weston. It's on the west side of The Dells. It's centrally located to the search. There weren't a lot of vacancies. I guess this is prime vacation season. Everybody's here with their kids, a last fling before school starts."

Please, Liz, let me come before school starts. Jenny had called her at work. It had been a crazy summer for Liz. One of the other partners had been gone from work for months. He'd had a heart attack, and Liz had worried that the rest of the staff would have one, too, if they kept up the pace. Everyone was working six days a week, twelve hours a day. But still, when Jenny had called, she'd agreed to let her come. Jenny, at sixteen, loved the city. Its diversity, its energy, its passion for music and art.

Liz had managed to squeeze out time to shop, to go out to eat and even for a concert at Grant Park. Four days after she'd arrived, Liz had kissed Jenny goodbye and sent her home on the train. Three months later, Jenny had been dead.

"What are you thinking about?" Sawyer asked. "You look like you're a million miles away."

Liz debated whether she should tell him. Even after three years, it was difficult to talk about Jenny and the hole that her death had made.

"My little sister used to visit me in the summers. She told me it was better than a weekend at Six Flags."

Sawyer laughed. "Not bad. You edged out an amusement park. How old was she?"

"Sixteen." She'd always be sixteen in Liz's mind.

"Wow. A lot younger than you. Second marriage for one of your parents?"

"No. Just a bonus baby. I was thirteen when she was born."

"She in college now?" Sawyer asked.

"No." Liz gripped the edge of the Formica-topped table. "She's… Jenny's dead."

She could see his chest rise and fall with a deep breath. "I'm sorry," he said. "What happened?"

"She killed herself. In the bathroom of my parents' house. She bled to death in the bathtub."

He didn't know what to say. "Did she leave a note?"

"No. I'm not sure if that makes it more or less horrible."

"Do you have any idea why?"

"She was eight weeks pregnant. According to her best friend, the father of the baby had taken back his ring just two days before."

Sawyer shook his head. "I'm sorry."

He was sorry, and she hadn't even told him the worst part. The part that had almost destroyed her until she'd found OCM.

"I guess I understand why it's so important for you to help Mary."

He had no idea. "Let's just say I don't want another girl to fall through the cracks." It was the same thing she'd told Jamison. There wasn't really a better way to sum it up.

"Right." Sawyer folded up his paper napkin. "You know," he said, his voice hesitant, "Mary might be hiding in one of those cracks. She and Mirandez. She had the chance to point the finger at him. But she wouldn't."

"I don't know why," Liz said. "Maybe she's afraid of him?"

"If she's smart, she is. If she's lying about him being the father, maybe she's trying to get him to marry her? Maybe he's a meal ticket?"

It was possible. She might see it as a better alternative than working her whole life. "When we find them, I'll ask her."

Sawyer slid out of the booth. "I hope like hell you get the chance."

Chapter Nine

At each place, it was the same. Liz showed Mary's picture first, then Mirandez's. Then she'd tell the story. She'd been working in Europe for the past year and had missed her sister's wedding. Having just returned, she hoped to surprise the bride and groom.

Everyone had looked at the pictures, shaken their heads, taken her card and agreed to call her if the couple checked in. Sawyer had concocted the story, hoping that people's inherent love of a good surprise would keep any clerk from telling Mary and Mirandez that someone had asked about them. And if someone did have loose lips, perhaps Mirandez wouldn't be too nervous if he thought only Liz had followed Mary.

They'd stopped at ten places before noon. "How's that bagel holding up?" Sawyer asked.

"We can stop if you're hungry," she said.

"You don't eat lunch?"

She waved a hand. "Sure I do."

"Uh-huh. What did you have for lunch yesterday?"

Liz chewed on her lip. "Chips and a can of pop."

"The day before?"

"Oh, for goodness' sake. I had…chips and a pop."

He leaned across the seat and inspected her. "You don't *look* like you've got scurvy," he said.

She let out a huff of air. "I take a multivitamin every day. Oh, damn." She smacked herself on the forehead. "I think I forgot my vitamins."

Sawyer shook his head. Ten minutes later, he turned the car into a gas station. Half the building was a convenience store. "I'll get us some lunch." He opened his door. "So, what kind of chips do you like?"

She smiled. "You're not going to try to reform me?"

"I'm smarter than that. Do you want to come in?"

"No. I need to call Jamison. I left a message on his machine early this morning. That was before I knew we would be traveling together."

"What's he going to think about that?"

"He'll be thrilled. He'll think I'm safer."

"You like Jamison, don't you?"

"He's a great boss. He trusts all of us. He knows we work hard, and he's really loyal in return. He treats us more like good friends than employees."

"He and Fraypish are friends, right?"

"For over twenty years. Jamison really respects Howard's legal judgment." Liz pulled out her cell phone and started dialing. "And he works at the right price, too."

Sawyer slammed the door shut. He didn't really care about what Jamison thought about Fraypish. He wanted to know what Liz thought about the man.

Why? He pushed open the door of the convenience store. Why did it matter? He and Liz had shared a couple kisses. Okay, a couple of really hot kisses that had made his knees weak, but still, it meant nothing. They would hopefully find Mary safe. She'd turn on Mirandez, and months from now, if he and Liz happened to run into each other at the grocery store, they'd nod politely and go their separate ways.

He grabbed an extralarge bag of potato chips. What did he care if she got fat and had bad skin?

He walked over to the counter and picked out two ham-and-cheese sandwiches. He stuck two cans of pop in the crook of his arm. A young woman at the cash register stopped filing her nails so that she could ring him up.

"Will that be all?" he asked.

"You don't happen to stock multivitamins?"

She shook her head.

"Got any fresh fruit?"

She pointed to the back of the store. "Bananas. Fifty cents apiece."

"I'll take six." When he got to the car, Liz was just snapping shut her cell phone. He dropped the bag into her lap. She reached inside and pulled out the chips.

"A big bag," she said, looking pleased. She pulled out the soda. "Thank you very much," she said. She handed him the bag, but he didn't take it.

"There's something else for you," he said.

She peered inside the plastic bag. A smile, so genuine that it reached her pretty green eyes, lit up her face. "You bought me bananas."

You'd have thought it was expensive perfume or something that sparkled. He opened his own soda and took a big drink. Liz Mayfield made a man thirsty. "I can probably find us a picnic table somewhere," he said.

She shook her head and ripped open her bag of chips. "Let's just keep going."

They stopped at another eleven places before Sawyer finally pulled into the parking lot of Lake Weston. It was after seven, they hadn't had dinner and Liz looked exhausted. She had dutifully gotten out at each stop, given her spiel and returned to the car, looking more and more discouraged.

"Look, here's our place. I think we should call it a night," Sawyer said. "Neither of us got much sleep last night. Let's get checked in, I'll find us some food, and you can crash."

"No."

It was the first word she'd said in two hours.

"What?"

"No. We have to keep going. Let's just grab a sandwich. We can probably hit three or four more places tonight."

"Liz, be reasonable. It'll be dark in another hour. We'll get a fresh start in the morning."

Liz picked the map up and spread it across her lap. "Look, there're two places just ten miles or so up the road. We're wasting time."

He was going to have to strap her down. But he didn't think he had the energy.

He shook his head. "We have to get checked in. They close the office at eight. We need to get a key to our cabin."

"Cabin?" she repeated.

"I got a *two*-bedroom cabin. It was all they had. I hope you don't mind sharing a bath."

"Oh. No, of course not. It sounds great. I mean, it sounds like it will suit our needs. Enough space, you know."

She was blushing. He didn't get it. Had she really thought he'd only book one room? Maybe in his wildest dreams. "You're going to have to register. It's in your name. If Mirandez happened to track you back here, I didn't want there to be any record of me. Only problem is, you'll have to put it on your credit card. The department will reimburse you."

"That's fine." She opened her car door. "I'll get us registered. And then we're going to the next two on the map. Their offices might close around eight, too. We'll need to hurry."

The woman was a workhorse. "Fine. We'll go to those two. But then we're done. And I'm picking the restaurant. Get prepared because there may not be chips on the menu."

IT WAS ALMOST NINE O'CLOCK when Sawyer ordered steaks for both of them. He'd found a supper club alongside the highway. The parking lot had been full, and he'd taken that as an endorsement.

The lighting was a little too dim, the music a little too loud. But the chairs were soft, and the cold beer he held in his hand tasted really good.

He thought Liz might fall asleep in her chair. Her eyes were half-closed. She looked pale, tired and defenseless. And it made him want to slay dragons for her.

If—or when, he corrected himself, trying to think a bit more positively—he found Mary, he would kick her butt for making this woman worry. For making the two of them traipse across the country in a hot car that didn't have a working air conditioner.

He wished he'd learned that little piece of information earlier. Like before he'd left his own car at the station and decided to take a road trip in the Toastermobile. He'd turned the knob just after breakfast this morning, when the temperature had already hit the low nineties, and hot air had blown in his face. He'd looked at Liz, and she'd shrugged her shoulders and looked the happiest she had all morning.

Looking back, it had been an omen of how the day would go. One big bust.

But through it all, Liz had moved forward without complaint. He'd driven, and she'd read the map, directing him from place to place. Her instructions had been clear and succinct. At each stop, she'd gotten out and flashed her pictures. She hadn't whined or complained. Hell, she could probably slay her own dragons. She was tough enough.

"We'll go north tomorrow," he said. He picked up a roll, buttered it and held it out to her. She shook her head no. He kept his hand extended and raised one eyebrow.

"I'm too tired to fight," she said, and she grabbed it out of his hand.

He waited until she took a dainty little bite before continuing, "Thank you. You don't eat enough."

"I ate a banana."

"So you did. Maybe that will be enough to keep you from falling down."

"If it's not, just prop me up and drive to the next place."

He laughed until he realized she was half-serious. "You're not going to give up, are you?"

"No. I can't. I won't."

"What happens if we don't find Mary?"

"We will. If we look hard enough, we will."

God, he hoped he didn't have to disappoint her. "Probably no need to start so early tomorrow. Maybe you could catch up on your rest."

"I'm not tired."

No, of course not. "Yeah, well, I am."

She blinked twice. "No, you're not." She shook her head at him. "You think by saying that you're tired that I'll implicitly understand that it's okay if I'm tired."

Why did she have to be a psychologist? Why couldn't she have been an accountant or an engineer?

"Did it work?" he asked.

"No. I'm fine. Don't worry about me."

"Okay. But could you at least drink your water? Just being in the car today was enough to dehydrate a person."

"Where did you get your medical degree?"

He didn't take offense. She'd smiled at him. The first one of those he'd seen in a couple of hours.

"Off the street of hard knocks. It's a fast-track program. You do your internship at a homeless shelter and your residency in the emergency room at Melliertz Hospital. They don't have metal screeners there for nothing."

"I'll bet you've seen a lot of violence, huh?"

She leaned her head back against the chair. The flickering

light from the cheesy candle on the table danced across the long lines of her graceful neck. She was a beautiful woman.

"I'll bet you've *heard* about a lot of violence," he replied. "I wonder what's worse. Seeing it or hearing about it."

A cloud of sadness drifted across her face. "I think seeing it," she said. "When you hear about it, you can't imagine how horrific it really is. Your mind just won't let you go there."

He had a bad feeling about this. He figured there was only one way to ask the question. "You're the one who found your sister?"

"Yes."

"What happened?" He braced himself, having investigated a few of those types of calls over the years. It was gruesome, ugly work.

"I tried her on the telephone but didn't get an answer. After a couple of hours, I drove out to my parents' house. They were gone for the weekend. She'd been dead for several hours when I found her."

He knew exactly what it had looked and smelled like. He hoped like hell that they didn't run into something similar with Mary. That Mirandez hadn't spirited the girl away just so he could kill her and dump her body up in the boondocks. "I'm sorry," he said, thinking it sounded a bit inadequate.

"I am, too," she said, her voice trembling just a little. "But thank you. It's still hard for me to talk about it. For some reason, you made it easier."

It wasn't a dragon but close. A sense of satisfaction, a sense of peace, filled him.

The waiter arrived at their table, his arms laden with heavy serving platters. He set two sizzling steaks down in front of them with sides of baked potato and fresh green beans.

Sawyer picked up his fork. "Bon appétit," he said. In return, she smiled and picked up her own utensils.

Twenty minutes later, the dishes had all been cleared away. Sawyer sipped a cup of steaming-hot coffee and watched Liz. She'd done better with dinner than she had with breakfast or lunch. She'd managed to eat at least half the steak and most of the potato. "Let's get out of here," he said when he saw her head jerk back. She was literally falling asleep sitting up. Within a couple of minutes, he'd settled the bill and walked her out of the restaurant. He kept his hand firmly planted underneath her elbow. It felt so right that he refused to think about all the reasons it was wrong.

A ten-minute drive got them back to the cabin. "Let me check it out," Sawyer ordered. He opened the compartment between the two seats and pulled out the gun that she'd seen him shove inside earlier. When he got out, he quickly walked to the cabin door, the barrel of the gun pointed upward. He twisted the doorknob, evidently found it locked, because she watched as he unlocked the heavy door with the real key the office had given them. Then in one fluid motion, he swung his body inside. Within seconds he was back, motioning for her to get out of the car. "Looks okay," he said. He waited for her to get inside, then pulled the door shut behind them, turned the lock and looked with some disgust at the flimsy chain before hooking it.

"What were you expecting?" she asked.

"I didn't know. A good cop just expects something."

Sawyer Montgomery was a very good cop. She stood somewhat awkwardly by the door. The cabin wasn't big but comfortable enough. The small sitting area had two chairs, a lamp table and a stone fireplace. A sign posted on the fireplace warned against actually using it. To the right, pushed up against the wall, was a double bed. To the left, two doors. She walked across the scarred but clean wooden floor and peeked into the first one.

Okay. Small but neat. The bath had a white tile floor and

pale blue walls. Above the shower stall was a small, high window with a faded yellow shade.

She moved on to the second door. Reaching inside the door, she found the light switch. A single bed with a dark green bedspread and small dresser almost filled the space. The switch controlled the floor lamp next to the bed. Its dim light barely reached the corners of the room.

"It's kind of a two-bedroom," Sawyer said, standing directly behind her.

"It's fine," Liz said. "Which bed do you want?" she asked.

Sawyer edged past her and in four steps walked across the small room. He lifted the inexpensive white plastic blinds and inspected the windows. They were double-paned and locked from the inside.

"I'll take the one in the other room."

The room with the door that had the no-real-protection lock. Yes, Sawyer Montgomery was a good cop. Even though she was more than a hundred miles from home, physically exhausted and in a cabin with a man she'd only known for a couple days, she felt safe.

"If you hear anything, and I mean anything," he continued, "you come get me. I'm a light sleeper."

Thinking about him sleeping just twenty feet away from her did funny things to her insides. "I'm sure it'll be fine," she said.

"Just don't hesitate," he said. "Why don't you use the bathroom first? I've got to make a couple calls and check messages." He pulled one of the chairs closer to the lamp table. Liz grabbed her bag by the door and took it into the bathroom with her.

Sawyer waited until he heard the shower running before dialing Robert's cell phone. When it rang four times, Sawyer got worried that Robert had some hot date. He breathed a sigh of relief when it was answered on the seventh ring.

"Why, it's Fisherman Sawyer," Robert said.

There were times when caller ID was inconvenient. "I figured the lieutenant would fill you in."

"Oh, yeah. Where are you?"

"Halfway between Madison and Hell."

Now it was Robert's turn to laugh. "I've been there. Lots of potholes and greasy-spoon restaurants. Is our little piranha biting?"

"No. I didn't really expect him to. I think I'm on a wild-goose chase."

"How's Liz?"

Wonderful. Gorgeous. Strong. "Fine. A little tired. It's been a long day."

"You planning on letting her get any sleep tonight?"

Sawyer could hear the tease in his partner's voice. It didn't matter. *Liz* and *bed* in the same sentence wasn't funny. "None of your business," he said.

"She's gotten to you, hasn't she?" Robert asked, his voice more serious than usual.

"She's…interesting."

"Six-legged spiders are interesting."

"Them, too. Look, I better go."

"Well, before you do, you might want to know this. Fluentes thinks Mirandez has a sister somewhere in Wisconsin."

"What? I don't think that's possible." Sawyer ran his hands through his hair. "I've never seen any mention of siblings. Not anywhere."

"Well, rumor has it he's got a much older sister. Hardly anybody has ever seen her, but she evidently came home for their old man's funeral a few years ago."

A sister? Was it possible that Mirandez had sought refuge with his family?

"Fluentes have a name?" Sawyer asked. "Was the sister married?"

"I told you everything I know."

"Okay. Thanks." Sawyer hung up just as Liz came out of the bathroom. She had on clean shorts and a T-shirt. She gave him a quick wave and slipped into the bedroom, closing the door behind her.

Liz closed the door and flipped the light switch off. In two steps, she reached the bed. She pulled the bedspread and thin blanket back all the way, leaving them at the end of the bed. She slipped under the cool sheet and hoped for sleep.

She rubbed her elbow. In the shower, she'd almost scrubbed it raw, in some silly hope that she could erase the feel of Sawyer's hand as he'd cupped her elbow and guided her across the parking lot. She could still feel his heat, his strength, his goodness.

It had been a long time since a man had taken care of her. The last serious relationship she'd had, she'd taken care of the man. Not in the physical sense certainly but in almost every other way.

She'd been a twenty-five-year-old virgin when she'd met Ted. Theodore Rainey. They'd dated for two years before he'd asked her to marry him. She'd accepted both his engagement ring and the invitation to sleep in his bed. A year later, after three wedding dates had come and gone, canceled due to Ted's work schedule, it had seemed as if they'd never manage to get married.

She knew she should have looked beyond his feeble excuses and tried to understand the real reason he avoided marriage. She supposed that was why psychologists never treated themselves. They had no objectivity. Had one of her patients described the relationship that Liz had with Ted, Liz would have advised her to get out of it.

In the end, they'd parted almost amicably. By that time, the sex was infrequent, generally hurried and rarely fulfilling. It had been a relief not to have to pretend anymore.

Liz pulled the sheet up another couple of inches, snuggling into the cool bed. As she drifted off to sleep, she thought about the lucky woman who shared Sawyer's bed, knowing in her heart that that woman wouldn't spend much time pretending.

Chapter Ten

Liz woke up when she heard the shower turn on. The walls of the cabin were perhaps not paper-thin but pretty darn close. She heard a thud and a soft curse. Sounded as if Sawyer was having a little trouble with the narrow stall.

She slipped out of bed, walked over to the window and peeked through the slats of the blinds. Looked like a pretty day. Bright sunshine with just a few puffy clouds. Maybe it would be a few degrees cooler than the day before. It had been a real scorcher. She'd known her air-conditioning didn't work, but in some juvenile way, it had been her way of one-upping Sawyer. He'd been so high-handed about coming with her that she figured she owed him one.

But then later, when he remained in the hot car while she at least got a few breaks going into the mostly air-conditioned offices, and he didn't complain even once, she began to feel bad. When he'd bought her bananas, she'd felt very stupid and very petty. She intended to start this day off better. She'd seen the sign in the office area last night that promoted the free continental breakfast for guests. She could go grab a couple cups of coffee, maybe some chocolate doughnuts if she got really lucky and be back before Sawyer got out of the shower.

She slipped her feet into sandals and grabbed her purse off the old dresser. When she opened the front door, she sucked in a deep breath, cherishing the still-cool early-morning air. It was probably not much past seven. When she got to the office, she had to wait a few minutes while a young family, a man, woman and three small children, worked their way past the rolls and bagels, assorted juices and blessed coffee.

No chocolate doughnuts but there was a close second— pecan rolls. She put two on a plate and then grabbed a bagel and cream cheese for good measure. Sawyer ate a lot. She poured two cups of coffee and balanced them in one hand, grateful for the summer she'd spent waiting tables. When she got to the door, the young man who'd gotten his family settled around the one lone table got up and opened it for her.

Liz strolled across the parking lot, loving the smell of the hot coffee. Unable to resist, she stopped, took a small sip from one of the cups, burned her tongue just a bit and swallowed with gusto. Little topped that first taste of coffee in the morning.

When she got outside the cabin door, she carefully set both coffees and the plate of pastries down on the sidewalk. She used her key to open the door. Then she bent down, picked up her cache and pushed the door open the rest of the way with her foot. She went inside and turned to shut the door. And then she almost dropped her precious brew.

Sawyer, wearing nothing but a pair of unsnapped jeans, had a gun pointed at her chest.

"What the hell do you think you're doing?" he asked.

What was *she* doing? "Are you going to shoot me?"

"Don't ever do that again," he instructed, ignoring her question.

"Do what?" She threw his words back at him. Darn, he had some nerve. He'd scared ten years off her, and he acted as if *he'd* been wronged. Before she dropped them, she put the coffees and the pastry plate on the table.

He closed the gap between them, never taking his dark

brown eyes off her face. He carefully placed his gun next to the plate. "Well, for starters," he said, his words clipped short, his accent more pronounced, "don't ever leave without telling me where you're going."

He acted as if she'd been gone for three days. "Sawyer, you're being ridiculous. I walked across the parking lot."

He grabbed both of her arms. "Listen to me. You don't open a door, you don't answer a phone, you don't—"

She tried to pull away, but his hold was firm. "I'm not your prisoner. You're not responsible for me."

He was close enough that she could see the muscle in his jaw jerk. "I am. Make no mistake about that. You do what I tell you to do when I tell you to do it. This is police business, and I'm in charge."

"I thought you might appreciate coffee. If I'd known that I might get shot for it, I wouldn't have bothered."

He stood close enough that she could smell him. The clean, edgy scent of an angry man. His bare chest loomed close enough that all she had to do was reach out and she would be touching his naked skin. She let her eyes drift down across his chest, following the line of hair as it tapered down into the open V of his unbuttoned jeans.

Oh, my.

She flicked her eyes up. His breath was shallow, drawn through just slightly open lips. His eyes seemed even darker.

And then he closed the distance between them and pulled her body up next to his, fitting her curves into his strength. He pushed his hips against hers, confirming what her eyes had discovered.

He was hard.

"This is crazy," she said. "We can't—"

"Just shut up," he murmured, and then he bent his head and kissed her. As wild as his eyes had been, she expected the kiss to be hard, brutal. But it wasn't. His lips were warm and soft, and he tasted like mint. She opened her mouth, and he angled his head, bringing them closer until she no longer knew where he stopped and she began. He rocked against her, and she thought she might split apart because the pleasure was so intense.

She moved her hands across his broad back, then lower, dipping her fingertips just inside the waistband of his jeans. She lightly scraped her nails across his bare, hot skin, and when he groaned, she felt the power of being a woman. It soared through her, heating her.

He moved his own hands, pushing them up inside her loose shirt. When all he encountered was bare skin, his big body literally shuddered. She pushed her hands deeper into his jeans, under the cotton material of his briefs, cupping each bare cheek. He pulled his mouth away from hers. "You're driving me crazy."

That made her braver, made her feel even more powerful. She found his lips again and kissed him hard. And she arched against his body, greedy with her need to touch him everywhere. "I want you to—"

The shrill ring of a cell phone cut her off. Sawyer pulled away from her and reached across the table to check his phone.

"It's mine," Liz managed. "It's in my purse."

She grabbed the still-ringing phone. Remembering his orders that she couldn't answer the phone without his permission, she looked at him. The phone rang two more times before he nodded. Liz hurriedly pushed a button. "Hello," she said.

"Liz, you were supposed to call me yesterday."

Howard Fraypish. She'd forgotten all about him. "I'm sorry, Howard. I had a few things to take care of."

She covered the mouthpiece with her hand and whispered to Sawyer, "I'll be just a minute. It's Howard."

Sawyer raised an eyebrow.

"We're working on a placement."

"Sure. Whatever." He walked across the room. She watched him pull a T-shirt out of his bag. He pulled it on in one smooth motion.

"…and I need to make sure that Melissa hasn't changed her mind. The Partridges don't want to be disappointed."

She'd totally missed the first part when she'd been ogling Sawyer's bare chest. "No, Howard. I spoke with her just a couple days ago. She's definitely giving the baby up for adoption. I don't think she's going to change her mind. She should deliver by the end of next week. And then two weeks after that, she leaves for college."

"Call me the minute she delivers."

"I will, but don't worry. She knows you're handling the legal work. I told you that I'd told her to call you directly if she can't reach me."

"Oh, yeah."

He sounded so distracted. "Is something wrong, Howard?"

"What could be wrong? I'm just busy. Really busy. I've got to go. Goodbye, Liz."

Liz snapped her phone shut. Sawyer stood next to the table, drinking one of the cups of coffee.

"You want the bagel?" he asked.

So, he wanted to pretend that the past ten minutes hadn't happened. That they hadn't argued, that they hadn't practically swallowed each other up. No, she wouldn't let him do it. Even if it meant that she had to admit that she'd come close to begging him to take her to bed.

"What's going on here, Sawyer?"

He stared at her for a long minute. "When I got out of the shower and I couldn't find you, I got worried. It was less than a week ago that somebody made a threat to your life.

Now, I know you think that it was just some kid but maybe not. Even if it was, we're on this crazy chase after Mirandez. I know you don't understand how dangerous he is. But if you're right that he and Mary are here and he finds out that you're looking for him, there's no telling what he might do. The man has no conscience. He kills people like the rest of us kill bugs."

Well, okay. "I'm sorry. I should have said something before I went for coffee."

He shrugged his shoulders. "Just forget it."

Forget that he'd kissed her? Was it that easy for him? "We got a little carried away here," she reminded him.

He nodded. "You're right. I'm attracted to you, Liz. But to act upon it would be absolutely wrong on my part. Whether you like it or not, I am responsible for this operation. And that includes you."

"I'm a big girl, Sawyer. I take responsibility for my own actions."

"And I take responsibility for mine."

He didn't sound too happy about it. "Sawyer, I don't understand why we can't—"

"Because I can't lose focus. My job is to find Mirandez. And to arrest him, with solid enough evidence that the guys in suits have no trouble getting a conviction."

"I'm trying to help you."

"I appreciate that. But what happens when Mary is part of that evidence? What happens if I have to arrest her, too? I can't let you and how you feel about Mary keep me from doing my job."

"I wouldn't ask you to do that," she said, not understanding why he couldn't see that. She'd never put him in that position.

"You wouldn't have to," he said, his voice soft.

IF POSSIBLE, LIZ THOUGHT the temperature had shot even higher than the day before. By ten o'clock, after just a couple hours in the car, they both looked a little wilted. They'd already been to four smaller campgrounds. One hadn't even had an office, so they'd had to be content with just driving through the camping area, looking at the various campsites. At the other three, the response had been virtually the same.

"Nope. They don't look familiar. But then again, we get a lot of people passing through. It would be pretty hard to remember everybody. Sure, you can check back. We're here from sunup to sundown most days."

Good old-fashioned Wisconsin charm. Liz wondered why she felt compelled to wring the next person's neck. Between the heat outside, the worry about Mary and the sexual tension radiating off Sawyer, she thought murder looked like a fairly good alternative.

He hadn't touched her again. Hadn't really said more than ten words to her. But each time she got out of the car and walked into one of the campground offices or when she walked back, she knew, just knew, that he watched her every step of the way. And while it seemed a little crazy, she thought she saw a hunger in his eyes. But then she'd get in the car and he'd be all business, all silent business, and she decided she had a case of wishful thinking and wicked thoughts.

She wanted Sawyer. She wanted to kiss him. After all, the man had the kind of lips that you could kiss for about three straight weeks without coming up for air. And then she wanted him naked.

She'd only ever slept with one man. But now all she could think about was getting it on with a man she'd known for less than a week.

It made her feel disloyal to Mary. Mary had to be the priority. And Liz knew what happened when priorities got mixed up. She couldn't bear for that to happen again. Mary deserved more. Liz respected Sawyer's ability to stay on task. She felt slimy that her focus had slipped momentarily. It had been jarred by the incredible warmth of his body pressed up against hers.

But thankfully, Sawyer had pulled back in time. He'd done the right thing. So, she needed to stop being mad at him.

"How much farther north?" she asked.

Sawyer risked a quick look at her. He'd told himself he might get through the day if he just didn't have to look at her. Didn't have to see her pretty green eyes with the dark eyelashes that had literally fluttered down across her cheeks when he'd kissed her. Or her pink lips, the bottom one fuller than the top, that literally trembled when he'd brushed his hands across her breast.

She'd gathered her long hair up, twisted it in that way that only women knew how to do and clipped it on top of her head. In deference to the heat, she had on a white sleeveless one-piece cotton dress, the kind of shapeless thing that seemed so popular these days.

Not that the dress did him much good. He could still remember what every one of her curves felt like. Hell, the woman even had curvy feet. She had white sandals on that showed off her red-painted toes and the delicate arch of her small foot.

He put his eyes back on the road. Safer by a long shot. "I thought we'd go about thirty miles. Then we'll need to cross over and come down the other side. If we don't get it all done today, we'll have to come back tomorrow."

"Then what?"

"Tomorrow we'll go west toward Route 39. That's one of the main roads. Lots of tourists head up this way. There're a couple large lodges and camping areas."

"This is kind of like looking for a needle in a haystack, isn't it? I guess I didn't fully appreciate how difficult it might be."

"You want to turn back? You could be in your apartment by midafternoon."

"No. Absolutely not. I'm not giving up."

He hadn't expected any different. Liz seemed almost driven to help Mary.

"You must care a great deal about Mary," he said.

"I know it may be hard to understand. She's not all that easy to be around. She's at the stage of her life where she's very inner focused. Her needs, her wants, her pleasures take priority."

"Sounds like most teenagers."

"True." Liz smiled and he felt better. Lord, she was sunshine, all wrapped up into a nice portable package.

"Thankfully, most people grow out of it," she said. "Some never do. Some can't ever love another more than they love themselves."

It was the opening he'd waited for. He just didn't know if he had the courage to ask the question. "Sounds like you're speaking from experience?"

"Years of study."

Right. *Be bold or go home.* That was what the bumper sticker said that Robert had tacked up on his computer a couple years ago. "How's Howard feel about your leaving town with me?"

"Howard?" She looked genuinely puzzled. "How would he know?"

"He doesn't know you're with me? I thought that's why he called."

"He called about an adoption that he's working on."

"I figured that was just a pretense. I thought Jamison probably called him, and Fraypish decided it might be in his best interests to remind you not to forget him. I'm surprised he didn't demand that you come home. I know if you were dating me, you wouldn't be spending the night in a cabin with another man."

"Dating you?"

Now she looked a little green. Clearly the idea didn't have a lot of appeal. "Never mind," Sawyer mumbled. He sucked at bold.

"I'm not dating Howard."

"You two looked pretty friendly at the dance."

"We were dancing. It's hard to look like strangers when you're doing that. Howard wanted to take a date. I didn't have one. So, when he asked, I said yes. We met there. He didn't even pick me up."

"Hard to believe that you wouldn't have a date." *Lame. Lame. He was so lame.*

She chuckled. "There are worse things."

"Agreed. Still, seems like you'd have them lined up outside your door." He kept his eyes on the road, too scared to look at her and say the words.

She didn't say anything for a minute. He wondered if he'd offended her. He risked a quick look over.

"I almost got married a few years back," she said so matter-of-factly that he almost missed it. A hundred pounds, like barbells falling from a rack, seemed to land square on his lungs, making it hard to breathe.

"Married?" He managed to spit the word out.

"Someone that I used to work with," she said. "He's a nice enough guy. We just didn't want the same things."

He could imagine what the guy wanted from her. What every man, including him, would want. "What did you want?"

"Marriage. I suppose children."

She should have that. "Sounds reasonable," he managed

to say. Not for him, but then again, they weren't talking about him.

"Have you ever been married, Sawyer?"

"No."

"Come close?"

"Once."

"What happened?"

He wanted to tell her. Wanted to tell her about the whole stupid mess. But then she'd know he was a failure. That he hadn't been able to protect his son. That he hadn't been smart enough or brave enough. And then he'd see the pity in her eyes, the same pity he'd seen in the nurses' eyes, the doctors' eyes, the hospital chaplain's eyes. He couldn't stand that.

"We were both young," he said. "It probably wouldn't have worked out."

"Do you ever see her? Run into her at class reunions?"

"She's dead."

"Oh. I'm sorry."

"Yeah. Me, too." He meant that. He'd hated her. Hated her for what she'd done to his son. But even so, when he'd heard that she'd died of a drug overdose, just a couple years later, he'd mourned her loss. Another tragedy caused by drugs. And by the people like Mirandez who bankrolled the drugs into the country and then built a distribution system, mostly of kids, that rivaled those found at blue-chip companies.

"You must have loved her very much," Liz said.

He knew what she was thinking. She thought he was still in love with his dead girlfriend. He really wished it was as simple as that. "Sure," he said, choosing to let her continue down that path.

"Don't you think she'd have wanted you to go on?"

No. She hadn't really cared if he'd lived or died. All she'd cared about was where she was going to get her next hit of heroin. "It doesn't matter. I know what's best for me."

"I guess we'd all like to think we do," she said.

"If we don't, who does?"

"Sometimes it's difficult for us to see ourselves as clearly as others can see us."

She was probably right. But he didn't want her looking too closely at him. Otherwise, she'd see that he had a hole, a big, dark hole, all the way down to his soul. "Is that Liz or Liz the psychologist talking?"

She looked a little offended. His goading tone had done what he'd intended. "I'm not sure I can separate Liz from Liz the psychologist. It's who I am."

For the hundredth time, he was glad he'd managed to put on the brakes at the cabin. She deserved better. Better than some guy who was so afraid of losing what he loved that he wouldn't love at all. He didn't need a damn psychologist to explain it to him. "Well, I'm hot and hungry. Let's keep going."

Chapter Eleven

The next morning, Liz woke up with the birds. They were singing outside her window, welcoming the new day with their high-pitched tune of joy. She turned over, reached out her hand and with one finger separated the blinds. The bright sun made her squint her eyes.

Darn it. She'd overslept. They should have been on the road two hours ago. Why hadn't Sawyer woken her up? Was it possible that he'd overslept, too? Swinging her legs over the edge of the bed, she grabbed a pair of shorts from her suitcase and slipped into them, stuck her feet into her sandals and left the room.

Sawyer's bed was empty. The bathroom door stood half-open, telling her that he'd left the cabin. She made a quick trip to the small room and felt immeasurably better after having brushed her teeth and washed her face. She walked out of the cabin, saw her car and wondered where Sawyer might be.

Maybe he'd gone to the office for coffee today. Oh, she wished she had a gun. She'd love to just shock the heck out of him. He'd open the door, and maybe she'd shoot at his feet just to give him a taste of his own medicine. And then she'd kiss the heck out of him again.

As delightful as that sounded, with nothing more threatening than a nail file, Liz tossed that option. Still, the coffee sounded good. She walked across the parking lot to the office and helped herself to a large black coffee. She passed on the sweets. A few more days of pecan rolls and she'd be one big roll.

On her way back, she discovered Sawyer almost hidden behind the cabin. He was doing push-ups. She didn't know how many he'd done before she started watching, but she saw him do thirty. Then he flipped over onto his back and started in on the sit-ups.

Her throat went dry. The man had on a pair of loose cotton shorts but no shirt. Sweat clung to his skin, and the sun glinted off his broad chest. With each sit-up, the muscles in his stomach rippled. A hundred sit-ups later, he collapsed on his back, his legs spread.

She felt a bit like a voyeur.

When Sawyer sprang up from the ground in one fluid motion, she realized she must have sighed.

"Liz?"

"Good morning," she said. "I'm sorry. I didn't mean to disturb you." *Or stop you.*

"No problem. I needed to stretch out a bit."

"We have spent a lot of time in a car lately."

"Yeah."

Okay. If he could pretend that she hadn't been staring at him, she could, too. "I'm sorry I slept so late."

"You must have needed it."

"Right. Do you want to shower first or should I?"

"You go ahead. I'm going to run for a little while. Just around the parking lot. The cabin won't be out of my sight."

She wondered if she stood on her tiptoes if she could catch a glimpse out the bathroom window. Sawyer was being vigilant in protecting her. She was just being greedy. "Well, I'll see you in a few minutes, then."

He nodded.

By the time she'd showered and dressed and Sawyer had done the same, she felt almost calm. Not at all like a woman who had almost thrown herself on a sweaty, half-naked man in a hotel parking lot.

They drove into town and grabbed a quick breakfast at one of the local eateries. Back in the car, Liz spread the map across her lap. She looked at it then folded it.

"What's wrong?"

"Nothing. I figure you know where you're going."

"I do. South. Then we'll work our way back up on the other side."

It sounded an awful lot like yesterday and the day before. A day of stops and starts and disappointments. Liz resisted the urge to pound her head against the window.

As if Sawyer had read her mind, he asked, "You up for this? We can always go back to the city."

Giving up wasn't an option. Being late had grave consequences. These were the lessons she'd learned. "No, let's go. The sooner we get started, the sooner we find them."

To his credit, Sawyer didn't even respond. He just started driving.

By the middle of the afternoon, Liz felt horrible. She'd worn her most lightweight shirt and shorts, but still the material clung to her skin. It had to be ninety-five degrees in the shade. They'd already stopped at seven campgrounds, two parks and four small motels that crowded the river.

"Next stop is Twin Oaks Lodge," Liz said, holding the map a couple inches off her legs. If she let it rest, it would probably stick to her.

"Yeah, that sounds right. I actually tried to get a cabin there, but they were full. Said they book up by the beginning of April for the whole summer."

"Not a bad position to be in," Liz said.

"It's not all gravy. They have long, cold winters up here," Sawyer reminded her.

"So? We have long, cold winters in Chicago."

With that, he turned the wheel, pulling the car into the large parking lot of Twin Oaks Lodge.

As usual, he pulled off to the side, out of view of the office windows. His cell phone buzzed just as Liz opened her door. He scanned the text message.

"Is it work? Is it Mary?" Liz asked.

"It's work, and I don't know if it's Mary."

"If it's Mary..."

"Then I'll tell you what I can. I just have to respect the privacy and the security of the person who's calling me. Even having you listen in on one side of the conversation could jeopardize that. I won't do that to this person."

"This person? I can't even know if it's a man or a woman?"

"No. Better for you and better for the person."

She nodded, apparently realizing he wasn't going to budge. There was a lot he probably should apologize for, but this wasn't one of the things.

"Fine. I'm going to go into this office, ask my questions and pretend to look at the brochures. If I—" she paused for effect "—would happen to get us both a cold drink, will you promise not to shoot me when I come back?"

It took him a minute to realize that she was kidding, that she was in some way trying to smooth things out between the two of them. He shrugged. "It depends. Make sure it's a diet."

"It's always the details that get a person into trouble, isn't it?" Liz opened the car door and walked across the parking lot. He watched her until she got inside.

He dialed Rafael Fluentes. The man had infiltrated the organization deeper than any other undercover cop had been able to. His calls rarely meant good news.

"It's me," Sawyer said when Fluentes answered.

"I hear you're working the river. How's the fishing?"

"Nobody is biting."

"Sucks everywhere. There's talk of a rumble," Fluentes said.

Damn. It was an unusual night when there wasn't an intergang slaying. Turf battles waged fierce and frequent. Fluentes wouldn't have called about that. This must be a big-time, bring-out-your-big-guns war call. "When?" Sawyer asked.

"Soon."

Sawyer regretted being two hundred miles away. Robert would keep him informed, but it wasn't the same as being there. "Hope the fish bite better there."

"Yeah, me, too. I don't care if the small ones slip through our nets, but I'd like to hook a few of the big ones. By the way, I've got a little info on the sister fish. Mirandez is the only child of Maria and Ramon Mirandez. However, Maria had a child ten years before she married Ramon. We're not even sure Ramon knew about the kid. In any event, Mirandez has a much older half sister out there somewhere."

Maybe that made some sense. She'd come to Mirandez's father's funeral. If Ramon Mirandez hadn't known about the child, Maria Mirandez would have finally been free to have both her children with her to comfort her in her time of need.

"What's her name?"

"Angel."

"Angel what?"

"I don't have a last name. Maria's maiden name was Jones."

"Jones?" Sawyer frowned at the phone.

"Yeah. Mirandez's grandfather was as white as you and me."

"Bet that's not well-known in the hood."

"Remind him of it when you arrest him."

"Angel Jones," Sawyer repeated. "Or Angel whatever. She's probably married by now. Where's she live?"

"Not sure. Maria Mirandez moved to one of those independent living centers a couple years ago. A real nice expensive one."

Sawyer couldn't help but interrupt. "Guess what's paying for that?"

"I know. If we didn't have the drug money, the economy would be in real danger. Anyway, we got one of her old neighbors to talk. She remembers Maria visiting a daughter who lived up north."

"Up north?" Sawyer repeated, even more discouraged than before. "That's it? That's all you got?"

"Maria evidently never drove at night. She could get from her daughter's place to home all in daylight. So, I'm guessing it's not Alaska."

"You're funny."

"Hey, I said it wasn't much. But at least we know there's a sister."

"Yeah, I know. I'm sorry. I'm just getting discouraged."

"Patience is the fisherman's friend. Try to remember that," Fluentes said before he hung up.

Sawyer wouldn't brag about catching Mirandez. But he would get some real pleasure out of seeing him stuffed and mounted on a plaque and hung on somebody's wall. Not his. He didn't want to look at the son of a bitch every day.

He'd been off the phone for three minutes before Liz came out of the office. She was carrying two big cups. She got in and handed him one. He opened the straw, poked it into the hole and took a big drink. "I like a woman who can follow directions."

"Just tell me what to do and I can do it."

She hadn't meant it to be provocative. He could tell that by the sudden blush on her face. But the double meaning hadn't been lost on either one of them. He rubbed his jaw, and his whole damn face felt hot. What a bunch of idiots they were.

"News about Mary?" she asked.

He shook his head. "Mirandez has a sister. A half sister on his mom's side."

"Where?"

"Nobody knows. They'll keep digging. I've got a name. Angel. Might be Angel Jones. Every place we go from now on, we ask for her, too. Maybe we'll get real lucky."

TWO STOPS LATER, luck struck. Liz flashed the picture, told her story and waited for the standard answer. When the young man behind the desk gave her a crooked smile and said that she'd be able to find Mr. and Mrs. Giovanni at cabin number seven, she almost wept.

"My sister's pregnant," Liz reminded the clerk, wanting so desperately to believe but knowing she couldn't be too optimistic.

"I know. I was surprised when her husband told me that the baby wasn't due for another couple of months. They wanted to rent a boat yesterday, and I was nervous as heck. Thought she'd probably pop that kid out when she hit the first wave. But they docked it back in last night, safe and sound. Although I don't think your brother-in-law knows much about fishing. Your sister had to show him how to bait a hook."

"Yes, she's a talent. Well, I can't wait to see them. My car is in the parking lot. If I just keep driving on this road, will it take me past cabin seven?"

"Sure thing. And if they aren't there, look for them out at the dock. That's where they seem to spend most of their day. She reads books, and he throws his line in the water and spends most of the day on his cell phone. That's not how I'd spend my vacation. But since your brother-in-law tips twice as good as anybody else, I ain't gonna judge."

Easy to tip when it was with dirty money.

"Well, I'm going to try to surprise them. You won't call them or anything, will you?"

"Couldn't if I wanted to. Cabins don't have phones."

"Well, okay, then. I guess I'll see you later."

"Sure. Just make sure your brother-in-law knows how helpful I was."

Liz managed a smile. She walked quickly back to the car, opened the door and slammed it shut before she turned to Sawyer. "They're here. Cabin seven. Mr. and Mrs. Giovanni."

Sawyer's eyes lit up, and his hands clenched the steering wheel. "Giovanni," he repeated.

"Dark hair. Dark eyes. Guess he figured people in Wisconsin wouldn't know the difference between Hispanic and Italian."

"Suppose. It's not like he could have picked Anderson or MacDougal."

"Now what?" They hadn't really ever talked about what would happen if they actually found them.

"We call for backup. Damn, I wish Robert were here."

"What do I do?"

"Stay here. Once I make the call, I'm going in for a closer look. I want to get the layout of the cabin."

"The clerk said they might be down at the lake. There's a path that runs behind all the cabins."

"Okay. Thanks."

"I don't want Mary getting hurt. You need to let me get her out of there."

"You're not going anywhere near Mirandez. He'll kill you. Without hesitation, without second thoughts."

"But—"

"But nothing," he said. "Don't fight me on this, Liz. I've

been straight with you all along. This is a police operation. You have to stay here. You have to stay safe."

She didn't intend to give up that easily. "You'd have never found her if it wasn't for me. Why can't I just go look around with you?"

"No. Mirandez is a crazy man. Look, Liz, I'll do my best to make sure Mary doesn't get hurt. You've got to trust me."

She would trust him with her life. If Capable Sawyer couldn't handle the trouble, the trouble had a destiny. But she couldn't walk away from Mary now. Not when she was this close.

"It's not a matter of my trusting you. Mary doesn't trust you. She doesn't like you. She's not going to listen to you. She'll do something stupid."

He seemed to consider that. "You'll do exactly what I tell you to do?"

"Yes."

"You won't call out to her or say anything until I give you the sign?"

"No."

Sawyer shook his head as if he couldn't believe what he was about to do. "All right. But don't make me regret this." He picked up his cell phone and dialed the number he'd evidently memorized. He gave the party on the other end a terse description of their location and the suspected location of Mirandez and Mary. He listened for a minute, responded with a terse yes and hung up.

"Who was that?"

"Miles Foltran. He's the sheriff of Juneau County. I made contact with him before we left Chicago so that he knew we were in the area. He'll have backup here in ten minutes."

"Now what?" Liz asked.

"I never should have listened to Fischer," Sawyer muttered.

"What?"

"Never mind. Just be quiet. I need to think."

Liz wasn't even offended. The man had more on his mind than being polite to her.

"Now we go take a look," he said, starting the car. He threw it into Drive and slowly eased out of his parking spot.

"Shouldn't we wait for backup?"

"We are. We're going to keep a nice safe distance away."

Sawyer drove down the narrow blacktop road, keeping his speed around twenty. They saw the first cabin and then ten or twelve more look-alikes. Sawyer continued past cabin seven, all the way until a stand of evergreens took over where the road stopped. He turned his car around, angling it so that he could get a view of the shorefront that ran behind the cabins.

"I don't believe this." Sawyer reached between the seats and pulled out his gun.

"What?" Liz craned her neck to see.

"Look between those two cabins, about a hundred yards out. That's Mirandez."

A short, thin man, wearing a baggy white T-shirt and blue jean shorts that fell below his knees, paced up and down the dock. He had a beer in one hand and a phone in the other.

"Keep talking," Sawyer muttered. "Keep talking, you bastard."

But almost as if that had been the kiss of death, Mirandez lowered his arm, snapped the cell phone closed, walked over to the lawn chair at the edge of the water, held out his hand and helped Mary pull herself out of the chair.

"Mary," Liz murmured, more scared now than ever that she'd actually seen Mary. "You've got to make sure she doesn't get hurt," Liz said. "Promise me."

"Damn," Sawyer said, totally focused on Mirandez. "They're leaving."

Liz stared at the young couple. Sure enough, Mary and

Mirandez were walking toward the black SUV that was parked almost on the sand. Mirandez evidently hadn't wanted his vehicle far from him.

Before she could even think about what to do, Sawyer threw the Toyota into Drive and pulled up to the end of the driveway. "Get out now. My side."

He opened the door, stepped out, grabbed her arm and literally pulled her from the car. He gave her a quick, hard kiss. "Run like hell for the trees."

"What are you doing?"

"What I ain't gonna do is let the bastard get away. He can't get around me. He's going to have to go through me. Now get the hell out of here."

Liz heard Mirandez's SUV engine kick to life, and she knew she had mere seconds. "Mary," she managed to choke out.

Sawyer spared her a quick glance. "I'll do the best I can."

She ran for all she was worth, reaching the trees just when she heard the horn. Mirandez leaned on it, obviously irritated that someone had the audacity to block his way. Liz could see him looking around, and she prayed that he wouldn't see either her in the trees or Sawyer, who had somehow managed to get behind a big oak tree about twenty yards to the left of the car.

When she heard the scrunch of car on car, she knew that Mirandez had gotten tired of waiting. With the bumper of his SUV, he pushed the rear of her car aside. In another fifteen seconds, he'd have enough space to squeeze out.

And almost as if in slow motion, Sawyer stepped out from the tree, fired twice, hitting the front wheel of the SUV. Mirandez reached his arm out of the open window, a deadly-looking gun extended from his hand, and fired at Sawyer, who had slipped once again behind the tree.

Liz wanted to scream but knew she couldn't distract Sawyer. The bullets bounced off the tree, the only protection Sawyer had against the horrible gun. Liz, almost without thought or intent, grabbed some rocks from the ground, and with all her strength, she flung them across the road, straight toward the cabin. One hit the door, another the roof and the rest scattered across the ground.

It was enough to momentarily distract Mirandez, and Sawyer didn't miss his opportunity. With Mirandez's attention on the cabin, Sawyer swung his big frame out from behind the tree.

The bullet caught Mirandez's forearm, and his gun fell to the ground.

Sawyer ran to the SUV, kicked the gun a hundred feet, all the while keeping his own gun leveled at Mirandez's head. "Police," Sawyer announced. "Turn off the engine."

Mirandez looked up, maybe to judge his chances, and Liz held her breath. Then, with a slight shake of his head, as if he couldn't believe what was happening, he turned off his vehicle.

"Mary, get out of the car," Sawyer instructed, his voice steady.

For just the briefest of seconds, Mary didn't move. Then she almost tumbled out in her haste.

Liz met her halfway. She reached for her and held her as close as the pregnancy allowed. She thanked God. They'd found her in time. This time she hadn't been too late.

Mirandez screamed and yelled obscenities at Sawyer. But when Sawyer took a step toward Mary, Mirandez changed tunes.

"Get the hell away from my baby," the drug dealer yelled. "You don't have any right. I'll kill you. I swear to the Holy Mother that you're a dead man."

His baby. Liz pulled away from Mary, wiping a gentle hand across the girl's teary face. What the heck was going on?

"Oh, Liz," Mary cried, "I was so scared. I didn't think I'd ever see you again. I—"

Just then, four squad cars rounded the corner. Six officers piled out, guns drawn.

"I'm a police officer," Sawyer called out. "The man in the SUV is Dantel Mirandez. He's wanted on suspicion of murder."

The tall one in the front of the pack held his hand up in the air, motioning those behind him to stop. "Detective, your voice sounds about right. But given that I've only talked to you on the phone, put your gun down now and show us some ID."

Sawyer nodded. "That's fine. Come a little bit closer. If he moves, shoot him. He dropped his gun. It's to my right, twenty-five feet out."

Sawyer laid his own gun on the ground and watched while the officers secured Mirandez's gun. He unclipped the badge on his shirt pocket that he'd hastily attached right before he'd pushed Liz from the car and run for cover himself. He tossed it at the man who'd spoken.

The man glanced at it for a moment, and then a big grin spread across his face. "Welcome to Wisconsin, Detective Montgomery. Looks like you've had quite a day."

Sawyer thought he might have the same silly-ass grin on his own face. "Watch him," he warned again before he picked up his gun and put it back in the car. Then he strode over to Liz and Mary.

"You both all right?" he asked.

"We're fine," Liz answered.

Sawyer took a long look at Mary. She looked tired and pale, and she was holding on to Liz so tightly that he was surprised Liz could still breathe. "What's the story here, Mary?"

"He's a monster," Mary answered, her voice brimming with tears.

"Did he hurt you?" Sawyer asked. "The baby?" Suddenly he knew killing Mirandez wouldn't be enough. He'd have to torture him first.

Mary shook her head and took a couple of loud sniffs. "Dantel has a sister who lives around here. She's a nurse. They were going to cut me up. And then take my baby."

"What?" Liz asked.

"But they had to wait. His sister said I had to be at least thirty-six weeks so that the baby would be big enough."

"But aren't you almost thirty-eight weeks, honey?" Liz brushed her hand gently over Mary's hair.

"Yeah. But he didn't know that. He was gonna keep me up here until his sister thought I was ready."

"It's not his baby, is it?" Sawyer asked. Liz had been right. Suddenly it was all starting to make some sense. "But he thought it was."

"Dantel treated me like a queen, bought me anything I wanted, took me anywhere I wanted to go. I couldn't tell him I was already six weeks pregnant before we ever slept together."

More lies. When would the damn lies stop? Sawyer pushed the disgust back. "He wants the baby?"

"His mother is dying. She wants a grandchild before she dies. His sister can't have any kids."

Sawyer wanted to make some sick joke about Mirandez being a mama's boy. But he couldn't. Dying mothers weren't funny. "How'd you find out what he had planned?"

"I didn't know at first. When we left Chicago, he said that he just wanted to get away and relax for a few days. I didn't want to go but you…you can't turn Dantel down. He doesn't like it."

Sawyer bet not. "Then what?"

"I thought we were going fishing. But he didn't have a

clue what he was doing. I started getting scared. There isn't even a phone in the room."

"What happened?"

"We went to his sister's house. At first she was really nice, talking to me about the baby and everything. But then I had to pee so I went upstairs to the bathroom. When I came down, I heard her telling Dantel that it would be a couple weeks before she could take the baby. That she didn't want to take a chance on the lungs."

The devil seed had taken root and sprouted in the Mirandez family. "Then what?" Sawyer asked.

"I pretended that I didn't hear them. I ate dinner with that horrible woman and pretended that nothing was wrong. I thought I might have a chance to get away. Dantel had been on the phone all the time. Another gang issued a challenge. There's going to be a big fight soon."

"Where?" Sawyer asked. "Did you hear him say where and when?"

"Yes. Maplewood Park. On Sunday night."

"Good girl," Sawyer said. "That information is going to be very helpful."

"Dantel hated that he wasn't in Chicago to control things. He went crazy on the phone one night, talking to somebody. I thought it might be my chance. But he saw me. I told him I stepped outside for some air, but I knew he didn't believe me. Since then, he's been watching me like a hawk." Her lower lip trembled, and a fresh set of tears slid down her face.

The girl had a lot of guts. "You did good," Sawyer told her. "You saved yourself and your baby. You should be proud."

When Liz threw him a grateful glance, Sawyer felt his heart, his stone-cold heart, heat up just a bit.

He was about to do something stupid like thank her when Sheriff Foltran interrupted him. "We've read him his rights, Detective. He needs medical attention. We'll see that he gets that at the local emergency room, and then we'll get him booked. My friend Bob owns this place, and I don't think he'll appreciate us hanging around until all his other guests show up."

Sawyer nodded at the man. "Right. Put him in one of your cars. I'll ride with you." He turned back to Liz and Mary. "I'm going to have to deal with this. He crossed state lines, so it's a bit more complicated to get him back into our jurisdiction. And then I need to arrange secure transport back to Chicago."

"How long will that take?" Liz asked.

"Probably a day or so. You two can go back now. Take the car. I think it will still run."

"It's over?" Mary asked.

"This part is over. I still need your testimony."

Mary nodded. "I want the bastard to pay. He was going to let that woman cut my baby out."

"You'll testify about the murder you saw?"

Mary didn't say anything for a full minute. She just stared at the ground. Then she looked at Liz. "Dantel said he'd kill me," she said, her voice very soft. "He said he'd kill you, too. He sent you that letter just to scare you. And he shot up your office just so we'd both know he was serious and that he could get to us anytime he wanted. He had the bomb put there, too. I don't know how but he did it. I'm so sorry."

"It's okay," Liz assured her. "He'll be in jail."

God willing, Sawyer thought. God and a smart jury. His gang would still be on the prowl. Sawyer wondered if Liz had any idea the risk Mary was taking. He should tell her.

"He beat that man and killed him," Mary said. "He was laughing while he did it. The guy was screaming and crying, and there was blood everywhere."

Hell, maybe he ought to do everybody a favor and manage to drop Mirandez in the Wisconsin River. With a fifty-pound sack of cement around his neck.

But he wouldn't. Even given the number of times he'd seen the system fail the community it served, Sawyer still believed in it. Believed that if he did his job right, the next guy would do the same, and so on. It was what separated them from the animals, both the four-legged and the two-legged like Mirandez.

Right now what he wanted most in the world was to take Liz into his arms. But he knew that couldn't happen. Even with Mirandez in custody, it wouldn't be fair to Liz to pursue a relationship. He didn't intend to offer marriage. He couldn't offer children. He needed to make a clean break of it now.

"I'm going to be pretty busy for a few days. He'll need to be processed."

Liz nodded.

"I need your written statement," Sawyer said to Mary.

"Now?"

"That would be best." He pulled the ever-present notebook out of his shirt pocket.

"Don't I have to sign a form or something?"

"You write it, date it and sign it. I've accepted statements written on crumpled-up paper towels. It doesn't matter what it looks like. What matters is what it says."

Mary assessed him for a long moment. "You know, you're not so bad for a cop."

Didn't rank up there with Liz looking at him as if he walked on water but it still made him feel real fine. "You're not so bad yourself. What are you two going to do when you get back to town?"

Mary was back to her shrugging.

Liz saw it, too. "Mary, I want you to stay with me. For at least a couple of days."

He didn't miss the pure relief that crossed Mary's face.

It reminded him of how much of a kid she really was. That didn't stop him from wishing that Liz hadn't made the offer. Mary attracted trouble. He didn't want Liz getting caught in the cross fire. He wouldn't be there to protect her.

"Your car should drive fine even though Mirandez did dent it up a little. I'm going to call Robert and ask him to meet you at your apartment. Just to make sure it's still secure."

"What?" Liz looked at him as if he'd lost his mind.

"I think we have a good chance that the judge will deny Mirandez bail. He's clearly a flight risk. We'll keep the lid on the fact that Mary's going to put him in the hot seat. Given that he still thinks Mary's pregnant with his baby, she's probably safe for now. You, too. But I don't want to take any chances. I'd feel better if Robert meets you there."

"Oh."

He knew immediately that if it were just her, she'd argue until she turned blue. But she wouldn't take a risk with Mary.

"You remember him, right?"

She nodded. "It's just a bit embarrassing."

"What?"

"The last time I saw Robert, I wasn't exactly dressed for success."

Sawyer remembered exactly how she'd been dressed. Or mostly undressed. He'd bet his last dime Robert did, too. "He won't even mention it." Sawyer would make damn sure of that.

Chapter Twelve

Liz was an hour from home when her cell phone rang. She answered it, keeping one hand on the wheel. "Hello."

"Everything okay?"

She'd left Sawyer more than two hours ago. Capable Sawyer clearly didn't like having things out of his immediate control and he probably figured he was due an update. "We're fine. No trouble."

"Good," he said.

The relief in his voice made her insides do funny little jumps. *Slow down, girl. He's a cop. With a misguided sense of responsibility.*

"I called Jamison and told him everything," Liz said. "Now that Dantel Mirandez is in police custody, he wants to reopen OCM, especially since we know Mirandez sent that letter to me. Do you have any concerns about that?"

Sawyer didn't answer right away. When he did, he didn't sound too happy. "I guess not," he said. "There's always some risk. But I don't think we can expect the man to keep his business closed forever."

"He'll be glad to hear that."

"I suppose you're planning on going back right away?"

"Of course. Why wouldn't I?"

He sighed. "By the way, I talked to Robert. Pull into the alley behind your building. He'll meet you there."

"Okay."

"If you don't see him right away, don't get out of the car. Just keep driving until you get to the closest police station. And call me."

"I'm sure everything will be fine."

"I know. It just doesn't hurt to have a plan B."

She imagined Capable Sawyer always had a plan B. "Mary has slept most of the way."

"That's good. By the way, I read her statement again. She did a good job. Lots of detail that will be helpful. Just remember, when she wakes up, remind her not to tell anyone that Mirandez isn't the father. That's the best protection she has right now."

"What happens when she delivers within a couple weeks and it's obvious the baby is full-term? What happens if Dantel tries to claim that he's the father?"

He didn't answer right away. When he did, he surprised her. "If Mary's telling the truth, a simple blood test will rule out Mirandez's claim. Of course, then her life won't be worth the paper that the test is printed on. When Mirandez finds out that she's going to testify against him, she's going to be in real trouble."

"What is she going to do?"

"She's going to have to get out of town, Liz."

"Are you crazy?"

"No. Don't say anything to her yet. I don't want her freaking out."

Liz gave Mary a quick glance. The girl snored, her head at a strange angle against the headrest.

"Well, I'm freaking out. She hasn't signed adoption paperwork yet. What if she decides to keep her baby? She can't just go off on her own with a newborn. She's going to need help."

"That can be arranged."

Liz realized with a sinking heart that he'd had time to

think it through. He'd known from the moment Mary confessed that this was how it had to end. Liz stepped on the gas a bit harder, wishing it was his head. "You should have told her. Before she confessed that she'd been there. You should have told her that her life would never be the same again."

"We need her. She's the one who can put Mirandez away. I never pretended anything—"

"But leaving town?" Liz interrupted. "That's huge. It means…it means I'll never see her again."

There, she'd said it. She didn't want to lose Mary.

For a minute, she thought he'd hung up. There was absolutely no noise on the other end of the phone. When he did speak, he sounded a bit strange. "Liz, I'm sorry. I probably should have said something. I couldn't. I just couldn't give Mary a reason to not do the right thing. A man died that night. Mirandez killed him, and he needs to pay for that. I know this is tough. But Mary would have drifted out of your life sooner or later. This way you'll know she's safe."

She absolutely hated that he made sense.

She wanted to hang on to her anger, to somehow let it soothe the pain of loss. But really the person to be angry at was Dantel Mirandez. It wasn't Sawyer's fault. "So, this is real-life witness-protection stuff?"

"Yeah. It doesn't just happen on the television shows."

"She's not going to take this well."

"Don't tell her yet. I just wanted you to have a chance to hear it first. When I get back to town, we'll tell her together."

She let up on the gas, and her stomach started doing those funny little jumps again. "Thank you, Sawyer." It sounded awfully inadequate, but she couldn't yet verbalize her feelings. They were too fresh, too unexpected, too much.

"It'll be okay, Liz. I promise. Just trust me on this one."

"I've always trusted you, Sawyer." *Even before I loved you.*

She jerked the wheel when the right-side tires swerved off the highway.

She felt hot and cold and sort of dizzy. "Traffic's picking up," she said. "I've got to go."

"Okay. Be careful. Please."

Careful? It was a little late for that. She'd fallen in love with Sawyer Montgomery.

Forty-five minutes later, she pulled into the alley and found her regular parking space. She'd barely turned the car off when someone tapped on her window. Even though she'd been expecting Detective Hanson, she still jumped several feet.

He smiled at her, but when a blue car pulled into the alley and headed toward them, his smile and easy demeanor vanished. "Get as close to the other door as you can. Lie down on the seat," he ordered.

Liz did as she was told, grateful that Mary still slept, slumped down in the seat. She saw that Detective Hanson had left the car door open and moved behind it. He had his gun out.

Liz held her breath and waited for the shots. All she heard was the engine of a car badly in need of a tune-up. It sounded as if it never even slowed down as it went past.

"It's okay." Detective Montgomery stood up. "Two old ladies. Both with blue hair."

Liz laughed. "Not part of Mirandez's gang?"

"I doubt it." He looked at Mary. "She sleep all the way here?"

"Yes. I don't think she's had much sleep the past couple of days."

"Let's get her inside. Street is pretty quiet. I've been here for about fifteen minutes and haven't seen anything unusual. I don't expect any trouble."

"Okay. Mary." Liz leaned over to tap the girl on her shoulder. "Wake up, sweetie. We're home."

Mary's eyes fluttered open. She looked at Liz first, then at Detective Hanson. "Who are you?" she asked.

"Detective Robert Hanson."

"Oh, yeah. I remember you. You were with Detective Montgomery. I guess you're the babysitter?"

Detective Hanson didn't look particularly offended. "I'll bet you can't wait for my microwave popcorn."

Mary snorted.

He ignored it. "Let's go," he said. "Stay close. Do what I tell you to do when I tell you to do it."

Liz knew the past several days had taken their toll on Mary when she didn't argue with Robert.

They got inside without incident. Robert checked each of the rooms. Mary stood in the kitchen, waiting for him to finish. When he did, she gave Liz a hug and went off to sleep in the spare bedroom. Liz gave her an extra blanket and shut the door behind her. Then she sank down onto her couch, loving the feel of the leather fabric. It was good to be home.

"Can I ask you something, Ms. Mayfield?" Detective Hanson asked. He stood near the kitchen counter. "How is Sawyer?"

"Stubborn. Bossy. Opinionated." She held up three fingers and ticked off the list.

Robert rubbed his hands together. "I knew it. I knew it from the first day I saw the two of you together. Like a match and dry kindling."

"Oh, but we're not…" She stopped, unwilling to share the private details of her relationship.

Robert laughed. A quiet chuckle. "Well, I hope you are soon. Otherwise, he's going to be a real pain in the ass to work with."

WHEN THE PHONE RANG late that night, Liz practically vaulted off the couch. The apartment had gotten very quiet after Robert had left and Mary had gone to bed. "Hello?"

"Ms. Mayfield?"

She didn't recognize the voice. "Yes."

"This is Geri Heffers from Melliertz Hospital. Melissa Stroud asked me to call you. She had a baby girl tonight."

Melissa. She wasn't due for another week. "Is everything okay?"

"Everything's fine. I understand you're Melissa's counselor and that you've been helping her arrange for an adoption. She's going to be released the day after tomorrow."

Liz knew what that meant. Melissa needed to sign the paperwork before she left the hospital. According to state law, she'd have seventy-two hours to change her mind. The baby would either stay in the hospital or be released to temporary care in a foster home until that time period elapsed. Only then could she go to the adoptive parents.

"I'll be there tomorrow. I'll come late afternoon." Liz promised the nurse and hung up. She dialed Howard's number from memory.

When he answered, she didn't waste words. "Howard, it's Liz. Melissa Stroud had her baby today at Melliertz. It's a girl. Healthy. She wants to sign papers tomorrow. Can you meet me there around four in the afternoon?"

"Excellent. The Thompsons really wanted a girl."

"The Thompsons? I thought Mike and Mindy Partridge were the adopting parents."

"No, they wanted to wait another couple months. Mike's traveling a lot these days."

"Have I met the Thompsons?"

"No. But they're great. I've done a full background check. You couldn't ask for better. I've talked to Jamison about them."

She didn't like it when she hadn't met the adopting parents. This had happened before. But when she'd mentioned something to Jamison, he'd told her not to worry about it and that he trusted Howard's judgment. "I'd like to see the background report," she said.

"Oh, sure," Howard said. "I'll bring it with me to the hospital."

Liz hung up the phone and went to check on Mary. She'd been right. It looked as though Mary would sleep through the night. The pregnancy, the worry, it had worn out the young girl.

Liz wished for just a bit of Mary's sleepiness. She turned on the television. Ten minutes and bits and pieces of three sitcoms later, she turned it off. She picked up a new magazine that had been waiting for her in the mailbox. Flipping page by page, she got halfway through it before she admitted defeat.

She couldn't stop thinking about Sawyer. What was he doing? Was he still interrogating Mirandez? Had he had dinner? Had he returned to the cabin? Had he gone to bed?

That was where her thoughts got her into trouble. She wondered if he slept in underwear. She didn't have to imagine whether he wore basic white. That little puzzle had been solved when he'd greeted her at the door with a gun and a pair of unsnapped jeans.

She'd been so darn busy looking at his zipper and the equipment underneath that she'd barely given the gun more than a passing thought. She hadn't worried that Sawyer would shoot her. Capable Sawyer didn't make mistakes like that.

Robert thought they were like a match and dry kindling. What he didn't know was that with a few choice words about responsibility and professionalism, Sawyer had effectively doused the flames, looking every bit like a man afraid of fire.

It made her wonder exactly what or who had burned Sawyer in the past. She'd wanted to ask Robert but knew it would be useless. Sawyer was his friend. He would guard his secrets.

Why hadn't Sawyer called? He'd said he *might* call, not that he *would* call. Why would he call? When she picked up a paper and pen, no longer content to silently argue with herself, and actually started to make a list of whys and why nots, she knew she'd gone around the bend.

Nothing would ever be the way it was before she'd met Sawyer. Heck, she'd never even be able to enjoy a big bowl of gumbo again. If she saw flowering vines climbing up a wrought-iron railing, she'd probably burst into tears. She'd never be able to go south of the Mason–Dixon line again.

Liz got up and walked over to the shelf where she kept her favorite CDs she'd purchased years ago. She pulled out two, walked into her kitchen, opened the cabinet door under her sink and dumped them into the trash.

She was done with New Orleans jazz.

She returned to the couch and reached an arm toward the light switch. She might not sleep, but at least she could brood in the dark.

LIZ ALMOST SLEPT through her appointment with Howard. She had gotten up once, around nine, and fixed breakfast for Mary. She steered Mary toward the television and then went back to bed. When she woke up the second time, she had a headache, a stuffy nose and a sore throat. As irrational as it was, she blamed Sawyer.

She showered and got dressed as fast as her ailing body allowed. She walked out to the kitchen and poured half a glass of orange juice. Her throat was so sore she knew she'd be lucky to get it down. "You doing okay, Mary?"

"I didn't know you had cable," Mary said, holding the remote control.

"Enjoy. I've got to go meet OCM's attorney. I'll be back by dinner. There are snacks in the cupboard. Help yourself."

Mary waved and flipped channels. Liz left the apartment. Halfway to the hospital, her stomach rumbled with hunger, but unless she could find somewhere that pureed eggs and bacon, she was out of luck.

Howard waited for her outside the front doors of the hospital. When he bent to kiss her cheek, she pulled back. "Don't get too close. I have a sore throat. I'm probably contagious."

When he jumped back a full foot, she couldn't help but compare him to Sawyer. Somehow she just knew that little short of the plague would keep Sawyer Montgomery from kissing his girl.

Oh, God, how she wanted to be that girl.

"You look horrible," Howard said.

"Thank you. I worked all night on this look."

He frowned at her. "If you didn't go gallivanting around the countryside, you'd probably stay a lot healthier."

Gallivanting? She'd saved an unborn baby from a crazy woman's knife. She couldn't have a lot of regrets. "Did you bring the background report?" she asked.

Howard put a hand over his mouth. "Oh, no. I completely forgot. Trust me, it's fine. They're great people."

"I'm not comfortable with this," Liz said.

"Come on. We're both here. You don't feel well. You surely don't want to stick around while I run all the way across town to get them from my office. You won't want to come back later. You'll probably be sleeping. So, let's just get this over with."

Unfortunately, everything he'd said was true. "Okay. But fax them to me tomorrow. Please don't forget. I need the information for my files."

After a quick stop at the hospital gift shop to pick up a box of candy, they checked in at the nurses' desk on the Maternity floor. They got the room number and walked down the long hallway. When they got there, they saw Melissa sitting up in her bed, watching a game show.

"Hi, Melissa," Liz spoke softly from the doorway, not wanting to scare the young woman. "How are you?"

"Hi, Liz. I'm okay, I guess."

Liz smiled at her client. Melissa Stroud had graduated from high school just three months earlier. She'd been the valedictorian of her class. Her gown had been big enough that the visitors, all the parents and aunts and uncles and grandparents proudly coming to see their offspring, probably hadn't realized that she was six months pregnant.

They'd have all been shocked that a smart girl like that could have gotten herself in trouble.

The father of the baby had been the salutatorian. First and second in their class.

Two smart kids having dumb sex.

"I've brought Howard Fraypish with me. You've talked to him on the phone."

"Okay."

Liz wasn't worried that the girl didn't show more emotion. Generally, that was how most of the girls got through the adoption process. They simply shut off their feelings.

"How's the baby?" Liz asked.

"Good. The nurses said she was real pretty."

Liz thought she caught just the hint of pride in the girl's voice. "You haven't seen her?"

"No. They said I could. Even after I told them I was giving her away. But I couldn't. I just couldn't." And suddenly, a tear slipped out of Melissa's eye, running down the smooth surface of her eighteen-year-old face.

She brushed it away with the back of her hand. "It's stupid to cry. I'm giving her away. That's what I want. That's what I planned on."

Liz felt her own tears threaten to fall. She blinked her eyes furiously. No matter how right the decision was, it was always painful. "You're a very brave girl, Melissa."

The girl shook her head. "I'm never going to sleep with another boy again as long as I live."

Liz smiled and patted the young girl's arm. "Someday you will meet a fine man. He'll make your heart race and your palms sweat." Just like Sawyer did to her. "The two of you will get married, and you'll have beautiful, brilliant children. Your heart will heal. Trust me."

Melissa sniffed. "It's hard to think about things like that. I hope she understands why I had to do this. I hope she realizes that it wasn't because I didn't love her."

"She'll understand," Liz assured the young girl, whose circumstances had forced her to become mature fast. "After all, she has a very smart mother. She'll understand all kinds of things."

Melissa smiled. "Well, let's get it over with."

Howard pulled up a chair. He opened his briefcase and pulled out a stack of papers. In a matter of minutes, Melissa had officially given away her child.

"Do you want me to stay?" Liz asked.

"I think I'd rather be alone. But thank you. I don't think I could have gotten through this without you."

Liz knew from previous experience that Melissa wasn't through it yet. She'd spend many hours sorting through the myriad of feelings, traveling down the dozens of paths her mind would wander around and through until she came to terms with her decision.

Liz hugged the girl. "I'll call you tomorrow."

Liz took the time to stop at the grocery store on the way home. She was anxious to get back to Mary, especially after seeing Melissa, and she was still feeling as if she'd gotten run over by a bus, but her cupboards were pretty bare. She needed to stock up if she intended to have a houseguest. She knew that Mary should have milk and fruit and vegetables.

Thinking about that reminded her of Sawyer buying her bananas, and she walked through most of the grocery store with tears in her eyes. Lord, she was an emotional mess.

She drove home and lugged her sacks inside. She set them on the floor next to the fridge.

"Mary," she called out. "I got Double Stuf Oreos."

No answer. The television was off. Liz listened for the shower. But nobody was running water in her apartment. In fact, she couldn't hear anything. Her apartment sounded empty. The truth hit her, almost making her stagger backward.

Mary was gone.

Chapter Thirteen

She ran from the kitchen to the spare bedroom. The bed was sort of made with the sheets and blankets pulled up, just not tucked in. A white sheet of notebook paper lay on the pillow.

It took every ounce of courage that Liz had to close the ten-foot gap. The message was short and sweet.

Liz, thanks for everything. You and that cop saved my life. By the way, he's not such a bad guy. I've talked to an old friend. She's going to let me share her place. I'll call you soon. Love, Mary.

Liz wanted to rip somebody's head off. Either that or sit down and cry for about a week. Or something in between those two extremes. She felt as if she was on a seesaw. She'd been high in the air, and the other person had just jumped off, causing her to hit the ground with a thud. Every bone in her body ached with the pain of betrayal, of abandonment.

She wanted to damn Mary to hell and back.

Why couldn't the girl have stayed put? What possessed her to leave? Why couldn't she just accept Liz's help?

Liz didn't have any answers. All she knew was that she wouldn't be able to rest until she was sure Mary and the baby were safe. She got herself off the floor, walked over to the phone and dialed Sawyer's cell phone. She'd given the number out so many times in Wisconsin that she knew it by heart.

He answered on the third ring. "Montgomery." His voice sounded so good, so solid.

"Sawyer?" she said. "It's Liz."

"What's wrong?" he asked immediately.

She laughed. She couldn't help it. So much for trying to hide anything from Capable Sawyer. "Mary's gone. She left a note."

There was a long silence on the other end of the phone. She realized that Sawyer wasn't surprised. It made her angry with herself that she hadn't seen it coming, as well.

"You're not surprised, are you?" she asked. "That's why you made her write down her statement. You knew she wouldn't be around to do it later."

Another pause, although this one was shorter than the last. "I didn't know," he said. "Not for sure. I had an idea she might run."

"I didn't see it." It broke her heart to admit it. How could she keep her girls safe if she didn't anticipate, if she didn't plan ahead?

"Liz," Sawyer said, "don't beat yourself up. She's a fickle kid."

A kid living in an adult world with adult dangers. "I've got to find her. I've got to know she's okay."

"No! That's crazy talk. You aren't going after her again. You know what happened the last time."

Sawyer's tone no longer held sympathy, but now a warning. A couple weeks ago she'd have taken offense. Now she could hear the caring behind his harsh tone.

"I'll be careful," she said. "I won't do anything foolish."

"You're not listening. You won't do anything. It's over. She's gone. Let her go."

"I can't do that." She knew he didn't understand. Knew that he couldn't. She needed to help him. "Sawyer, I told you that my sister, Jenny, died. What I didn't tell you was that I had the chance to save her."

"What?"

"Two days before she killed herself, Jenny left a message on my machine. 'Call me,' it said. I tried. No one answered. I wasn't worried. She'd left messages like that before. I got home from work the next night, and there was another message. 'Please call me,' it said." Her voice cracked, and she swallowed hard, knowing she needed to get through this.

"Liz, sweetheart, it's okay. You can tell me later."

"No. I need to tell you now. I didn't call. My friend and I had tickets to the opera. I'd left work late. She was already waiting outside my apartment when I got home."

She heard him sigh. It made her want to reach through the phone and hug him.

"I tried first thing the next morning. Couldn't get an answer. I remembered that my parents were out of town for the weekend. So, I drove to the house. You know the rest."

"I'm sorry," he said. "It's not your fault. There's no way you could have known."

"Perhaps not. But what I learned is that people reach out for help in different ways. I don't know if Mary's reaching out. Maybe she's not. Maybe she's pulling away and I'm just scared to let go. But I can't take the chance."

There was a long silence from his end. "Promise me," he said finally. "Promise me that you won't do anything until I get there. I'll leave in fifteen minutes. I won't stop for gas, for dinner, for anything. I'll be at your apartment in three hours."

No doubt about it—Sawyer Montgomery defined good. "I'll wait," she promised.

"Thank you," he said, and then he hung up.

THREE HOURS and twenty-seven minutes later, Sawyer pulled his borrowed car up in front of Liz's apartment building. He owed Sheriff Foltran a case of cold beer. That was the price the older man had quoted.

After Sawyer had hung up with Liz, he'd called him, given him a brief update and asked where he might rent a car. The sheriff had quickly set him straight, telling him that wasn't how it was done in the country. Within fifteen minutes, Sawyer had been on the road in a 2004 Buick, courtesy of the sheriff's wife.

He knocked on Liz's door. "Liz, it's Sawyer."

And when she opened it and walked into his arms, it felt right. He held her close, his chin resting on her head, content to let the heat of her body warm his soul.

"Thanks for coming," she said.

Three simple words. But the way she said it, it didn't seem simple at all. It seemed huge, bigger than life itself. It filled his heart, his whole being.

He bent his head to kiss her.

She jerked back. "I had a really sore throat this morning. It's better, but you still might catch it."

He shook his head. "I don't care." He reached for her again.

She slipped into his arms. "I knew you wouldn't care," she said. "I just knew it." She lifted her lips and kissed him.

He felt as if he'd come home. He wanted to consume her, to take sustenance from her strength, her goodness, her essence.

When he slipped his tongue inside and swallowed her answering groan, he knew, beyond the shadow of a doubt, that life would never be the same.

He kissed her for a very long time then wrapped his arms around her slim body and held her close.

"I missed you," he said.

"I know," she said, her words muffled, her lips pressed against his chest.

"Are you okay?" he asked. He put his fingers under her chin and lifted her face up for inspection. She had her long hair pulled back in a rubber band, and she didn't have a speck of makeup on. She looked pure and sweet and so beautiful.

"I'm fine," she said. "Now that you're here, I'm fine."

His chest filled with something that threatened to overtake him, to humble him, to bring him to his knees. "What happened, sweetheart?"

She grabbed a sheet of notebook paper off the lamp table and handed it to him. He turned it over and read it. "Damn kid," he said.

He noticed Liz didn't bother to defend her. But he doubted that her resolve to find Mary had lessened.

"Any thoughts on where she might be?" he asked.

"I want to go back to the bookstore. On the way here, before she went to sleep, Mary talked about getting more books for the baby. I don't know if that woman will tell me anything, but I have to try."

"Okay. I'll take a ride down there. I'll let you know what I find."

"I'm going with you."

"That's not necessary. You stay here. You don't feel well."

She shook her head. "I need to do something. I can't stay here."

He knew better than to try to argue. She had such strength, such sense of purpose, such commitment to a goal. He respected that. It was one of the things he loved about her.

Loved her. It hit him like a bullet against a Kevlar-lined vest. Bruising him, shaking him, shocking him. No longer sure his legs would continue to hold him, he sat down on the couch, hard.

"Sawyer, are you okay? What's wrong?"

Everything. Nothing. He shook his head, trying to make sense of it. He didn't want to love her. He didn't want to love anybody. If you didn't love, then it didn't hurt when you lost.

He needed air. "Let's get out of here," he said, standing up in one jerky movement.

She cocked her head, clearly not understanding his quick turnaround. Hell, he didn't understand it, either. He didn't understand much anymore.

"Sawyer, you're scaring me," she said.

He scared himself. "Liz, let's go. We're wasting time here."

"Are you sure?" she asked.

Oh, yeah, he was sure. Sure he loved her. Just not sure what to do about it.

He nodded. "Let's go. I'd like to get out of that neighborhood before it gets too late."

Sawyer called Robert from the car. "Hey, partner, where are you?" he asked.

"I'm working," Robert said. "Where the hell are you?"

"I'm working, too. Look, I need you to help me with a little surveillance at the corner of Shefton and Terrance."

"Are you in town? I didn't think you were coming back until tomorrow."

Sawyer looked at Liz. He'd used the hands-free speakerphone because of heavy rush-hour traffic. "My plans changed."

"What's at Shefton and Terrance?" Robert asked.

"There's a porn store on the corner of Terrance."

"That desperate, huh?" Robert laughed at his own joke.

"Funny. Mind your manners," Sawyer said. "I've got a lady in the car."

"Hi, Robert," Liz interjected.

"Hi, Liz," Robert said. "Sawyer, you did say *porn store?*"

Sawyer shook his head. "We'll be there in ten minutes.

Meet us at the corner of King and Sparton—that's two blocks north of the target. I'll fill you in then."

"Can you give me a hint?" Robert asked.

"Sure. We're looking for Mary Thorton," Sawyer said. "She's AWOL. The porn store is one of her old haunts. I don't think it's a trap, but I don't want to take a chance."

Ten minutes later, Robert walked into the porn store while Sawyer and Liz waited in the car, a block away. He returned ten minutes later carrying a brown paper sack. They watched him get into the car. Within thirty seconds, Sawyer's phone rang.

"Store's empty," Robert said, "with the exception of a greasy-haired old guy in overalls behind the counter."

"No woman, about sixty with gray hair?" Sawyer asked.

"Not that I saw."

Sawyer looked at Liz. "Maybe Grandma Porn only works the day shift?"

"At night, she bakes cookies for her grandchildren," Liz replied.

"Anything is possible," Sawyer said. "When it comes to Mary, I'm beginning to expect the unexpected."

"Let's talk to the guy in the store. Maybe he knows something."

"Okay. Hey, Robert, we're going in."

"Take money. The guy will probably block the door if you try to leave without buying something."

Liz pulled a twenty out of her purse and stuffed it into her shirt pocket. "Thanks, Robert," she said. "By the way, what did you buy?"

Robert laughed. "None of your business. All you need to know is that I'll be right outside the back door."

Sawyer pulled his car up in front of the store. When he and Liz entered, the man never even looked up from watching the small television behind the counter. Liz could just make out the familiar sounds of CNN.

They walked around the store for a few minutes. Finally, the man looked up. "Can I help you find something?" he asked.

"You must be Herbert," Sawyer said.

Liz wanted to smack herself on the head. She'd completely forgotten that the woman had mentioned her man friend Herbert. But Sawyer hadn't. Once again, he amazed her.

"That's me," the man replied.

"We're friends of Mary Thorton's. She talks about how nice you and Marvis have been to her."

"She's a great girl."

"The best," Sawyer agreed. "In fact, she called this afternoon and left a message on our machine. She said she was back in town after being gone a couple of days."

Liz wondered how he did it. The lies just rolled off his tongue.

"She was in Wisconsin," said Herbert.

"That's what she said. Nice time of year to go north," Sawyer added. "Anyway, she must have been having a blonde moment because she told us to call her later, but she didn't leave a number."

"Let me think." The man rubbed his whiskered chin. "I don't have her number. But Randy's place is just a few blocks from here."

Randy? Liz desperately wanted to ask, but Sawyer was on a roll.

"Good enough," Sawyer said. "We bought a stroller for the baby. We might as well deliver it."

Herbert picked up a notepad and scribbled an address on it. He held it in his hands. "You folks need anything as long as you're here?" he asked.

Liz pulled the twenty from her pocket. She walked over

to the stack of boxed condoms. She picked out the brightest, most garish design. She handed Herbert the twenty. "Thanks for asking. These should last a couple days," she said.

She heard Sawyer make a choking sound behind her.

"Keep the change," she said. "We'll tell Mary hello from you."

"You two come back anytime." Herbert handed her the slip of paper.

The phone rang seconds after they got back to the car. "Montgomery," Sawyer answered, leaving the phone on speaker. Liz noted he still sounded a bit hoarse.

"Everything okay?" Robert asked.

"Yeah. We got an address. Follow us."

"No problem. By the way, what's in *your* bag, Liz?"

"None of your damn business," Sawyer said and hung up.

"That wasn't very nice," Liz scolded him.

"When this is over," Sawyer said, his voice barely audible, "when we don't have the shadow of Mary or Mirandez or anything else standing between us, we're going to have a long talk."

The heat from Sawyer's body filled the small car. He wanted her. He might deny it, fight it and condemn himself for it. But he wanted her. "Take it from one who knows," she said, "talk isn't always the answer."

She heard the sharp intake of his breath and knew that he'd gotten her point.

She picked up the sack, opened it and peered inside. "I'm glad I bought a big box," she said, happy to let him chew on that for a while.

ONCE AGAIN, ROBERT COVERED the rear of the building, in the event Mary tried to make a run for it. Liz and Sawyer waited for him to get into position before knocking on the apartment door that matched the address Herbert had given them. When Sawyer gave her a nod, Liz rapped on the door.

"Just a minute," a female voice called from within.

Not Mary's voice. Liz looked at Sawyer and knew that he'd had the same thought. When the door opened, Liz knew why the voice sounded familiar. She looked different, of course, without a couple pounds of makeup on, but Liz recognized her. It was the girl from the bar. The one who had given her the original lead on Mary.

She didn't say anything, just simply stared first at Liz and then at Sawyer.

Liz looked past her. Mary sat on the couch.

"Liz?" Mary maneuvered her pregnant body off the cushions. "How did you find me?"

Sawyer stepped into the apartment. His eyes swept the room. "Anybody else here?" he asked.

"No," both girls answered at the same time.

"Mind if I look around?" Sawyer asked.

"You are such a cop." Mary shook her head at him in disgust. "Look around, peek in the closets, look under the beds. I really don't know what Liz sees in you."

Liz felt the hot heat of embarrassment flow through her. Had the two of them been that obvious?

Sawyer looked as if he couldn't care less that she'd put two and two together and come up with four. "Where's Randy?"

The girl who had opened the door held up her hand. "That's me. With an *i*, not a *y*."

"That your real name?" Sawyer asked.

"Yeah. My dad wanted a boy. Hey, if he's lucky, he'll get a grandson." She rubbed her stomach and laughed at her own joke. "Of course, he'll never know. I haven't talked to him in two years."

"Her dad's a bigger jerk than mine," Mary interjected.

Liz dismissed the comment. Now wasn't the time to try to deal with it. "Are you all right, Mary?" Liz asked.

"I'm fine. I left you a note," she said.

"You did," Liz acknowledged. "I appreciate that. I was still worried. You hadn't said anything about leaving."

"I didn't have anywhere to go. Then I called Randi, and she said I could stay here."

Liz looked around the room. Not much furniture but clean. The biggest mess was on the couch, where Mary had been sitting. When she'd gotten up, the big bag of chips on her lap had spilled. An open carton of milk, propped against the cushions, tilted dangerously.

"I know what I'm doing, Liz. Getting mixed up with Dantel was stupid. I'm not going to make a mistake like that again. But I can't live with you. I need to take care of myself. I need to prove that I can do it."

Liz didn't answer; she couldn't. She walked over to the couch and moved the milk carton from its precarious position to the lamp table, all while trying to sort out her chaotic thoughts. Chips and milk. A contradiction. Just like Mary. Sweet, yet bitter. Young, yet mature beyond her years. Considerate, yet selfish. Independent, yet so dependent.

Liz knew she needed to take a step back. Hated it, but knew it all the same. Otherwise, she ran the risk that she'd alienate Mary and cause her to cut off ties completely. She looked across the room. Sawyer stood absolutely still, watching her. She wanted to run to him and beg him to help her, to tell her what to do. But she knew she had to make the decision. She had to live with the consequences, good or bad.

"OCM is reopening next week. Will you come see me?" she asked.

Mary nodded. "Sure."

Liz swallowed hard, pushing the tears back. She pointed to the chips. "Eat some vegetables, okay?"

"No problem. Randi fixes broccoli every day. She said that we're going to have smart babies because they're getting lots of folic acid."

"You're both going to have beautiful and smart babies," Liz said. She gave Mary a hug first, then Randi. "Take care," she said. "Call me if you need anything."

She walked out of the apartment, hoping she'd make it to the car before she made a complete fool out of herself. Sawyer didn't say a word, somehow knowing that she needed a few moments of silence to sort out her thoughts.

He picked up the phone and held it to his ear, choosing not to use the speaker. He dialed. "Mary's fine," Sawyer said. "Thanks for your help, Robert."

Sawyer paused, listening. "Yeah, she is," he said. Another pause. "I'm not sure. I'll see you tomorrow." Then he hung the phone up.

"What did Robert have to say?" Liz asked.

Sawyer looked very serious. "He said you were a hell of a woman, and he wondered what I was going to do about it."

"Oh." She knew what *she* wanted him to do about it.

"I'm proud of you," he said.

She hadn't done it for Sawyer. But it felt darn good to hear him say those words. She leaned over toward him and kissed him on the cheek. "Thank you. That means a lot to me."

Sawyer put the car in Drive and pulled away from the curb. Neither of them said a word until they were just blocks from Liz's apartment. "You're awfully quiet," Sawyer said. "Are you sure you're okay?"

"I'm fine," Liz lied, knowing that she wasn't a bit fine. She was needy and wanting, but it had nothing to do with Mary and everything to do with Sawyer. Did she have the guts to tell him? If not now, when? When it would be too late? She'd just have to take the chance.

"I want you to make love to me. Tonight. Now."

Sawyer gripped the steering wheel so tightly that his fingers were white. He didn't say a word.

"Don't tell me it would be a mistake," she said. "Don't tell me that it would be inappropriate. It's all I've been thinking about for days."

"Stop," he said. "We'll be at your apartment in five minutes. Don't say another word until we get there."

It took them eight minutes. During that time, Liz didn't spend time regretting acting on the impulse to tell him. She contemplated all the ways she might make love to him. By the time the car stopped, she was practically squirming in her seat.

Sawyer put the car into Park and with deliberate movements turned off the engine and pulled the keys from the ignition. When he turned toward her, her heart plummeted. Liz knew what he'd done in the eight minutes. He'd figured out a way to tell her no. She could see the answer on his face.

"A man would be half-crazy not to want to take you to—"

"Don't give me your speech," she interrupted, refusing to let him walk away. There was more than one way to get her point across. She leaned over the seat and kissed him on the lips. She ran her tongue across his bottom lip.

She heard the quick intake of breath, and she felt the absolute stillness of his body.

"You want me," she stated.

He didn't deny it. She felt her confidence soar.

"Liz," he said, looking miserable, "I'm sorry. It would be a mistake. I can't give you what you want."

"I think you can," she said, looking pointedly at his zipper, which did little to hide his state of readiness.

He blushed. In her lifetime, she'd never expected to see Sawyer Montgomery blush.

"I can't pretend not to want you," he said. "I can't pretend that I don't go to bed hard at night for wanting you."

He spoke softly, but his words had an icy edge to them. She felt the answering heat pummel through her body, landing right between her legs. "There's no need to pretend," she said.

"You want commitment. You want marriage. I'm not offering that. I can't."

The words seemed torn from his soul. She didn't want him to suffer. She wanted them to celebrate life.

"You didn't bring a ring?" she asked, her voice full of accusation.

"No. Listen, I'm not…"

"Sawyer, I'm kidding. It was a joke."

He held her at arm's length. "I don't understand," he said.

"That's what I wanted from Ted. That's not what I want from you."

He looked a bit shocked, then fury crossed his strong features. He chuckled a dry, humorless noise. "Now, that's sweet," he said. "I'm good enough to sleep with but—"

"Sawyer," she said, "I'm sorry. I said that poorly."

He didn't respond.

She needed him to understand. "You're only the second person that I've ever told about Jenny. I told Jamison when I applied for the job at OCM. I thought he deserved to know what had driven me to his little counseling center. I told you because I wanted to share with you the joy of Jenny's life and the despair of her death. I wanted you to understand that both of those experiences make me who I am today."

"I'm glad you told me," he said.

"I want you to hear the rest. Jenny was a bright spot. For sixteen sweet years, she lit up my life. Since her death, I've been mourning that the time wasn't longer. I should have been celebrating the light."

She put her head against his chest. "People pass in and out of your life. They leave you changed, forever different.

You helped me understand and accept that Mary, too, will pass in and out of my life. I can't control that."

"Damn kid." He said it without malice.

"She's very brave."

"She is," he admitted. "Damn brave kid."

She lifted her head from his chest and looked him squarely in the eyes. Now wasn't the time to duck her head, to hide her feelings. "You're going to pass in and out of my life. You've been honest about that from the beginning. I'm not asking for forever. I'm asking for now."

He looked very serious. "I don't deserve you," he said.

She saw the hunger, the pure need, and knew it matched her own. It gave her courage.

"Take me inside," she urged. "Make love to me."

"I cannot resist you," he said. And then without another word, he opened the door and the two of them tumbled out of the car. He walked so quickly to the building that she almost had to run to keep up. When they got to her door, he took the key. Once inside, he shut the door, flipped the bolt lock and kissed her. Long and hard until both of them struggled for breath.

He moved her so that her back was against the wall. He pressed up against her, his chest against hers, his hips grinding into hers. So strong, so big, so much. She pushed her hands up inside his shirt, running her fingers across his bare stomach. His skin burned, and she could feel the muscles underneath. She traced his ribs and, with the tips of her thumb and index fingers, gently pinched each flat nipple.

He groaned and arched his back.

It made her feel powerful, as if she could tempt him beyond thought. It made her feel in control. But when he pulled away suddenly and grasped the hem of her shirt, she knew how quickly control shifted. "I want to see you," he said. "All of you." He yanked her white T-shirt over her head and ran his fingers across the edging of her bra, then lower, just lightly grazing her nipples. And when they responded to his touch, he bent his head and sucked her, right through the sheer material.

"I've been dreaming of this," he whispered against her skin. "Of what you'd look like in lace. You're more beautiful than I could have ever imagined."

His words, his barely there voice, floated around her, assuring her. But then his mouth was back, first on one nipple, then the other, and she couldn't think at all. His mouth moved across her body, lavishing wet kisses on her warm skin. He nipped at her collarbone, sharp licks of his tongue against her neck, before returning his lips to her mouth to kiss her thoroughly.

He reached behind her, releasing the clasp on her bra. She shrugged out of it, never taking her mouth off his. And when he slipped his warm hands into her shorts and cupped her bottom, pulling her against him, she ground her hips into his.

He pulled her shorts and panties down in one quick jerk. They pooled around her feet. Only then did he tear his mouth away. He stepped back a foot and looked at her. He didn't say a word for a moment, just looked at her. Then he took his hand and ever so lightly, with just the very tips of his fingers, brushed her cheek, tucking a strand of hair behind her ear. He let his hand drift downward, across her breast, then down, lingering just moments on her stomach, stopping just at the apex of her thighs. "You're perfect," he said, his voice soft.

He made her feel beautiful. She moved her feet apart, spreading her legs, inviting him to touch her. But he lifted his hand, moving it to the back of her head, working his fingers into her hair, and gently pulled her mouth to his. He kissed her gently, barely touching her at first, stroking her lips with his tongue, nipping at her bottom lip. He angled his lips, thrust his tongue into her mouth and kissed her.

When her knees started to buckle, he swept her up into his arms. With sure and confident steps, he carried her to the bedroom. He lay her down on the bed and gently pulled both her arms above her head. Moving across her body, he nudged her thigh aside. She spread her legs and he kneeled between them.

"Oh, my God," he whispered, running his fingers across her naked body. She shivered, and he gave her a smug smile. Then he bent down, kissing first one breast then the other.

"I need you." She arched her back, pressing her nipple into his mouth. She would beg soon.

He sucked her, sending shivers from her breast all the way to her very core. When he pulled back, he moved his strong hands under each thigh, pulling her legs wide. He moved his mouth down her stomach, coming finally to the place where she needed him most. She forgot about being embarrassed, forgot about wanting to please him, forgot about being lady-like, and she simply enjoyed. She took and took from him, the pressure building inside of her until it burst out of control, the waves of pleasure slamming through her.

He held her. He stretched out next to her and pulled her close, his arms wrapped around her. With every ounce of strength she had left, she threw one bare leg over his.

Oh, my God. She'd come apart, and he still had every stitch of his clothes on. Sensing her distress, he held her just a bit tighter. "Relax, sweetheart. It'll be my turn soon."

"But that's not fair," she protested, her voice weak.

"You don't have any idea, do you, what it does to a man to have a woman do that for him? To know that he's brought her pleasure?"

She realized he sounded just a bit smug.

She let him enjoy it for just a moment, then she reached

up and slipped a hand underneath his T- shirt. When her fingers crossed his nipples, she rubbed the tiny nubs. Breath hissed out from between his lips. He had his eyes closed. She trailed her finger down his stomach, following the line of hair. She ran her fingers across his jeans, tracing the ridge of his erection. He arched his hips off the bed. "Oh, sweetheart. You make me feel like a sixteen-year-old again."

His confession gave her courage. She moved quickly, straddling his hips with her legs. She rubbed against him, and he reached up, stilling her. But she wouldn't be stopped. She pulled his T-shirt up. Then she moved down so that her knees touched his. She unsnapped his jeans and pulled his zipper down slowly. He literally groaned.

"I'm a dead man," he said. She laughed. Then with a sure hand on each side of his hips, she pulled his jeans and briefs down.

She made love to him. Her fingers, her lips, skimmed his body, teasing, caressing. When she wrapped her hand around him, his whole body jerked, coming inches off the bed.

"I want to be inside of you," he said.

"I want that, too," she answered.

With one swift movement, he gently flipped her onto her back. He positioned himself above her and gently pushed himself into her. He held himself back, allowing her body to stretch, to adjust to him.

"Oh," she said.

He kissed her face, soft, gentle brushes of his lips. "It's okay. Just a little bit more."

She forced herself to relax and to take him.

"Perfect," he said, his voice a mere whisper.

And then he started to move. Within minutes, she shattered once again. Barely before she could catch her breath, he pounded into her, faster and faster, until his whole body tensed, and with one last powerful thrust, he exploded inside her.

For long minutes, there was no sound at all in the room. Then, with a sigh, he lifted his weight off her. He kissed her—a long, gentle kiss. Then he carefully pulled away from her, then fell onto his back in a clumsy movement. He threw one bent arm over his forehead. "That almost killed me," he said.

It was hard to keep the smile off her face. Now who was feeling smug? she thought.

"I liked it," she said. "Can we do it again?"

He opened one eye and stared at her. "You liked it? You *liked* it?" he repeated. "People *like* apple pie and long walks on the beach."

"I like cherry pie and long walks in the woods. A lot. But trust me on this—I don't like either one of those things as much as I liked this."

"*This* almost gave me a heart attack."

"I know CPR," she said. She boldly wrapped her hand around him, winking at him when he immediately responded.

"Oh, baby." He flipped her onto her back and proceeded to make her own heart race not once but several times over.

Chapter Fourteen

Sawyer woke up happy and warm. Liz slept on her side, her naked body wedged up against him, her bare back against his chest. He had an arm wrapped around her, and her breast filled his hand.

He moved just a bit. She stretched in response. He let go of her breast, pulled his arm back and gathered her long hair in his hand and moved it out of the way. Then he gently kissed the back of her neck. "Good morning," he said.

"I'll give you a dollar if you make coffee," she said.

He laughed. "I'll give you five dollars if you make breakfast."

She rolled over and laid on her other side, facing him. "I'll give you my last twenty if you'll make love to me again." She winked at him.

"Your last twenty? What happens then?"

"I'm hoping you'll take pity on the poor. I could be your own personal charity."

He rolled onto his back and pulled her on top of him. "I've been known to be a very generous man in the past. Giving of my own personal assets."

"Donate away, baby," she said.

And he did.

And later—much later—when they finally stumbled into

the kitchen, it was closer to lunch than breakfast. "Be careful," she said.

He thought the warning probably saved him a broken leg. He'd surely have tripped over the piles of soup cans, cereal boxes, pots and pans, glasses, silverware and cleaning products scattered on the kitchen floor.

"I like to clean when I'm nervous," she said. "I had some time to kill yesterday between when Mary left and you arrived."

"Anything left *in* the cupboards?"

She shook her head. "Nope. I'm nothing if not thorough."

"Next time you get really nervous, come to my house. My cupboards haven't been cleaned since I moved in."

"Yuck. Sounds gross."

She started coffee and he started lunch. For the first time in seventeen years, he started to think about a future.

"I'm going to go take a shower," she said.

"Okay." Good. He needed time alone, time to sort out his thoughts.

He loved her. He loved her playfulness, her sense of humor, her dedication to her clients, her willingness to help others. He loved her body.

She had wanted commitment and marriage from another man. She didn't expect it from him. He was, in her words, just passing through. He flipped the grilled cheese with more force than necessary, sending it flying out of the pan. It landed on the counter. He picked it up, dusted it off and returned it to the skillet.

Just maybe, *he* wanted a little commitment.

He opened a can of tomato soup. By the time it was hot, Liz had not only returned to the kitchen but he also had a plan.

"If you don't have anything else to do today," he said

carefully, "I thought we might go to Navy Pier. You like Ferris wheels?"

"I love Ferris wheels. But I can't. I have to get my office organized at OCM. I'd brought a lot of my files here. I'll need them back at work when we reopen."

Okay. She wasn't saying no just to say no. She had a commitment to work. He knew how important her work was to her. That was one of the things that made this perfect.

"You really like your job, don't you?" he asked.

"I love my job. Just like you love yours."

Yeah, Sawyer thought as he poured himself a second cup of coffee. Liz didn't need all those things that he couldn't give. She didn't seem concerned about her biological clock like most of the women he'd met over the years. She'd mentioned wanting children, but that was before. Now she had her career. A job she loved. One that she was passionate about.

He wouldn't get in the way. He'd make sure she understood that he didn't intend to disrupt her work. That he valued her dedication. He'd also make sure she realized they weren't ships passing in the night. He'd convince her that she could have both a career and a relationship with a man.

She'd wanted marriage at one time. He'd give her time to adjust to the idea again, and then once she saw that it could work between the two of them, he'd pop the question.

But for now, he'd give her space. He got up from the table, intending to put the dishes in the dishwasher.

"We didn't use my condoms," she said.

She spoke so matter-of-factly, as if she might be discussing the weather or what to have for dinner. He felt the world tilt, causing all the good and beautiful things that had happened last night to slide together, combining into a dark and ugly mess. He held on to his dirty plate tightly, afraid that he might drop it.

He should tell her now. He should have told her before. But now, if she had questions or concerns, it was the right thing to do.

No. He hadn't had a chance to win her over, to convince her of his love.

"I just want you to know that I think the chances are pretty good that we're safe. But if I'm wrong and I am pregnant, I won't expect anything from you. I can handle it myself."

Tell her, you fool. Tell her. "You'll let me know?" he asked.

"Of course. I'd never hide something like that."

Coward. "No problem. I'm sure it will be fine. I'll call you later today."

"HE'S NOT GOING to call," Liz moaned, her head resting in her cupped hand. It was late afternoon, and she'd worked like a dog all day, trying to reestablish connections with all her clients.

"It's been five hours," she said, looking at the clock.

Jamison walked past her office. He poked his head in, looking around. "Who are you talking to?"

"Myself."

"Fascinating. By the way, Sawyer called."

"What?"

"You must have been on your phone. It rolled over to my line. I told him you'd call him back."

"Oh." She'd been waiting all day, and now that he'd finally called, she didn't know what she was going to say to him.

"Snap out of it, girl," Jamison said. "Just remember. Play a little hard to get. It'll make you more interesting."

"Really?"

"I read it in one of Renée's magazines."

She was about ready to try anything. She picked up the phone and dialed.

"Montgomery."

"Hi, Sawyer. It's Liz."

"Hi. Thanks for calling. Is this a bad time?"

"No, it's fine. Jamison and I were…we were just discussing a case."

"Everything okay with Mary?"

"Yes. Thanks for asking."

There was an awkward moment of silence. Could that be the only reason Sawyer had called? She felt the loss, the sense of disappointment spread through her body.

"I was wondering if you'd have time for a late dinner tonight. I know you're busy and all."

Play a little hard to get. Jamison's advice rang in her ears. Hell. It would be hard to pull that off when she threw herself at him later. "I'd love to."

"Great. I'll pick you up at seven."

Come naked. "I'll be ready." Liz hung up the phone.

When Mary walked by unexpectedly ten minutes later, Liz still stared at her blank computer screen, unable to get much past the fact that in just a few short hours, she'd have another opportunity to seduce the very serious Sawyer Montgomery.

"Hi, sweetie," she said when the young girl dropped into the chair in front of her desk. "How are you?"

"I'm starting to waddle."

"It always looked good on Donald and Daisy."

"I saw the doc this morning. He thinks the baby is already over seven pounds."

No wonder she beamed. "Good. Your due date is coming up fast."

"I know. I've been a real pain about this adoption thing.

I know you've been worried that time is going to run out. I've made up my mind."

"That's wonderful, Mary. I know it's been difficult. What do you want to do?"

"I'm giving her up for adoption."

"Her?"

"They did an ultrasound. The doc is ninety-nine percent sure the baby is a girl."

"And you're sure? About the adoption?" In her heart, she believed the decision was best for Mary and for the baby. Mary probably knew that, as well. Knowing it and acting upon it were two different things.

"Yes. I'm too young to raise a baby. I need to go back to school and get an education. I don't want to work in some stupid job my whole life. I'm going to go to college. Maybe that's selfish, but that's what I want."

"It's not selfish, Mary. You're young. You have hopes and dreams. College is one way to make those things a reality."

"You know what made me decide adoption was the right thing?"

"What?"

"I was thinking about all those things, and then I realized that I wanted my baby to have all the same things. But I'd never be able to give her that. That's what made me decide."

Mary wiped a tear off her face. Liz hoped she could be strong for both of them. "I'll contact our attorney. We'll get the paperwork done immediately."

"No."

"But, Mary, you just said—"

"You didn't let me finish. I'm giving her up for adoption under one condition. I want you to adopt her."

Liz felt the floor tip. "Mary. Sweetheart. I…I'm flattered. Really. But I can't possibly adopt your child."

"Why not? You already have your education and you

have a great job. You're home at night and on the weekends. You live in a safe apartment. You can give her everything she'll need."

She could. But that wasn't the point. "Mary," she said, not sure where to begin. "Any number of people have the means to provide for a child. That does not mean that they would be good parents."

"I know that. You couldn't grow up in my house and not realize that. But with you, it would be different. You would be such a great mom."

A mom. A single mother. A statistic. A concern.

But those were the black-and-white facts and figures. Liz knew better. While it wasn't a perfect solution, single mothers were quite capable of raising great, well-adjusted kids. But could she do it?

She hadn't thought about babies for herself. At least not since it had become abundantly clear that Ted never intended to marry her. While they'd been engaged, she often thought about the children she hoped to have. They'd talked about it. But when she'd finally stopped waiting for him, she'd stopped thinking about children, never considering pursuing motherhood on her own.

Why not? Why the heck not? Mary was right. She had a good job. Even if OCM wasn't around forever, she had the background and the credentials to land another job quickly. She had a nice savings account courtesy of her previous work. She was healthy and strong. She was—

"But the most important thing," Mary said, interrupting her thoughts, "is that you'll love her. And she'll love you."

Now Liz and Mary were both crying.

"Oh, Mary. Are you sure?"

"I'm sure. More sure about this than anything. Please say you'll do it."

It wasn't really much of a decision. How could she say no?

She loved Mary. By default, she loved the baby that Mary carried. She had a connection to this baby that would carry her through the difficult months to come. She could do this. She wanted to do this.

What would Sawyer think? Did it matter? She knew it did. They'd never even discussed children. There'd been no need to. She hoped he'd be happy for her, that he'd understand what a gift Mary had given her.

"I'd be honored, Mary. I will love her and care for her. When she grows up, I'll tell her about her biological mother and what a wonderful young woman she was."

Mary wrapped her arms around Liz. "Thank you. Now I know everything will be okay."

LIZ HAD A THREE-PAGE LIST by the time her hand cramped up, and she was forced to lay down her pen. So much to do and so little time. She had to get the spare bedroom decorated. She needed a crib, a car seat. Clothes. She needed to tell Jamison. He'd be worried about the appearance of things. After all, someone on the outside looking in would say it was unethical for a counselor to adopt the child of one of her clients. But that was the legal mumbo jumbo. On paper, it might look weird. In her heart, Liz knew it made perfect sense. She also knew that once Jamison got past his shock, he'd do everything he could to help her.

She didn't want to wait another minute to do it. She walked up the stairs to his office. He sat at his desk, calmly reviewing the budget numbers, not having any idea that she was about to upset his world. She almost felt sorry for him.

"I just talked to Mary Thorton. She's agreed to put her baby up for adoption."

"That's probably a good decision on her part."

"Yes. Here's the kicker, Jamison. She wants me to adopt the baby."

He pushed his chair back from the desk. "You told her no, I assume."

She shook her head, almost laughing when all color left his face. She felt so good about the decision that his doubts couldn't dispel her joy. "No. I said I would."

She gave Jamison a moment to recover before continuing, "I know it's highly irregular. I know others might question the decision. But you know me, Jamison. You know I wouldn't agree to this if it weren't the right thing for me and for the client. I can do this. I can adopt this baby and make a difference in the baby's life."

"But, Liz, you're a single woman. You know we always try to place the babies with two-parent families."

"I know. But we've made exceptions in the past. This is at the client's request. We always give special consideration to that."

He stared at her. Then he stood up, walked around his office twice, then sat down again. He didn't say a word. "You're sure?"

"Absolutely. I'm scared. I'm not going to try to lie about that. It's such a huge commitment. What if I'm no good at this?"

"You've been good at everything you've ever done."

Liz walked around the edge of the desk and placed her hand on Jamison's shoulder. "You know what drove me to OCM."

"Is that why you're doing this? Is this more of the same? More of having to make up for not being there?"

Liz didn't take offense. Jamison had always known her better than most. "No. Jenny's gone. I will forever miss her. I'm not doing this for her or because of her. I'm doing it for me. I pray that I'll be the kind of mother this sweet child deserves."

Jamison put his head in his hands. "We're going to need an ironclad release from Mary."

"She'll sign it," Liz said.

"I don't want her coming back in five years claiming that you coerced her into the decision. You don't want that."

She understood the legal issues. "You're right. That's why I'm here. I want you to handle the paperwork from here. I know you won't miss anything."

He looked up and let out a big sigh. "Okay. Let's call Howard. He's going to have to work his magic."

But Howard didn't answer. Jamison left a message on his machine. Liz got up from her chair, walked around the desk and kissed Jamison. "Thank you," she said. "Thank you for supporting me."

"What's your friend the cop going to say about this?"

She couldn't wait to tell Sawyer. Mary had barely been out the door, and Liz had been reaching for the telephone. She'd dialed the first five numbers before common sense prevailed. She couldn't just call him, chat about the weather for a couple of minutes and drop the bomb. *Hey, Sawyer. Great news. I'm adopting a baby.*

He might be worried that a baby would change their relationship. After all, she wouldn't be able to drop everything to go out to dinner. But babies did sleep. Maybe they could still work in sex and breakfast.

"I'm not sure what he'll say," she said. "I'll see him tonight."

Chapter Fifteen

Sawyer rang her doorbell at seven minutes before seven. She looked out the peephole. He had on a blue sport coat, tan slacks and a white shirt. He looked good enough to eat.

She opened the door. "I've missed you," she said.

"Really?"

"Oh, yeah." She reached out, caught his striped tie in her hand and hauled him into the apartment. She released the tie, cradling his face with both hands. Then she kissed him. Hard.

She squirmed, pressed and arched, her hands racing across his back. She yanked at his coat. He helped, never taking his lips off hers. She pulled his shirt out of his pants, then grabbed for his belt buckle. Unzipping him, she boldly stuck her hand down his pants, wrapping her hand around him.

He bit her lip and pushed her against the wall. "Damn," he said.

"I want you inside me."

He grabbed her bottom, whipping his head up when he found nothing but skin under her dress. He stepped back and shucked his pants. Then he picked her up, braced her back against the wall, wrapped her legs around his waist, and in less than a minute, when she started to climax, he followed her over the edge.

Sawyer, his chest heaving, having come so hard he thought

he might pass out, gently unwrapped Liz's legs from his waist. He held her steady when she swayed. He rested his forehead against the wall, not certain if he'd ever be able to move.

The mantel clock chimed. Seven delicate rings.

Liz looked up and kissed his chin. "Thanks for coming early," she said.

He chuckled, knowing he didn't have the strength to laugh. He lifted his head and stepped back. His sport coat lay near the door. His pants and underwear a mere foot away. He'd taken her with his shirt and tie still on.

"You okay?" he asked.

"Wonderful."

"You look happy," he said.

"I am. I had a great day. How was yours?"

"Okay. I've got news about Mirandez," he said. He tucked his shirt in and zipped his pants. "Let's sit on the couch."

"Tell me," she said.

"We got Mirandez back to Chicago today. He's taken up residence at Cook County Jail. There's a hearing tomorrow. The judge will deny bail. That's a given."

"That's great."

"Yeah. There's something else. We had to turn over Mary's statement to his attorney. We put it off as long as we could."

"What should I tell Mary?"

"Tell her that we've arranged for her to go to a safe place. There's a hospital nearby. We've also arranged for help for a few weeks after the baby's born."

Mary wouldn't need help. "That won't be necessary."

"Are you sure? It's not a problem."

"Mary's giving the baby up for adoption. She wants to go to school. If there's no college nearby, you're going to have to pick a new place."

He looked a little shocked. "Yeah, actually, there's a grea

school about twenty minutes away. When did she decide all this?"

"Just today." This wasn't how she'd planned to tell him. He'd surprised her. It shouldn't matter. Maybe it just made everything easier. "Oh, Sawyer. The most wonderful thing has happened. Mary asked me to adopt her baby."

If he'd looked shocked before, now he looked absolutely stunned. She could see the color drain out of his face.

"What did you say?"

"Yes. I said yes. I'm adopting the baby. We think it's a girl."

"Are you crazy?" He stood up and paced around the room. "Have you lost your mind?"

She'd expected surprise. The anger hadn't even been on her radar screen. "Sawyer, what's wrong? You're acting weird."

"How could you do this? You have your career. You love your job. You told me so."

"I do love my job. But this gift, this totally unexpected, wonderful gift, has been given to me. I want the baby. I want to love her and watch her grow. I want to make a difference in her life. I want her to make a difference in mine."

"No."

He said the word as if it had two syllables, as if it had been torn from his soul.

"Sawyer, for God's sake, tell me what's wrong."

"I love you," he said. Where his voice had been loud before, it was now quiet. She could barely hear him. "I've loved you for weeks."

It should have made her dance with joy. But the anguish in his voice stopped her happiness cold.

"I wanted to give you time to get used to the idea. I didn't want to push. I wanted you to get used to me."

"Sawyer, I didn't know. I—"

"Now," he said, interrupting her, "everything has changed. I can't be with you."

Her chest hurt. She clenched her hands together.

"I don't understand," she said.

"I had a son," he said. "He died. In my arms. His tiny heart just couldn't do it."

A son. Why hadn't he ever told her?

"His mother?" she asked.

"Terrie was a young drug addict. I didn't know it when I got her pregnant. It was painfully clear by the time she'd had the baby. My son paid for her sins. He paid for my sins."

"Your sins?"

"I didn't protect him. I failed."

It started to make sense, in some horrible kind of way. "That's the girl who died? Your baby's mother died?"

"The drugs killed her, too. Just took a few years."

Oh, the pain he'd suffered. Liz wanted to reach out to him, to hold him, but she knew she had to hear it all.

"We never got married. I only saw her once after our son died. But I still didn't want her to die. It was just one more damn useless death."

His relentless passion for tracking Mirandez suddenly made a lot more sense. "Sawyer, I'm so sorry that happened to you. It must have been horrible."

"You have no idea."

She let that one pass. She hadn't lost a child. But she had lost a sister. She knew the emptiness, the absolute gray that had filled her world for months. She wouldn't try to compare her loss to his. To do so would trivialize both. "It was a long time ago, Sawyer. You have to move on."

"I moved on. I made a decision that I'd never father another child. I had a vasectomy ten years ago."

Well! How could she have fallen in love with a man she didn't really even know?

That wasn't exactly true. She knew Sawyer Montgomery. She knew what she needed to know. He was a good man, a loving man, capable of sacrificing his own safety to help a young, pregnant teen. She didn't want to lose him. "Sawyer, you have to let go. Not of the person, but of the anger, the absolute rage that you've lost someone."

The look he gave her was filled with contempt. "I'm not some jerk paying a hundred bucks an hour so that I can lie on your couch and you can try to heal me."

"Sawyer, that's not what this is. This is Liz and Sawyer, having a conversation. Nothing more. Nothing less."

"I'm not angry," he said. "Who the hell would I be angry at? A dead woman?"

She knew better than that. Even as a kid, Capable Sawyer would have wanted to handle everything. But he hadn't been able to handle this. He still hadn't forgiven himself. He tried to find peace. With every scumbag of a drug dealer he put away, he tried to buy peace. Only, peace wasn't for sale. It had to be delivered. That only happened when a person gave up the hate, the absolute despair of being left behind.

"You're asking me to choose between this baby and you," she said. "That's not fair. I shouldn't have to choose."

He looked at her, and a tear slipped out of his very brown eyes. He didn't bother to wipe it away. "No, you shouldn't," he said. "I can't let another child into my life. I won't risk it."

Liz's heart, which had started to crumble away at the edges, suddenly broke right down the middle. The pain, as real as if the strong muscle really could just crack, sliced through her body.

With trembling legs, she walked over to the door and opened it. Not able to look at him again, she stared at the floor. "I'm sorry about your son. If I had known, I'd have done this differently."

"You're saying you wouldn't adopt the child?"

"No, I'm not saying that. But I wouldn't have just blurted it out. You should have told me. Everything now seems like such a lie."

He slammed his hand against the wall. "I never lied to you."

"You let me think you were in love with your dead girl-friend. I had no idea that there had even been a child. You lied by omission. For God's sake, Sawyer. You let me worry about an unplanned pregnancy."

He didn't respond. She didn't really expect him to. She suddenly felt very old, as if her bones might splinter. She forced herself to straighten up, to lift her head. "I don't want to see you again," she said. "Jamison can be your contact. Give him the details about the arrangements for Mary."

LIZ HAD BEEN IN BED for just a few minutes when the tele-phone rang. "Hello," she answered.

"Liz, it's Mary. My water just broke."

Liz sat up in bed, fear and excitement making her heart race. "Have you been in labor long? How far apart are your contractions?"

"Hey, you sound strange. What's wrong?"

Liz covered the phone and cleared her throat. She'd spent the better part of the past hour crying. Her eyes burned, she could barely swallow and her head felt as if she'd been kicked. "I've got a touch of a cold. Nothing to worry about. Now, what about the contractions?"

"I'm not having contractions. I don't think I'm even in labor."

"You're sure? No pain of any kind?"

"My back has ached all day," Mary said.

While Liz was no expert on childbirth, she had heard about back labor. She wanted Mary at a hospital. Now. "Honey, do you think you can take a cab to the hospital?"

"Yeah."

"Perfect. I'll meet you there. We should arrive about the same time. Just hang on. And breathe. Don't forget to breathe."

She'd arranged just that morning for her car to be picked up and the dents repaired. She grabbed the phone book out of the drawer, dialed the number for the cab company and waited impatiently while it rang three times. They said ten minutes and she was ready in eight. The ride to the hospital seemed to take forever. Yet, still, she beat Mary's cab by ten minutes. When it finally pulled up, she yanked open the back door. She helped Mary out and threw a twenty at the driver.

"How are you?" she asked, hoping she didn't sound as scared as she was.

"I don't want to have a baby," Mary said. "I'm not doing this."

Liz wrapped her arms around the girl, holding her close. "Don't worry. It'll be over in no time."

No time turned out to be twelve hours later. Twelve long, ugly hours filled with swearing, yelling, moaning, groaning and crying. But when Liz placed the beautiful baby girl in Mary's arms, the look on the girl's face told her that it had all been worth it.

"She's so pretty," Mary said, stroking the baby's head and face. "Isn't her mouth just perfect?"

Liz nodded. The baby was a healthy seven pounds and two ounces and just eighteen inches long. Almost plump. The doctor had delivered her and said, "Look at those cheeks." He hadn't been talking about her face.

"She's gorgeous," Liz said.

Mary stared at the baby. "I love her," she said, her voice filled with awe. "I just love her so much."

How could anyone not love something so perfect, so absolutely perfect in every way? Liz swallowed, almost afraid to ask the next question. She'd known she was taking a chance by letting Mary hold the baby. But Mary had been explicit. She wanted to see her child.

"Having second thoughts about giving her up for adoption?" Liz asked, wondering if she could slip back into the role of counselor after having embraced the role of mother.

"I'm not giving her up."

Liz nodded, afraid to speak.

"I'm giving her to you. That's different. I'm giving her to someone that I know will care for her and love her and give her all the things that I can't give her."

Liz didn't think her legs would continue to hold her. She sank down onto the edge of the bed. "Are you sure, Mary? Are you absolutely sure?"

"Yes. I've screwed up most of my life. I'm not screwing this up. She's my daughter. That will never change. But she's your daughter, too. She's going to call you Mom. And you're going to take her to her first day of kindergarten and make her Halloween costumes and make sure she has braces and gets into a good college. I know you'll do that. If you're half as good to her as you've been to me, she'll be a very happy girl."

Liz couldn't have stopped the tears if she'd tried. But she didn't. She let them fall, in celebration of mothers and daughters, in thanks of second chances, in hopes that Mary would someday have another daughter to love. In a different time, in a different place.

Mary held the baby out to Liz. "Here, take your daughter. She needs to start getting used to you. What are you going to name her?"

"I don't know. I hadn't thought about it."

"Would you call her Catherine? That was my mother's name."

Liz swallowed hard. "Catherine is a beautiful name. She fits it perfectly."

LIZ HELD CATHERINE for two hours before finally returning her to the nursery. She left the hospital, choosing to walk instead of catching a cab. She needed the fresh air. It had been a long stretch in a stuffy hospital.

She also needed to call Jamison. He had to get Mary's signature on the adoption agreement and get Catherine released to a temporary foster home for a couple of days. Liz hated that part. She wanted to bring her daughter home right away. But she knew the rules. She wasn't going to do anything that would jeopardize the legal standing of the adoption.

By the time Liz could pick up Catherine, she assumed Mary would be well on her way to her new home. Mary had accepted the news that she would be relocated under the witness-protection program with cautious optimism. Liz knew the young girl was scared but that she also welcomed the chance to have a new life.

At one point in the discussion, Mary had joked about calling Sawyer to thank him. Liz hadn't been able to even smile. The pain of losing Sawyer tasted too fresh, too bitter.

She would go on. She had Catherine. She had her work. Assuming Jamison would let her bring Catherine with her. That was just one more thing to talk to him about. She pulled her cell phone out of her purse. She'd called him shortly after she and Mary had arrived at the hospital last night. But then things had gotten a little hectic.

Jamison answered on the first ring. "Yes," he said.

"Jamison, it's Liz. It's over. She had a little girl. She's a beauty."

"Mom and baby okay?"

"Yes. Pretty tough delivery but Mary did great."

"Did she hold the baby?"

"Yes. And then she handed her to me and said that I better get to know my daughter."

For once, Jamison seemed speechless.

"Have you heard from Detective Montgomery?" Liz asked.

"Yes. He called late last night. I told him Mary was in labor. He said he would have some guards posted outside of Mary's room. Did you see them?"

She had. She'd appreciated them, but it had been just one more painful reminder of the man she'd loved and lost. He took care of things. He made things happen. He made it tough on the bad guys. "Yes, I did."

"I'm supposed to call him once I talk to you. They want to move Mary as soon as possible. He was going to have somebody talk to the doctor."

She knew it was for the best, but it still hurt to know that she would soon lose Mary from her life. "She can't be moved until she signs the adoption agreement. Or, at the very least, she needs to be moved somewhere we can get to her. You need to call and tell him that."

"Why can't you call him?"

She didn't bother to answer.

"What's going on here?" Jamison asked.

She didn't want to talk about it. Not yet. She'd managed not to think about Sawyer the entire time Mary had been in labor. She couldn't let her mind go there yet. She wasn't ready. "Jamison, I know I'm not making much sense. But you need to trust me."

"I don't understand."

"I'm not going to be seeing Sawyer again. I want something that he won't let himself have."

"It's still not all that clear," Jamison said.

"I don't understand it. Why should you?"

"You okay?"

Trust Jamison to get down to the nitty-gritty. "Yes. I'm fine. And next week, I'll be better. And in a year or two, I might even be good."

"Anything I can do?"

"Yes. Get that paperwork to Mary. I want to bring my daughter home."

Liz put her cell phone away. She walked another two blocks to the grocery store. There she filled her cart with bottles, formula, diapers and lotion. The next stop was a department store. She got some blankets, T-shirts and one-piece sleepers. She knew she'd need a hundred more things but she could always ask Carmen or Jamison to help her out.

Funny. When Mary had first asked her to adopt the baby, Liz had thought Sawyer would be around to help. Had looked forward to sharing the baby with him. That wouldn't happen. And she needed to stop hoping, stop praying that it might change. He was gone. She better start getting used to it.

When she got home, she dropped her purchases on the kitchen counter and went back to her bedroom, taking her clothes off on the way, leaving just her bra and panties on. She lay back on the bed, closed her eyes and assumed sleep would come. After all, she'd been up for thirty-some hours. But sleep, being a slippery fellow, danced just out of her grasp. She tossed and turned, her body too keyed up to get any real rest. After an hour, she got up.

She made herself a cup of tea and a grilled-cheese sandwich. She checked her voice mail. No calls. Not able to be patient, she dialed Jamison's number.

"Yes," he said.

"Have you been to see Mary? Did she sign?"

"You should be sleeping, Liz."

"I know. Well?"

"It's the strangest thing. I can't get in touch with Howard. He's not answering his cell phone. I've left four messages on his pager, and his assistant doesn't know where he is."

Howard Fraypish was never unreachable. He carried a backup cell phone just in case his primary one went dead. "Are you sure you have the right number?" She rattled it off.

"I know the number. I've left messages. I can't do anything until I get the paperwork from him."

If Mary hadn't gone into labor a week early, Liz would have had all the loose ends tied up. Now she needed Howard. "I'll go over to his office."

"He's not there."

"Maybe his assistant can find the documents on his PC. She'll print them off for me. I've known her for years."

On her way out of the apartment, she stopped to check her mailbox in the odd event that Howard had mailed the information to her. She opened the slot and pulled out an assortment of bills, a magazine and…a plain white envelope with her name scratched across it.

She slid her thumb under the flap and pulled out the single sheet.

Stay away from Mary Thorton and her baby. Otherwise, they die. You don't want that on your conscience.

Liz slammed her mailbox shut. Damn it. It was supposed to be over. Mirandez was in jail. She waited for the fear to hit her, but all she could feel was bone-deep anger. Somebody had threatened Catherine. Her child.

She would not let them win.

She grabbed both the envelope and the sheet of paper by the edges and slid them into her purse. Once she'd seen Howard, she would take the letter to the police.

"I'M SORRY, LIZ. Howard didn't leave any paperwork for either you or Jamison."

She was not in the mood to be put off. "Can't you just get it off his computer?"

The woman looked a little shocked. "I don't know his password," she said. "Even if I did, I'm not sure that would be appropriate."

"Look, Helen. What's inappropriate is for Howard to have left his office without providing us with the necessary paperwork to complete this adoption. Now he won't return any calls. I want to know what's going on. This is so unlike him."

Now the woman looked really nervous. "I…I'm not sure what's going on," she confessed. "Howard has been acting so strange. Real nervous. Almost jumpy. Have you seen him lately?"

"Yes." She'd seen him at the hospital when Melissa Stroud had her baby. "He seemed a little scatterbrained but nothing unusual for Howard."

"Twice in the past week, I've caught him sleeping at his desk in the middle of the afternoon. When I arrive in the mornings, I can tell he's been working all night."

It didn't sound good, but then again, she had her own sleep issues. "Maybe he's just working too hard. Does he have new clients?"

The woman shook her head. "No, just the opposite. Business is off. If it wasn't for OCM and a couple other agencies that he works with, I'm not sure I'd have a desk to sit at. Last week I wanted to order a new fax machine and he told me to hold off—that cash was a little tight this month."

Liz did not have time to worry about Howard. She had plenty of her own worries. She stood up and slung the strap of her purse over her shoulder. "If you talk to him, tell him it's imperative that he call Jamison. We need the paperwork, and we need it now. If I don't have it within twelve hours,

I'm going to recommend to Jamison that OCM find a new attorney."

Liz left Howard's office and tried to grab a cab to take her to the police department. Two passed her by without even slowing down. In her hurry to leave the apartment, she'd forgotten her cell phone. She changed her path and headed back toward her apartment. Once there, she could call for a cab.

She was four blocks from home when three men jumped out of the bushes. All three wore dark coats and blue jeans, and each had a ski mask over his face.

Liz looked around for help, but the residential street was empty. "What do you want?" she asked, forcing words around her fear.

"Shut up," one man said. Then he put his hand on her shoulder and pushed her hard. Liz stumbled back and stuck both arms out, breaking her fall. Sharp rocks cut into the palms of her hand. She scrambled to her feet, unwilling to let them tower over her.

Another man grabbed for her purse, yanking it so hard that the shoulder strap broke. Liz didn't try to fight him for it. The first man stepped forward again. Liz braced herself for another push. She didn't expect the fist to her jaw, sending rockets of pain through her whole face.

She tasted blood.

"You stay away from Mary Thorton and her baby," the third man said. "If you don't, you'll be sorry. This is just a little sample. Just because Dantel's in jail doesn't mean he's not still in charge." Then he hit her in the stomach. She doubled over. When she managed to catch her breath and straighten up, they were gone.

It had all happened in less than a minute. She'd been attacked in broad daylight. She took stock of her injuries. She gently moved her jaw back and forth, very grateful when everything seemed to work. Blood oozed from several small cuts on the palms of her hands. She bent down to pick up her purse, and pain shot through her midsection. Damn. She probably had a broken rib or two. She sank to her knees and managed to grab the strap. Awkwardly, she got to her feet and half walked, half ran the rest of the way to her apartment.

Once inside, she got to the sink and spit out the blood in her mouth. She walked over to the telephone, careful not to look in the mirror on the way, and dialed 911.

Chapter Sixteen

Two officers and an ambulance responded. The police questioned her briefly. She gave them the best description she could of the men and told them what they'd said about Dantel Mirandez. She handed over the letter and envelope. Then the ambulance transported her to the hospital, the same one she'd left just hours earlier literally walking on air. Now she lay flat on her back, wheeled in, presented to the nurse on duty like a stuffed turkey on Thanksgiving Day.

The doctor put six stitches in the inside of her cheek, where her teeth had cut into the tender flesh. He also cleaned out the rocks in her hands and wrapped them up in white gauze. Then someone else took films of her ribs and substantiated that one was cracked. The doctor didn't even bother to wrap it, just told her to move carefully for a couple days.

She'd just snapped her jeans when Sawyer burst into the exam room. When he saw her, he stopped so suddenly that his body almost pitched forward over his feet.

He stared at her. First at her swollen jaw, then at her wrapped hands. When he finally spoke, his voice seemed rusty, as if he hadn't used it for a while.

"Are you okay?" The minute he said it, he knew it was an insane question. One look at her told him she wasn't okay.

"How did you know I was here?" she asked.

"The responding officers ran Mirandez's name through

the database. I came up as the arresting officer. So, they called me."

It sounded so simple. It didn't give any clue to the absolute terror he'd felt when they'd told him about her injuries. "He'll pay for this," Sawyer told her. "I promise you. He will pay for this."

She didn't say anything. Just stood there, holding her blouse together with one hand. He could see the pale blue silk of her bra against her soft skin. So beautiful. So fragile.

It was his fault this had happened. He never should have let Lieutenant Fischer talk him into taking her to Wisconsin in the first place. Mirandez wouldn't have any reason to be going after her now.

"I'm sorry," he said. "I'm sorry that bastard hurt you. I'm sorry I let him."

She looked at him as if he'd lost his mind.

He tried again. "I expected him to go after Mary. I never thought you'd be the target. That was stupid of me. Now you're paying the price."

She dismissed his concerns with a wave of her free hand. "How could you have known? He's been told the baby isn't his. Why would he care about warning me away from Mary or the baby? Did they tell you about the letter?"

"I swung by the station and took a look at it. He spelled your name right this time," Sawyer said, feeling the disgust well up in the back of his throat.

"I guess I didn't notice," she said.

"What exactly did the men say to you?" Sawyer asked. "Word for word, if you can remember."

"They told me to stay away from Mary and the baby. Then they said that just because Dantel was behind bars it didn't mean he wasn't still in charge."

Sawyer rubbed his forehead. He had a hell of a headache. It didn't make sense. None of it. Not that he questioned that

Mirandez had been able to communicate with his gang. That happened all the time. Prison bars didn't prove to be a very strong barrier. Sometimes it was a phone conversation in code. Other times, a dirty guard willing to carry messages back and forth for a price.

Perhaps the order had come down before Mirandez learned that the baby wasn't his. Whatever the reason, Sawyer would find out. "Is it okay for you to leave?" he asked.

She nodded. "Yes."

"I'll take you home."

"No." The word exploded from her. He hadn't expected less.

"Liz, be reasonable. You're hurt. You can't walk home. Just let me drive you." He wanted to make sure she got safely inside her apartment. It was the least he could do.

"No," she repeated. "I'm not ready to leave. I want to see Mary as long as I'm here."

"I'll wait," he said.

"That's not necessary," she said.

She looked as if she'd rather be anywhere but with him. He couldn't blame her. "We're moving Mary tomorrow," he said. "Guards will remain outside her door until then. We're placing a plainclothes cop in the nursery just in case he'd go for…the baby."

"Her name is Catherine."

Catherine. He didn't want to know that. Didn't want to know anything about the baby. But Liz deserved to know that her baby would be safe. "Your boss told me that the baby goes to a temporary foster home for a couple days. The detective can go with her just in case."

She chuckled, a dry, humorless laugh. "The foster parents should love that."

"It's not great, I agree. But it beats the alternative."

"What happens when I bring her home? Does the detective stay until she's in college?"

He could hear the sarcasm. "I don't think that will be necessary. But maybe for a couple of weeks. We're having the doctor certify that Mary was at or near a full-term pregnancy. We'll provide that to Mirandez's attorney. Just in case, we're asking permission from the court to run a DNA match. We need to get a blood draw from Mirandez. That will prove conclusively that he's not the father. But it will take several weeks before those results are available."

"Capable Sawyer."

"What?"

"Never mind. It was stupid. I'm just tired. I need to see Mary. You need to leave." She buttoned her shirt. He looked away, not wanting to watch her hands, not wanting to think about how his own hands had unbuttoned her shirt, how he had literally shook with wanting her.

Because perhaps, in a lifetime or two, he might forget.

He heard her groan. She had her sweater half-on with one sleeve hanging free. The arm that should have filled it was wrapped around her waist. She was even paler than before. "What's wrong?"

"Cracked rib."

He hadn't thought he could hate Mirandez any more than he already did. "Any other injuries that I can't see?" he asked. He knew she hadn't been raped. When the officers had contacted him, he'd asked that. Knowing that if she had, he'd have killed the men responsible. He would have laid down his badge and gone after them and ripped their hearts out.

She shook her head. "No. All in all, I think I got lucky."

Lucky. As absurd as it sounded, she was right. With no witnesses to stop them, it would have been easy for Mirandez's men to slit her throat or put a bullet through her temple. But they hadn't. They'd roughed her up and scared her, but they'd left her standing.

He took a step forward, then another, stopping just a foot away from her. Gently, he took her arm and pushed it through the sweater sleeve. With unsteady hands, he pulled both sides together, fastening the top button. Then the second one. The third.

Liz didn't breathe. Couldn't. Sawyer had his head bent, concentrating as he worked the buttons into the small holes, his strong fingers being so careful, so gentle. She thought her legs might not hold her. The man was helping her, dressing her like an adult would a child, and it was the most erotic thing that had ever happened to her.

When he finished with the last button, he lifted his head, meeting her eyes. He leaned forward, and ever so softly, he brushed his lips across her sore and swollen jaw. Then he reached for her bandaged hands, raised each one to his lips and gently kissed the tips of her fingers.

Then he gathered her small hands in his much larger ones, brought them to his chest and bent his head forward so that his forehead rested on hers. She could feel the beat of his heart pulsing through her body, sending crazy, wild, zigzag waves through her. His breath was hot, his skin cool, his body strong. She felt safe and protected. Yet weak and wanting for more.

"I love you," he said, his voice just a whisper in her ear. "I'm so sorry you got hurt."

She took in a deep breath, wanting to always remember the scent of Sawyer. She focused on his hands, which were still wrapped around hers. She wanted to remember the feel of his skin, the lines of his bones, the strength of his muscles. It wouldn't be enough. But it would be all she had.

"Sawyer, you need to go." She said it softly, all the malice gone. He was a good man. He'd suffered a great loss. She didn't want to drag out the goodbyes, making either one of them suffer more.

He nodded and pulled his hands away. He looked her straight in the eye. He slowly raised his right hand, reaching toward her face. She caught his fingers with her own and gently pushed his hand back to his side. Then she deliberately and carefully reached up and on her own, all on her own, tucked the wayward strand of hair behind her ear.

He gave her a sad half smile. Without another word, he left the room.

THE NEXT MORNING, Sawyer waited impatiently while they brought Mirandez up to see him. The door opened, and his slimy attorney came in first, carrying a briefcase almost bursting at the seams. Mirandez shuffled in next, his hands cuffed in front of him.

Sawyer hadn't wanted to come. He didn't want to even look at the murdering bastard. But he'd come up empty-handed in his search for the men who had terrorized Liz. Even the guys on the inside couldn't shake loose any information.

"This is highly irregular, Detective," the attorney said, setting his briefcase down on the table with a thud. "What is it that's so important that you had to talk to my client at the crack of dawn? It's barely seven o'clock."

He didn't care whose butt he'd had to drag out of bed. He'd been up all night. But still he had nothing. "Your client arranged to have Liz Mayfield beaten and threatened."

"That's impossible," the attorney said, disregarding Sawyer's statement.

Sawyer didn't bother to respond. He'd been studying Mirandez. For the briefest second, the man had looked surprised, then he'd completely closed down, pulling his usual sneer back in place.

"Are you charging him?"

"I want to ask him some questions."

"Under the circumstances, I will advise my client not to answer."

Mirandez sat up straighter in his chair. "Shut up, Bill. You talk too damn much."

The attorney's face turned red. Sawyer almost felt sorry for him until he remembered that the guy made his living defending killers. He deserved to be treated like dirt.

Mirandez rocked back in his chair. "Do you lie awake at night thinking these things, Cop?"

Mirandez was half-right. Since he'd let Liz slip out of his life, Sawyer had spent most of his nights staring at the ceiling, afraid to close his eyes, afraid to give in to the temptation to remember what it felt like to be wrapped in her arms. Last night, after walking away from her yet again, he'd worked himself to death, poring over reports, talking to informants, hoping he could forget the look in her eyes when she'd told him goodbye.

"You need to hire better help," Sawyer said. "Your guys ID'd you. They said you sent them. We've got both letters. You're not going to get away with this."

"You bore me." Mirandez put both hands on the table and twirled his thumbs. "What do you think I am? Stupid?"

"I think you're the scum of the earth."

Mirandez laughed. "Yes, well, I think you're pretty much an SOB yourself."

"Mr. Mirandez," the attorney began before a sharp look from his client had him shutting his mouth.

Mr. Mirandez? How freaking much was Mirandez paying the guy to get him to suck up that way? There wasn't enough money in the world. *Mr. Mirandez?* It made Sawyer sick. Nobody in his right mind would give Mirandez that kind of respect.

As suddenly as that, Sawyer figured it out. Mirandez. Not Mr. Mirandez, not Dantel Mirandez. He only went by Mirandez. Mary called him Dantel. Nobody else did. Nobody in his gang would. They probably didn't even know his first name.

"The baby isn't even mine. I don't care what happens to it."

Whoever had sent the men hadn't known that the baby wasn't Mirandez's. The men had warned Liz to stay away from Dantel's baby. Someone smart enough to throw the blame on Mirandez had hurt Liz. Why? Who? Would they try again?

Sawyer stood and grabbed his coat.

"Hey, what's your hurry?" Mirandez looked around the room. "While it's not Vegas, I thought we might play some cards. I'll stake you a couple hundred. I know you cops don't make much of a living."

"At least we make it honestly," Sawyer said and left before he followed through on his urge to slam Mirandez up against the wall.

He walked to his car, dialing Liz's number on his cell. The phone rang four times then the voice mail kicked on. He didn't want to leave a message. Wasn't sure what he even had to tell her. Just knew he needed to talk to her, needed to hear her voice. Needed to know that she was okay. He dialed OCM's main number next. Jamison answered on the second ring.

"Yes."

"Jamison, it's Sawyer Montgomery. I'm trying to get in touch with Liz. Is she there by any chance?"

"No. I haven't heard from her. She's supposed to be here at noon. We're meeting with Howard Fraypish. I talked to her early this morning. She had some errands to run and then she planned to stop by. I'll let her know to call you."

"Do that."

He redialed Liz's number. This time, when the voice mail kicked on, he left a brief message. "Liz, it's Sawyer. I don't think it was Mirandez's guys who attacked you. So, be careful, okay? Please call me. I know you probably don't want to talk to me. But just let me know you're okay. That's all you have to do. Just let me know."

He hung up before he started to beg. He couldn't shake the feeling that Liz was in danger. Not knowing what else to do, he drove. He went to Liz's apartment and pounded on the door. He dialed her number again and again. When her voice mail kicked on the last time, he said, "Liz, damn you, where are you? Call me."

He called Mary's room at the hospital. She hadn't seen her. He got the number of Randi's apartment and called there just in case. No luck. He called Robert and told him what was going on.

He was going to be too late. Something horrible had happened to Liz, and he was going to lose her. She'd never know how much he loved her. He hadn't been able to tell her. He'd chosen to let her believe that it wasn't enough.

Life is about choices. That was what she'd told him. Liz had chosen to live. She'd survived her sister's death, she'd learned to let go, to forgive herself for not being there. She'd chosen to make a difference in the lives of countless young women, allowing them to fully understand and appreciate that no matter how desperate the situation, they always had a choice.

They could lie or tell the truth. Give or take. Laugh or cry. Love or be empty forever.

Sawyer wiped the tears from his eyes as he drove down the familiar street. Without thinking, he went to the one place that gave him peace. He found his regular spot and parked the car. It had started to rain. It didn't matter. The cold, wet day couldn't touch him. He opened the gate of the small cemetery nestled between a church and a school. He took the path to the left. Then he knelt next to his son's grave and placed a hand on the shiny marker.

When he'd left Baton Rouge, his son had come with him. It had been the only choice.

The rain fell harder, hitting his head, his face, mixing with the tears that ran freely down his cheeks. He couldn't hear a thing besides the beating of his own heart.

Choices. He didn't want to give up his last chance to make the right one.

So, he bent his head, all the way to the ground, and he kissed the wet, cold earth that sheltered his child. He didn't kiss him goodbye. Never that. His son would always have a special place in his heart. But his heart needed to be bigger now. It needed to hold Liz and Catherine.

He'd been a coward. He knew now that he'd rather have one minute, one day, one week with Liz than a lifetime of being alone and afraid.

He knew he couldn't keep Liz or Catherine safe from all harm. He couldn't wrap them up in cotton and hide them from the danger that lurked in dark corners. They might get hurt. They might get sick. But he wanted to be there every step of the way, holding them, supporting them, making sure they knew they were loved more than life itself.

WHEN HE GOT BACK to the car, he tried Liz's apartment again. Still no answer. He checked his machine at work. No messages. Damn it.

He checked the time. Ten minutes after ten. Jamison had said they had a meeting with Fraypish at noon. Not knowing what else to do, Sawyer tried Jamison again.

"Yes," Jamison answered.

"It's Sawyer Montgomery. Any word from Liz?"

"No. I've tried a couple times. I swear this meeting is doomed. I can't reach Howard, either."

Fraypish. Liz had gone to see him and then been attacked. "Jamison, how well do you know Howard Fraypish?"

"We're like brothers. Why?"

"I don't know. It's just that there's something about him that nags at me."

"He's odd, but if you're thinking that he would harm Liz, that just wouldn't happen. When Liz got that first death threat from Dantel, Howard was just outraged."

Sawyer remembered Liz standing outside the hotel, whispering, *He doesn't know about the letter. Please don't tell him.*

"How did he know about the letter, Jamison?"

"I don't know. I might have mentioned it, I suppose."

A slow burn started in Sawyer's stomach. Mirandez's goons hadn't written the second letter. No, it had been somebody who knew about the first letter but hadn't actually seen it. Somebody who hadn't realized that Mayfield had been spelled wrong or that the grammar had been rough. Somebody who knew how to spell *conscience* and what it meant. Somebody who knew Mirandez as Dantel. That was what Mary called him. Sometimes Liz, too, especially after she'd been talking with Mary. Jamison had just referred to him as Dantel. That was likely the name he'd used when he'd been chatting with his buddy.

Sawyer turned a sharp left. "Jamison, what's Fraypish's address?"

The man hesitated, then rattled it off.

Sawyer hung up, called for backup and started praying. He couldn't lose her now. Not when he'd just found himself.

When he got there, he parked his car in front of the three-story brownstone. He took the steps two at a time. He had his fist just inches away from the door, ready to knock, when he heard a crash inside the house. He put his ear to the door and pulled his gun out of his holster. He could hear Liz and then another voice. An angry voice. A man's voice.

She was alive. He stepped away from the door, pulled out his cell phone and called for backup. He debated all of two seconds before he tried the handle. Locked. He heard a car pull up and realized that Jamison had also come.

He held up a finger warning the man to be quiet. "Do you have a key?"

"Yes. I feed his cats when he's not home." Jamison pulled out a ring and pointed at a gold key.

Sawyer inserted it quietly and opened the door just inches. He could hear their voices more clearly. Fraypish was yelling.

"You stupid woman. I am not going to let you ruin everything."

"Howard, you're never going to get away with it."

"I've been getting away with it for months. Your boss, Jamison, my good buddy, always was a trusting soul. And a fool."

"Why, Howard? At least tell me why you had to sell the babies."

"I'm not lucky at cards. At craps, either."

"How could you?"

Sawyer could hear the disgust in Liz's voice. Silently, he made his way down the hall.

"Easy. You'd be amazed at how desperate some people are to have a baby. Especially healthy, white infants like your little Catherine. They'll borrow from friends and family, mortgage their house. Whatever it takes. They'll drop a hundred thousand without blinking an eye."

"You make me sick," Liz said.

"You don't understand, Liz. I tried to convince you to stay away from that baby. When that didn't work, I hired a few guys to make my point. But still, you won't stop. I have to stop you."

"Howard, please, don't do this. We'll talk to Jamison. We'll get you help."

"It's too late. I borrowed money from the wrong people. If I don't make regular payments, they'll hurt me. Bad. They're due a check this week. I don't have any other babies in the pipeline. I need yours."

"You'll never get away with it. Jamison will figure it out."

"No, he won't. When you don't show up for the noon meeting, Jamison and I'll come looking for you. We'll find the body, I'll console Jamison, and your little Catherine will be on the market by dinnertime."

With that, Sawyer came around the corner. With one sharp downward thrust on Fraypish's arm, he knocked the gun out of his hand. Then he tackled the man, sending his fist into the guy's jaw. That was for the bruised jaw. He hit him again. That was for the cracked rib. He had his arm pulled back, ready to swing again, when two sets of hands pulled him off Fraypish.

"That's enough, Detective. We'll take it from here."

Sawyer shook his head to clear it. Two officers stood on each side of him. He took a step back. Liz sat on the bed, her arms wrapped around her middle. Tears ran down her face.

He pulled her into his arms.

"Thank you for getting here in time," she whispered. "I feel so stupid. I had no idea."

He held her. "Me, neither, honey. I focused on Mirandez, and I missed Fraypish."

"It's not your fault," she assured him.

Maybe not but he couldn't even think about what might have happened if he'd arrived five minutes later. He pulled back, just far enough that he could see her eyes. "I love you," he said, not willing to go another second without her knowing exactly how he felt. "I've been a stupid fool. I don't want to lose you. Tell me I haven't lost you. Tell me I'm not too late."

"What about your son?"

He brushed a tear off her cheek. "I loved him before he was born. Once I'd held him, he was the moon and stars and everything that was perfect. And when you love that much and you can't hold on to it, it hurts. It rips you apart. I didn't ever want to hurt like that again."

She kissed him, a whisper of lips against his cheek. "I never meant to hurt you."

"You were right. Life is about choices. When you love someone, there's a risk. You can choose to avoid risks, to never take the big leap off the cliff into the water, but then you never know the absolute joy of coming to the surface, the stunning glory of the bright sunshine in your eyes. I don't want to stand at the top alone."

"What are you saying?"

"Liz, I'm ready to jump. You have my heart. Take my hand. And together, with Catherine, we'll build a family. I'll take care of you, I promise. I love you. Please say you'll try."

She kissed him on the lips, and he allowed himself to hope. "You are the kindest, most loving and most…capable man I've ever met. I know you'll take care of me. I want a chance to take care of you." She reached out and took his hand. "And I want us to take care of our daughter together."

* * * * *

A VERY SPECIAL DELIVERY

BRENDA HARLEN

Brenda Harlen is a former attorney who once had the privilege of appearing before the Supreme Court of Canada. The practice of law taught her a lot about the world and reinforced her determination to become a writer—because in fiction, she could promise a happy ending! Now she is an award-winning, national bestselling author of more than thirty titles for Harlequin. You can keep up-to-date with Brenda on Facebook and Twitter or through her website, brendaharlen.com.

Chapter One

When she woke up the morning of November first staring at water stains on a stippled ceiling, Julie Marlowe wondered if she was having a bad dream. Then she remembered that uncomfortable twinges in her lower back had forced her to take a break on her journey home the day before, and the closest available accommodations had been at the Sleep Tite Motor Inn.

She managed to roll her pregnant body off the sagging mattress and swing her feet over the edge. The bathroom's tile floor was cold beneath her feet, and the trickle of spray that came out of the shower head wasn't much warmer. She washed quickly, then dried herself with the threadbare but clean towels on the rack. She had another long day of travel ahead of her, so she dressed comfortably in a pair of chocolate-colored leggings and a loose tunic-style top. Then she slipped her feet into the cowboy boots she'd bought "just because" when she'd been in Texas.

Seven months earlier, she'd had a lot of reasons for wanting to leave Springfield. But after traveling eight thousand miles through twenty-seven states and sleeping in countless hotel rooms, she was more than ready to go home.

She missed her family, her friends and the comfortable and predictable routines of her life. She even missed her father, despite the fact that he could be more than a little stubborn and overbearing on occasion. The only person she could honestly say that she didn't miss was Elliott Davis Winchester the Third—her former fiancé.

Julie had told her parents that she needed some time and some space to think about her future after ending her engagement. Lucinda and Reginald hadn't understood why she needed to go—and how could she expect that they would when there was so much she hadn't told them?—but they'd been supportive. They'd always been unflinching in their support and unwavering in their love, even when she screwed up.

When she left Springfield, Julie was determined to ensure that she didn't screw up again.

She felt a nudge beneath her rib, and smiled as she rubbed a hand over her belly. "You weren't a mistake, baby," she soothed. "Maybe I didn't plan for you at this point in my life, but I know that you're the best thing that ever happened to me, and I promise to be the best mommy that I can."

The baby kicked again, clearly unconvinced.

Julie couldn't blame her for being skeptical. Truthfully, she had more than a few doubts of her own. She and Elliott had talked about having children and neither wanted to wait too long after the wedding before starting a family, but she hadn't known she was pregnant when she gave him back his ring and left town.

After a quick visit to the doctor confirmed that she was going to have a baby, she wasn't even tempted to change her course. Though she'd known Elliott for two years—and had been engaged to him for six months—she'd suddenly realized that she didn't really know him at all. What she did know was that he wasn't the kind of a man she wanted to marry, and he certainly wasn't the kind of man that she wanted as a father for her baby.

Of course, that didn't change the fact that he *was* the father of her baby, but she hadn't been ready to deal with that reality in the moment. Maybe she'd been running away, but over the past few months she'd accepted that she couldn't run forever. In fact, in her current condition, she couldn't run at all anymore. The best she could manage was a waddle.

And she was ready to waddle home.

Lukas Garrett snagged a tiny box of candy from the orange bowl on the front desk—the remnants of the pile of Halloween candy from the day before—and emptied the contents into his mouth.

Karen, the veterinarian clinic receptionist and office manager, shook her head as he chewed the crunchy candy. "Please tell me that's not your lunch."

He swallowed before dutifully answering, "That's not my lunch."

"Lukas," she chided.

"Really," he assured her. "This is just the appetizer. I've got a sandwich in the fridge."

"PB & J?"

"Just PB today." He reached for another box of candy and had his hand slapped away.

"You need a good woman to take care of you."

It was a familiar refrain and he responded as he usually did. "You're a good woman and you take care of me."

"You need a wife," she clarified.

"Just say the word."

Karen, accustomed to his flirtatious teasing, shook her head.

"Go eat your sandwich," she directed. "As pathetic as it is, I'm sure it has slightly more nutritional value than candy."

"I'm waiting to have lunch after I finish with the morning appointments." He glanced at the clock on the wall, frowned. "I thought for sure Mrs. Cammalleri would be here with Snowball by now."

"She called to reschedule," Karen told him. "She didn't want to leave the house in this weather."

"What weather?" Luke turned to the window, then blinked in surprise at the swirling white flakes that were all that was visible through the glass. "When did it start snowing?"

"About an hour ago," Karen told him. "While you were ensuring that Raphael would never again be controlled by his most basic animal urges."

He moved closer to the window. "Did the forecast call for this?"

She nodded. "Twelve to fifteen inches."

He frowned. "How does global warming result in early season snowstorms?"

"We live in a Snowbelt," she reminded him. "And the current catchphrase is 'climate change.'"

"I'd prefer a climate change that included warm sun and sandy beaches."

"So book a vacation."

"I've been thinking about it," he admitted. And while an island getaway held a certain appeal, he had no desire to go on a holiday alone. Nor was he interested in venturing out solo with the goal of finding an anonymous female someone to share a few days of sun, sand and sex. That kind of thing had lost its appeal for Luke before he'd graduated college.

"Well, another thing you should think about is closing up early," Karen suggested. "Mrs. Cammalleri was your last scheduled appointment and the way the snow's already falling hard and fast, if we don't get out of here soon, we might not get out of here at all."

"The clinic's open until three on Fridays," he reminded her. "So I'll stay until then, but you go ahead."

"Are you sure you don't mind?"

"Of course not. There's no need for both of us to stay, and you've got a longer drive home than I do."

Karen was already tidying up her desk, straightening a pile of files, aligning the stapler with the edge of her desk calendar, putting the pens in the cup.

Luke took advantage of her distraction to snag another box of candy. "If this keeps up, the kids will be building snowmen tomorrow."

"Hard to believe they were trick-or-treating just last night, isn't it?"

"Yeah." He couldn't help but smile as he thought about his almost five-year-old nephews, Quinn and Shane, who had dressed up as SpongeBob and Patrick. Their baby sister, Pippa, was too young to go door-to-door, but even she'd been decked out in a pumpkin costume with a smiling jack-o'-lantern face on the front and a hat with stem and leaves.

His eldest niece—his brother Jackson's twelve-year-old daughter, Ava—had skipped the candy-grabbing ritual in favor of a Halloween party with some friends at the community center. And Jack had chaperoned. Luke wasn't at all surprised that his brother, who had earned quite the reputation as a heartbreaker in his youth, was a slightly overprotective father. The surprising part had been finding out that he was a father at all—especially to the daughter of the woman who had been Luke's best friend since fifth grade.

He was still surprised, and a little annoyed, that Kelly Cooper had managed to keep her weekend rendezvous with Jack a secret for more than twelve years. It was only when she'd moved back to Pinehurst with her daughter at the end of the summer that Luke had learned that his brother was Ava's father and that his designation as "Uncle Luke" was more than an honorary title. He still wasn't sure that he'd completely forgiven her for keeping that secret for so long, but he was genuinely thrilled that Kelly and Jack were together now and making plans for an early December wedding.

"From carving pumpkins to throwing snowballs in the blink of an eye," Karen noted as she turned to retrieve her coat and purse from the cabinet behind her desk—then muttered a curse under her breath as she nearly tripped over Einstein, Luke's seven-month-old beagle puppy.

He'd been one of a litter of eight born to a severely malnourished and exhausted female who had been abandoned on the side of the road. A passerby had found the animal and taken her to the veterinarian clinic. The mother hadn't survived the birth, and Luke had been determined to ensure that her efforts to give life to her pups weren't in vain.

Thankfully, Karen had stepped up to help, and between the two of them, they'd made sure that the puppies were fed and nurtured and loved—and then they'd given them to good homes. But Luke had always known that he would keep one, and Einstein was the one he'd chosen. And he loved the crazy animal, even if he wasn't exactly the genius of his namesake.

When the puppies were first born and required almost constant care, it made sense for them to be at the clinic. Luke also believed it would help with their socialization, getting them accustomed to being around people and other animals, and so he'd continued the practice with Einstein long after his brothers and sisters had gone to other homes. Unfortunately, one of Einstein's favorite places in the clinic was wherever he could find Karen's feet.

"I swear that animal is trying to kill me." But despite the annoyance in her tone, she bent to rub his head, giving him an extra scratch behind his left ear because she knew that was his favorite spot.

"Only if he could love you to death," Luke assured her.

She shook her head as she made her way to the door. "You should go home, too," she said again. "No one's going to come out in this weather."

As it turned out, she was right. Aside from Raphael's owner who came to pick him up, the front door didn't open and the phone didn't ring. So promptly at three o'clock, Luke locked up the clinic and headed out to his truck with Einstein.

Of course, this was the puppy's first exposure to snow, and when he stepped out onto the deck and found himself buried up to his chest in the cold, white fluff, he was not very happy. He whined and jumped, trying desperately to get away from it. And when he couldn't escape it, he decided to attack it. He barked and pranced around, clearly under the impression that he was winning the battle.

Luke couldn't help but chuckle at his antics. The animal would probably play in the snow for hours if he let him, so he finally picked up the pup and carried him to the truck. He sat him on the floor of the passenger side and let the heater blow warm air on him while Luke cleared the thick layer of snow off of his windows.

Luckily he'd found an old hat and a pair of gloves in his office, and he was grateful for both. The unexpected snowfall might have been fun for Einstein, but driving through it was a completely different story, even with all-wheel drive. The snow had been falling steadily and quickly and the plows hadn't yet been around, so he knew the roads would probably be slick—a fact that was proven when he fishtailed a little as he pulled out of the clinic's driveway and onto the street.

Warm and dry once again, Einstein hopped up onto the passenger seat and pressed his nose against the window, his breath fogging up the glass. When Luke finally turned onto

Terrace Drive, the pup barked excitedly, three quick little yips. The snow was still falling with no indication that it would let up anytime soon, and he was as happy as Einstein to know that they were almost home.

The cold had come after the snow, so the first layer of flakes had melted on the road, then frozen. Now there was a dangerous layer of ice beneath everything else, and Luke suspected the tow trucks would be working late into the night. It would be too easy to slide off the road and into a ditch in these conditions—as someone had apparently done right in front of his house.

Julie clenched the steering wheel with both hands and bit down on her bottom lip to hold back the scream of frustration that threatened to burst from her throat. A quick detour through Pinehurst to meet with a friend of her brother's from law school had seemed like a great idea when she'd called and made the appointment a few hours earlier, but that was before the snow started.

Still, she'd no intention of being dissuaded by some light flurries. Except that those light flurries had quickly escalated into an actual blizzard. Weather reports on the radio had warned people to avoid unnecessary travel. Since Julie had been on the highway between Syracuse and Pinehurst at the time and pulling off to the side of the road in order to be buried in snow didn't seem like a particularly appealing option, she decided her travel was necessary.

And she'd almost made it. According to her GPS, she was less than three miles from Jackson Garrett's office—but it might as well have been thirty. There was no way she could walk, not in her condition and not in this weather.

Tears of frustration filled her eyes, blurred her vision. She let her head fall forward, then jolted back again when the horn sounded. Great—not only had she driven into a ditch, she'd just drawn attention to the fact by alerting anyone who happened to be passing by. She didn't know if she was more relieved or apprehensive when she realized that no one seemed to be anywhere in the vicinity.

She was sure she'd seen houses not too far back. In fact, she specifically remembered a sprawling ranch-style with a trio of grinning jack-o'-lanterns on the wide front porch, because she'd noted that it wouldn't be too long before those pumpkins were completely blanketed by snow.

She closed her eyes and silently cursed Mother Nature. Okay, maybe she had to accept responsibility for the fact that she'd been driving through a blizzard with no snow tires—but who the heck would have thought that she'd need snow tires on the first day of November?

She felt a spasm in her lower back in conjunction with a ripple of pain that tightened her whole belly. Julie splayed a hand over her tummy, silently trying to reassure her baby that everything was okay. But as the first tears spilled onto her cheeks, she had to admit—if only to herself—that she didn't know if it was. She didn't know how being stuck in a ditch in the middle of nowhere during a freak snowstorm could possibly be "okay."

She drew in a deep breath and tried to get the tears under control. She didn't usually blubber, but the pregnancy hormones running rampant through her system had been seriously messing with her emotional equilibrium. Wiping the trails of moisture from her cheeks, she tried to look on the bright side.

She knew she wasn't lost. She wasn't exactly sure where she was, but she'd followed the directions of her GPS so she wasn't actually in the middle of nowhere. She was in Pinehurst, New York. An even brighter side was found when she pulled her cell phone out of her purse and confirmed that her

battery was charged and she had a signal. Further proof that
she wasn't in the middle of nowhere.

Confident that she would be able to get some roadside assistance, Julie leaned over to open the glove box to get the
number and gasped as pain ripped across her back. Gritting
her teeth, she blew out a slow, unsteady breath and prayed
that it was just a spasm. That the jolt of sliding into the ditch
had pulled a muscle in her back.

On the other hand, it could be a sign that she was in labor.
And right now, that was *not* a scenario she wanted to consider.

"Please, baby—" she rubbed a hand over her belly
"—don't do this now. You've got a couple more weeks to
hang out right where you are, and I'm not even close to being
ready for you yet."

Moving more carefully this time, she reached for the folio
that contained her vehicle ownership and warranty information and—most important—her automobile association card.
Hopefully there wasn't any damage to her car and as soon as
it was pulled out of the ditch, she could be on her way again.

Except that when she dialed the toll-free number on the
card, she got a recorded message informing her that all of
the operators were currently busy assisting other customers
and to please hold the line if she wanted to maintain her call
priority. She disconnected. It would probably be easier—and
quicker—for her to find the number of a local company and
make a direct call. Or maybe, if she was really lucky, a Good
Samaritan with a big truck conveniently equipped with tow
cables would drive down this road and stop to help.

A flash of color caught the corner of her eye and she turned
her head to see a truck drive past, then pull into a driveway
she hadn't even noticed was less than ten feet from where
she was stranded. The vehicle stopped, the driver's side door
opened and then a gust of wind swirled the thick snow around,
obliterating her view.

She thought she heard something that sounded like a dog barking, but the sound quickly faded away.

Then there was a knock on her window, and her heart leaped into her throat. Not thirty seconds earlier, she'd been praying that a Good Samaritan would come to her rescue, and now someone was at her door. But how was she supposed to know if he had stopped to offer help—or if his intentions were less honorable?

Her breath was coming faster now, and the windows were fogging up, making it even harder to see. All she could tell was that he was tall, broad-shouldered and wearing a dark cap on his head. He was big. The road was mostly deserted. She was helpless.

No, she wasn't. She had her cell phone. She held it up, to show him that she was in contact with the outside world, then rolled down her window a few inches. A gust of cold air blasted through the scant opening, making her gasp.

"Are you okay, ma'am?"

Ma'am? The unexpectedness of the formal address in combination with the evident concern in his tone reassured her, at least a little. She lifted her gaze to his face, and her heart jolted again. But this time she knew the physiological response had nothing to do with fear—it was a sign of purely female appreciation for a truly spectacular male.

The knit cap was tugged low on his forehead so she couldn't see what color his hair was, but below dark brows, his eyes were the exact same shade of blue-green as the aquamarine gemstone ring her parents had given to her for her twenty-first birthday. His nose was just a little off-center, his cheekbones sharp, his jaw square. He had a strong face, undeniably masculine and incredibly handsome. His voice was low and soothing, and when he spoke again, she found her gaze riveted on the movement of his lips.

"Ma'am?" he said again.

"I'm okay. I'm just waiting for a tow truck."

He frowned. "I'm not sure how long you'll have to wait. I managed to squeeze through just as the police were putting up barriers to restrict access to Main Street."

"What does that mean?"

"It means that the primary road through town is shut down."

She sighed. "Any chance you have tow cables in your truck?"

He shook his head. "Sorry."

She gasped as another stab of pain slashed through her.

"You *are* hurt," he decided. "Let me call an ambulance."

She shook her head. "I'm not hurt. I think...I'm in labor."

Chapter Two

"Labor? As in having a baby?" Luke couldn't quite get his head around what she was saying. Not until he noticed that her hand was splayed on her belly.

Her very round belly.

How had he *not* noticed that she was pregnant?

Probably because his most immediate concern, when he'd spotted the vehicle in the ditch, was that the driver might be injured, maybe even unconscious. He hadn't given a passing thought to the driver's gender. And then, when she'd rolled down the window, he'd been absolutely spellbound by her wide and wary blue-gray eyes.

But now, with his attention focused on the bump beneath her shirt, the words that had seemed undecipherable suddenly made sense. "You're pregnant."

Her brows lifted in response to his not-so-astute observation. "Yes, I'm pregnant," she confirmed.

She was also a pretty young thing—emphasis on the

young. Early twenties, he guessed, with clear, flawless skin, high cheekbones, a patrician nose and lips that were surprisingly full and temptingly shaped.

He felt the subtle buzz through his veins, acknowledged it. He'd experienced the stir of attraction often enough in the past to recognize it for what it was—and to know that, under the circumstances, it was completely inappropriate.

Young, beautiful *and pregnant,* he reminded himself.

"Actually, I don't think it is labor," she said now. "I'm probably just overreacting to the situation."

But he wasn't quite ready to disregard the possibility. "When are you due?"

"November fifteenth."

Only two weeks ahead of schedule. He remembered his sister-in-law, Georgia, telling him that she'd been two weeks early with Pippa, so the timing didn't seem to be any real cause for concern. Of course, Georgia had also been in the hospital. The fact that this woman was stuck in a ditch and nowhere near a medical facility might be a bit of an issue.

He took a moment to clear his head and organize his thoughts, and saw her wince again.

"Are you having contractions?"

"No," she said quickly, and just a little desperately. "Just… twinges."

Apparently she didn't want to be in labor any more than he wanted her to be in labor, but that didn't mean she wasn't.

"I think I should call 911 to try to get an ambulance out here and get you to the hospital."

"It's probably just false labor."

"Have you been through this before?"

"No," she admitted. "This is my first. But I've read a ton of books on pregnancy and childbirth, and I'm pretty sure what I'm experiencing are just Braxton Hicks contractions."

He wasn't convinced, but he also wasn't going to waste

any more time arguing with her. Not with the snow blowing around the way it was and the condition of the roads rapidly getting worse. He pulled out his phone and dialed.

"911. Please state the nature of your emergency."

He recognized the dispatcher's voice immediately, and his lips instinctively curved as he recalled a long-ago summer when he and the emergency operator had been, at least for a little while, more than friends. "Hey, Yolanda, it's Luke Garrett. I was wondering if you could send an ambulance out to my place."

"What happened?" The clinical detachment in her tone gave way to concern. "Are you hurt?"

"No, it's not me. I'm with a young woman—"

He glanced at her, his brows raised in silent question.

"Julie Marlowe," she told him.

"—whose car went into the ditch beside my house."

"Is she injured?"

"She says no, but she's pregnant, two weeks from her due date and experiencing what might be contractions."

"Twinges," the expectant mother reminded him through the window.

"She insists that they're twinges," Luke said, if only to reassure her that he was listening. "But they're sharp enough that she gasps for breath when they come."

"Can I talk to her?"

He tapped on the window, and Julie lowered the glass a few more inches to take the device from him. Because she was inside the car with the window still mostly closed, he could only decipher snippets of their conversation, but he got the impression that Yolanda was asking more detailed questions about the progress of her pregnancy, possible complications and if there were any other indications of labor.

A few minutes later, Julie passed the phone back to him.

"If I thought I could get an ambulance through to you, I'd

be sending one," Yolanda told Luke. "But the police have completely shut down Main Street in both directions."

"But emergency vehicles should be able to get through."

"If they weren't all out on other calls," she agreed. "And the reality is that an expectant mother with no injuries in the early stages of labor, as Julie seems to think she might be, is not an emergency."

"What if the situation changes?"

"If the situation changes, call me back. Maybe by then the roads will be plowed and reopened and we can get her to the hospital."

"You don't sound too optimistic," he noted.

"The storm dumped a lot of snow fast and there's no sign that it's going to stop any time soon. The roads are a mess and emergency crews are tapped."

He bit back a sigh of frustration. "What if the baby doesn't want to wait that long?"

"Then you'll handle it," she said, and quickly gave him some basic instructions. "And don't worry—I reassured the expectant mom that Doctor Garrett has done this countless times before."

"Please tell me you're joking."

"I'm not." There was no hint of apology in her tone. "The woman needed reassurance, and I gave it to her."

And although her statement was technically true, she'd neglected to mention that the majority of the births he'd been involved with had been canine or feline in nature. He had absolutely no experience bringing human babies into the world.

Luke stared at Julie, who gasped as another contraction hit her. "You better get an ambulance here as soon as possible."

Julie was still mulling over the information the dispatcher had given her when she saw her Good Samaritan—who was apparently also a doctor—tuck his phone back into the pocket of his jacket.

"Let's get you up to the house where it's warm and dry."

She wished that staying in the car was a viable option. She was more than a little uneasy about going into a stranger's home, but her feet and her hands were already numb and she had to clench her teeth together to keep them from chattering. She took some comfort from the fact that the emergency operator knew her name and location.

She rolled up the window—no point in letting the inside of the car fill up with snow—and unlocked the door.

As soon as she did, he opened it for her, then offered his other hand to help her out. He must have noticed the iciness of her fingers even through his gloves, because before she'd stepped onto the ground, he'd taken them off his hands and put them on hers. They were toasty warm inside, and she nearly whimpered with gratitude.

He walked sideways up the side of the ditch, holding on to both of her hands to help her do the same. Unfortunately the boots that she'd so happily put on her feet when she set out that morning had smooth leather soles, not exactly conducive to gaining traction on a snowy incline. She slipped a few times and no doubt would have fallen if not for his support. When she finally made it to level ground, he picked her up—scooping her off her feet as if she weighed nothing—and carried her to the passenger side of his truck. She was too startled to protest, and all too conscious of the extra twenty-nine pounds that she was carrying—and now *he* was carrying. But when he settled her gently on the seat, he didn't even seem winded.

He drove up the laneway, parked beside the house. When he inserted his key into the lock, she heard a cacophony of excited barking from the other side of the door.

"You have dogs?"

"Just one." Her rescuer shook his head as the frantic yips continued. "We just got home. I let him out of the truck at the end of the driveway when I saw your vehicle, and he raced ahead to the house to come in through the doggy door, as he always does. And every day when I put my key in the lock, he acts as if it's been days rather than minutes since he last saw me."

"They don't have much of a concept of time, do they?"

"Except for dinnertime," he noted dryly. "He never forgets that one."

He opened the door and gestured for her to enter. But before Julie could take a step forward, there was a tri-colored whirlwind of fur and energy weaving between her feet.

"Einstein, sit."

The dog immediately plopped his butt on the snow-covered porch right beside her boots and looked up with shiny, dark eyes, and his master scooped him up to give her a clear path through the door.

"Oh, he's just a little guy. And absolutely the cutest thing I've ever seen."

"He's cute," the doctor agreed. "And he hasn't met anyone he doesn't immediately love, but sometimes he's too stubborn for his own good."

She slipped her boots off inside the door, and when he put the puppy down again, it immediately attacked her toes with an enthusiastic tongue and gentle nips of his little teeth.

"Einstein, no!"

The pup dropped his head and looked up, his eyes filled with so much hurt and remorse, Julie couldn't help but laugh.

The doctor looked at her with a slightly embarrassed shrug. "He's got some kind of foot fetish. I'm not having a lot of luck in trying to curb it."

"No worries, my feet are too numb to feel much, anyway."

"Come on." He took her arm and guided her down the hall

and into what she guessed was a family room. The floor was a dark glossy hardwood and the walls were painted a rich hunter-green, set off by the wide white trim and cove moldings. There was a chocolate leather sectional and a matching armchair facing a gorgeous stone fireplace flanked by tall, narrow windows. The lamps on the mission-style side tables were already illuminated, but as he stepped through the wide, arched doorway, he hit another switch on the wall and flames came to life in the firebox.

"You should warm up quickly in here," he told her. "I converted to gas a few years ago. As much as I love the smell of a real wood fire, I prefer the convenience of having heat and flame at the flick of a switch."

"You have a beautiful home," Julie told him. And, it seemed to her, a big home, making her wonder if he had a wife and kids to help fill it. She hadn't seen a ring on his finger, but she knew that didn't prove anything.

"I like it," he said easily.

She moved closer to the fireplace, drawn by the flickering flames and the tempting warmth. "Do you live here alone?"

"Me and Daphne and Einstein," he clarified.

She was reassured by this revelation that she wouldn't actually be alone with a stranger. "Daphne's your…wife?"

"No."

He responded quickly—so quickly she couldn't help but smile. The immediate and predictable denial was that of a perennial bachelor with absolutely no desire to change his status.

"Daphne's a three-year-old blue Burmese, and not very sociable. Unlike Einstein, you'll only see her if she decides you're worthy of her presence."

Which meant that they *were* alone—except for a cat and a dog. But he was a doctor, and the emergency operator had vouched for him, and she had to stop being wary of everyone just because her experience with Elliott had caused her to doubt her own judgment. "It's a big house for one man and two pets," she noted.

"Believe me, it felt a lot smaller when I had to share it with two brothers."

"You grew up here?"

He nodded. "Born and raised and lived my whole life in Pinehurst, in this house. Well, I wasn't actually born in this house—my mother wanted to do things more traditionally and give birth in the hospital."

"That was my plan, too," she admitted.

"Sliding into a ditch and going into labor during an unexpected snowstorm was a spur-of-the-moment decision?" he teased.

"I'm not in labor," she said again. "My baby isn't due for another two weeks and first babies are almost never early."

"Almost isn't the same as never," he told her, and pushed the oversize leather chair closer to the fire so that she could sit down.

When she lowered herself into the seat, he sat cross-legged on the floor facing her and lifted her feet into his lap. "Your feet are like ice," he noted.

She was startled by the boldness of the move and felt as if she should protest—but only until he started to rub her toes between his hands, then she closed her eyes and nearly moaned with pleasure.

In fact, she probably did make some kind of noise, because Einstein bounded over, eager to play with her feet, too. But one sharp look from his master had him curling up on the rug in front of the fire.

"Don't you own winter boots or a proper coat?" the doctor asked her.

"Of course I do, but it wasn't snowing when I started out this morning."

"Started out from where?"

"Cleveland," she admitted.

"Then you obviously did a lot of driving today."

"About seven hours."

"Heading back to Boston?"

She eyed him warily. "What makes you think I'm going to Boston?"

"I saw the Massachusetts plates on your car, and there's just a hint of a Boston accent in your voice."

"I wasn't planning on going any further than Pinehurst today," she said, deliberately not confirming nor denying his assumption. Then, because she'd rather be asking questions than answering them, she said, "Is Luke short for Lukas?"

"It is." He set down the first foot and picked up the second one.

"I've been researching baby names," Julie told him. "Lukas means bringer of light."

And she thought the name suited him, not just because he'd rescued her—bringing her hope if not necessarily light—but because it was strong and masculine.

"Have you narrowed down your choices?"

She nodded.

"Any hints?"

She shook her head, then gasped when the pain ripped through her again.

Luke released her foot and laid his hands on the curve of her belly. She tried to remember everything she'd read about Braxton Hicks and how to distinguish those false contractions from real labor, but in the moment, she was lucky she remembered to breathe through the pain.

After what seemed like forever, the tightness across her belly finally eased.

"Twinge?" Though his tone was deliberately light, she saw the concern in his eyes.

"Yeah." She drew in a deep breath, released it slowly.

"I'm going to put the puppy in the laundry room, just so that he's out of the way in case things start to happen." Then he took the dog away, returning a few minutes later with an armful of blankets and towels and a plastic bin filled with medical supplies. He covered the leather chaise with a thick flannel sheet, then folded a blanket over the foot of it.

"Is there anyone you should call?" the doctor asked. "Anyone who's going to worry about where you are?"

She shook her head. Her parents wouldn't know that she'd been caught in this storm because they hadn't known about her intention to detour through the Snowbelt on her way home.

"Husband? Boyfriend?" he prompted.

"No." She could see the direction he was going with his questions, and she was almost grateful when her body spasmed with pain again. It was easier to focus on the contraction—whether false or real—than on the reasons why her relationship with her baby's father had fallen apart.

She was gripping the armrests of the chair, but noticed that he was looking at his watch, counting the seconds. She panted softly and tried to think of something—anything—but the pain that ripped through her. The books she'd read talked about focal points, how to use a picture or some other item to evoke pleasant memories and a feeling of peace. Right now, all she had was Luke Garrett, but his warm gaze and steady tone—proof of his presence and reassurance that she wasn't entirely alone—somehow made the pain bearable.

"Ninety seconds," he said. "And I'd guess less than five minutes since the last one."

"It doesn't look like my baby's going to wait for a hospital, does it?"

"I'd say not," he agreed. "Did you take prenatal classes?"

"No."

"Your doctor didn't recommend it?"

"I've been traveling a lot over the past few months, so I didn't have a chance."

"Traveling where?"

"Pretty much everywhere."

"Work or pleasure?"

"Both."

She knew it sounded as if she was being evasive, and maybe she was, but it wasn't in her nature to share personal information with someone she didn't know and whom she probably wouldn't ever see again when the roads were finally cleared and her car was pulled out of the ditch.

"I'm just making conversation," he told her. "I thought it might take your mind off of the contractions."

"I was counting on an epidural to do that," she admitted.

His lips curved. "Well, it's good that you have a sense of humor, because an epidural isn't really an option right now."

She liked his smile. It was warm and genuine, and it made her think that everything was going to be okay. "I knew it was too much to hope that you rented a spare bedroom to a local anesthesiologist."

He took her hand, linked their fingers together and gave hers a reassuring squeeze.

"I'm scared," she admitted.

"You're doing great."

"I don't just mean about giving birth," she told him. "I mean about being a parent."

"Let's concentrate on the giving birth part for now," he suggested.

She sucked in another breath and gritted her teeth so that she didn't embarrass herself by whimpering. Or screaming. The pain was unlike anything she'd ever experienced, and she knew it would continue to worsen before it got better.

"Breathe," Luke said, and she realized that she wasn't

doing so. She released the air she was holding in her lungs in short, shallow pants. "That's it."

"Okay," she said when the contraction had finally eased.

"Two minutes," he announced, not very happily.

She could understand his concern. Her contractions—and she knew now that they were definitely contractions—were coming harder and faster. The idea of giving birth outside of a hospital was absolutely terrifying, but somehow, with Luke beside her, she felt confident that she would get through it. More importantly, she felt that her baby would get through it.

"Should I get undressed now?"

It wasn't the first time he'd had a woman say those words to him, but it was the first time they'd come at Luke completely out of the blue.

And apparently Julie realized that her casual statement might be misinterpreted, because her cheeks flooded with color. "So that you can examine me," she clarified.

Examine her. Right. She was an expectant mother and he was the doctor who was helping to deliver her baby. Of course she would expect him to examine her.

He mentally recalled the brief instructions he'd been given by the 911 operator. Thankfully the human birthing process wasn't very different from that of other mammals, but Luke felt more than a little guilty that Julie was offering to strip down for him because she thought he was an MD.

It should have been simple enough to think like a doctor. But he couldn't forget the quick punch of desire he'd felt when his eyes had first locked with hers. Before he'd realized that she was eight and a half months pregnant. Still, the fact that she was about to give birth didn't make her any less attractive, although he would have hoped that this tangible evidence of her involvement with another man should have cooled his ardor.

But the combination of her beauty and spirit appealed to something in him. She'd found herself in a tough situation, but she was dealing with it. Sure, she was scared. Under the circumstances, who wouldn't be? But she'd demonstrated a willingness to face that fear head-on, and he had to respect that courage and determination. And when he looked into those blue-gray eyes, he wanted to take up his sword to fight all of her battles for her. Not that she would appreciate his efforts—most women preferred to fight their own battles nowadays, but the desire to honor and protect was deeply ingrained in his DNA.

He wasn't interested in anything beyond that, though. Sure, he liked women and enjoyed their company, but he wasn't looking to tie himself to any one woman for the long term. His brothers had both lucked out and found partners with whom they wanted to share the rest of their lives, and he was happy for them, but he didn't see himself as the marrying kind. Certainly he'd never met a woman who made him think in terms of forever.

Which was just one more reason that he had no business thinking about Julie Marlowe at all. She might be beautiful and sexy but she was also on the verge of becoming a mother—no way would she be interested in a fling, and no way was he interested in anything else.

So he gave her privacy to strip down—and his plush robe to wrap around herself. He was trying to think about this situation as a doctor would—clinically and impartially. But how was he supposed to be impartial when she had those beautiful winter-sky eyes and those sweetly curved lips, sexy shoulders and sexy feet? And despite the baby bump, she had some very appealing curves, too.

When he returned to the family room, he was relieved to see that she was wearing the robe he'd left for her so she wasn't entirely naked beneath the thin sheet she'd pulled up over herself. But she still looked vulnerable and scared, and every last shred of objectivity flew out the window.

She was panting—blowing out short puffs of air that warned him he'd missed another contraction. "I thought I had a pretty good threshold for pain," she told him. "I was wrong."

He knelt at the end of the chaise, and felt perspiration beginning to bead on his brow. She was the one trying to push a baby out of her body, and he was sweating at the thought of watching her do it. But when he folded back the sheet and saw the top of the baby's head, everything else was forgotten.

"The baby's already crowning," he told her.

"Does that mean I can start to push?"

"Whenever you're ready."

He talked her through the contractions, telling her when to push and when to pant, trying to ensure that her body was able to adjust to each stage and rest when possible.

Of course, it was called labor for a reason, and although it was progressing quickly, he knew it wasn't painless. Her hands were fisted in the sheet, and he covered one with his own, gave it a reassuring squeeze. "It won't be too much longer now."

"Promise?"

He looked up and saw that her stormy eyes were filled with tears and worry. "I promise."

As she pushed through the next contraction, the head slowly emerged. The soft, indignant cry that accompanied the baby's emergence from the birth canal confirmed that its lungs were working just fine.

"You're doing great," he told Julie. "Just—"

He didn't even have a chance to finish his sentence before the baby slid completely out and into his hands.

Chapter Three

Luke stared in awe at the wet, wrinkled infant that was somehow the most beautiful creature he'd ever seen. And when the baby looked at him with big blue eyes wide with innocence and wonder, he fell just a little bit in love with the little guy.

He wiped the baby's face carefully with a clean, soft towel to ensure that his nose and mouth were clear of fluid. Then he wrapped him, still attached by the cord, in a blanket and laid him on his mother's chest.

"And there he is," he told her.

Julie blinked, as if startled by this statement. *"He?"*

"You have a beautiful, healthy baby boy," he confirmed. "Born at 4:58 pm on November first."

"A boy," she echoed softly, her lips curving just a little. "My baby boy."

Tears filled her eyes, then spilled onto her cheeks. She wiped at them impatiently with the back of her hand.

"I'm sorry. I'm not usually so emotional."

"It's been an emotional day," Luke said, feeling a little choked up himself.

It took her a few minutes to get her tears under control before she spoke again, and when she did, she surprised him by saying, "I thought he'd be a girl. I *wanted* a girl." After a moment she continued. "I don't even feel guilty admitting it now. Because looking down at him, I know that I couldn't possibly love him any more if he had been a she. All that matters is that he's mine."

"Why did you want a girl?" he asked curiously.

"I guess I thought it would be easier to raise a girl, since I was once one myself. I don't know anything about little boys. Or big boys." She glanced up at him and offered a wry smile. "And personal experience has proven that I don't understand the male gender at all."

"Are you disappointed that he's a he?"

She shook her head. "No. I'm not disappointed at all. He's...perfect."

"That he is."

"I never expected to feel so much. I look at him, and my heart practically overflows with love." But she managed to lift her gaze from the baby to look at Luke now. "Thank you, Dr. Garrett."

He didn't know how to respond to her gratitude, especially when he felt as if *he* should be thanking *her*. Because in his entire life, he had honestly never experienced anything more incredible than helping to bring Julie's beautiful baby boy into the world.

What he'd told her earlier was true—the hard part was all hers. And he couldn't help but be awed by the strength and determination and courage she'd shown in face of the challenge. He felt honored and privileged to have been a part of the experience, to have been the very first person to hold the brand-new life in his hands.

By the time he'd cut the cord and delivered the placenta, Julie had put the baby to her breast and was already nursing. And Luke finally let himself exhale a silent sigh of relief.

He tidied up, gathering the used sheets and towels, then left mother and child alone while he stepped away to call Yolanda to let her know that an ambulance was no longer a priority. She offered hearty congratulations and a smug "I knew you could handle one little baby" then signed off to deal with other matters.

After putting a load of laundry in the washing machine, Luke fed Einstein, then realized that his stomach was growling, too. And if he was hungry, he imagined that Julie was even more so. He put some soup on the stove to heat, then peeked into the family room again.

"How are you feeling now?"

"Exhausted," she admitted. "And ecstatic. I don't know how I can ever repay you for everything you've done."

"I'm just glad I was here to help."

She smiled at that. "And if an ambulance could have got through the storm, you would have shipped me off to the hospital in a heartbeat."

"Absolutely," he agreed without hesitation.

"Since I am still here, there is something I wanted to ask you."

"Sure."

"What do you think of the name Caden?" She looked at him expectantly, trying to gauge his reaction.

"What does it mean?" he asked.

"Fighter or battle."

He nodded. "I like it."

She smiled down at the baby before lifting her eyes to

meet his again. "Then let me formally introduce you to Caden Lukas Marlowe."

She saw surprise flicker in his eyes, then pleasure. He offered his finger to the baby, and Caden wrapped his tiny fist around it, holding on tight. "That's a lot of name for such a little guy," he noted.

"You don't mind the 'Lukas' part?"

"Why would I mind?"

She shrugged. "I wanted him to have a small part of the man who helped bring him into the world. I know we probably won't ever see you again after we leave Pinehurst, but I don't want to forget—and I don't want Caden to forget—everything you've done."

"You're not planning to go anywhere just yet, are you?"

"Not just yet," she assured him. "But I figured you'd want to get us out of here as soon as the roads are clear."

Of course, she couldn't go anywhere until her car was pulled out of the ditch and any necessary repairs were made, but she didn't expect her Good Samaritan to put them up for the duration.

He shrugged. "As you noted, it's a big house for one person and two pets."

She wasn't entirely sure what he was suggesting. Was he really offering to let them stay with him? And even if he was, she could hardly stay in the home of a man she'd just met. No matter that she already felt more comfortable with him than with the man she'd planned to marry.

Before she could ask, she heard the sound of footsteps stomping on the porch. Despite the fact that the roads were still closed, Lukas didn't seem at all surprised to have a visitor—or that the visitor, after a brisk knock, proceeded to open the door and walk right into the house.

Einstein had been released from the laundry room and cautiously introduced to the baby. Since then, he hadn't left Julie's side. But he obviously heard the stomping, too, because he raced across the room and down the hall to the foyer, barking and dancing the whole way.

The sharp barks startled the baby, and Caden responded with an indignant wail of his own. Julie murmured reassuringly and snuggled him closer to her chest, and by the time the visitor had made his way down the hall to the family room, he was settled again.

"This is a friend of mine," Lukas told her, gesturing to the tall, dark-haired man beside him. "Cameron Turcotte." Then to Cameron he said, "This is Julie Marlowe and Caden."

"Are the roads clear now?" Julie asked him. She assumed that they must be if he was able to get through, although she couldn't begin to fathom why he would have chosen to visit a friend in the middle of a snowstorm.

"The plows are out in full force, but it's going to take a while," he told her. "Main Street is technically still shut down, but I knew the officer posted at the barricade and told him that I had to get through to deal with a medical emergency."

"Are you a doctor, too?" Julie asked him.

Cameron's brows lifted. "Too?"

"Yolanda wanted to reassure Julie that she was in capable hands with Doctor Garrett," Lukas told his friend.

The other man chuckled.

"Why do I feel as if I'm missing something?" Julie asked warily.

"The only thing that matters is that you and your baby are okay," Cameron said. "And since I was on my way home from the hospital, Luke asked if I could stop by to check on both of you. With your permission, of course."

She looked questioningly at Lukas. "I don't understand. You said everything was okay. Is something—"

"Nothing's wrong," he said, answering her question before

she could finish asking it. "But you may have misunderstood my qualifications."

She frowned. "What do you mean?"

"I'm a DVM, not an MD," he told her.

It only took her a few seconds to decipher the acronym, and when she did, her jaw dropped.

"My baby was delivered by a *vet?*"

Lukas nodded.

Julie was stunned.

And mortified.

Dr. Garrett wasn't a qualified medical doctor—he was an animal doctor.

She drew in a deep breath and tried to accept the reality of the situation. And the truth was, neither of them had had any other choice. She'd been stranded in his house in a blizzard with no one else around to help. Her options had been simple: accept his assistance or try to deliver her baby on her own. And, in his defense, he hadn't claimed to be a doctor— it was the 911 operator who had offered that information.

And she'd grasped at it with both hands. It wasn't how she'd wanted to deliver her baby but knowing that she had no chance of getting to a hospital, she'd considered herself lucky that her car had gone into the ditch by a doctor's house. Proving once again that she had a tendency to see what she wanted to see.

"I didn't intend to deceive you," Lukas said to her now. "But you seemed to find comfort in believing that I was a medical doctor, and I didn't want to cause you undue stress by correcting that impression."

And she'd willingly stripped out of her clothes because a doctor—especially an obstetrician—was accustomed to his patients doing that. Glancing at the veterinarian who had delivered her baby, she didn't doubt that he was accustomed to women stripping for him, too, although probably not in a clinical setting.

"So." She cleared her throat. "How many babies have you delivered?"

"One," he admitted.

"And it looks to me like he did a pretty good job for a first-timer," Cameron—*Doctor* Turcotte—commented.

"But I think we'd both feel better if Cameron checked Caden over, just to make sure I didn't miscount his toes or something."

She could smile at that, because she'd already counted his fingers and toes herself.

"And you might want some numbers—weight and length, for example—to put in his baby book," Cameron said.

"I guess 'tiny' is somewhat vague," she admitted, relinquishing the swaddled infant to the doctor.

He measured Caden's length and the circumference of his head, then he used a kitchen scale to weigh the baby.

"Not as tiny as I thought," he said, handing the infant back to his mother. "Just about seven and a half pounds and twenty inches. A pretty good size for thirty-eight weeks. You obviously took good care of yourself throughout your pregnancy."

"I tried to exercise regularly and eat healthy," she said, then felt compelled to confess, "but I sometimes gave in to insatiable cravings for French fries and gravy."

"Well, I don't think those French fries and gravy did any harm to you or your baby," Cameron assured her.

He opened a backpack she hadn't seen him carry in. "Newborn diapers and wipes," he said, pulling out a bunch of sample packs. "Some receiving blankets and baby gowns."

"Thank you," Julie said. "I've got a few outfits and sleepers in the trunk of my car, just because I wandered through a baby store the other day, but I didn't think I'd be needing diapers just yet."

"Well, there should be enough here to hold you for a couple of days, until you can get out—or send Luke out—to stock up on supplies." Then he said to his friend, "You did a good job—for someone who doesn't specialize in obstetrics."

Lukas narrowed his gaze in response to Cameron's grin, but he only said, "Julie did all the work."

"Knowing you, I don't doubt that's true," the doctor teased. "Now I'm going to get home to my wife and kids, while I still can. If the storm doesn't blow over, you might be snowed in for the whole weekend," he warned Julie. "But if you have any questions or concerns, please call."

"I'm sorry."

They were Luke's first words to Julie when he returned to the family room after seeing Cameron to the door.

"I'm not," she told him. "I'm grateful."

He sat down across from her. "You're not even a little bit mad?"

She shook her head. "I'm a little embarrassed. Okay, more than a little," she admitted. "But the truth is, I couldn't have done it without out you."

"It was an incredible experience for me, too."

"Could you do one more thing for me, though?"

"What's that?"

"Not tell anyone that you got me naked within an hour of meeting me."

"Not even my brothers?"

"No one," she said firmly.

He chuckled. "Okay, I won't tell anyone. But speaking of telling—was there anyone you wanted to call? Or have you already posted newborn photos from your phone on Facebook or Twitter?"

She shook her head. "I don't do the social media thing."

His brows lifted. "Do you do the telephone thing?"

"Of course, but I don't think any of my friends or family is expecting to hear any news about a baby just yet."

"He's only a couple weeks ahead of his due date," Lukas reminded her.

Which was true. It was also true that no one was expecting any birth announcement because no one had known that she was pregnant. Not even her parents, because it wasn't the type of news Julie wanted to tell them over the phone. She'd wanted to talk to her mother in person, to share her joy—and her fears—with the one person she was sure would understand everything she was feeling. But she'd been traveling for work for the past seven months and hadn't had a chance to go home. In fact, no one aside from her boss at The Grayson Gallery knew, and it wasn't Evangeline's voice that Julie wanted to hear right now—it was her mother's.

But more than she wanted to hear Lucinda's voice, she wanted to see her, to feel the warmth of her arms around her. Julie wondered at the irony of the realization that never had she more craved the comfort of her own mother than after becoming a mother herself.

"I guess I need to figure out a way to get home."

"You're not going anywhere until this storm passes," Lukas pointed out to her.

Watching the snow swirl outside the window, she couldn't dispute the point.

She'd hoped to be home before the weekend. She'd only taken this detour through Pinehurst to discuss some issues with the lawyer her brother had recommended. Of course, she hadn't admitted to Daniel that she was the one in need of legal advice, because he would have demanded to know what the issues were and insisted that he could handle whatever needed to be handled.

Instead, she'd told him that she had a friend in New York State—because she hadn't been too far away at the time and heading in that direction, suddenly aware that she couldn't go home until she had answers to some of the questions that had plagued her over the past several months—who was looking for a family law attorney and wondered if he had any contacts in the area.

"I guess you're stuck with us for a little bit longer, then," Julie finally said to Lukas.

"It's a big enough house that we won't be tripping over one another," he assured her.

"When the snow stops, I'll have my car towed and make arrangements for someone to come and get me."

"I already called Bruce Conacher—he owns the local garage and offers roadside assistance—to tell him that your car was in the ditch. He's put you on the list but warned me that there are at least a dozen vehicles ahead of yours."

"I'm not sure if that makes me feel better or worse— knowing that I wasn't the only one who slid off the road in that storm."

"You definitely weren't the only one," he assured her. "And I'm sure there will be more before the night is over. But on the bright side, the storm hasn't knocked out the power lines."

She shuddered at the thought.

"It's past dinnertime," he pointed out. "Are you hungry?"

"Starving," she admitted.

"How does soup and a grilled cheese sandwich sound?"

"It sounds wonderful," she said.

Luke headed back to the kitchen where he'd left the soup simmering. He ladled it into bowls, then flipped the grilled cheese out of the frying pan and onto the cutting board. He sliced each sandwich neatly in half, then transferred them to the plates he had ready. He carried the soup and sandwiches to the table, then went to the drawer for cutlery.

"It smells delicious," Julie said, coming into the room with Caden carefully tucked in the crook of one arm.

"Of course it does—you're starving," he reminded her.

She smiled at that, drawing his attention to the sweet curve of her lips.

He felt his blood pulse in his veins and silently cursed his body for suddenly waking up at the most inappropriate time. Because yes, he was in the company of a beautiful woman, but that beautiful woman had just given birth. Not to mention the fact that she was in his home only because there was a blizzard raging outside. There were a lot of reasons his libido should be in deep hibernation, a lot of reasons that feeling any hint of attraction to Julie Marlowe was wrong.

But after six months of self-imposed celibacy, his hormones apparently didn't care to be reasoned with. Not that he'd made a conscious decision to give up sex—he just hadn't met anyone that he wanted to be with. At least not longer than one night, and he was tired of that scene. He was looking for more than a casual hookup.

He could blame his brothers for that. Until recently, he hadn't wanted anything more than the casual relationships he'd always enjoyed with amiable members of the opposite sex. And then he'd started spending time with Matt and Georgia, and Jack and Kelly, and he'd realized that he envied what each of them had found. He'd even had moments when he found himself thinking that he'd like to share his life with someone who mattered, someone who would be there through the trials and tribulations.

But he figured those moments were just a phase. And the unexpected feelings stirred up by Julie Marlowe had to be another anomaly.

She was simply a stranger who had been stranded in a snowstorm. He'd opened up his home to her because it was what anyone would have done. And he'd helped deliver her baby because circumstances had given him no choice. The fact that his body was suddenly noticing that the new mom was, in fact, a very hot mama, only proved to Luke that no good deed went unpunished.

She moved toward the closest chair, and he pulled it away from the table for her. As she lowered herself onto the seat, he caught just a glimpse of shadowy cleavage in the deep V of the robe she wore before the lights flickered. Once. Twice.

Then everything went dark.

He heard Julie suck in a breath. Einstein, who had positioned himself at his master's feet as he was in the habit of doing whenever there was food in the vicinity, whimpered. Beyond that, there was no sound.

No hum of the refrigerator, no low rumbling drone of the furnace. Nothing.

And the silence was almost as unnerving as the darkness.

"So much for the power holding out," he commented, deliberately keeping his tone casual.

Thankfully, he had an emergency flashlight plugged into one of the outlets in the hall. It ran on rechargeable batteries and automatically turned on when the power went out, so the house wasn't completely pitch black. But it was pretty close.

While he waited for his eyes to adjust to the darkness, he reached for Julie's free hand, found it curled into a fist on top of the table. He covered it with his own, squeezed gently.

He heard the distant howl of the wind outside, a sound even more ominous than the silence. Julie heard it, too, and shivered.

"I've got some candles by the stove," he told her. "I'm just going to get them so we can find our food."

He found half a dozen utility candles in the drawer, set a couple of them in their metal cups on the counter and lit the wicks. The scratch of the head against the rough paper was loud in a room suddenly void of all other sound. He lit a couple more and carried them to the table.

They were purely functional—a little bit of illumination so that they could see what they were eating. And yet, there was something about dining over candlelight—even if the meal was nothing more than soup and sandwiches and the lighting was necessity rather than mood—that infused the scene with a romantic ambiance he did not want to be feeling. But somehow the simple dishes and everyday glassware looked elegant in candlelight. And when he glanced across the table, he couldn't help but notice that Julie looked even more beautiful.

"Dig in before it gets cold," he advised.

She dipped her spoon into the bowl, and brought it up to her mouth. Before her lips parted to sample the soup, they curved upward and her gaze shifted to him. "Chicken and Stars?"

"So?" he said, just a little defensively.

"So it's an unusual choice for a grown man," she said.

"It's my niece's favorite."

"How old is your niece?"

"I have two nieces," he told her. "Two nieces and two nephews. Matt's daughter, Pippa, is only a baby. Jack's daughter, Ava, is twelve going on twenty."

Her brows drew together, creating a slight furrow between them. "Is Jack short for Jackson?"

"Yeah," he admitted. "Why?"

"Your brother is Jackson Garrett?"

Now it was his turn to frown. "You know Jack?"

"Actually, he's the reason I came to Pinehurst," she admitted.

Luke carefully set his spoon down in his bowl, the few mouthfuls he'd consumed settling like a lead weight in the pit of his stomach. "Please tell me that he isn't the father of your baby."

Chapter Four

"What?" Julie lifted her head to look at him, her blue-gray eyes wide. "No. Oh, my God, no! I've never even met the man."

Luke exhaled a long, slow breath. "Okay," he finally said. "So why were you coming to Pinehurst for a man you've never met?"

"Because my brother, Daniel, knows him. They went to law school together." She picked up half of her sandwich, nibbled on the corner. "Why would you ask if your brother was the father of my baby?"

"Because it was only a few months ago that I found out Ava—the niece who likes Chicken and Stars soup—was Jack's daughter."

"She's twelve and you only met her a few months ago?"

"No—I've actually known her since she was a baby," he clarified. "But I didn't know that my brother was her father."

"I'm having a little trouble following," she admitted.

"Ava's mother, Kelly, was one of my best friends growing up. When she was in college, she had a fling with some guy and got pregnant, but she never told me who that guy was."

Julie's gaze dropped to her bowl again. "She must have had her reasons."

"She had reasons," he acknowledged. "But I'm not sure anything can justify that kind of deception."

"Is your brother still as upset about it as you are?"

His smile was wry. "Is it that obvious?"

"There was a bit of an edge to your tone."

"I was—maybe still am—upset," he admitted. "I was the first person she told when she found out she was pregnant, because I was her best friend. When Ava was born, Kelly asked me to be the godfather, but she never told me that her baby was actually my niece."

"And you didn't even suspect the connection?"

"No, I didn't suspect anything. Because I didn't know that Jack and Kelly had been involved, however briefly."

"So why didn't your brother guess that the child she was carrying might be his?"

"Because he didn't know she was pregnant. Kelly made me promise not to tell anyone," he confided. "I thought she'd met someone when she was away to school, fallen for the wrong guy and ended up pregnant. So I promised, because I never suspected that her baby was my brother's baby."

"Why didn't she tell him that she was pregnant?" Julie asked curiously.

"I guess she was planning to tell him, but by the time she knew about the baby, he was engaged to someone else."

She winced. "That would hurt."

"Yeah." He could acknowledge that fact without accepting it as justification.

"How did his wife react to the news that he had a child with someone else?"

"She never knew. They were divorced more than five years ago," he told her. "And now Jack and Kelly are engaged."

"Apparently your brother has forgiven her for keeping their child a secret."

"It took him a while, but he did. And Ava is thrilled that she's finally going to have a mother *and* a father."

"In a perfect world, every child would have two parents who loved him or her and one another," she said.

Which told him absolutely nothing about her situation. Where was Caden's father? Was he part of their lives? Luke didn't think so, considering that she hadn't wanted to contact anyone to let them know that she was in labor, or even later to share the news that she'd had her baby.

"I feel fortunate that I grew up in that kind of home," he said, in the hope that offering information to Julie would encourage her to reciprocate.

But all she said was, "That is lucky."

And then, in what seemed an obvious attempt to change the topic of conversation, "How long do you think the power will be out?"

Or maybe she was genuinely worried. He heard the concern in her voice and wished he could reassure her, but he didn't want to give her false hope. "I don't know. I think it depends on what caused the outage."

"So it could be a while," she acknowledged.

"It could," he agreed. "But we've got the fireplace and lots of blankets, candles and flashlights, and a pantry full of canned goods. I promise—you might be bored, but you won't freeze, get lost in the halls or starve."

Her lips curved. "If nothing else, today has proven to me that there's no point in worrying about things I can't control."

He could tell that she was trying to stay upbeat, but he didn't blame her for being concerned. She was a first-time mother with a brand-new baby, trapped in a stranger's house without any power in the middle of a snowstorm.

"Speaking of starving," she said. "I think this little guy's getting hungry."

By the flickering light of the candles, he could see that the baby was opening and closing his mouth and starting to squirm a little despite being snugly swaddled in one of the receiving blankets Cameron had brought from the hospital.

"Just hold on a second," Luke said, and went down the hall to retrieve the emergency flashlight.

He came back with the light and guided Julie the short distance back to the family room.

"While you're taking care of Caden, I'll get some blankets and pillows," he told her.

"Okay."

It didn't take him more than a few minutes to gather what they would need, but he took some time to putter around upstairs, giving the new mom time to finish feeding her baby. He didn't know a lot about the nursing process. Matt's wife, Georgia, had only recently weaned Pippa, and while she'd been pretty casual about the whole thing, Lukas had always averted his gaze if he was around when she was breastfeeding the baby. Not that he was uncomfortable with the act of a mother nursing her child—he just didn't think he should be looking at his brother's wife's breasts.

Of course, the whole train of thought was one that should definitely—and quickly—be derailed. Because now he was thinking about Julie's breasts. And since there was no family connection between them, and therefore no intrinsic moral conflict, he couldn't seem to shift his thoughts in a different direction.

He changed out of his jeans and shirt and into a pair of pajama pants and a long-sleeved thermal shirt. Bedtime usually meant just stripping down to his boxers and crawling beneath the sheets of his king-size bed, but he didn't want to be too far away from Julie and Caden in case either of them needed anything through the night. Not to mention that it would probably get a little chilly in his bedroom if the power stayed out through the night.

He remembered that Julie was still wearing the robe he'd given to her earlier, and while it had served the purpose of providing some cover during the childbirth process, he didn't think she would be very comfortable sleeping in it. He rummaged through his drawers until he found a pair of sweatpants with a drawstring waist and a flannel shirt with buttons that ran all the way down the front so that it would be easier for her to—

Trying *not* to think about that, he reminded himself sternly.

Instead, he turned his attention to the storm. He could hear the wind howling outside and the brush of icy snowflakes battering against the windows. If it didn't stop snowing soon, it would take him forever to clear his driveway. And if the power stayed out, it would take even longer because his snowblower required an electric start.

The starter on the gas fireplace was electric, too, so he was grateful he'd turned it on when they'd first come in from the storm. The fire would keep the family room toasty warm, which wouldn't just make it more comfortable to sleep through the night but was absolutely essential for the newborn.

He gathered up the clothes for Julie—adding a thick pair of socks to the pile—and the blankets and pillows and carted everything down the stairs. Having lived in this house his whole life, he wasn't worried about missing a step or bumping into a wall, but he was worried about Einstein getting tangled up in his feet. However, the dog was conspicuously absent as Luke made his way down the stairs, causing him to wonder where the pint-size canine had disappeared to and what mischief he might be getting into.

He found the puppy curled up beside the sofa, close to Julie and Caden.

She was obviously exhausted after her busy—and traumatic—day, and she'd fallen asleep with the baby still nursing. The sight caused an unmistakable stirring in his groin, and Luke chastised himself for the inappropriate reaction. She was a stranger, in his home and at his mercy because of the storm. She'd just given birth to a baby, and he was ogling her as if she was a centerfold.

Except that he had never seen anything as beautiful as the sight of the baby's tiny mouth suckling at his mother's breast. The tiny knitted cap that Cameron had brought from the hospital had fallen off Caden's head, revealing the wisps of soft dark hair that covered his scalp. His tiny little hand was curled into a fist and resting against his mother's pale, smooth skin.

Luke tiptoed closer to set the bundle of clothes beside her on the couch. As he neared, Einstein lifted his head, his tail thumping quietly against the floor.

"Good boy," he whispered, patting the dog's head.

Then he unfolded one of the blankets and gently laid it over the lower half of her body, careful not to cover the baby. The little guy looked up at him, those big blue eyes wide and completely unconcerned. His mother didn't even stir.

Luke took another blanket and a pillow for himself and settled into a chair nearby, prepared for a very long night.

When Julie awoke in the morning, she found the bundle of clothes Lukas had left for her on the sofa. Though she had more than a few changes of clothes in the suitcases in the trunk of her car, she didn't want to trudge through the snow to retrieve them while wearing nothing more than her host's robe, so she gratefully donned the borrowed shirt and sweats.

He'd also put a few toiletries out on the counter of the powder room: hairbrush, new toothbrush and a tube of toothpaste, all of which she put to good use.

Her first clue that the power had been restored was that the light in the powder room came on when she automatically hit the switch. Her second was the tantalizing aroma of bacon that wafted from the kitchen as she made her way down the hall. Though her grumbling stomach urged her to follow the scent, she knew she needed to take care of her baby's hunger first. Because she had no doubt that Caden would be hungry, too.

She'd lost count of how many times he'd woken her in the night, his avid little mouth instinctively seeking her breast and the sustenance it provided. And while he never seemed to nurse for extended periods of time, he nursed frequently. The books she'd read offered reassurance that this was normal, but reading about it and living it were two entirely different scenarios. She understood now why new mothers were always exhausted—feeding a newborn was pretty much a full-time job.

Of course, she also realized that she wasn't really feeding him yet, and that the frequent nursing sessions were necessary to help her milk come in. Throughout her pregnancy, she'd gone back and forth on the breast versus bottle issue but, in the end, she was persuaded by all the benefits found in breast milk—not to mention the simplicity of the method.

"Something smells delicious," she told Lukas when she finally made her way into the kitchen.

"Hopefully better than the bread and jam you would have got if the power had still been out," he told her.

"Right now, even that sounds good," she told him.

"How do bacon, eggs and toast sound?"

"Even better."

"How are you doing this morning?"

"I'm a little sore," she admitted. "And tired."

"I don't imagine you got much sleep with Caden waking you up every couple of hours."

She winced at that. "Obviously he woke you up, too."

He shrugged. "I'm a light sleeper. Thankfully, I don't need a lot of sleep, so I feel pretty good. Of course, being able to make my morning pot of coffee helped a little."

"I gave up coffee six months ago," she admitted, just a little wistfully.

"So what can I get for you?" Lukas asked. "Juice? Milk?"

"Juice is great," she said, noting that there were already two glasses poured and at the table.

He gestured for her to help herself, then pointed to the carton of eggs on the counter. "Scrambled or fried?"

"Whichever is easier."

"Which do you prefer?"

"I like both," she assured him.

He shook his head as he cracked eggs into a bowl. "You're a pleaser, aren't you? The type of person who says yes even when she wants to say no, who goes out of her way to avoid conflicts or disagreements."

She laughed. "No one's ever accused me of that before," she told him. "But I do try not to be difficult—at least not until I've known someone more than twenty-four hours."

"So how do you like your eggs?" he prompted.

"Benedict," she told him.

He chuckled. "Okay. But since I don't have hollandaise sauce, what's your second choice?"

"Scrambled," she decided.

"That wasn't so hard now, was it?" He added a splash of milk to the bowl, then a sprinkle of salt and pepper and began to whisk the eggs.

"I'll let you know after I've tried the eggs."

He grinned as he poured the mixture into the frying pan.

"My brother and sister-in-law are going to stop by later today, as soon as Matt finishes clearing his driveway."

She moved closer to the window. "I can't believe it's still snowing out there."

"It's just light flurries now," he noted. "Nothing like what we had yesterday."

"Everything looks so pretty, covered in a pristine blanket of snow."

"Take a look out the back," he suggested. "It's not quite so pristine out there."

She carried Caden to the window at the back of the room, noted that the snow there had been thoroughly—almost desperately—trampled. And then she spotted the culprit. Einstein, Lukas's puppy, was racing around as if being chased by the hounds of hell. He had his nose down and was using it like a shovel to tunnel through the cold white stuff and then, when he'd pushed enough to form a mound, he'd attack it.

She chuckled. "What is he doing?"

"I have no idea," Lukas admitted. "*He* has no idea."

"It's his first snow," she guessed.

"Yeah. He's been out there for half an hour and every few minutes, he spins in a circle and barks at it."

"Pets are a lot like kids, aren't they?" she mused. "They give you a fresh perspective on things we so often take for granted."

"Some of them," he agreed. "Daphne's perspective is neither sociable nor very sunny."

She laughed again. "Considering I haven't seen more of her than a flick of her tail, I can't disagree with that."

"She ventured downstairs last night to sleep by the fire, but I'm sure it wasn't for company but only warmth."

"It was warm," Julie agreed. "I even threw the blanket off a couple of times in the night."

"I thought about turning the fire off, but until the power came back on, I was reluctant to lose our only source of heat."

"I really can't thank you enough," she said. "When I think about what could have happened if you hadn't come home and found me in the ditch last night—"

"There's no reason to think about anything like that," Lukas told her.

"Well, I'm grateful. I don't know anyone else who would have done everything that you've done—for me and Caden."

"If the people you know would have left a laboring mother trapped in a ditch, you need to meet new people."

She managed to smile at that. "Okay—most of my friends would have opened their doors under those circumstances, but I don't know that their hospitality would have outlasted the storm."

"Are you suggesting that I should throw you out into a snow bank now?"

"Well, maybe you could wait until after you've fed me breakfast," she suggested.

He set a plate in front of her, then reached for Caden.

Julie transferred the baby to him without any protest or hesitation. After all, this man had helped bring her son into the world. And even if that hadn't been her choice at the time, she couldn't fault his competence—and she couldn't forget the expression of awe and wonder on his face as he'd gazed down at her newborn baby. Or the sense of absolute rightness that she'd felt in the moment that he'd placed the tiny, naked body in her arms so that he could cut the cord.

It was as if that act had somehow forged a bond between them—two strangers brought together by circumstances neither of them could ever have foreseen.

"He really is tiny, isn't he?" Lukas said, settling the sleeping baby into the crook of his arm. "I'll bet he doesn't weigh half as much as Einstein."

"You wouldn't say he was tiny if you'd had to push him out of your body," Julie told him, and dug into her eggs.

He winced at the thought as he picked up his own plate to take it to the table. "You're probably right about that."

She nibbled at a slice of crisp bacon and hummed with pleasure as the salty, smoky flavor flooded her taste buds. "Why is it that the foods that are so bad for you always taste so good?"

"I never really thought about it," he said, scooping up a forkful of eggs.

"You wouldn't."

"What's that supposed to mean?"

"You're a guy. You don't have to count calories or worry about fat content or carbs."

He shrugged as he chewed. "I pretty much eat what I want to eat."

"For the past several months, I have, too," she admitted. "I figured a pregnant woman should be allowed some latitude. Of course, I'll probably regret it when those extra ten pounds keep me in maternity clothes for another couple of months."

"You don't look as if you're carrying ten extra pounds," he told her.

"Right now it's more like twenty."

"Then you were too skinny before."

She picked up another slice of bacon. "No one ever accused me of being skinny, either," she assured him.

He studied her from across the table for a minute before he asked, "Why would you want to be?"

It wasn't a question anyone had ever asked her before. All of her friends—everyone she knew—wanted to be thinner, prettier, richer. It was every American woman's dream. Wasn't it?

"I've never understood why women obsess so much about their bodies," Lukas continued.

"Yeah, because men never judge us on the basis of our appearance," she said dryly.

He didn't deny it. "A pretty face and an appealing figure usually catch our attention," he admitted. "But men are simple creatures. We're not looking for perfection—we're just looking for a woman who's willing to get naked with us."

Her brows lifted. "Really?"

"Pretty much."

"I'll be sure to share that insight with my friends when we're sweating through Zumba classes."

He grinned. "We also like women who aren't afraid to shake their stuff."

Julie couldn't help smiling at the predictably male response. And as she finished her breakfast, she found herself marveling over the fact that she'd known Lukas for such a short period of time but somehow felt comfortable and at ease with him.

At home in Springfield, she knew a lot of people through her job at The Grayson Gallery and through her association with Elliot. As a result, she felt as if she had a certain image to uphold. She would never pop out for a quart of milk unless her hair was neat and her makeup immaculate. She rarely wore blue jeans and the only gym shoes she owned were exclusively for use in the gym.

Now she was wearing borrowed clothes that didn't fit, her hair was in a haphazard ponytail and her face was bare of makeup. And maybe it was because Lukas had held her hand as she sweated through labor and childbirth, but he seemed unaffected by the absence of mascara on her lashes and he honestly didn't seem to care who she was. He'd come to her aid simply because that was the kind of man he was, with no ulterior motive or hidden agenda. It wasn't just a surprising but a liberating revelation.

As was the fact that when he talked to her, he actually

seemed to listen to what she was saying—even if they were having a nonsensical conversation about carb counting or Zumba classes. He was charming and funny and genuine, and she'd never known anyone quite like him.

And whenever he smiled at her, she felt a subtle clenching low in her belly that made her just a little bit uneasy. Not because she worried that he would do or say anything inappropriate, but because she was worried that her response to him was inappropriate.

The last time she'd had sex was probably the night that Caden was conceived. In the eight and half months since then, she'd hardly thought about it—she certainly hadn't missed it. So why was she thinking about it now?

Was this flood of hormones through her system simply a side effect of the birth experience? Or was it connected to the sexy man who had rescued her from a blizzard and delivered her baby?

If she'd met Lukas Garrett in a different time and place— and if she wasn't the new mother of a beautiful baby boy— she would probably strike up a conversation, flirt with him a little, see if there was any evidence that the sizzle she felt was reciprocated.

But it wasn't a different time or place, and Caden was her priority. She didn't have the leisure or the energy for any kind of romantic complications.

As she pushed away from the table to carry her empty plate to the sink, she couldn't help but feel just a little bit disappointed by the fact.

Chapter Five

The window by the sink overlooked the driveway, and as she glanced outside, she realized that she'd been so focused on the snow earlier she hadn't noticed that it was cleared.

"How did you have time to shovel your driveway already?" she asked.

"I didn't. Jon Quinlan came by first thing this morning with his plow."

"Is he a neighbor?"

"Not exactly."

It was an evasive response from a man who had impressed her as being anything but, and it piqued her curiosity. "Then what is he—exactly?"

"He owns a landscaping and yard maintenance company."

"So why didn't you just say that you hire someone to clear it?"

"Because I didn't hire him," he admitted. "And he won't let me pay him."

"He must not have a very successful business if he works for free." She returned to the table and took the baby again.

"That's what I keep telling him, but Jon thinks he owes me. His daughter has a poodle-mix named Sparky. A few years back, Sparky had a hernia, but Jon had just been laid off from his job and didn't have the money for the surgery."

"But you did the surgery, anyway," she guessed.

He lifted one shoulder. "I couldn't let the animal suffer."

And in that moment, she realized it was true. Someone else might have turned the man away, but Lukas Garrett couldn't. It simply wasn't in him to do nothing when he could help. She also realized that he wasn't comfortable talking about what he'd done because he didn't think it was a big deal.

So instead of commenting on his generosity, she asked, "What kind of pet does Mrs. Kurchik have?"

He was visibly startled by her question—so she tapped a finger to the label that advertised "Mrs. Kurchik's Peach Jam" on the jar.

He shrugged again. "An aging basset hound and a battle-scarred tabby cat."

"The joys of living and working in a small town?"

"Pinehurst isn't nearly as small as it used to be, but the population growth hasn't affected the sense of community," he told her.

Before she could comment further, she heard something that sounded like a thud from behind the door to the laundry room. "What was that?"

"Einstein," he admitted. "He can come in and out through the doggy door, but I closed the inside door so that he doesn't race in and track snow through the house."

She frowned as another thump sounded. "Is he...knocking?"

He laughed. "Maybe he does think that's what he's doing. It's certainly a better explanation than that he likes to bang his head against the door." He pushed away from the table. "I'd better go dry his paws and let him in before he gives himself brain damage—if it's not already too late."

While Lukas was dealing with the dog, Julie decided to give her parents a call. She bypassed the handset on the table for her cell phone. Not just because she didn't want her host to incur long-distance charges for the call but because she didn't know how to explain a stranger's name and number showing up on her parents' call display. It was easier all around to call from her cell, as she was in the habit of doing.

When she heard her mother's voice on the other end of the line, her throat tightened and her eyes filled with tears.

"Hello?" Lucinda said again when Julie was unable to respond. Then, confirming that her mother had checked the display, "Julie—is that you?"

She cleared her throat. "Yes, it's me. Hi, Mom."

"Is everything okay?"

"Of course," she said. "I think the connection just cut out for a second."

"I'm so pleased to hear from you. I was going to call from the car on the way to the airport, but I wasn't sure of your schedule."

"You're going to the airport?"

"We're on our way to Melbourne." Lucinda practically sang out the announcement. "Your dad booked the tickets for our thirty-fifth anniversary."

Julie wondered for a minute if she'd somehow overlooked the milestone because of everything going on in her own life, but she knew that she hadn't. "Your anniversary isn't until the end of the month."

"But Reg wanted us to be there for our anniversary," her mother explained. "To celebrate thirty-five years together at the place we met."

Julie knew the story, of course. Her mother had been an

American student studying in Melbourne, her father had been on vacation after his first year of law school, and they'd met at a café near Brighton Beach.

"We always said we would go back some day, but we never did. After we got married, we got so busy with other things. Your father was building his career, and I was focused on raising four children."

"You sound really excited about this," Julie said, wishing that she could share her mother's enthusiasm. For the past several months, she'd been looking forward to going home. Now her return was almost imminent, but her parents weren't even going to be there. And she was more than a little apprehensive about the prospect of returning to Massachusetts—and facing Elliott—while they were away.

"We both are," Lucinda told her. "It's been a long time since we've been on vacation together, just the two of us."

"Then it's definitely long overdue," she agreed with false cheerfulness. "When will you be home?"

"December seventh."

"You're going for more than a month?"

"Thirty-five days—one for each year we've been together."

Which, Julie had to admit, was an incredibly romantic gesture on her father's part. And it was incredibly selfish of her to be upset because her parents were leaving the country rather than hanging around at home to welcome the grandchild they didn't know they had.

"That's…wonderful," she finally said.

"You'll be home by then, too, won't you?" Lucinda asked her.

"I'll be home by then," Julie promised, gently tracing the curve of her baby's cheek with her fingertip. "With a surprise for you."

"For me?" Lucinda sounded delighted.

"For both you and Dad."

"I can't wait," her mother said. "Although honestly, it's enough to know that you're finally coming home. We've missed you, baby."

She felt the sting of tears in the back of her eyes. "I've missed you, too. All of you."

"You're doing okay, though?" Lucinda prompted.

"I'm doing better than okay," Julie assured her. "I needed the time away, to figure some things out, but I'm looking forward to coming home." And it was true, even if the thought of seeing her former fiancé tied her stomach into knots.

"Where are you now?"

"In Upstate New York."

"I saw on the news that there's a big storm moving in that direction. You make sure you keep an eye on it," her mother advised.

Julie had to smile. "I'll do that."

"Oh, your father's tapping his watch," Lucinda said regretfully. "I have to run."

"Okay. Give my love to Dad. And have a fabulous time."

After Einstein was dry, Lukas carried him into the kitchen to ensure that he didn't try to jump all over their guests. Except that when he opened the laundry room door, he found Julie's chair was empty and both mother and son were gone.

His heart gave a little jolt—an instinctive response that he didn't want to think about too deeply—but settled again when he heard her voice in the family room. At first he thought she was talking to Caden, but as he finished tidying up the dishes from breakfast—not an easy task with the dog tucked under his arm—he realized that she was on the phone. Though he wasn't trying to listen to her conversation, he couldn't help but hear bits and pieces of it. She sounded cheerful and upbeat, so he was surprised—and distressed—to enter the family room after she'd ended the call and see tears on her cheeks.

From the time they were kids, his brothers had always teased him about his protective instincts. He never liked to see anyone or anything hurting. It was one of the reasons he'd become a vet—to help heal injured creatures. It still broke his heart when he couldn't save one of them, and it still brought him to his knees whenever he saw a woman in tears.

"Julie?" He crouched down beside the sofa, setting Einstein on the floor by his feet. "Is everything okay?"

She wiped at the wet streaks on her cheeks, but the tears continued to fall. "I'm sorry."

"Don't apologize," he said. "Just tell me what I can do to help."

She offered a wobbly smile but shook her head. "Nothing. I'm just being a big baby."

Which he didn't believe for a minute. "Do you want to tell me about the phone call?"

"My mom," she admitted. "I guess, now that I'm a mom, too, I really wanted to hear her voice and to tell her that I would be home in a few days. I haven't seen them in a while—my fault, because I was working out of town—and I just found out that she and my dad are going to Australia for a month."

He frowned. "They couldn't postpone their trip to see you and meet their new grandson?"

"They probably could—and they would."

"But?" he prompted.

"But it's their thirty-fifth anniversary and the trip was a surprise for my mom from my dad, a journey back to the place they first met."

"You didn't tell them that you had the baby, did you?"

"No," she admitted.

"Will there be anyone else at home when you get there?"

She shook her head. "My youngest brother, Ethan, is at school in Washington. He won't be home until Christmas break. Daniel lives in Boston and Kevin in New Haven."

"Are you going to tell them about Caden?"

"I can't tell them before I tell my parents," she said matter-of-factly.

"What about…" He wanted to ask about Caden's father, but he let the words fade away. He was undeniably curious, but he had no right to ask. They had been brought together by circumstances beyond anyone's control, and he didn't want to make her uncomfortable by pressing for information she didn't want to give.

She looked up at him, waiting for him to finish his question. She seemed to tense, as if she anticipated what he was going to ask and didn't want to answer. But instead he only said, "What do your brothers do?"

"Daniel's a corporate attorney, Kevin's the producer of a talk radio station and Ethan is still trying to figure out what he wants to be when he grows up."

"How old is he?"

"Twenty-seven," she admitted.

"You're the youngest."

"Is that a statement or a question?"

"It's a guess," he admitted. "But you don't look like you're even close to thirty."

"I'm the youngest," she confirmed, but didn't actually tell him how old she was.

"And the only girl."

She nodded.

"How was that—growing up with three older brothers?"

"Most of the time it was great," she said, then one corner of her mouth quirked upward in a half smile. "Except when it wasn't."

Being one of three brothers himself, he knew what she meant.

"Any of them married? Kids?"

"Just Kevin. He and Brooke recently celebrated their second anniversary, and they're expecting their first child in March."

"So Caden is the first grandchild for your parents?"

She nodded.

He frowned. "That's a pretty big milestone for most people."

She just nodded again.

He sensed that there was something she wasn't telling him, something she didn't want to tell him. And although he knew it wasn't any of his business—after all, they were only strangers whose paths would never have crossed if not for an unexpected snowstorm—he couldn't help but comment. "I know Caden came a couple of weeks early, but I wouldn't have thought they'd make plans to go anywhere when you were so close to your due date."

She finally lifted her gaze to meet his. "They wouldn't have—if they'd known I was pregnant."

He couldn't quite get his head around what she was saying. "Are you telling me that you managed to keep your pregnancy a secret from your family for the better part of nine months?"

"I didn't intend to keep it a secret," she admitted. "I wanted to tell them. But when I first left town, I didn't know I was pregnant."

"When did you know?"

"A few days later. And then, I didn't know *how* to tell them. It didn't seem like the kind of news I should share over the phone, and I was sure I would see them soon. But my job kept me so busy, I never had a chance to go home."

"You haven't been home in nine months?"

"Actually, it's more like seven months—since April," she admitted.

"And that kind of extended absence isn't unusual?"

"It was an extraordinary career opportunity," she explained. "As an art curator at The Grayson Gallery, I was invited to travel to select galleries around the United States with Evangeline Grayson's private collection of impressionist and post-impressionist art."

"Has it been that long since you've seen Caden's father, too?" Luke asked.

"Caden doesn't have a father," she said coolly.

His brows lifted. "I might not have any kids of my own, but I'm pretty sure I understand the basics of reproduction."

"Then you know that donating sperm doesn't make a man a father."

He didn't believe that her child had been conceived through intrauterine insemination. She seemed too young to have chosen that route—and too defensive. Which suggested that the story of Caden's father was a little more complicated than she wanted him to know.

And while he had a lot more questions, he accepted that she had no obligation to tell him anything. He also suspected that if he pushed for answers, she might lie, and he'd rather wait until she trusted him enough to tell him the truth.

So all he said was, "I just got a message from Bruce. He's towed your car, but he won't have a chance to look at it until Monday at the earliest."

"Monday?" she echoed, obviously disappointed.

He shrugged. "He's going to be busy the rest of the day hauling cars out of ditches, and he doesn't work on Sundays."

"I guess I should make some kind of arrangements, then."

"Arrangements for what?" he asked.

"Transportation to a hotel."

"We don't have a hotel in Pinehurst," he told her. "There are a few bed-and-breakfasts, and one roadside motel on the outskirts of town, but no hotel."

She frowned at that. "I guess I could try the motel."

"Why would you want to try somewhere else when there's plenty of room for both you and Caden here?"

She was shaking her head even before he finished speaking.

"Why not?" he challenged.

"Because we've imposed on you too much already."

"It's not an imposition."

"How is having a stranger and her newborn baby in your home *not* an imposition?"

"Because I want you to stay," he told her honestly. "At least until the weather clears and your car is fixed."

He didn't need to point out that there was no one waiting for her at home, as her response confirmed.

"I feel like I should decline your invitation, but considering that my options are extremely limited right now, I'll say thank you instead."

"You're welcome. I made up the bed in the first room at the top of the stairs," he told her. "It has a private en-suite bathroom, so you don't have to worry about sharing one."

"Does it have a shower?"

"As a matter of fact, it does."

"Because I would really appreciate being able to... Oh, no."

"What's wrong?"

"My suitcases are in the trunk of my car, and my car's on its way to Bruce's Body Shop."

"Your suitcases are already upstairs in the spare bedroom."

"They are?"

He shrugged. "You mentioned that you'd been travelling, so I figured you'd have some essentials with you. I got your luggage out of the trunk this morning."

"Thank you," she said sincerely. "After a shower and some clean clothes, I just might feel human again."

The guest room was bathed in natural light that poured through the pair of tall narrow windows. The double bed was covered in a beautiful sage-green comforter in a rich suede-like fabric. The dressers had strong but simple lines and were made of light-colored wood, and—as promised—her suitcases were on top of the blanket chest at the foot of the bed. The overall effect of the room was both warm and welcoming, and Julie wanted nothing as much as she wanted to fall into the bed and sleep for several hours.

Actually, that wasn't entirely true. As much as she wanted sleep, she wanted a shower even more. She opened the biggest suitcase and found her robe, then dug around for the toiletry bag with her shampoo, body wash and feminine hygiene products. Thankfully, she'd thought to stock up a few weeks earlier, because she wouldn't want to have to ask Lukas to make a trip to the pharmacy for her. On the other hand, the man had willingly stepped in to deliver her baby, so there probably wasn't much that fazed him.

The en-suite bathroom not only had a glass-walled shower with an adjustable showerhead but a separate soaker tub. For just a few seconds, Julie imagined herself sinking into a tub filled to the rim with frothy, scented bubbles, but she didn't want to chance taking a bath without checking with a doctor first. She also didn't want to leave Lukas with Caden for too long. Her host seemed comfortable and easy with the baby and she appreciated his willingness to help with him, but her son was her responsibility and a quick shower would have to suffice.

The towels on the rack were the same sage color as the spread in the bedroom, and thick and fluffy. There were apothecary jars filled with cotton swabs and cotton balls on the granite countertop and an assortment of decorative soaps in a basket on the apron of the tub.

She reached into the shower to turn on the faucet, then quickly stripped out of her clothes. When she stepped under the spray, the warm, pulsing water felt so good she nearly whimpered with relief. She poured a handful of body wash into her hand, then slicked it over her skin. She'd always figured that they called it *labor* because it wasn't a walk in the park, but she hadn't expected it to be such sweaty work. In retrospect, however, she was grateful that the process had gone so smoothly.

Since she'd learned of her pregnancy, Julie had been focused on doing everything she could to take care of herself and her unborn child. Everything she'd done over the past eight months had been with the goal of giving birth to a healthy baby.

Of course, she hadn't planned to give birth on a stranger's family-room couch, but when the only alternative was the frigid interior of a ditched car, it was undoubtedly the better option.

She'd thought about the birthing process a lot in recent months, but she'd always imagined herself in a brightly lit and sterile hospital room with a team of doctors and nurses around her. She'd never considered a home birth. That was fine for other people, if they chose, but not for her. She wanted to be in a hospital with medical personnel and pain-numbing drugs and emergency equipment in case of any complications.

It had been scary, the realization that there were none of those supports available when she went into labor, and she was sincerely thankful that there had been no problems. She was even more thankful that Lukas had been there to deliver her baby. Yeah, the realization that he was a veterinarian and not a medical doctor had thrown her for a minute, but in the end, all that really mattered was that he'd helped bring Caden into the world, because there was no way she could have done it without him.

It wasn't just that he'd been there to catch the baby—his calm demeanor and patient reassurance had alleviated a lot of her doubts and fears so that the process wasn't quite as terrifying as it might otherwise have been. She hadn't planned on having anyone in the delivery room with her and had resigned herself to going through the process alone.

In the end, however, she didn't feel as if she'd been alone at all. Lukas Garrett might have been a stranger, but he'd been there for her. And now, after everything they'd shared, she really felt as if he was a friend—someone she could count on.

Trust didn't come easily to her, especially not since the incident with Elliot, but she trusted Lukas. Of course, she'd had no choice but to trust him when she was in the middle of labor. She couldn't get to the hospital and her baby refused to wait to be born. But with every look, every word and every touch, he'd been compassionate and gentle and reassuring. And when she'd finally pushed her baby out into the world, she'd been grateful not just that someone was there to receive him, but that it was Lukas.

She squirted shampoo into her hand, scrubbed it through her hair. Through the whole childbirth experience, she'd been so preoccupied with the process and trying not to panic that she hadn't thought about anything else. She'd barely even noticed her rescuer's impressive physical attributes—but she hadn't been nearly as preoccupied this morning.

A brand-new mother probably shouldn't be aware of the incredible sexiness of a well-built man, but she was still a woman, and Lukas Garrett was definitely a man. A man who made her blood hum and her skin tingle, and those were very definite warning signs that Julie should keep a safe distance from him.

She'd been hurt by Elliott. Not just by his actions and his words, but by the realization that she hadn't known her fiancé nearly as well as she'd thought she did. She'd seen only what she wanted to see, and she'd made the wrong choice. Again.

Her father—a baseball aficionado—was fond of the expression "three strikes and you're out." So after Julie's third strike in the romance department, she'd accepted that it was time to walk off the field. That was it—she was finished with dating and done with men.

Travelling across the country with Evangeline's collection, she'd had more than a few handsome men cross her path. But none of them had made her feel anything. She chatted, she flirted—it was part of the job, after all, to be sociable—but she didn't feel anything. In fact, she'd been certain that she wouldn't ever feel anything again, that what Elliott had done had left her numb inside.

She wasn't feeling numb now.

She knew that her body was flooded with hormones as a result of the pregnancy and childbirth processes. It was entirely possible that her physiological response had absolutely nothing to do with Lukas Garrett personally and everything to do with the fact that she had an overabundance of estrogen and progesterone zinging through her system that wanted to rendezvous with the testosterone in his.

Except that she hadn't had the same reaction to Cameron Turcotte. The other man was arguably just as handsome as the veterinarian, but her pulse hadn't even fluttered when he'd walked into the room. Of course, he'd also worn a wide gold band on the third finger of his left hand, so maybe her hormones weren't completely indiscriminate, after all. Or maybe it was the emotional connection that had been forged through the sharing of the childbirth experience with Lukas that was stirring her up inside.

Whatever the reason, it was a complication she didn't need or want. Thankfully, this awareness or attraction or whatever she was feeling wouldn't be an issue for long. As soon as Bruce checked over her car and deemed it road-worthy, she would be on her way back to Springfield and would probably never see Lukas Garrett again.

With that thought, she flicked off the tap and reached for a towel. Every inch of her skin felt hypersensitive, almost achy, as she rubbed the thick terry cloth over her body. It had been a long time since anyone had touched her—since she'd even thought about a man's hands on her. But she was thinking about it now. And wanting.

Muttering an oath of frustration, she wrapped the robe around herself and knotted the belt at her waist. Her hair was dripping wet, and she'd forgotten to get her hair dryer out of the suitcase, so she strode back into the bedroom to retrieve it—and let out a startled gasp.

Chapter Six

Luke didn't realize Julie had finished in the shower until he heard her gasp.

"Sorry." His apology was immediate and sincere. "I didn't hear the water shut off, and I didn't expect you to finish in the shower so quickly." Which was true, even if it didn't begin to explain his presence in her bedroom.

She tugged on the lapel of her robe, no doubt to close the open V that he couldn't help but notice dipped low between her breasts. "What are you doing in here?"

"I found something in the attic that I thought you could use."

She glanced at Caden, lying on his back in the middle of the bed, as if to reassure herself that he hadn't been abandoned or neglected. "What is it?"

"Come and have a look," he invited, and stepped aside so that she could see.

Her gaze shifted, her eyes went wide. "Oh. Wow."

Her instinctive response obliterated any lingering doubts about his impulsive gesture.

She took one step forward, then another. She knelt beside the cherry wood cradle, her lips curving as she ran a hand over the smooth, glossy wood. "This is…beautiful."

"It's old," he admitted.

"Timeless," she whispered, almost reverently. Then looked up at him. "Was it yours?"

He nodded. "But it was Jack's before it was mine, and Matt's before that."

She trailed a finger down one of the spindles. "I've never seen anything like it."

"It was handmade by Rob Turcotte—Cam's father. He was a really good friend of my dad's—and an incredibly talented carpenter. He made it as a gift to my parents when my mom was expecting Matt."

Luke was babbling, but he couldn't seem to stop himself. Because he hoped that conversation would help focus his attention on something—*anything*—but the sexy curves of the woman in front of him.

He knew that he should look away, but he seemed to be suffering a momentary disconnect between his eyes and his brain. Or maybe he was simply a red-blooded man facing a beautiful, mostly naked woman. Looking at her now, he never would have guessed that she'd given birth just about eighteen hours earlier.

Her skin was rosy from the shower, and droplets of water glistened on her skin. The short silky robe belted at her waist did nothing to hide her distinctly feminine shape, and the hem skimmed just above her knees, drawing attention to her long, sexy legs.

His gaze skimmed upward again, and he couldn't help but notice that her wet hair tumbled over her shoulders, dripping onto her robe so that there were wet patches on the fabric just above her breasts. And when he realized that the nipples of those breasts were taut beneath the silky fabric, his mouth went completely dry and the blood in his head started to quickly migrate south.

He took a deliberate step back, a tactical retreat.

She cleared her throat, then gestured to the suitcases at the end of the bed. "I forgot my, um, hair dryer."

He nodded. "Clothes," he said, his voice sounding strangled. "You might want some clothes, too."

Her cheeks flushed prettily. "Yeah."

"I'll get out of your way," he said, and hurried out of the room.

After Julie's hair was dried and she was dressed in a pair of yoga pants and a tunic-style top, she fed Caden again before carrying him back downstairs to the family room. Apparently Lukas had found more than a cradle in the attic, because he was now in the process of putting together something that looked like a playpen.

"This doesn't have any sentimental value," he said, when she entered the room. "It's just old. And it probably doesn't comply with current safety guidelines, but since Caden isn't rolling around yet, it should suffice if you want to put him down for a few minutes without having to worry about Einstein climbing over him."

She eyed the structure dubiously as she settled back on the sofa. Although Lukas's puppy had actually shown incredible restraint around the baby so far, she wasn't convinced that the well-spaced spindles would keep him out. "Are you sure Einstein can't squeeze through those bars?"

"I'm sure," Lukas said. "He's tried three times already and he keeps getting his head stuck."

"Oh, the poor thing." She rubbed behind the puppy's ears,

and his whole back end wagged happily in response to the attention.

"The 'poor thing' should have learned after the first try," Lukas grumbled.

"Isn't perseverance a virtue?"

"What you think of as perseverance others might consider stubbornness or stupidity," he said, with a stern look at the puppy.

Einstein, obviously sensing his master's disapproval, dropped his head and looked up at him with sad eyes.

Julie had to bite down on her lip to hold back a smile. "I think he's a lot smarter than you give him credit for."

Before he could respond to that, the back door slammed, and she heard a female voice say, "Snowsuits and boots off." The command was followed by the rustle of outerwear being shed and the thump of boots hitting the floor, then footsteps pounded.

Lukas winced. "It sounds like Matt may have brought the whole family," he warned.

She was afraid to ask what "the whole family" entailed, but the first part of the answer was apparent when two dark-haired boys raced into the room. They were similarly dressed in jeans and hooded sweatshirts, one red and the other blue, and Einstein raced to greet them, dancing around their legs.

"Where is he?" The one in red pushed ahead. "I wanna see him."

"Me, too," his brother chimed in.

Lukas stood in front of Julie—a human barrier between the new mom and the eager twins—and held up his hands. "Slow down, boys."

"But we wanna see the baby," red shirt entreated. "We don't have a boy baby at our house."

"We just gots a girl," blue shirt said.

"You *have* a girl," an authoritative female voice said from the doorway.

The boy in red tilted his head to peek around Lukas. "Her name's Pippa," he told Julie. "She's our sister."

"And who are you?" she asked him.

Now that the boys weren't barreling full-speed ahead, Lukas stepped aside so that they could talk to Julie—and see the baby.

"I'm Quinn." He nudged his brother closer. "This is Shane."

"And I'm their mother." The other woman set an overflowing laundry basket on the floor beside the sofa. "Georgia."

Her smile was warm and genuine, and Julie found herself responding easily. "Julie Marlowe. And this is Caden."

"Oh—he's absolutely gorgeous," Georgia said, crouching down for a closer look.

"Speaking of gorgeous—where is Pippa?" Lukas asked.

Georgia slapped a hand to her forehead. "I knew I was forgetting something."

Julie actually felt her heart skip a beat. Had she really—

Then the boys giggled.

"You didn't forget her," Quinn assured his mother. "She's with Daddy."

"We gots a new daddy," Shane told Julie. "'Cuz our first daddy went to heaven."

Julie didn't have a clue how to respond to that, so she was relieved when Georgia spoke up.

"There are some more things in the van," she told Lukas. "And the boys insisted on bringing Finn and Fred, too, so I'm sure Matt would appreciate a hand."

"I've got two I can lend him," he said, and headed out to do that.

"Who are Finn and Fred?" Julie wondered.

"Our puppies!" Quinn announced.

"From the same litter as Einstein," Georgia elaborated.

"The local softhearted vet was stuck with eight orphaned puppies, and somehow convinced his brother to take two of them."

"What's a orphan?" Shane wanted to know.

"*An* orphan is someone who doesn't have a mommy or a daddy," his mother explained.

"How was he born if he didn't have a mommy?"

Georgia forced a smile. "Can we save this conversation for home? We came here to meet Julie and her baby, remember?"

Shane nodded. "He's even smaller than Pippa."

"She was about the same size as Caden when she was born," Georgia told him. "Although it's probably hard to remember that now."

"I never heard of the name Caden," Quinn told Julie. "But we gotsa Cain in our kinnergarden class."

"He eats glue," Shane informed her solemnly.

Julie had to chuckle at that. "Well, hopefully I'll teach Caden not to do that before it's time for him to go to school."

The boys crowded closer to get a better view of the baby. Caden looked back at them, his big blue eyes wide. For a whole minute, neither of the twins moved, they just watched intently.

Finally Quinn's gaze shifted to Julie. "Does he do *anything?*"

"Not really," she admitted. "Right now, he eats a lot and sleeps a lot."

"Does he poop a lot, too?" the boy wanted to know. "'Cuz Pippa does."

Julie found herself laughing again. "Well, he hasn't done a lot of that yet, but he was only born yesterday."

She saw movement in the doorway, and glanced over just as Lukas walked back in. Two seconds later, she realized that it wasn't Lukas, after all, but a man who looked so much like him, he had to be his brother. And the baby on his hip—an adorable little girl dressed in pink overalls with tiny pink sneakers on her feet—had to be Pippa.

"There's my girl," Georgia said.

Pippa smiled widely, showing four tiny pearly white teeth, and held her arms out to her mother.

"She is gorgeous," Julie said.

"That's because she looks just like her mama," Matt said, touching a hand to his wife's shoulder.

"Another unbiased opinion," she said dryly.

He just grinned. "I'm Matt," he said, offering his hand to Julie. "The *real* Dr. Garrett."

"Not that he has much more experience than Lukas when it comes to delivering babies," Georgia said.

"I did an obstetrics rotation in med school," he pointed out.

"How many years ago was that?" his wife challenged.

"More than I'm willing to admit."

"Well, according to Dr. Turcotte, Lukas did just fine," Julie told him.

"Lukas had the easy part," Matt told her.

"I'm not sure how easy it was to keep me from going into full-scale panic when I realized I wasn't going to make it to the hospital to have my baby," she admitted. "But he did it."

"Those Garretts know how to get what they want," Georgia told her.

"That we do." Her husband's admission was accompanied by a quick grin.

"I wanna play outside," Quinn said. "In the snow."

"Me, too," Shane said.

"That sounds like a terrific idea," their mother agreed. "Especially if Daddy and Uncle Lukas go with you."

Both boys turned to Matt. "Yeah, Daddy. *Pleeease.*"

He looked at Georgia, his brows lifted. "Trying to get rid of me?"

"Just so that Julie and I can share labor stories and talk about babies and breasts and—"

"I'll go play with the boys," he said.

"Yay!" They raced out of the room with as much energy and enthusiasm as they'd raced into it.

Matt dropped a kiss on the top of his wife's head and walked out of the room.

"I'm so sorry," Georgia apologized when they were gone. "I really tried to entice the boys to stay at home with Ava— Jack and Kelly's daughter—but even though they absolutely adore their cousin, they didn't want any part of that today."

"I'm glad you brought them," Julie assured her. "They're fabulous kids."

"Most days," Georgia acknowledged with a weary smile.

"And Matt—does he always do what you tell him to?"

"Usually." The other woman grinned. "Of course, it helps that it's usually what he wants to do, anyway. And he loves spending time with the kids—it gives him an excuse to act like a kid himself."

"Do you mind if I ask you another question?"

"Ask away."

"How did you manage two of them? I feel as if I didn't sleep at all last night, and Caden's only one baby."

"I wasn't on my own when the twins were born. Their dad worked a lot of long hours, but it seriously helped me get through the day just knowing that I could pass one or both of them off to him when he got home. So if you have any kind of support network, I would strongly recommend you utilize it."

"I'll keep that in mind," Julie said.

She was relieved that Georgia hadn't asked about Caden's father. She didn't want to lie but she didn't know any of these people well enough to tell them the truth. Still, she knew that she needed to tell someone, which made her think again about the appointment she'd missed with Jackson Garrett.

Since her reasons for wanting to consult with a lawyer hadn't changed, she should reschedule that appointment. Except now that her brother's friend was also the brother of the man who had delivered her baby, the situation was a little more complicated, making her doubt whether she should confide in him or find different legal counsel.

"Another thing to keep in mind is that it will get easier," Georgia told her. "It will take a while, but you and Caden will establish rhythms and routines, you'll start to anticipate his needs and adjust your schedule accordingly."

"Fingers crossed," Julie said.

"And when things get really crazy and you want to outscream your screaming baby, just try to remember that incredible feeling of love and joy that filled your heart when he was first placed in your arms."

"I still feel that," Julie admitted. "Every time I look at him."

"Savor it," Georgia advised.

"What aren't you telling me?"

The other woman hesitated, then shrugged. "Pippa went through a colicky stage, which was pretty much pure hell for about three months."

Julie looked at the smiling, cooing baby. "Neither of you looks any the worse for wear."

"Not now," Georgia agreed.

"You have a beautiful family."

"I'm a lucky woman—although it took me a while to get settled here in Pinehurst and realize how very lucky."

"You're not from here?"

Georgia shook her head. "I moved from New York City last February."

"That's a major change—not with respect to geography so much as lifestyle, I would think."

"You'd be right. But I needed to make a major change.

Phillip, my first husband, passed away when I was pregnant with Pippa, and I found it more than a little overwhelming to be on my own with two toddlers and another baby on the way. So when my mother invited me to move in with her, it seemed like a perfect solution." She smiled wryly. "And it was until four months later when she moved to Montana."

"Why Montana?"

"She fell in love with a cowboy." Georgia smiled. "Which was great for her but a little unsettling for me, since I'd moved here to be closer to her. And then Matt moved in next door to me."

"That's how you met?"

She nodded. "And three months later, we got married."

"Fast work," Julie mused.

"On his part or mine?"

"I guess you'd have to tell me."

Georgia chuckled. "I wasn't looking for happily-ever-after. I wasn't even looking for a relationship. I had my hands more than full enough with three kids, but Matt found a way to be there, to fit in, to be everything I never knew I needed. How could I not fall head over heels in love?"

Julie didn't envy the other woman her happiness. Georgia had obviously traveled a difficult road to get to where she was at. But she did wonder what it would be like to fall head over heels in love and to know, as Georgia obviously did, that she was loved the same way in return.

Julie had never experienced that depth of emotion. She'd had intense crushes and serious infatuations, all of which had eventually faded or fizzled. She'd thought she was in love with Elliott—she never would have agreed to marry him otherwise—but she also would never have described herself as head over heels. Their affection for one another had grown over time, a result of common goals and shared interests. Which, in retrospect, seemed more like the foundation for a strong business partnership than a successful marriage. And then even that foundation had crumbled.

"Of course, the Garrett men are all charmers," Georgia continued. "Which might explain why Luke is the only one in Pinehurst who's still single. Is your baby's father in the picture?"

The question came at her so unexpectedly, Julie found herself shaking her head before she realized it.

"Good."

"Why is that good?" she asked curiously.

"Because of the vibes in the air between my brother-in-law and you."

"I think you're misinterpreting something."

"Am I?" the other woman mused.

She felt her cheeks flush. "I don't even know him."

"You don't have to know a man to be attracted to him," Georgia said matter-of-factly.

"I suppose not," she agreed.

"But I didn't mean to make you uncomfortable."

"You didn't. I'm not," Julie said. "I'm…confused."

Georgia smiled. "Yeah, I remember that feeling, too."

Julie didn't know what to say to that, so she was grateful that the other woman didn't seem to expect a response.

"But I didn't come over here to play matchmaker, only to bring a few things that you might be able to use for Caden."

"It looks like more than a few things," Julie noted, relieved by the change of topic.

"I had twins," Georgia reminded her. "Which means that I had to have two of everything, including infant car seats. I'm still using one for Pippa, but you're more than welcome to the other one. The base secures into your vehicle, and the carrier pops in and out, which is great for carting a baby around or even just as a place for him to sit while you're doing something else.

"When the twins were babies, I used to put them in their car seats on the floor in the bathroom while I was in the shower, because I was absolutely paranoid that something would happen if I didn't have my eyes on them every single minute."

Julie smiled at that. "Glad to know it's not just me."

"It's not just you. In fact, it's probably most new mothers."

"I just feel so completely unprepared. I thought I'd have more time to get ready. My own fault for listening to a friend who assured me that first babies never come early."

"They are more often late than early, but each baby comes in his own time," Georgia told her.

"It would have been nice if Caden had waited to come until after the storm had passed."

"But now you have an interesting story to tell when he asks about when and how he was born."

Julie would never forget the circumstances of her son's birth—or the connection that she now felt to the man who had helped deliver him. "There is that," she agreed.

"Mommy!" Clomping footsteps came through the kitchen, then a snow-covered bundle appeared in the doorway. Wrapped up as he was in the bulky snowsuit with a red hat pulled down to his eyes and a matching scarf wrapped around his throat, Julie couldn't tell if it was Quinn or Shane. But if she had to guess, she would say Quinn, since he seemed to be the more talkative and outgoing of the two brothers.

"Uncle Luke sent me in to get a carrot," he announced.

Georgia rose to her feet. "A carrot?"

"We made a snowman!"

"You look like a snowman," his mother told him.

The child giggled. "Shane 'n me made angels in the snow, too."

"Well, you're dripping all over Uncle Lukas's floor," Georgia chided. "So come back to the kitchen while I find you a carrot."

Since Caden was asleep again, Julie set him down in the playpen and followed them to the other room. "I think I want to see this snowman."

"It's out there." Quinn pointed a red, snow-covered mitten toward the back window.

Julie had made her share of snowmen as a kid, but even with the help of her older brothers, she'd never managed to put together anything of the scope or scale that the twins, along with their new daddy and uncle, had assembled.

It was a larger-than-life creation, with arms that reached up to the sky. There were mittens on its hands, a striped scarf around its throat, and a matching knitted hat on its head. The eyes were probably dark stones but they looked like coal and the mouth was made up of smaller stones curved into a lop-sided but undeniably happy grin.

But as impressive as the snowman was, it was Lukas, wrestling in the snow with his shy nephew, who captivated her.

Georgia joined her at the window.

"Isn't he awesome?" the little boy said.

Yes, he is, Julie thought, before she tore her attention from the flesh-and-blood man and shifted it to the one made of snow.

"I almost expect him to start dancing," she told Quinn.

"You'd need a magic hat for that," Georgia advised.

"Do we have a magic hat?" he asked hopefully.

"Nope. Just a carrot," the boy's mother said, and handed him the vegetable.

When Frosty's nose was in position, Matt decided that the boys' hard work had earned them big cups of hot chocolate with lots of marshmallows on top. Of course, this suggestion sent them racing back into the house to beg their mother to make it, which warned Luke that his brother wanted to talk to him without the twins overhearing their conversation.

A suspicion that was confirmed when Matt said, "So what's her story?"

There was no point in pretending he didn't know who the "her" was that his brother was asking about. "I don't know many of the details," he admitted. "She tends to skirt around personal questions."

And though his brother probably wasn't concerned with her financial status, Luke suspected that Julie came from a family with money. The car Bruce had towed out of the ditch was a late-model Audi A6 that he knew, from a trip to last year's auto show, was worth a pretty penny. The watch on her wrist was also pretty—and costly—and her clothes were likely designer. He wasn't familiar enough with any specific label to be able to identify what she was wearing, it was more in the way they fit, the quality of the fabrics and the cut. On the other hand, he suspected that Julie would look equally stylish dressed in an old potato sack.

"Did she say anything about the baby's father?" Matt pressed.

Luke shook his head.

"Did you ask?"

"Of course not."

"Why not?"

"Because I figured if she wanted me to know, she'd tell me."

"Aren't you curious?"

"Sure," he admitted. "But it's really none of my business."

"She's living under your roof."

"She was stranded in a storm." Luke felt compelled to point out the obvious. "I haven't put her on the title to the property."

"I know," his brother admitted. "Just…be careful."

"Careful of what?"

"Falling for her—and her baby."

He snorted. "I'm not the falling type."

"There's a first time for everything," Matt warned.

"No need to worry," he assured his brother. "She's not going to be here long enough for me to even lose my balance."

"It doesn't take long."

Of course, Matt would know. Seven years earlier, he'd accepted the daddy role not just easily but eagerly when he'd learned his girlfriend was pregnant—only to find out, three years after their wedding, that the child she'd given birth to wasn't his. And yet, that experience hadn't prevented him from falling all over again—this time for a young widow and her three children. Thankfully, that story had a much happier ending.

"And I've seen the way you look at her," Matt added.

He frowned at that. "How do I look at her?"

"The same way you used to look at the green mountain bike in the window of Beckett's Sporting Goods store when you were a kid."

Luke remembered that bike—and the quick thrill that had gone through him when he'd seen it in the family room with a big bow on it the morning of his twelfth birthday. A thrill not unlike what he felt whenever Julie walked into the room.

"She's a beautiful woman," he said, careful to keep his tone light.

"She is that," his brother agreed. "But there's something about her—a vulnerability that reminds me too much of the wounded strays you were always bringing home."

"First a bike, then a puppy—I wonder if Julie would appreciate either of those comparisons."

"I'm not worried about her. I'm worried about you."

"I'm thirty-four years old," he reminded Matt.

"And starting to think that it's time to settle down and have a family?"

"No." Luke shook his head. He was happy for both of his brothers, pleased that they were happy, but he didn't want what they had. Marriage and kids? Not anywhere on his radar.

At least not before he'd heard Caden's first indignant cry and looked into those wide, curious eyes trying to focus on a whole new world. In that moment there had maybe—just maybe—been the tiniest blip on Luke's radar. Not that he would ever admit as much to his brother.

"Right now, the only thing I'm thinking about is hot chocolate," he said, and turned to follow the path his nephews had taken back into the house.

Chapter Seven

"I really like your brother's family," Julie said to Lukas after Matt and Georgia had packed up their kids and puppies and gone.

"He definitely lucked out when he bought the house next door to Georgia," Luke agreed. "She's one in a million."

"He must be one in a million, too—a man willing to take on the responsibility of her three kids."

"Not just willing but eager," he admitted, remembering how he and Jack had both worried about their big brother's single-minded pursuit of the widowed mother of three. "Of course, Matt's always wanted a big family. And he couldn't love those kids any more if they were his own."

"You can see it in the way they are together—like all of the pieces just fit." She sounded just a little bit wistful.

"They do fit," he agreed. "But that doesn't mean it was easy."

She looked down at her baby, snuggled contentedly in

her arms. "That's what I want for Caden," she told him. "A real family."

Luke waited for the warning bells to start clanging inside of his head, but nothing happened. Okay, so maybe he was overreacting. After all, she hadn't been looking at him when she'd said it, but at the baby. There was no reason—aside from a possibly overinflated ego—to think that she imagined him anywhere in the picture of that family she wanted.

In fact, it was entirely possible that she wasn't thinking about him at all but the man who was her baby's father. Which, recalling his brother's warnings, seemed the perfect opportunity to ask about him.

"Maybe Caden's father wants the same thing," he suggested.

"I told you—Caden doesn't have a father."

Of course, he knew that wasn't true. He also knew that whatever had happened between the man and Julie didn't negate his parental rights and responsibilities. But she obviously wasn't ready to tell him anything about that relationship. Maybe he'd cheated on her—or maybe he'd been cheating *with* her. If the man already had a family with someone else, he wouldn't be in a position to give Julie the family she wanted for her son.

"Well, I'd say he's off to a good start, because he's got a great mother, anyway," he told her.

Her lips curved, but the smile didn't reach her eyes, and he suspected that she didn't trust he was willing to drop the subject of Caden's father. "I'm flattered you think so," she said. "But the truth is, I have absolutely no idea what I'm doing."

"Fake it till you make it."

"That's interesting advice."

"I'm an interesting guy," he said immodestly.

She looked at him now, her gaze speculative. "And far too charming for your own good," she decided.

"Since when is an excess of charm a bad thing?"

"When it's part of a package that includes a too-handsome face and a smile that makes a woman's knees weak."

There was no way he could not smile in response to that. "You think I'm handsome?"

"It's not an opinion but a fact," she told him.

"Do I make your knees weak?"

"Right now, I'm weak from hunger," she told him. "Breakfast was a long time ago and that chili your sister-in-law brought over smells fabulous."

His teasing smile faded. He was accustomed to being on his own and not having to think about anyone else, and it was only now he realized they'd skipped lunch. Which wasn't unusual for him, but probably wasn't advisable for a nursing mother.

"You should have said that you were hungry," he admonished. Then he shook his head. "No, you don't have to tell me—just help yourself to anything you want. And if there's something that you want that I don't have, let me know so I can get it for you."

She touched a hand to his arm, silencing his rambling apology.

"I'm not really starving," she assured him. "But that chili does smell good."

"I'll dish it up."

Julie decided to try Caden in the car seat/carrier that Georgia had brought over. When he was buckled in, she sat him across from her at the table while Lukas sliced a loaf of crusty bread to accompany the chili.

Conversation throughout the meal was casual and easy, and Julie began to relax again. She'd enjoyed the teasing banter they'd exchanged earlier, had felt comfortable with Lukas. And then she'd touched him—just a casual brush of her fingertips to his sleeve—but the sparks that had flown from the contact had unnerved her.

"Fiction or nonfiction?" he asked, pushing aside his now empty bowl.

"Sorry?"

"What do you like to read?"

"Almost anything," she told him. "But I'm not a fan of the horror genre. What about you?"

"Mostly nonfiction," he said. "Rock or country?"

"Alternative."

His brows lifted at her response. "Me, too," he admitted. "Romantic comedies or action flicks?"

"Depends on my mood."

"What are you in the mood for tonight? There's a Sandra Bullock, Hugh Grant movie on TV or we can choose something from my James Bond collection."

"You don't have to entertain me," she told him.

"I don't see how sliding a DVD into a player qualifies as me entertaining you."

"I just figured you had better things to do than hang out with me."

"I can't imagine anything better than spending a few hours in the company of a beautiful woman," he countered.

Julie was flattered—and tempted. Because as tired as she was, she was even more tired of being alone. For the past seven months, she'd moved from city to city, gallery to gallery. Yes, she'd routinely been introduced to new people, but at the end of each day, she'd gone back to an empty hotel room alone. She'd kept in touch with her family and friends, but the distance had been lonely.

Now the show was over, Evangeline's collection had been carefully packed up and shipped back to The Grayson Gallery, and Julie was officially on the three-month maternity leave that she'd negotiated with her employer. She didn't have to be "on" anymore, she didn't have to present a polished and professional image. What Lukas was offering her right now—the chance to sit and relax and tuck her feet up beneath her on the sofa—sounded too good to refuse. And she wasn't going to.

"Despite the blatantly inaccurate but much appreciated compliment, I would enjoy watching a movie with you," she told him.

"So what will it be? Rom-com or double-oh-seven?"

"Double-oh-seven," she said without hesitation. "I'm still feeling a little emotional and I don't know you well enough to want to bawl my eyes out in front of you twice in one day."

"You didn't bawl earlier," he denied. "You were just a little teary."

"That doesn't make me feel better," she told him.

"Okay—any particular Bond flick you want to see?"

"Do you have the latest one?"

"Is it your favorite?"

"I haven't actually seen it yet."

"Then that's what we'll watch." He stood up to carry their bowls to the dishwasher. "Did you, uh, want to nurse the baby before we start the movie?"

She glanced at the slim, white-gold watch on her wrist. He noticed that the elegant oval was ringed with diamonds and the name on the face said Cartier. "I probably should," she said in response to his question.

"I'll tidy up in here and make popcorn while you're doing that," he said.

"Popcorn? We just finished dinner."

"There's always room for popcorn," he insisted.

She frowned. "Isn't that Jell-O?"

"Sorry, I don't have any Jell-O."

She was shaking her head when she carried Caden out to the family room.

Luke puttered around in the kitchen for a while, putting

away the leftovers, loading the dishwasher, checking that both Einstein and Daphne had water in their respective dishes. The popcorn would only take a few minutes in the microwave but it would take Julie longer than that to nurse Caden.

When the popcorn was popped, he dumped it into a bowl and carried it, along with a can of cola for himself and a glass of water for Julie, to the family room.

"Can I ask you a question?"

"Sure," he agreed easily.

"Does being around a nursing mother make you uncomfortable?"

"No," he immediately responded, though his gaze shifted away. "I think it's one of the most incredible and beautiful things I've ever seen."

"Then why do you jump up and leave the room every time you think Caden's hungry?"

"Because I thought you might be uncomfortable, nursing in front of a stranger."

She shrugged. "My body stopped being my own when I got pregnant. And considering that you helped deliver my baby, it seems pointless to be self-conscious about baring a breast when you've seen much more intimate parts of me."

"Okay, then," he said, because his brain suddenly seemed incapable of generating a more articulate response.

"And it's your house," she reminded him. "So if I'm uncomfortable, I can go to my room. And if you're uncomfortable, you can send me to my room."

"Seeing you nurse your baby doesn't make me uncomfortable," he assured her. "This conversation, on the other hand…"

She laughed. "Okay—conversation over."

"Thank you," he said, and picked up the remote.

Luke wasn't surprised that Julie fell asleep before the end of the movie. What did surprise him was that when she did succumb to slumber, her head tipped toward him, then nestled against his shoulder.

He could smell the scent of her shampoo, and it reminded him of fruity drinks and tropical beaches. Her hair was soft and shiny and a thousand different shades of gold. Her skin was flawless and pale, her cheekbones high, her lashes long and thick. Her lips were exquisitely shaped, and temptingly full.

He felt a stirring low in his belly, tried to ignore it. She was an attractive woman so it wasn't unexpected that he would be attracted to her. But under the circumstances, it would be completely *in*appropriate to act on that attraction.

So though he was tempted to dip his head, to brush his lips over the sweet, soft curve of hers and wake her with a long, lingering kiss, he knew that he couldn't. She wasn't *his* sleeping beauty and he wasn't anyone's prince.

Even if, for just a minute, he wanted to be.

Luke loved all of his nieces and nephews, and he got a kick out of hanging out with the kids, but that was good enough for him. He had no desire to tie himself to one woman—who would want that when there were so many fascinating and interesting women to choose from?—and no concern about carrying on the family name—and why would he, when his brothers already had that covered? In fact, he couldn't remember the last time he'd been involved in a relationship that had lasted even six months. And that was okay, because he'd never seen himself as the type to settle down with a wife and a couple of kids.

But his mind had started moving in a different direction when he'd helped deliver Julie Marlowe's baby. There was something about the little boy that had taken a firm hold on his heart. Maybe it was the fact that his hands had been the first to hold the newborn infant, but whatever the reason, he felt as if there was a real connection between them.

Unfortunately, he knew that when Julie decided to go back to Massachusetts he'd probably never see her or Caden again. The prospect left him feeling strangely empty inside.

And it wasn't just the little guy that he would miss. Though he'd barely known Julie for twenty-four hours, they'd been through a lot together in that short period of time. He didn't know her well, but he knew that she was smart and strong and brave and spunky, and he knew that he wanted some time to get to know her better.

Whether it was fate or providence or luck, she wasn't going anywhere for at least a few days. Not while the snow was still falling and her vehicle was at Bruce's Body Shop. And maybe, by the time the storm passed and her car was fixed, she would want to stay a little longer.

Or maybe by then he'd be ready for them to go.

Okay, so he didn't think *that* was a likely scenario, but living with a woman and her baby was completely outside of his realm of experience so he wasn't going to assume anything.

The end credits rolled, and still she didn't stir. With sincere reluctance, he finally nudged her gently with his shoulder.

"Come on," he said. "I don't want to sleep in a chair again tonight."

Her eyelids flickered, then slowly lifted. It took a moment for her soft blue-gray gaze to focus, but the moment that it did, she pulled away from him. "I fell asleep," she realized. "I'm so sorry."

"No need to apologize to me." He lifted the baby from her arms, then helped Julie to her feet. "Although Daniel Craig would probably be upset to know that he put you to sleep."

"I *wish* Daniel Craig was here to put me to sleep."

He sighed and shook his head. "Runner-up again."

"Actually, you're better than Daniel Craig," she told him. "He's just a fantasy, but you're real. And you saved my baby."

He wasn't comfortable being thrust into the role of a hero.

Especially when anyone else would have done the same thing under the circumstances. So he ignored the latter part of her comment and said, "Come on." He nudged her toward the stairs. "Let's get you up to a real bed."

When they reached the guest room, he turned on the bedside lamp, then gently laid Caden down in the cradle.

"Do you have pajamas?" he asked Julie, who was already tugging back the covers on the bed.

"I'm too tired to get changed," she said.

He didn't argue with her. And when she'd crawled between the sheets, he moved over to the bed and dropped a chaste kiss on her forehead. "Sweet dreams."

"You, too," she said, her eyes already shut.

As Luke made his way to his own room down the hall, he suspected that he would be tossing and turning all night. Thinking about the woman down the hall, and wanting what he couldn't have.

When Julie awoke the next morning, she didn't remember if she'd dreamed, but she'd definitely slept better than the night before. She was still up countless times to nurse and change and cuddle with Caden, but she didn't have any trouble falling back to sleep in between. And Caden had slept well in the cradle—if not for any longer than three hours at a time.

After his morning feeding, Julie took another shower and changed into a clean pair of yoga pants and a wrap-style sweater. A quick glance at the clock revealed that it was after 8:00 a.m. She hadn't heard any activity from down the hall, and she wondered if Lukas was already up and about or if he was still sleeping.

As she started down the stairs, she noticed Einstein waiting for her at the bottom, dancing around in excited anticipation.

She bent to pat his head, and he fairly quivered with excitement. For an active and exuberant pup, he was surprisingly restrained around the baby, which she appreciated.

He raced down the hall, then back again. She didn't have any trouble interpreting his silent message, and she followed him to the kitchen.

"Pancakes okay?" Lukas said by way of greeting when she appeared in the doorway.

"Very okay," she said. "But you don't have to cook for me all the time."

He shrugged. "I was cooking for myself, anyway."

She settled Caden into his carrier as Lukas put a platter of food on the table. Along with a generous stack of fluffy pancakes was a pile of crisp bacon strips.

"You made bacon again?"

"You don't have to eat it if you don't want it," he told her.

"The problem is that I do want it," she admitted, and snagged a piece from the platter.

"Would you feel less guilty if I told you it was turkey bacon?"

"Yes." She bit into it. "Is it?"

"No, but I'll lie if it will make you feel better."

She took a couple more slices, then added a couple of pancakes to her plate. Lukas sat down with her and proceeded to slather his pancakes with butter and drench them with syrup.

They chatted while they ate. Lukas teased her with hints about what parts of the movie she'd missed when she'd fallen asleep the night before—although she was skeptical about his claim that James Bond had to battle a one-legged Gypsy bank robber and his buxom transgendered girlfriend. He made her smile and laugh, and he made her forget all the reasons that she'd run away from Springfield more than seven months earlier and appreciate the fact that she was with him here in Pinehurst now.

He was halfway through his stack of pancakes when a low hum sounded from across the room. "Sorry," he apologized, pushing his chair away from the table. "That's my pager."

He read the message on the display, then disappeared into his office, no doubt to make a call. Julie finished her breakfast, stealing another piece of bacon from the platter and chatted with Caden while she waited for Lukas to return.

When he came back to the table, he wasn't smiling. Without a word, he picked up his plate and scraped the contents into the garbage.

"Is everything okay?" she asked tentatively.

He shook his head. "No. I have to go see a patient."

"I didn't know vets made house calls."

"Sometimes." He grabbed his keys from the counter, and Einstein was immediately at his feet, tail wagging. Lukas shook his head. "Sorry, buddy. Not this time." When the puppy's ears dropped, he bent to give the dog a quick scratch.

"I'll be back soon," he said.

Julie wasn't sure if he was talking to her or the dog, and then he was gone.

Despite his promise to be back soon, Lukas was gone for most of the day. Julie wasn't concerned by his absence so much as she was concerned about him, because it was apparent that whatever had called him away from home on a Sunday morning had been serious.

Early afternoon, she made herself a peanut butter sandwich and washed it down with a glass of milk. After she'd fed and changed Caden, she sat him on her lap and read out loud to him from one of the picture books that Georgia had brought over.

The DVD was still in the player from the night before, so

Julie fast-forwarded to the part where she'd fallen asleep and watched the end of the movie.

When it was over, she fed Caden—again, and changed him—again. Then she laid him on a blanket on the floor for some "tummy time" because it was supposed to help develop upper body strength for crawling.

As soon as Einstein heard the key in the lock, he was racing toward the door, dancing and barking in excited anticipation of his master's return. Julie scooped Caden up from the floor and carried him to the hall to greet Lukas.

From the wide doorway, she could see that he was seated on the deacon's bench beside the closet, a takeout bag beside him and Einstein in his lap. His boots were still on his feet, there was a light dusting of fresh snow on his jacket, and though his eyes were closed, tension was evident in the clenched muscles of his jaw.

She took a quick step back, not wanting to intrude on what was obviously some private pain, and retreated to the family room again. She'd turned on the TV after the movie finished, more for the background noise than because she had any interest in the crime investigation show that was playing out on screen, but she settled back on the sofa now and feigned rapt attention.

A few minutes later, Lukas spoke from the doorway. "I picked up Chinese."

Caden, who had just started to drift off to sleep, woke up again. His eyes opened wide and immediately began searching for him. The realization that her son already recognized the man's voice was both startling and unnerving for Julie, but it was Lukas's avoidance of her gaze that worried her.

She followed him into the kitchen and put Caden in the portable car seat.

"I'm sorry," he said, still not looking at her. "I didn't think I'd be gone so long."

"I'm just a stranger passing through town," she reminded him lightly. "You don't have to clear your schedule with me."

He got plates from the cupboard, retrieved cutlery from the drawer. "I know. But I didn't even think about the fact that you were stranded here without a vehicle—"

"There wasn't anywhere I needed to go," she interjected gently.

He started to unpack the bag of food, still not looking at her. "I got spring rolls, chicken fried rice, orange beef—"

Julie deliberately stepped in front of him, so that he had no choice but to look at her. And when he did, the stark pain evident in his blue-green eyes hit her like a fist.

She took the foil container from his hands and set it aside. "Why don't you leave the food for a minute and tell me what happened?"

"It's not a story with a happy ending," he warned her.

"I kind of figured that."

He blew out a breath. "It was Mrs. Boychuk who called about her seven-year-old boxer." One side of his mouth kicked up in a half smile. "Sweet'ums.

"Even as a pup, the dog was built like a tank and with the proverbial face that only a mother could love, but to Mrs. Boychuk, he was Sweet'ums. Six months ago, he was diagnosed with osteosarcoma—bone cancer."

"What kind of treatment do you offer for that?"

"We don't have the ability to offer any treatment locally," he admitted. "So Mrs. Boychuk took him to a clinic in Syracuse for radiotherapy. The treatment seemed to be successful, at least initially, but a couple of months ago we found that the cancer had spread to his lungs."

And she could tell by the flat tone of his voice that there was nothing to be done at that point.

"She lost her husband to cancer three years ago—she didn't want to lose her companion, too. She refused to believe the diagnosis. But over the past couple of days, Sweet'ums really began to struggle with his breathing and yesterday he stopped showing any interest in food."

"She called you to put him down," Julie realized, her eyes filling with tears.

He nodded.

She swallowed around the lump in her throat. She wanted to say or do something to help ease his pain, but she felt completely helpless. He obviously cared about his animal patients and losing this one was tearing him up inside.

And although Julie didn't know Mrs. Boychuk or Sweet'ums, she felt as if she knew Lukas, and it hurt her to see him hurting. In the end, she went with her instincts, lifting her arms to wrap around his neck and holding him tight.

For a brief second, he went completely and utterly still, and she wondered if she'd overstepped the boundaries of their fledgling friendship. Then his arms came around her, too, and he hugged her tight. She felt a shudder run through him, an almost-physical release of the grief he was holding inside, and then the tension seemed to seep from his muscles.

After a long moment, he finally eased away.

"Are you okay now?" she asked gently.

"No," he admitted. "But I'm doing much better. Thanks."

And he impulsively touched his lips to hers.

She felt the jolt of the fleeting contact all the way down to her toes. And when he took a quick step back, she knew that he'd felt it, too.

She cleared her throat, focused her gaze on the takeout containers on the counter. "Orange beef?"

He nodded. "Are you hungry?"

"Always," she said, and forced a smile.

What she didn't admit was that she was suddenly craving something other than Chinese food. Because that teasing brush of his lips had triggered a hunger for more of Lukas Garrett's kisses.

Chapter Eight

Luke was at the clinic before eight o'clock Monday morning. Not surprisingly, Karen's vehicle was already in the parking lot. He hung his coat on a hook in the staff room/kitchenette, then traded his boots for shoes before heading out to the front to retrieve the files for his morning appointments.

When he opened the door to reception, he heard Karen lift the top off the jar of doggy treats that she kept on her desk. She frowned when he came around the corner and there was no dancing puppy at his feet.

"Where's Einstein?"

"He decided to stay at home today," Luke told her.

"*He* decided?"

"Yeah." He shook his head, still baffled by the animal's unusual behavior. "He seems to have assigned himself as the baby's protector and doesn't like to be too far away from him."

Her brows lifted. "Baby?"

"Sorry—I guess a lot of things happened on the weekend that you don't know about."

"I saw Sweet'ums's file on top of the stack this morning," she said, her voice quiet, her eyes filled with compassion.

He just nodded.

"But since that doesn't explain Einstein staying home with a baby, maybe you should fill me in."

He did—briefly summarizing the details of discovering Julie's car in the ditch and inviting the laboring mother into his house to help deliver her baby.

"That was Friday?" Karen asked.

He nodded.

"And this woman and her baby are still at your place?"

"Her car's at Bruce's shop," he pointed out. "What was I supposed to do—call a cab to take them to a bed-and-breakfast?"

"It sounds like you did more than enough," she told him. "I would have thought *she* might have called her baby's father to come and pick them up."

"I don't think he's in the picture," Lukas admitted.

Karen's brows rose again. "You don't *think?*"

"She hasn't volunteered very much information about her personal life."

"And that isn't waving an enormous red flag in your mind?"

Of course it was. Julie's reluctance to talk about Caden's father did give him cause for concern. But he wanted to give her the benefit of the doubt. He wanted to believe that she had legitimate reasons for the secrecy. And he hadn't demanded answers or explanations because he wanted her to trust him enough to tell him those reasons of her own volition.

If he thought about it, he might wonder why he wanted her to open up to him, why it mattered so much to him. He'd only known her for three days. He barely knew her at all. But there was something about her that made him want to know her a whole lot better.

Part of that was the immediate and undeniable physical attraction he felt toward her. An attraction that hadn't dimmed when he'd realized she was pregnant nor even through the experience of childbirth. But he'd managed to downplay it—to convince himself that it didn't need to be a factor.

Of course, that was before he'd kissed her. Not that it had been much of a kiss. In fact, he would have argued that the brief contact barely met the most conservative definition of a kiss, except that he'd felt the impact of it in every cell of his body.

And if that wasn't reason enough to be wary, Karen had pointed out another: there was too much about Julie that he didn't know. He wasn't sure what to think about the fact that she'd never told her parents about her pregnancy. If she'd hidden the existence of her baby from them, had she also hidden it from her baby's father? This disconcerting possibility inevitably made him think about Jack, who hadn't learned about his daughter's existence until Ava was twelve years old.

And the effortless way that Caden had completely taken hold of Luke's heart made him remember that Matt had raised another man's son as his own for three years—until the child's biological father came back into the picture. Which wasn't something he should be worrying about after only three days with Julie and her son, except that after only three days, he already knew that he would miss them when they were gone.

He pushed those concerns aside when Megan Richmond came through the front door with her eighteen-month-old chocolate Lab. He loved his job and the familiar routines of his work. Not that the work was ever routine, but there were certain patterns and rhythms to his days at the clinic. The needs of the pets and the concerns of their owners were always his primary focus, but several times throughout the day on Monday, he found his attention drifting. He called home three times, just to see if Julie and Caden were doing okay, to ensure that Einstein wasn't being a bother, to inquire if there was anything they needed.

And when the last patient was gone from the clinic at the end of the day, he was the first one to head out, even before Drew—the animal tech—had finished wiping down the exam rooms.

He could smell the rich, savory scents of basil and garlic as soon as he walked through the door. Einstein came running when he tossed his keys on the counter, reassuring Lukas that the pup still did know who was his master, even if he'd chosen a mistress for today.

Then Luke looked up and saw Julie standing at the stove, and he felt an instinctive hum through his veins.

He was a decent cook. He didn't live on fast food the way some of his single friends did, but he did eat a lot of grilled cheese sandwiches in the winter and hamburgers in the summer—usually because, by the time he got home at the end of the day, he didn't have the energy or the imagination to make anything else. It was a pleasant change to walk in the door and have a meal waiting. And an even more pleasant change to find a beautiful woman in his kitchen.

"I didn't know what your after-work routine was and I didn't want to overcook the pasta, so I haven't put it in yet," she said.

"My after-work routine is to look in the fridge, then look in the freezer, then open a bottle of beer while I try to figure out what I want to eat."

She went to the fridge and retrieved a bottle of beer, twisted off the cap and handed it to him. "Tonight you're having chicken parmigiana and spaghetti with green salad and garlic bread. It will be on the table in fifteen minutes."

He grinned. "You just fulfilled a fantasy I never even knew I harbored."

"Do I want to know?" she asked cautiously.

"A sexy woman offering me a home-cooked meal at the end of a long day." He tipped the bottle to his lips, drank deeply.

She laughed at that as she used her thumb and finger to measure the pasta, then dropped it into the pot of boiling water. "If you think I'm sexy, you need to seriously reevaluate your standards."

As he swallowed another mouthful of beer, he realized that she wasn't being coy or fishing for compliments—she honestly believed what she was saying. "You really don't see it, do you?"

"See what?"

"How incredibly attractive you are."

"I had a baby three days ago," she reminded him.

"Yeah, I think I remember hearing something about that," he said dryly, and turned his attention to the infant securely strapped in the carrier on top of the table, where Julie could keep an eye on him—and vice versa.

"How was the little guy today?" he asked, tweaking Caden's toes through the velour sleeper. The baby kicked his legs instinctively in response to the touch, making Luke smile.

"Hungry. Sleepy. The usual." She lifted the lid of another pot, stirred the sauce that was simmering.

"Did you manage to get any rest?"

"A little." She stirred the pasta. "What did your day entail?"

"Along with the usual checkups and vaccinations, there was a calico with a mild respiratory infection, a diabetic Doberman, a Saint Bernard with a urinary tract obstruction and a ten-month old kitten whose owner was convinced she had a tumor in her belly."

She held her breath. "Not a tumor?"

"Not a tumor," he confirmed. "Pregnant."

Her lips curved. "So a better day than yesterday?"

"A much better day," he agreed.

"I'm glad."

"I also talked to Bruce Conacher today. He didn't have a number for you, so he called me."

"Is my car fixed?" she asked hopefully.

Luke shook his head. "Unfortunately, it's going to be out of commission for at least a few more days."

"Why?"

"You snapped the right front drive axle and Bruce has to wait on delivery from an out-of-town supplier. He was apologetic, but he doesn't do a lot of work on imports so he didn't have the part in stock or easy access to one."

She sighed. "Are you willing to put up with us for a few more days?"

"I told you, you can stay as long as you want," he reminded her. "And the few more days will only make your car drivable. If you want the damaged bumper and fender repaired, it will be a little bit longer than that."

"I guess, since my car's already at his shop, Bruce might as well fix everything that needs to be fixed."

"I'll let him know," Luke said. "And I promise—you'll be pleased with the results. He does good work."

She nodded. "Okay. Now wash up so we can eat."

He fed the animals first, then scrubbed his hands at the sink while she served up the meal. His brows drew together as he looked at the plate she set in front of him.

"You don't like Italian food?"

"What?"

"You're frowning," she noted.

"I love Italian food," he assured her. "But when you asked

if pasta was okay for dinner, I thought you'd cook some spaghetti and top it with canned sauce."

"This is canned sauce," she admitted. "You didn't have all the ingredients to make fresh, but I doctored it up a little bit."

"It doesn't look anything like what comes out of the can."

"I'll take that as a compliment."

"It was intended as one," he assured her. "I really didn't expect anything like this. You didn't have to go to so much trouble."

"It wasn't any trouble. I like to cook."

"Well, that's convenient because I like to eat."

"Then dig in."

So he did, and his taste buds nearly wept with joy. "This is really good."

"You didn't believe me when I said I could cook, did you?"

Truthfully, the luxury car, the diamonds at her ears and designer labels on her clothes had made him suspect that she was more accustomed to having someone cook for her than vice versa. "I didn't think you could cook like *this*," he admitted.

She smiled, choosing to be pleased by his obvious enjoyment of the meal rather than insulted by his skepticism. "Carla, my parents' housekeeper, was originally from Tuscany—although she would be the first to renounce this meal as American Italian and not *real* Italian."

The revelation about the housekeeper confirmed his suspicion about her privileged upbringing. And yet, she seemed perfectly at ease in his humble home, more than capable of looking after herself—and perfectly content to do so. "What is real Italian?"

"Simple recipes with quality seasonal ingredients," she said, then shrugged. "But I've always been partial to a good red sauce."

"This is definitely that," he agreed. After a few more bites, he couldn't resist asking, "What else did Carla teach you to make?"

"You'll have to wait until dinner tomorrow to find out."

The next night Julie made stuffed pork chops with garlic mashed potatoes and green beans. The night after that was broccoli and beef stir-fry with wild rice. On Thursday, it was chicken in a cream sauce with new potatoes and baby carrots.

"Did you want any more chicken?" she asked, when he set his knife and fork down on his empty plate.

"No, thanks." He rubbed a hand over his flat belly. "I couldn't eat another bite."

"You have to have room for dessert," she told him. "Caden napped a little bit longer than usual today, so I had time to make apple crisp."

"One of my favorites," he told her.

"And you've got French vanilla ice cream in the freezer to go with it."

"We never had dessert on a weeknight."

"Never?"

"Well, maybe a slice of birthday cake, if it happened to be someone's birthday."

"When is your birthday?"

"June twenty-second."

"I guess I won't be making a birthday cake anytime soon," she noted.

"When's yours?"

"March fifth."

"How old are you going to be?"

"That was a smooth segue," she told him. "If not exactly subtle."

He shrugged. "I've been trying to guesstimate, but I can't figure out if you're older than you look or younger than you seem."

"I'll be twenty-four on my next birthday," she admitted.

Which meant that she was only twenty-three now, eleven years younger than him. But so what? There were no age taboos with respect to friendship. And he really felt as if he and Julie were becoming friends. Or they would be if he could continue to ignore the way his pulse pounded and his blood hummed whenever he was near her.

"Apple crisp?" she prompted.

"Why not?"

She cut a generous square of the still-warm dessert and topped it with a scoop of ice cream.

"I am feeling seriously spoiled," he confessed, lifting his spoon toward his mouth. "I don't think I've ever eaten as well as I've eaten this past week."

"If you want to continue eating, you're going to have to make a trip to the grocery store," she said. "Since I'm going to be here for a while, I could make a list of some things that will help with the menu planning."

"Why don't you make that list and we can go out tonight?"

She seemed startled by the suggestion. "Tonight?"

"Sure. I figured, since you haven't been out of the house since you got here, you might enjoy a quick outing."

Her face lit up as if he'd given her a precious gift. "I would *love* to go out."

Julie had been so excited about the opportunity to get out of the house for a little while that she hadn't thought about the repercussions of going out with Lukas. What was intended to be a quick trip to the store ended up being an hour-long parade up and down the aisles as the local vet seemed to be acquainted with everyone in town—and everyone was curious about the unknown woman and baby who were in his company.

He was always polite and made a point of introducing her

to everyone who stopped to chat, but he didn't divulge any information about her aside from her name. After the third introduction, Julie realized that he was being deliberately secretive. When he put his hand on her back to nudge her along after a brief exchange of pleasantries with a bubbly blonde he'd introduced as Missy Walsh, the pieces started to come together.

"Why do you want people to think that we're together?"

"We are together," he said, deliberately misunderstanding her question.

Her gaze narrowed. "You know what I mean."

Before he could reply—and undoubtedly deny any complicity—they turned up the next aisle and crossed paths with someone else he knew. It was another woman, this one stunningly beautiful with long dark hair, warm golden eyes and a wide smile.

"Hey, stranger," she said, and touched her lips to his cheek in a way that confirmed they were anything but strangers. Her gaze shifted to take in Julie and Caden, then moved back to Lukas again. "I heard whispered speculation in aisle four about whether or not it was 'his baby,'—now I know who they were talking about."

He just shrugged. "People are always going to find something to talk about."

The brunette moved to take a closer look at Caden, then shook her head. "No way. He's much too cute to be your kid." She offered her hand to Julie. "I'm Kelly Cooper."

"Jack's fiancée," Lukas added, in case she hadn't made the connection.

"And one of Lukas's oldest friends," Kelly told her.

"It's nice to meet you," Julie said.

"Who was in aisle four?" Lukas asked.

"Tara Gallagher and Missy Walsh."

"Is there anything I can bribe you with to go back there and tell them that the baby is mine?"

Kelly shook her head. "It wouldn't matter. Not to Missy, anyway. I could say that you had a dozen kids by a dozen different mothers, and she would take that as hope she might bear the thirteenth." Then she turned to Julie. "Missy's been in love with Lukas since tenth grade, but he never gave her the time of day."

"Julie isn't interested in ancient history," Lukas said.

"It doesn't sound ancient to me," she couldn't resist teasing.

Kelly laughed. "I've got a lot more stories I could tell."

"And we've got to get to the produce department," Lukas said pointedly.

His friend rolled her eyes. "You could at least pretend to be subtle."

"Why?"

"To make a good impression on your houseguest."

"I'm trying to make a good impression—which is why I don't want her hanging around here to talk to you."

She poked her tongue out at him. Lukas kissed her cheek then started to push the cart away. Since Caden's carrier was attached to the cart, Julie automatically fell into step beside him. "It was nice meeting you," she said to Kelly.

"We'll finish our conversation another time," the other woman promised.

"I'll look forward to it."

After Julie had selected the fruits, vegetables and fresh herbs she wanted, they made their way to the checkout line. She always liked to have a list when she went to the grocery store, but she invariably added to the list as she shopped. She hadn't realized how much she'd added until Lukas was unloading the cart onto the checkout belt.

She tried to move past him, closer to the register so that

she would be in position to pay, but he deliberately blocked her path.

"I want to get this—"

He put a hand over hers as she reached into her purse. "We'll discuss this later."

"But—"

He dipped his head closer, his mouth hovering just a few inches above hers. "The gossip from aisle four just moved her cart into line behind us."

She lifted a brow. "What does that have to do with the price of free range chicken at the Saver Mart?"

"Nothing," he admitted. "But I wouldn't mind adding fuel to the speculative fires."

"You think she'd really believe that we're together?"

"Why not?"

To an outsider, it probably did look as if they were having an intimate conversation. Their heads were close and their voices pitched low so that only Julie and Lukas could know that they were arguing about who should pay the grocery bill. "Because I drove into town less than a week ago."

"Eight months after the brief but blistering hot affair we had when I was in Boston for a veterinary rehabilitation symposium."

His lips brushed the shell of her ear as he spoke, making her blood heat and her heart pound. It was an effort to focus her attention on their conversation, and she had to moisten her lips with the tip of her tongue before she could respond. "Were you really in Boston eight months ago?"

"Actually it was Baltimore," he admitted. "But Missy never had an aptitude for geography."

The clerk announced the total of their order and Lukas drew away to pull out his wallet. Julie's fingers tightened on the handle of the buggy as she exhaled a long, shaky breath.

She wanted to believe the flood of heat that made every

inch of her skin itch was nothing more than postpartum hormonal overload, but the more time she spent with Lukas, the more she was beginning to suspect otherwise.

She secured Caden's car seat into the truck while he loaded the grocery bags.

"I'm writing you a check when we get back to your place," she said, when he slid behind the wheel.

"We'll talk about it then," he said agreeably.

But she wasn't fooled for a minute. And since she knew he was going to give her grief about paying for a few groceries—even though she would be eating the food—she decided to give him some grief, too.

"I'm a little surprised that you'd be resistant to such an attractive woman."

He turned the key in the ignition. "Who?"

"Missy Walsh."

He pulled out of the parking lot and onto the road. "You don't know anything about the situation."

"I know that you're apparently afraid of a five-foot-tall curvy blonde in pink spandex."

"With good reason," he told her. "She adopted a kitten last year just so that she could make regular appointments to come into my clinic."

"You don't think it's possible that she just wanted a pet?"

"Within six months, she gave it away because she was allergic. Then she tried a dog—same problem."

"Maybe she's just a lonely woman who wants some company," she suggested.

"I told her to try a goldfish."

"And?"

"She brought the bowl in when the fish went belly up."

Julie couldn't help but laugh. "You're kidding?"

"I wish I was."

"Okay, that is a little strange," she admitted.

"The biggest problem is that she's really sweet," Lukas admitted. "She just tries too hard. She actually dated one of my friends for a while, and he really liked her at first. He said she was fun and interesting to talk to. But the more time they spent together, the more she assimilated his ideas and opinions. She liked everything he liked, wanted to do whatever he wanted to do, agreed with everything he said."

"I would think that's the kind of woman every man would love."

"Maybe for five minutes," he acknowledged. "After that, it would get pretty boring."

"So you've never gone out with her?"

"No. And I've never given her the slightest bit of encouragement. But that hasn't stopped Missy." He shook his head, obviously frustrated by the situation. "She came into the clinic a couple of weeks ago—coincidentally only a few days after Jack and Kelly got engaged—to ask my opinion about geckos."

"With one brother recently married and the other engaged, it's understandable that she might think you're ready for a committed relationship," Julie pointed out to him. And then she couldn't resist asking, "So why are you still single?"

"Never met the right woman, I guess."

"Really? That's your answer?"

"Or maybe I'm just not the marrying kind."

"That sounds like the response of a man who's been burned by love."

"It's the truth."

"How old are you?"

"Thirty-four."

She shifted in her seat so that she could see him more clearly. "Are you honestly telling me that you've never known a woman who made you think in terms of forever?"

"Not really."

"What does that mean?"

"Well, I did propose to someone once," he confided. "But she turned me down."

Which confirmed her "burned by love" theory but still didn't quite add up. "And that was it? One heartbreak and you gave up?"

"I wouldn't even call it a heartbreak," he admitted, turning into his driveway. "In retrospect, I'm not even sure I was in love with her, but I could imagine sharing my life with her."

"Now that's the foundation of a really romantic proposal."

Her dry tone made him smile. "My proposal was motivated by more practical considerations."

"And you wonder why she turned you down?"

He just shrugged.

"So if you weren't wildly in love, why did you want to marry her?"

"Because she was pregnant."

Her jaw dropped. "You have a child?"

"No," he said quickly. "It wasn't my baby."

"Oh." She thought about that for a minute. "Have you always had a hero complex—a desire to save the damsel in distress?"

He scowled. "I don't have a hero complex. She was a friend, and the baby's father was out of the picture, and I knew she was terrified by the thought of going through pregnancy and childbirth on her own.

"And," he confessed with a small smile, "for the few minutes that she took to consider my offer, I was absolutely terrified that she would say yes."

"I can understand why she would have been tempted," Julie admitted.

"Because I'm so tempting?" he teased.

"Because having a baby without a father is a scary prospect—even when it's the right thing to do."

"Right for whom?"

She didn't say anything, was afraid that she'd already said too much.

· "Who were you thinking about when you decided to have your baby on your own?" he pressed. "Yourself or Caden?"

"Both of us."

Then she unbuckled her belt and reached for the door handle, a clear signal that the conversation was over.

Chapter Nine

Kelly tried not to worry. She knew that Lukas was a grown man, capable of making his own decisions and accepting the consequences of those decisions. But he was also her best friend and, as such, she was entitled to pry—just a little.

And wasn't it a lucky coincidence that she had an appointment to take Puss and Boots—the pair of kittens her daughter had insisted on adopting from Lukas a few weeks earlier—to the clinic for their sixteen-week immunizations the following Tuesday morning?

The vet gave them a quick once over, nodded approvingly. "They're doing well. Thriving."

"Does that mean they're getting fat?" she asked. "Because every time I turn around, Ava's giving them treats."

"They're not getting fat. But as long as they're eating the right amount of food, treats should be reserved for special occasions."

"Tell your niece that."

"I will," he promised.

"She won't listen," Kelly warned. "I told her that they had to have their own bed—which they do. And they still sleep with her."

"So long as she has no allergies and they aren't interfering with her sleep, it shouldn't be a concern. In fact, for these two—because they were orphaned at such a young age—that close physical contact could be one of the reasons that they're thriving. Love is as necessary as food, water and shelter to living creatures."

"Even you?" she asked.

He glanced up at her, his brows raised. "Where did *that* come from?"

"It's a simple question," she told him. "I can't help but admire the life you've built for yourself. You have a successful veterinarian practice, a fabulous house—but no one to go home to at the end of the day."

"I have Einstein and Daphne," he reminded her.

"And now you have Julie and Caden."

"They're not mine."

"But you want them to be," she guessed.

"What are you talking about?"

"I'm talking about you playing house with a beautiful woman and her brand-new baby."

"I'm not playing house."

"And I'm concerned about you falling for her," Kelly admitted. "For both of them."

"I'm not falling for her," he said.

She didn't believe that claim for a second. "I don't want you to get hurt, Lukas."

"Don't you have more important things to worry about— like your wedding?" he said pointedly.

She shook her head. "Ava's taken care of every single detail—I don't have to do anything but show up."

"You're letting your twelve-year-old daughter plan your wedding?"

"She's almost thirteen," Kelly reminded him. "And she had very strong opinions about what she wanted. Since Jacks and I really just want to make it legal, we decided to put Ava in charge of the details."

"And is everything on schedule?"

"Almost everything." She let out a long sigh. "I still don't have a dress."

"You know that Jack will be happy to marry you if you show up at the church in old jeans and a T-shirt."

"Yeah," she said, and smiled because she did know it was true.

The smile slipped as her stomach pitched. She sucked in a lungful of air, trying to fight against the unexpected wave of nausea. *Not now. Please not now.* Unfortunately, her body refused to listen to the mental pleas, and she bolted out of the exam room and to the washroom.

After she'd expelled the meager contents of her stomach—and heaved a few more times just to make sure there was nothing left inside—she flushed the toilet. Her hands were shaking as she dampened some paper towels and wiped her face. When she was reasonably certain that her legs would support her, she returned to the exam room, where Lukas was waiting with the kittens.

He handed her a bottle of water. "Morning sickness?"

"I don't know." She lowered herself onto the stool beside the exam table and unscrewed the cap from the bottle. "It might just be a touch of a stomach bug that's going around. Ava was home from school two days last week."

"Do you have any other flulike symptoms? Fever? Chills?"

"No," she admitted. "Just the nausea."

"Then I'd guess *pregnant* over *flu*."

Kelly lifted the bottle to her lips, took a long swallow of

water. "Jacks and I both wanted to have another baby, and Ava has been asking for a brother or a sister almost since she could talk. But a baby in the abstract is a lot different than a flesh-and-blood child."

"You're scared," he realized.

"I'm almost thirty-four years old," she said. "The last time I had a baby I was twenty-one—too young and stupid to know that I should have been terrified."

"You're not alone this time," he reminded her.

"I know. I mean—assuming that there is a 'this time.'" She sighed. "He said that this is what he wanted—but what if it isn't? I know Jackson still thinks about everything he missed out on when Ava was a baby, and I understand that. But I don't know that he's truly ready for the reality of a baby."

"Is any parent ever truly ready?"

"Good point," she admitted. "Okay, on the way home I'll stop at the pharmacy and pick up a pregnancy test."

Lukas settled the kittens back in their carrier. "And you'll let me know?"

"If there's anything to know," she told him. "You'll be the first—*after* Jackson this time."

He grinned. "I can live with that."

While Kelly was at Lukas's clinic, Julie was at Jackson's law office.

After an extended delay waiting for parts that had be-ordered from an out-of-town supplier, Bruce had finished the repairs to her vehicle and delivered it to Lukas's driveway the previous afternoon. She'd been waiting to get her car back so she could continue her journey to Springfield, but with her parents out of the country, she wasn't really anxious to go home. Because going home meant facing Elliott, and she wasn't ready to do that just yet.

So when Lukas had assured her that she was welcome to

stay as long as she wanted, she found herself accepting his offer "for just a few more days." But she was grateful that having her car back afforded her the freedom to come and go as she pleased, because she was finally able to reschedule her appointment to see the lawyer.

She hadn't told Lukas about the appointment, although she couldn't have said why any more than she could have said why she felt as if she was going behind Lukas's back to meet with his brother. After all, Jackson Garrett was the reason she'd come to Pinehurst in the first place. It was just an odd twist of fate that his brother was the reason she'd stayed.

She was summoned into the office at precisely 11:15 a.m., and when she walked through the door, Jackson rose from the chair behind his desk.

"I've been trying to figure out why your name sounds familiar," he admitted, offering his hand. "But I don't think we've ever met."

"We haven't," she admitted. "I was looking for a family law attorney in the area and my brother, Dan, recommended you. He said you went to law school together."

"Dan Marlowe," he said, and smiled. "It is a small world, isn't it?"

"Smaller than I ever would have guessed," she agreed. "Because your brother Lukas delivered my baby."

"So this little guy is the one?" He crouched down to get a closer look at the sleeping infant. "Well, he doesn't look any the worse for wear."

"I feel very fortunate that your brother knew what he was doing—or at least how to fake it."

"Then you're not here to sue him for malpractice?" Jackson teased.

She managed a smile. "No. I just wanted some general information. At least, that's why I originally requested to see you."

"And now?"

"Now that Caden was born in New York State, I have some specific questions about registering his birth." She opened her purse, pulled out a checkbook. "How much do you need as a retainer?"

"I don't need a retainer at all if I'm only answering a few questions."

"I'd rather keep this official."

"The minute you walked through the door of my office, the rules governing solicitor-client privilege came into effect," he assured her. "I'm not going to repeat anything you say here to anyone—not even your brother or mine."

She dropped her gaze. "I feel a little disloyal," she admitted. "Talking to you instead of Lukas."

"If you need a rabies shot, my brother's your man. If you have legal questions, not so much."

She smiled again. "Fair enough. Okay, the first question is about the paperwork I have to fill out to register Caden's birth. Do I have to include his father's name?"

"Are you married to him?"

She shook her head. "No."

"Then there's no presumption of paternity," he told her. "He could sign an acknowledgment of paternity, in which case his personal information would be included on Caden's birth certificate, but if he isn't willing to do so, you would have to apply to the court to request a paternity test."

"What if I don't want him named on the birth certificate?"

He considered her question for a minute. "Your son's biological father has certain rights and responsibilities, regardless of what either of you wants," he finally said. "Has he indicated that he is unwilling to fulfill his responsibilities?"

She dropped her gaze to the sleeping baby. The beautiful baby who was the reason for everything she'd done since she'd learned of the tiny life growing inside her. The reason she was here now.

"He doesn't know about Caden," she admitted.

"I try not to make judgments," he told her. "Especially when I don't know the whole story."

"I appreciate that." And she knew it couldn't be easy for someone with his personal experience to remain objective. Lukas had told her about his fiancée keeping the existence of their child a secret for twelve years. But despite that history, they'd obviously worked things out and were together now.

Julie knew that she and Elliott would never work things out, because she would never forgive him for what he'd done—or herself for not taking control of her life sooner. And right now, she wanted to focus on her son, to be the best mother that she could be, and to keep him away from his father.

"But I can't give you legal advice specific to your situation if I don't know what that situation is," he told her. "So you're going to have to give me at least some of the details."

"I can do better than that." She reached into her purse again, this time pulling out a slim envelope of photographs. "I can show you."

When Julie looked at the calendar Saturday morning, she was surprised to realize it was the fifteenth of November. The month was already half over and her stay in Pinehurst had been extended from a few days to more than two weeks.

Even more surprising was the fact that she wasn't eager to leave. Part of her reluctance was because her parents were on the other side of the world, but another—maybe even bigger—part was that she enjoyed spending time with Lukas.

And she was starting to worry that she was enjoying this unexpected detour a little too much, and starting to seriously crush on the man who had delivered her baby. So when Lukas asked if she wanted to go over to Matt and Georgia's for a while after breakfast, she decided that was probably a good idea. Being around other people would help keep her focus off the man who occupied far too many of her thoughts.

She started questioning her decision when she stepped into the entranceway of Matt and Georgia's house and realized that the entire Garrett family was in attendance—adults, children and pets. Her reservations multiplied when Kelly said, "Don't take your coat off—we're kidnapping you."

Julie took an instinctive step back, holding Caden tight against her chest. "What?"

"Only for a couple of hours," Georgia said, her tone reassuring. "And you will thank us for it—I promise."

Her panicked gaze met Lukas's amused one. "Did you know about this?"

"Not until about two minutes ago," he assured her. "But I heartily approve of their plan."

"What is the plan?" she asked warily.

"A mini-spa retreat," Georgia said.

Wariness gave way to interest. "Really?"

Kelly grinned. "Massage, pedicure. A few hours of girl talk."

"No boys allowed," Jack's fiancée said firmly. "Not even baby boys."

"But—"

"No buts, either," Georgia said.

"I'm not sure about leaving Caden," Julie admitted. While she was undeniably tempted by the invitation, she couldn't help but think that abandoning her two-week-old baby into someone else's care made her a bad mother.

"Of course you're not," Georgia acknowledged. "It's the scariest thing in the world for a new mother to leave her baby for a few hours. But he'll be with Luke and Matt and Jack— they know what they're doing."

"Their hands will be full with the twins and two babies, three puppies and two kittens."

"Ava's here, too," Kelly reminded her.

Which made Julie feel a little better. Jackson and Kelly's daughter might be twelve, but she was mature for her age. She promised Julie that she had "tons of experience" looking after Pippa, and her easy confidence and obvious competence in handling the infant reassured the new mother.

But truthfully, Julie would never have even considered saying "yes" to the proposed outing if she didn't know that Lukas would be there, too. And she had pumped so that she'd have the option of giving Caden a bottle instead of nursing at Matt and Georgia's house, so she didn't have to worry about her baby going hungry if she wasn't around.

"You need this," Kelly told her. "And even if you don't think you do—*we* do."

Julie smiled at that.

"Everything is new and exciting now," Georgia told her. "But trust me, a few hours away from your baby to recharge your batteries will make you an even better mother."

"The new mother looked panicked at the thought of leaving her little guy for a couple of hours," Matt commented when the women had finally gone, leaving the men with the kids and a menagerie of pets.

"Maybe she was just panicked at the thought of leaving him with Lukas," Jack teased.

"I don't blame her," Luke said. "What do I know about babies?"

"A lot more now than a couple of weeks ago," Matt guessed.

"Which means you have more experience at this stage than I do," Jack admitted. "I never knew Ava when she was this young. In fact, I can't believe that she was ever this small."

"Next time around, you'll be there every step of the way," Matt said.

"The next time around is going to come sooner than either of us expected," Jack confided.

"Really?" Matt grinned. "Kelly's pregnant?"

"Due next summer—July twenty-seventh, to be exact."

"Congratulations," Luke said.

"It's hush-hush right now," Jack told them. "Because it's early days, but mostly because Kelly doesn't want to tell Ava until we're married."

"Yeah, you wouldn't want your twelve-year-old daughter to suspect you've had sex with her mother out of wedlock when your wedding isn't scheduled for another few weeks," Matt said dryly.

"We've had the talk," Jack said. "Ava knows all about the important role of the stork."

His brothers laughed.

"Seriously, though," Luke said. "You're good with Kelly's pregnancy?"

Jack nodded. "I'm thrilled. I think Kelly's a little apprehensive, because Ava's almost a teenager. But I know our daughter will be all for it. She desperately wants to be a big sister."

"She certainly enjoys being a big cousin," Matt commented. "She's great with the twins and Pippa. And she's jumped up to check on Caden every five minutes since he went down for his nap."

"Yeah—Luke's managed to limit his checks to every seven minutes," Jack said dryly.

He just shrugged.

"It's pretty obvious you've fallen for the kid," Matt said. "The question is—have you fallen for his mother, too?"

"I'm just helping her out," he said.

"By inviting her to move in with you?"

"She hasn't moved in," he denied. "She's only staying with me temporarily."

"Temporary is a couple of days," Jack said. "Julie's been sleeping in your bed for longer than that already."

"Jesus, Jack. She just had a baby two weeks ago—she's not sleeping in my bed."

His brother's brows lifted. "I was speaking figuratively. The house and everything in it is yours, including the guest room bed. Therefore, she's sleeping in your bed."

"But that was quite the vehement protest," Matt noted.

Luke glowered at him.

"She's a beautiful woman, you're both single and living in close quarters. You wouldn't be human if you hadn't thought about taking things to the next level."

"And what is the next level of friendship?"

Jack shook his head. "You can lie to yourself all you want, but you can't fool your brothers."

And, of course, they were right. Luke *was* attracted to Julie. But he had no intention of putting the moves on a woman who'd had a baby just two weeks earlier—he wasn't a completely insensitive idiot.

Unfortunately, her time in Pinehurst was limited. Exactly how limited, he wasn't sure. He'd half expected her to start packing up when she got her vehicle back, and the fact that her parents were away had obviously been a factor in her decision to stay in Pinehurst a little bit longer. But how much longer? And would she stay long enough for him to figure out if there was any fire to go with the sparks he felt whenever he was around her?

"You can't fool Missy Walsh, either," Matt interjected.

"What does any of this have to do with Missy?" Luke demanded.

"I heard she was absolutely distraught after seeing you cuddling up to Julie in the grocery store," Jack told him.

"I wasn't cuddling up to her," Luke denied.

"It's not like Missy to get her facts wrong. At least not where you're concerned."

"I was purposely flirting with Julie," he admitted.

"Is it possible to accidentally flirt with a woman?" Matt wondered.

"Actually it is," Jack told him. "If flirtation is perceived but not intended."

Matt turned back to Luke. "But you were purposely flirting with Julie."

"I just wanted to give Missy something to think about."

"How is Missy?" Jack teased. "Has she got a new pet yet?"

"I'm glad you think it's funny. But at least I haven't come home and found her in my bed," Luke retorted.

His middle brother winced at the memory of what a former client had done to try to win his affection. As if that scenario wasn't awkward enough, Kelly had been with him when they found the naked woman in his condo.

"Not yet," Matt warned.

"I can't imagine her trying to break in when she knows Julie and Caden are there."

"So it's the new mom-and-baby security system," Jack concluded.

"Which might work with respect to Missy but has to put a damper on the rest of your love life."

"It would if he had one," Jack scoffed. "He hasn't even dated anyone since Sydney Dawes—and how long ago was that?"

More than six months, but Luke wasn't going to admit that. Instead, he just shrugged. "I got tired of going through the same routine with different women, and I decided I wasn't going to do it anymore."

"You've given up dating?"

"I've given up dating for the sake of dating," he clarified.

"You've finally realized that all those meaningless relationships were…meaningless?" Matt teased.

"Just because I'm not looking to hook myself up 'till death do us part' like you guys doesn't mean I don't want to meet someone different, someone who matters."

"How can you possibly know if someone's different unless you get to know her—by dating her?" Jack demanded.

"You ask her to move in with you," Matt said, not entirely tongue-in-cheek.

"Julie and Caden are only staying at my place for the short term," Luke reminded his brothers.

"You just keep telling yourself that, and maybe you'll even start to believe it," Jack said.

"Or maybe," Matt suggested, "you'll figure out that a real relationship isn't such a bad deal, after all."

Chapter Ten

When the women arrived at Gia's Salon & Spa, they were escorted to individual treatment rooms. Julie enjoyed a head and neck massage with warm oils and scented wraps that worked out knots she hadn't even known existed. After that, she rejoined Georgia and Kelly in the pedicure area. It was set up like a private living room, with the chairs arranged in a semicircle facing the fireplace. Flames were flickering in the hearth and soft music was piped through speakers in the ceiling.

Totally relaxed now, they talked about everything and anything—from recent movies and favorite books to local events and sports legends—which, Julie learned, included the three Garrett brothers.

When their toenails were painted and they were sitting around waiting for the polish to dry, Kelly looked at Julie and huffed out a breath. "Dammit," she said. "I like you."

"Thank you," Julie said cautiously.

The other woman smiled. "I didn't want to like you," she admitted. "Because I know that Lukas is falling for you and I'm afraid that you're going to break his heart."

Julie felt a jolt of something—surprise? alarm? hope?—in her chest in response to Kelly's words, but she shook her head. She didn't believe it, couldn't let herself believe it.

She was just beginning to acknowledge to herself that she had feelings for Lukas. And under different circumstances, she knew that she could easily fall for him. But circumstances weren't different. Maybe he was the right man, but this was definitely the wrong time. Her life was simply too complicated right now to even consider a personal relationship, no matter how much she might wish otherwise.

"I think you're misreading the situation."

"I don't think so," Kelly denied.

"Lukas has been incredibly kind but—"

The other woman snorted.

"He *is* kind," Georgia confirmed, shooting a look at her soon-to-be sister-in-law. "But I think Kelly's suggesting that his motives aren't quite so altruistic where you're concerned."

Julie shook her head. "He knows that I'm not staying in Pinehurst, that my life's in Springfield."

"Is it?"

The question surprised Julie. But then she realized that Kelly was right to challenge her statement, because in the two weeks that she'd been in Pinehurst, she'd barely thought about her former life at all. She certainly didn't miss it.

Yes, she missed her family. But they were still her family and always would be, regardless of where she made her home. On the other hand, she had no reason to consider making her home in Pinehurst. Her growing feelings for a sweet and sexy veterinarian aside, there was nothing for her here.

"It used to be," she finally said. "Although the truth is, I've been on the road working for the past seven months."

"What do you do?"

"I'm a curator at The Grayson Gallery in Springfield, but I've been traveling with a private collection since April."

"You haven't been home in all that time?" Georgia asked.

Julie shook her head.

"I'm thinking there's a better reason than an art show to stay away for so long," Kelly mused.

"A lot of reasons," she agreed. "Although I fully intended to be home before my baby was born."

"Except that Caden had other ideas."

"Or maybe it was fated that you would get stuck in Pinehurst," Georgia suggested.

Kelly frowned, obviously not pleased to consider that stronger forces might have factored into setting up the current situation.

"It wasn't fate," Julie denied. "It was simply the combination of no snow tires and a freak blizzard."

"The snow melted last week," Kelly pointed out.

"I just got my car back from Bruce on Monday." Which even she knew was a lame explanation, considering that it was now Saturday and she was still there, still without any firm plans to leave or any set date to do so.

"Monday," Kelly echoed in a considering tone. "So maybe Lukas isn't the only one who's falling?"

Julie sighed. "I'm *not* falling. But I will say that Lukas is handsome and kind, sexy and sweet. He's smart, funny, warm, compassionate and probably the most incredible man I've ever met."

"She's definitely falling," Georgia confirmed. "Can you believe it—all of the Garrett brothers finding true love in the same calendar year?"

Kelly shook her head. "You read too many romance novels."

The mother of three shrugged, unapologetic. "I like happy endings."

"And you got your very own when you married Matt."

"Actually, I like to think of the day I married Matt as a happy beginning," her friend clarified. "And speaking of weddings…"

Kelly sighed. "I know—I need a dress."

"Not that you should rush into anything," Georgia said. "After all, you still have three whole weeks before the wedding."

Julie's jaw dropped. "You're getting married in three weeks and you don't have a dress?"

"I've got the groom," Kelly said, just a little smugly.

"And an appointment at Belinda's Bridal in Syracuse next Saturday," Georgia told her.

"Why do I have to go all the way to Syracuse to go shopping?"

"Because your daughter found a beautiful strapless satin Alfred Sung gown in stock and in your size, and she begged and pleaded and somehow convinced the manager to hold it until next weekend."

"She just wants me to go strapless so that she can go strapless," Kelly muttered.

"Possibly," Georgia admitted. "But she showed me a photo of the dress she picked for you, and it's gorgeous."

The bride-to-be still didn't look convinced. "Any dress looks good on an airbrushed model in a glossy magazine."

"Next Saturday," Georgia said firmly.

Kelly wiggled her painted toes, then looked at Julie. "Can we kidnap you again next Saturday?"

Julie grinned. "For shopping? Anytime."

Only later did she realize that none of them—herself included—had questioned the assumption that she would still be in Pinehurst a week later.

* * *

Julie enjoyed her visit to the spa with Kelly and Georgia, but by the time she slid her "Fabulous Fuchsia" painted toes into her shoes, she was anxious to get back to Caden and Lukas. Not that she would dare admit as much to either of the women in her company.

When they arrived at Matt and Georgia's house, they found a much quieter scene than the one they'd escaped from a few hours earlier. Lukas was in the living room with Caden in his lap, watching a football game and explaining the set plays and terminology to the baby. When there was a stoppage in play, he told them that Matt was in the basement playing video games with the twins, Pippa was napping in her crib upstairs and Jack was in the kitchen working on a science project with Ava.

As the other women went off to track down their respective partners, Julie crossed to the sofa and scooped her baby into her arms. She breathed in his sweet baby scent and noisily kissed both of his cheeks. "There's my big guy."

"And still in one piece," Lukas said proudly.

"If I hadn't been absolutely certain, I never would have left him with you."

"Did you leave him with me?" he asked. "Because Ava seemed to think she was in charge."

She smiled at that. "Kelly says she's desperate for a baby brother or sister of her own."

"And in the meantime, she's been practicing with Pippa—and now Caden."

"Did either you or Ava have any problems?"

Lukas shook his head. "Aside from the fact that he did *not* want to take the bottle you left for him."

"I wondered about that. The books warn that when nursing mothers attempt to bottle-feed, their babies can suffer from nipple confusion…" She let the explanation trail off as she felt her cheeks flush. "Sorry, I spent the last few hours with two women who have been through the same thing, I wasn't thinking about the fact that you probably don't need to hear those kinds of details."

He just shrugged. "He screamed for a while—and let me tell you, that boy has a very healthy set of lungs—but when you didn't miraculously appear to give him what he wanted, his hunger won out."

"I guess that's a good thing," she said. "But it almost makes me feel superfluous."

"It was one bottle—you're not superfluous."

"I know I'm being silly. It's just that I really missed him. I had a fabulous time, but I missed him."

"You look like you had a good time. In fact, you look..." He trailed off, as if not quite sure how to complete the sentence.

"Rested and refreshed?" she suggested. "Kelly promised that I would be both when Gia was finished with me, and that's definitely how I feel."

"I was going to say beautiful," he admitted.

"Oh." There was something about the way he was looking at her, the intensity in his eyes that started her heart pounding just a little bit faster again.

"But you're always beautiful," he continued. "Even the first time I saw you—through the foggy window of your car—you took my breath away."

"Of course, that was before I got out from behind the wheel and you saw me waddle like a penguin behind the belly of a whale," she teased.

"You never waddled," he denied.

"I was eight and a half months pregnant," she reminded him.

"And beautiful."

He brushed his knuckles down her cheek, but it was her knees that went weak.

"And I've been thinking about kissing you since that first day." His words were as seductive as his touch, and the heat in his gaze held her mesmerized as he lowered his head, inching closer and closer until his lips hovered above hers.

"You have the most tempting mouth." He traced the outline of her lips with his fingertip. "Soft. Shapely. Sexy."

"Are you still thinking about it?" she asked, the question barely more than a whisper. "Or are you actually going to kiss me?"

Luke breached the tiny bit of distance that separated their mouths and lightly rubbed his lips against hers.

They were even softer than he'd suspected.

Even sweeter.

He kissed her again, another gentle caress—a question more than a statement. She sighed softly, her eyes drifting shut—the answer that he'd been seeking.

He nibbled on her mouth, savoring her texture and flavor. Her response was unhesitating. Her lips yielded, then parted, and her tongue dallied with his. They were barely touching—it was only their mouths that were linked, and the taste of her made him crave more. He slid an arm around her waist, to draw her closer, and finally remembered that she had a baby in her arms. And that they were standing in the middle of his brother's living room.

With sincere reluctance, he eased his mouth from hers.

She looked up at him, her eyes clouded with desire and confusion.

"That wasn't an actual kiss," he told her.

She blinked. "Then what was it?"

He wasn't sure how to answer that honestly without scaring her off. Because the truth was, it had been just enough of a taste to make him realize that he was starving for her, and that he wanted to feast not just on her mouth but on all her delicious parts.

"Let's call it…a prelude to a kiss," he decided.

"So am I ever going to get a real kiss?"

It was reassuring to know that she was experiencing at least some of the same attraction that was churning him up inside. Unfortunately now wasn't the time or the place to figure out how much.

"Yeah," he promised. "But not when I have to worry that we might be interrupted by either of my brothers, their significant others, kids or animals, or any combination of the same."

When they were home and Caden was fed and settled down for a nap, Julie went to the laundry room to take the clothes out of the dryer. She carried the basket into the family room, intending to fold while she watched TV, and froze in the doorway when she saw Lukas was already there.

He was reading a veterinarian periodical and didn't even look up when she entered the room. She exhaled an unsteady breath and sat down on the edge of the sofa, with the basket on the coffee table in front of her.

At Jackson and Kelly's house, when Lukas had been looking at her and talking about kissing her, all she'd been able to think about was how much she wanted the same thing. Now that her mind wasn't clouded by his nearness and her hormones weren't clamoring for action, she was having second thoughts. Mostly because what he'd called a prelude to a kiss was actually one of the best kisses she'd ever experienced in her entire life.

"I'm not going to jump you, Julie."

But she jumped when his voice broke the silence, knocking the basket off the table and spilling its contents all over the floor.

He immediately crossed the room, dropping to his knees beside her to help gather up the laundry.

"I'm sorry," he said. "I didn't mean to make you nervous."

She wanted to say that she wasn't, but since it would obviously be a lie, she remained silent.

"Although I have to admit I'm a little curious about why you're suddenly so on edge," he continued. "Is it because you're afraid I'm going to really kiss you? Or disappointed that I haven't already?"

"I'm not sure," she admitted, picking up scattered baby socks. "Maybe a little of both."

His smile was wry. "At least you're honest."

She scooped up the last sleeper and dropped it into the basket.

"Your pulse is racing," Luke noted, and touched his fingertip to the side of her neck, just beneath her ear.

Her skin felt singed by the touch, and her throat went dry. She lifted her gaze to his, and saw the desire in his eyes. She hadn't seen it when he looked at her before. Maybe she hadn't wanted to see it. But there was no denying it was there now.

"It's the way you look at me," she admitted. "You make my heart pound."

He took her palm and laid it against his chest, so she could feel that his heart was pounding, too. And then his head lowered toward her, and her breath caught in her lungs.

"Can I kiss you now, Julie?"

She wanted him to kiss her. She wanted to feel his lips against hers so desperately she ached, but she also knew that if he kissed her, everything would change. And she wasn't sure she wanted anything to change.

She genuinely liked Lukas. She enjoyed spending time with him, talking to him. She even enjoyed being with him when they didn't have anything to talk about, because the silence was never awkward or uncomfortable. She didn't want things to get awkward between them.

But as his lips hovered above hers, she couldn't deny that she wanted his kiss a lot more than she wanted the status quo.

His hands—those wide-palmed, strong, capable hands—cradled her face gently. He tilted her head back, adjusting the angle to deepen the kiss. He touched his tongue to the center of her top lip, a light, testing stroke. She met it with her own, a response and an invitation. He dipped inside her mouth, and the sweep of his tongue sent shockwaves of pleasure shooting down her spine, leaving her weak and quivering with need.

After what seemed like an eternity—and yet somehow nearly not long enough—he finally eased his mouth from hers. "That was a kiss," he told her.

She made no attempt to move out of his arms, because she wasn't sure her legs would support her. "Maybe we should have stopped with the prelude," she said, when she'd managed to catch her breath.

"I don't think that would have been possible."

"I don't want to start something we can't finish. You know I'm only going to be in town for a few more weeks."

"How could I possibly forget when you keep reminding me every time I turn around?"

"I just don't want to give you mixed signals."

He tipped her chin up, forcing her to meet his gaze. "Are you attracted to me, Julie?"

"Do you really have to ask?"

He grinned. "Then I can be satisfied with that."

She eyed him doubtfully. "Really?"

"I'm not going to push for more than you're ready to give."

"I'm grateful for that," she told him.

"And until you trust me enough to talk to me, I can't see a few kisses leading to anything more."

"I do trust you."

"And yet you haven't said a single word to me about Caden's father."

Well, that was a complete mood killer. Except that she knew it wasn't unreasonable for Luke to want at least some of the details. "Not because I don't trust you," she told him. "But because I don't want to talk about him."

"As I said, I'm not going to push for more than you're ready to give."

She understood why he would have questions, and maybe it was time to give him some answers. She sat back on the sofa and drew in a deep breath. "His name is Elliott Davis Winchester III. He works in public relations at the Springfield Medical Center but has aspirations of a career in politics. I've known him for two years—well, I guess closer to three now, although I haven't seen him since I gave him back his ring seven and a half months ago."

Luke had been reluctant to push for answers—probably because he suspected he might not like what he learned. Her words confirmed it. "You were engaged to him?"

She nodded.

He wasn't really shocked by the revelation. Julie didn't seem the type of woman to get pregnant as a result of a one-night stand. But a relationship, however long-term, was different than an engagement. An engagement was a promise to marry, a plan for forever. If Julie had been engaged to Caden's father, she'd obviously been in love with him. Maybe she still was.

He cleared his throat. "What happened?"

"I realized he wasn't the man I thought he was—and he definitely wasn't a man I wanted to marry."

"Have you been in touch with him, to tell him that you had the baby?"

She shook her head.

"Don't you think he has a right to know?"

"Of course, the biological father has all kinds of rights, doesn't he?"

Something in her tone alerted him to the possibility that there was more to her situation than a jilted lover not wanting to fight over custody of her child. "Tell me what happened, Julie. Because I can't imagine that you went from making wedding plans one minute to hiding out with your baby the next without a pretty good reason."

His patient tone succeeded in dimming the fiery light in her eyes. "He hit me."

Luke hadn't seen that coming, and he almost felt as if he'd been punched.

"We'd been out to a political fundraiser and Elliott had been busy working the room, drinking and chatting with everyone who was anyone, telling jokes and laughing and drinking. When we got back to his place, he poured another drink and wanted to rehash every word of every conversation he'd had, but I was tired and just wanted to go to bed. He accused me of not being supportive, I said that he seemed more interested in Johnny Walker's company than mine, and he backhanded me.

"He only hit me once," she said, and touched a fingertip to her cheek where there was a tiny white scar he'd never before noticed. "But it was with the hand that proudly displayed the Yale class ring, and that was enough for me. I left.

"There was a pattern of escalating behavior, of course, that I only recognized after the fact. But the slap was—for me—the final straw."

"What else did he do?" Luke asked the question through gritted teeth.

"Does it matter? I left him. It's over. Now I just want to forget."

"Yes, it matters," he insisted. "Because unless you tell somebody about what he did, he gets away with it."

"Most of the time he was very courteous and considerate," she finally said. "But sometimes, when he was drinking, he would become impatient, angry, aggressive."

"What did he do?" he asked again.

"He'd berate my opinions, belittle my feelings. Outwardly, he would be attentive and affectionate, but he'd hold my hand a little too tight, or his fingers would bite into my skin when he took my arm."

"Did he leave bruises?"

"Not really. He never really hurt me before the night I left. But…"

"But what?" he prompted.

"I guess I knew it was escalating toward that," she admitted. "I wasn't really scared of him, but I was uneasy. I think that's one of the reasons that I didn't want to set a wedding date, because I was waiting for something like that to happen so I could leave him."

"Why did you need a reason to leave?"

"Because until he actually hit me, he seemed like the perfect man. My parents knew him, respected him. And for the first time in my life, they approved of a man I was dating. When we got engaged, they were thrilled."

"Do you think they would be thrilled to know that he'd hit you?"

"Of course not," she immediately denied. "Neither of them has any tolerance for domestic abuse."

Luke didn't, either. He'd never understood how anyone could hurt someone they claimed to love—spouse, child, parent or even pet. But he knew that it happened far too often.

"I understand now why you don't want him to be part of Caden's life, but I don't understand why you didn't immediately go to the police and press charges," he said.

"It was my first instinct," she confided. "My cheek was still burning when I reached for the phone. Elliott saw what I was doing, and there was a quick flare of panic in his eyes… and then he smiled.

"And he warned me that if I called the police—if I told anyone at all—he would destroy my father's career."

Chapter Eleven

Luke knew it didn't matter if the man had the ability to follow through on his threat, what mattered was that Julie obviously believed he did.

"How was he going to do that?" he asked her now.

"My father's a judge—a superior court judge, actually, with a reputation for being strict and unyielding. He built his career on a foundation of ensuring everyone had equal access to justice and was treated equally by the law."

"And it didn't occur to you that he might be a little bit upset that you gave in to your abusive fiancé's blackmail?"

"It occurred to me that he'd be devastated if his career was ended and I could have saved it."

"What do you think he did that you needed to save it?"

She picked up a sleeper out of the basket and carefully began to fold it. "Can I refuse to answer that question on the grounds that it may incriminate me?"

"This isn't a court of law," he reminded her. "You don't have to tell me anything that you don't want to."

"I don't want you to think badly of me," she admitted.

"I don't think I could."

She put the sleeper down, reached for another. "I had a very privileged upbringing," she confided. "I had the luxury of a stable home and a loving family, but I didn't always make smart choices.

"In my junior year of high school, a bunch of kids were planning to go to Mexico for spring break. My parents weren't thrilled with the idea, but they agreed that I could go if I paid for it. After Christmas, I went shopping with a few friends and there was this gorgeous Kate Spade handbag that I just couldn't resist. Except that, after buying the bag, I realized that I was almost two hundred dollars short for the trip and my parents refused to loan me the money."

"Which made you furious," he guessed.

She nodded and kept folding. "Because it wasn't that they didn't have the money—it was the principle, they said. They'd agreed that I could go if I paid for it, and I said that I would."

"So you didn't get to go on the spring break trip," he concluded.

"No—I went. When I told Tomas, my boyfriend at the time, that I didn't have the money, he said that he would loan it to me and let me pay him back in a few months. It seemed like the perfect solution to me, except that when we were ready to leave Mexico, Tomas wanted me to carry some souvenirs back for him as repayment for the loan."

He could see where she was going with this story and he really didn't want to hear anymore. But it was like passing the scene of a motor vehicle collision—he didn't want to see the carnage, but he couldn't seem to look away.

"I was young and naive, but I wasn't stupid," Julie continued. "I told him to carry his own drugs and I would reimburse him the cost of the ticket when we got home."

"Nothing about that sounds scandalous to me."

"No, that's just background—the first really bad choice that I made. Of course, I promised myself that I'd learned my lesson. Then, about six months later, I met Randy Cosgrove."

She'd finished with the sleepers and moved on to diaper shirts. "Randy was another bad boy. His father was a minister and Randy was the stereotypical preacher's kid who went in the opposite direction of everything his family believed. He was dark and brooding and sexy—the type of guy that all fathers warn their daughters about."

He wasn't sure how much more he wanted to hear about her relationship with Randy, but he wasn't willing to interrupt now that she was finally talking to him.

"My father warned me. My mother warned me. My brothers warned me. But I didn't listen. I was so sure they were wrong about him, and even if they weren't, I didn't care. Because I had fun with Randy—he was defiant, sexy and exciting, and I was totally infatuated with him.

"One night Randy came by to take me for a drive in a friend's car he'd borrowed. It was a candy-apple-red 1965 Ford Mustang convertible and it was a starry night, and we drove around for nearly an hour with the top down and the music blaring. And then the cops showed up and arrested both of us for stealing the car."

"How old were you?"

"Seventeen."

"That must have been a scary experience for you."

"I was terrified. I don't know how long I was at the police station before my parents came—probably not more than a few hours—but it felt like forever. Then my dad and the arresting officer were in conference for what seemed like several more hours, and when they finally came out, we went home."

"The way you told the story to me, you didn't even know the car was stolen."

"I didn't," she assured him. "But I didn't ask any questions, either. Not even the name of the friend Randy supposedly borrowed the car from. Randy did six months in juvie, and I walked away.

"Elliott told me that he could prove my dad had pulled strings and called in favors to keep me out of jail, that I wasn't charged because I got deferential treatment. If that's true, if he has proof, it will completely undermine my father's assertion that everyone is equal under the law."

"If you were never charged, what kind of proof could he have?"

"I don't know," she admitted.

"Then maybe you should consider that he manufactured whatever so-called evidence he has."

"I wish I could believe that was true, but I never told Elliott about that…incident. Which means that he must have gotten the details from someone else. Someone who was there, at the police station, and who knows what happened behind the scenes."

"Have you talked to your father about this?"

She shook her head.

"Why not?"

"I couldn't. At first, I couldn't because I didn't want to face my parents after what Elliott had done. And then—" she blew out an unsteady breath "—I was afraid to ask him about it."

"Afraid that it might be true?" he guessed.

She nodded. "I didn't want to believe it. At the time, I was so relieved that I didn't have to be photographed and fingerprinted and go to court, that I didn't even question it. But later, I started to wonder how I'd managed to slip out of that sticky situation so easily.

"Elliott's allegation that my father pulled strings and called in favors would certainly answer that question. And after everything my parents had done for me, there was no way I could do anything that would risk my dad's reputation and career."

"Instead, you let Elliott get away with what he did to you?"

She winced at his blunt assessment, though it was true. "I chose to end my relationship with Elliott and walk away. It seemed like the easiest solution at the time. Of course, that was before I knew I was pregnant."

"And now?"

"Now…I don't know," she admitted. "Elliott has political ambitions, and a strict timetable in which he wants things to happen. And I honestly don't know how he'll react to his ex-fiancée showing up with his out-of-wedlock child.

"I know I have to tell him about the baby, but one of the reasons I didn't tell him when I first discovered that I was pregnant was that I was worried he would try to force a reconciliation. He would say it was for the sake of our baby, but it would really be for the sake of his career. In politics, married men are viewed as more trustworthy and reliable than unmarried men—add a baby to the mix, and he'd be laughing."

"Do you think he'd still try to get you back?"

"I don't know," she admitted.

"Would you go back to him?"

"No." Her response was unequivocal and without hesitation.

"I'm sorry."

"For what?"

"Asking you to talk about this."

"You didn't push me for more than I was ready to give," she reminded him.

"Okay, then I'm sorry that talking about this undid all the good of Gia's massage."

She managed a smile. "Well, at least my toes still look good."

There was a definite chill in the air on Monday, so Julie decided to put a roast in the oven for dinner. She peeled carrots and potatoes to go with it, and figured she would try her hand at Yorkshire pudding, too.

Sunday had been a quiet day. Despite the passionate kisses she and Lukas had shared on Saturday night and her heart-wrenching confessions afterward, there was no lingering awkwardness between them.

There were also no more kisses, and although she was undeniably disappointed, the rational part of her brain reassured her that it was a good thing. It was scary to think about how much he meant to her already, how quickly he'd become not just a good friend but an important part of her world. And she knew that if there were more kisses, if they took their relationship to the next level, it would only be that much more difficult for her to leave.

After the basic prep for dinner was done, she spent some time playing with Caden—talking nonsense to him and showing him blocks and squeaky toys. Then they had a nap together, lying on a blanket on the floor with Einstein. When Julie woke up, she noticed that even Daphne had joined them. And when she reached a tentative hand out, the cat not only endured her gentle scratching but actually purred in appreciation.

She had just checked the potatoes when Lukas called to say that he was leaving the office. Caden wasn't on any kind of schedule yet, but she liked to nurse him before Lukas got home. Despite his claim that he was okay with the nursing thing, and although she knew her breasts were functional rather than sexual, the sizzle she felt around Lukas was so completely sexually charged that she'd decided it was best to keep her clothes on whenever he was around.

After Caden was fed and his diaper changed, Julie put him in a clean sleeper. She was just fastening the snaps when she heard the crash.

She raced down the stairs with the baby in her arms just as the back door opened and Lukas walked in.

They stood on opposite sides of the room, staring at the scene. The roasting pan had been upended in the middle of the kitchen floor, meat juices were spreading over the ceramic tiles and Einstein was in the middle of all of it, joyfully wolfing down prime rib.

It took Luke all of two seconds to accurately assess the situation. "Einstein!"

The dog cowered, his ears flat, his belly against the floor. Which meant that he was pretty much marinating himself in beef juice.

Julie was silent for a long minute, trying to comprehend the carnage, then her blue-gray eyes filled with tears.

Luke's first instinct was to go to her, to put his arms around her and reassure her that it wasn't a catastrophe of major proportions. But he knew that if he took a single step in her direction, Einstein would jump up, vying for his attention, and splashing in the au jus. Instead, he moved toward the dog, trying not to step in the gravy. He scooped him up and held him at arm's length.

"Let me get him cleaned up first, then I'll come back to deal with that," he told Julie, nodding toward the remains of Einstein's feast.

Of course, bathing a wriggling puppy who didn't like to be bathed wasn't an easy task. Einstein kept trying to jump out of the laundry tub, which meant that Luke ended up as wet as the puppy, and every time he plunked the animal back down in the water, he howled so desperately and pitifully that Luke started to feel guilty for forcing the bath.

When he finally drained the tub and rubbed the dog down, Julie had cleaned up the kitchen.

"I hope you're not hungry," she said, when he came out of the laundry room. "Because that was dinner."

"For what it's worth, it smelled really good."

"It would have been delicious." She glared at the dog. "He didn't even savor it—he scarfed it down like it was a bowl of three-dollar kibble rather than thirty dollars worth of prime rib."

Luke tried to look in the bright side. "I was kind of in the mood for pizza, anyway."

She just stared at him. "Pizza?"

"What's wrong with pizza?" Aside from the fact that it wasn't prime rib, of course. But he wasn't going to bring that up again.

"Nothing," she finally decided. "As long as we can get it with pineapple and black olives."

"I'll go along with the pineapple and black olives if I can add bacon."

"Are you that determined to clog your arteries before you're forty?"

"My doctor isn't worried."

"Fine. Pineapple, black olives and bacon," she agreed.

"Speaking of doctors," Lukas said. "Weren't you supposed to take Caden for a checkup soon?"

"We have an appointment with Dr. Turcotte on Thursday afternoon."

"What time?"

"Two o'clock."

"Do you want me to go with you?"

She lifted a brow. "You don't think I can manage to take the baby to a doctor's appointment on my own?"

"I'm sure you can," he agreed. "But I usually book surgeries on Tuesday and Thursday afternoons, and it just so happens that I don't have anything scheduled for this Thursday. Besides, I'm kind of curious to see how much the little guy has grown."

"You're not worried that going to see my baby's doctor with me might send the wrong message?"

"Cameron isn't the type to jump to conclusions," he assured her.

"I wasn't thinking about him so much as any other patients who might be in the waiting room—particularly those of the female variety."

"They can jump to all the conclusions they want."

She smiled. "So it's true."

"What's true? Who have you been talking to?"

"Maybe I'm just observant."

His gaze narrowed. "Kelly."

"Perhaps," she allowed.

"What else did she tell you?"

"I'm not dishing on our girl talk to you."

"Then I'll ask Kelly."

"You do that," she said, her tone reflecting certainty that Kelly would keep her confidence.

"We go back a long way," he reminded her.

"You were the first friend she had when she came to Pinehurst in fifth grade and still her best friend," she said, repeating what Jack's fiancée had obviously told her. "And the woman you once proposed to."

He winced. "Apparently she had no problem dishing to you."

"She wanted me to understand what kind of man you are,"

Julie explained. "But I already knew, and I'd already figured out that she was the woman you told me about."

"When she told me that she was pregnant—I knew she was terrified. And I didn't want her to think that she had to go through it on her own."

"And you were in love with her."

He frowned at the matter-of-fact tone of her statement. "Maybe I thought I was," he allowed.

"Of course you were," she continued. "And why wouldn't you be? She's a beautiful woman, you obviously shared a lot of common interests and history."

He was surprised—and a little unnerved—by the accuracy of her insights. No one else had ever known the true depth of his feelings for his best friend. No one had ever guessed that the real reason he'd never fallen in love with any other woman was that he was in love with Kelly.

Then he'd realized that she was in love with his brother— and that truth wasn't just a blow to his ego but a dagger through his heart. Until he'd seen them together and saw the way they looked at one another. Even when they were both still hurt and angry, there was no denying the love between them—and he knew they'd both tried.

And that was when Luke had finally let go. Because he knew that he could feel hurt and betrayed, but he couldn't continue to pretend that he and Kelly had ever been anything more than friends.

"We did share a lot of things," he admitted to Julie. "But never more than a single kiss when we were in seventh grade."

She held up her hands. "None of my business."

"I just want to make it clear that I didn't have any kind of romantic history with my brother's fiancée."

"Aside from the fact that you were in love with her."

"Infatuated," he clarified, because he understood now that unrequited love wasn't really love at all. He'd spent too many years comparing all the other woman he met to the ideal of the one he held in his heart, and now that he'd finally let go of that ideal, a different woman had taken up residence in his heart.

"To-may-to, to-mah-to," she countered.

He frowned, feigning confusion. "I thought you said bacon, pineapple and black olives?"

She rolled her eyes. "Why don't you actually order it so that we get to eat sometime tonight?"

So he did.

The pizza was delivered within twenty minutes, but even when the delivery boy rang the bell, Einstein didn't move from the corner to which he'd been banished. In fact, he even stayed there the whole time that Luke and Julie were eating.

But when the pizza box was empty and pushed aside, the pup slowly inched across the floor on his belly until he was beside her chair. Even when Einstein dropped his chin onto her foot, Julie pretended she didn't see him. Einstein, devastated by this rejection, licked her toes.

"He's trying to apologize," Luke pointed out to her.

"Well, I don't accept his apology," she said.

But in contradiction to the harsh words, one hand reached down to scratch the top of his head, and Einstein's tail thumped against the floor.

She had every right to be furious with the animal still, but her soft heart couldn't hold out against the obviously contrite puppy. It seemed to Luke further proof that she fit into every aspect of his life, and with each day that passed, he couldn't help wondering if she might change her mind about passing through.

He'd dated a lot of women in his thirty-four years, and he wasn't sure how to interpret his growing feelings for Julie. Was it just proximity? Was it the shared experience of Caden's birth that had forged a bond between them? Or was it because his brothers had both fallen in love so recently that he was looking to fill some void in his own life?

He knew that was a distinct possibility, except that he'd never felt as if there was a void in his life. He'd always been happy—he had a job he loved, good friends, close family and pets that lavished him with affection.

Okay, so that might be a bit of an exaggeration where Daphne was concerned, but he knew the cat loved him, too. Or at least appreciated being fed every day, having a warm bed to sleep in and a clean litter box at her disposal.

But with Julie and Caden under his roof, even though they'd been there only a few weeks, he felt as if they belonged. Which wasn't something he should be thinking when she was planning to go back to Springfield soon.

He didn't know exactly when, but he was hoping he could convince her to stay at least until her parents came back from Australia.

"Ava called me at the clinic today," he told her.

She was immediately concerned. "Is something wrong with Puss or Boots?"

"No. She just wanted to know if I'm bringing a date to the wedding. Apparently she's trying to finalize the seating plan for Jack and Kelly's wedding and the numbers would work better if I had 'plus one.'"

"I'm sure Missy Walsh would clear her schedule for you," Julie teased.

"I was actually hoping you might be available."

"You want me to go with you to your brother's wedding?"

"Sure."

She looked wary. "That's a pretty monumental occasion."

"The second wedding in five months for the Garrett brothers," he confirmed.

"That's why you want me there," she realized. "As a barrier against all of the single women in Pinehurst who will be looking at you and dreaming of orange blossoms."

"I've never understood the connection between weddings and orange blossoms."

"They've played a part in wedding traditions tracing back to the ancient Greeks and Romans."

"So they're just a myth?"

She rolled her eyes. "They're a symbol."

"Of what?"

"Of innocence, fertility and everlasting love."

"That's a weighty responsibility for one flower."

"And they smell nice," she told him.

"They don't have any mystical powers, do they? Because apparently I have to wear one in the lapel of my tux."

"No mystical powers," she assured him. "You don't need to be afraid that you'll fall in love with the third woman who crosses your path after the sun sets."

"I'm not afraid of falling in love," he denied.

"Says the only Garrett brother who's never sweated in a tux waiting for his bride to walk down the aisle."

"I never used to think that I wanted what my brothers have."

"Why not?" she challenged.

"Maybe I just never found the right woman," he said, his tone deliberately casual. "Until you."

Chapter Twelve

Julie's eyes went wide, wary. "You don't even know me."

"I know that my life is better—richer and fuller—since you and Caden have been part of it," Luke told her. "I know that I look forward to coming home at the end of each day because you're here. And I'm hoping that you'll stay in Pinehurst at least until the wedding."

She sighed. "Does anyone ever say 'no' to you?"

"Do you want to say 'no'?"

"No," she admitted. "And that's the problem."

"You're going to have to explain how that's a problem."

"Because you're a good man, Lukas Garrett, and I've never fallen for a good man before."

Although she hadn't come right out and said that she'd fallen for him, he was happy enough to accept the implication.

"In fact, I've always had notoriously bad taste in men," she continued. "I thought that had changed when I met Elliott, but even then, it turned out that he wasn't a good man—I only thought he was."

"And you're afraid that you might be wrong about me?" he guessed.

"I'm afraid that I'm totally wrong *for* you."

"You're not," he insisted.

"I'm a twenty-three-year-old single mother who ran away from home without even telling her parents that she was pregnant."

"You had a lot of reasons for running, but now you've stopped."

"Have I? Or is the fact that I'm still here and not in Springfield proof that I'm still running?"

It was a question that Julie spent a lot of time thinking about over the next few days, and still the answer continued to elude her.

As she kept reminding Lukas, her home was in Springfield. So why wasn't she in any hurry to go home? Part of the reason for her reluctance was that if she went back to Massachusetts now, she'd be alone in the house she'd grown up in. Another part of the reason was apprehension. When she returned to Springfield, it was inevitable that she would cross paths with Elliott, and she wasn't yet ready for that to happen. She wasn't afraid of him—at least not physically. But she was afraid of what it would mean for Caden when Elliott learned that he had a child.

But the primary reason that she was still in Pinehurst was that it was where she wanted to be. Not just because it was a picturesque town in Upstate New York, but because it was where Lukas was.

Julie felt more comfortable in Lukas's home than she'd ever felt in Elliott's condo. Her former fiancé hadn't liked her to cook. He'd preferred that they go out to eat, to be seen at the best restaurants, to be seen with people who could advance his career ambitions.

She couldn't remember ever tucking her feet up beneath her on his couch and falling asleep while they watched TV. Because they didn't watch TV—they went to the theatre and museums and political fundraisers and charity events.

She hadn't realized how tiring it was to always be "on" until she finally had the opportunity to turn "off" and just relax. She could relax with Lukas—so long as she didn't think about the physical attraction that had her on edge.

His nearness made her weak, the slightest touch made her quiver, and even from across the room he could make her all hot and tingly with just a look. And the way he looked at her, she knew he felt the same way.

But he hadn't kissed her since that day she'd been kidnapped by Georgia and Kelly, and that was probably for the best. She was already more involved than was smart, and when she finally left Pinehurst, she knew that she'd be leaving a big part of her heart behind.

It was Sunday night, just four days before Thanksgiving, and Luke and Julie still hadn't reached a consensus with respect to their plans for the holiday.

"Kelly called today to tell me that she borrowed a highchair for Thanksgiving—one that has a reclining seat specifically designed for infants so that Caden can be at the table with everyone else."

"That was very thoughtful of her, but we're not going to be there for Thanksgiving."

"You and Caden were invited," he reminded her.

"Thanksgiving is a family holiday, and we're not family."

"Thanksgiving is a time to celebrate with those we care about," he countered. "Family *and* friends."

Apparently she didn't disagree with that, because she said nothing.

"And it's Caden's first Thanksgiving—so it should be special."

She lifted a brow. "Are you really using my child as a negotiating tool?"

He grinned. "Whatever works."

"Not that," she assured him.

"Okay, what if I said that my brothers and I haven't had a real Thanksgiving in a lot of years and I'd really like you and Caden to be there?"

"What do you mean, you haven't had a real Thanksgiving?"

"For the past few years, Matt, Jack and I have ordered pizza and chowed down on it while watching football on TV. This year, Georgia and Kelly have promised a traditional turkey dinner with all the trimmings," he explained. "And I'd really hate to miss out on that."

"There's no reason why you should," she assured him.

"I can't go if you don't go."

"Of course you can."

"And leave the two of you here?" He shook his head. "My mother raised me better than that."

The look she gave him confirmed that he'd finally played the trump card. But when she spoke, she said, "You often mention your parents in casual conversation, but you've never told me what happened to them."

"It's not a favorite topic of conversation," he admitted. "They were on a yacht that ran into a bad storm near Cape Horn. The boat capsized and everyone on board drowned."

"You lost them both at the same time?"

He nodded.

"I'm sorry," she said sincerely. "I can't even imagine how devastating that must have been."

"It was a shock for all of us," he agreed. "But I think it was the best way. Neither of them would have been happy without the other."

"They must have really loved one another."

"They did. They didn't always agree about everything, but there was never any doubt of their affection."

"Do you have any other family?"

"A couple of aunts and uncles and cousins on my father's side, but they're all in North Carolina, so we don't see them much."

"How long have your parents been gone?"

"Six years," he told her. "For the first three, I didn't make any changes around the house. I couldn't even rearrange the furniture. It was Jack who finally asked me one day if I was going to live in Mom and Dad's house forever.

"The house had been left to all three of us, but both Matt and Jack had already moved out, so I secured a mortgage on the property to buy them out. When I reminded my brother that it was my house now, Jack said he just wanted to be sure that *I* knew it, because every time he walked in the front door, he felt as if he was walking into their house still—right down to the ancient welcome mat inside the front door."

"Because part of you was still hoping they would come home," she guessed.

"That might have been a factor. And maybe I needed some time to accept that they wouldn't. But about six months after that conversation with Jack, I started a major renovation. It wasn't enough to tear down wallpaper and buy new towels for the bath—I knocked out walls, added another bathroom upstairs, updated the kitchen cabinets, refinished the hardwood."

"Converted the wood-burning fireplace to gas," she remembered.

He nodded. "Jack convinced me that the instant ambiance would help me get laid. And I can't believe I just said that out loud."

But she laughed. "I can't imagine you needed any help with that."

"That sounds like a compliment."

"A statement of fact," she noted. "You're an extremely handsome man—smart, sexy, charming. You've got a good heart, and a generous nature."

"And a soon-to-be sister-in-law who will give me no end of grief if I show up for Thanksgiving dinner without you and Caden."

Julie sighed. "You're also relentless."

"Does that mean you'll come for dinner?"

"If I do go, I can't go empty-handed," she protested. "I want to make a contribution to the meal."

"Kelly assured me that she and Georgia have everything covered."

"Even dessert?"

"Even dessert," he confirmed. "But if you want, we could take a couple bottles of wine."

"And flowers."

He wrinkled his nose. "For the main meal or dessert?"

She swatted his arm. "For the hostess."

"Okay," he relented. "We'll take wine and flowers."

He was right. Georgia and Kelly had everything covered. Roast turkey with pecan cornbread stuffing, buttermilk mashed potatoes, gravy, maple-glazed sweet potatoes, buttered corn, baby carrots, green beans with wild mushrooms, cauliflower gratin, tangy coleslaw and dinner rolls. Of course, everything looked so good that Julie couldn't let anything pass by without putting at least a small spoonful on her plate.

And everything was absolutely delicious. But even more than the meal, Julie found she genuinely enjoyed the interactions that took place around the table. There were often several conversations happening at the same time, bowls of food being passed in both directions and across the table, glasses clinking and cutlery clanging. It was, in her opinion, the most chaotic—and the most enjoyable—Thanksgiving dinner ever.

She was seated between Lukas and Caden and across from Quinn. The baby had sat contentedly in the borrowed high-chair throughout most of the meal, but when Julie pushed her plate aside, she noticed that he was starting to fidget and rub his eyes. It was a sure sign that he was ready for a nap, and because he always fell asleep easier when he was being cuddled, she lifted him out of his chair.

Kelly and Georgia got up to start clearing away the left-overs and dishes to make room for dessert, so she passed the baby to Lukas in order to help.

She picked up the bowl that was mostly empty of butter-milk mashed potatoes and another with a few cauliflower florets and traces of cheese sauce, and headed toward the kitchen. But she couldn't resist turning back for one linger-ing look at the gorgeous man holding her baby. It wasn't just that he looked so comfortable with her son but that he looked so *right* with Caden in his arms.

Was it luck or fate that her car had slid into the ditch in front of his home? She didn't know, but she was grateful for whatever had brought him into her life. And she knew that her son was going to miss Lukas when she finally took him home to Springfield—maybe almost as much as she would.

Julie had just returned to the dining room when she heard Quinn say, "I was thinkin'."

The words made her smile, because the precocious twin had started a lot of conversations with the same preamble throughout the meal. Some of her favorite topics were the proposed marriage of his puppies, Finnigan and Frederick, with Ava's kittens, Puss and Boots, so that they could have "pup-tens"; having separate spaces for the boys and girls during carpet time at school so Shelby Baker couldn't sit beside him; and his confusion about why, if the glue at school was non-tot-sick (which Miss Lennon explained to him meant it wouldn't make kids sick) she worried about Cain eating it.

"What were you thinking?" Matt asked gamely.

As Julie gathered up a handful of cutlery, she waited to hear the child's response.

"There's lotsa mommies and daddies here."

"Sure," Matt agreed, a little cautiously.

"Me an' Shane an' Pippa have a mommy and daddy. And Uncle Jack and Auntie Kelly are Ava's mommy and daddy. But Caden only gots a mommy."

"Uncle Luke could be his daddy."

There was immediate and stunned silence, although Julie wasn't sure if it was the statement or the fact that Shane had spoken it that was the bigger surprise.

"Yeah," Quinn agreed, immediately onboard with that plan. "'Cuz he doesn't gots any kids."

"That's…an interesting idea," Lukas said. "But it isn't that simple."

"I know." Quinn nodded solemnly. "You'd hafta get married—like when Dr. Matt married Mommy so he could be our daddy."

"Yeah, it was all about you, kid," Jackson said dryly.

But Quinn's gaze was still focused on Lukas. "So—are you gonna do it?"

"I think we should focus on getting Uncle Jack to the altar before we start planning any more weddings," he replied cautiously.

"What's a altar?"

"It's where the wedding takes place," he explained.

"Uh-uh." Quinn shook his head. "Mommy and Daddy got married at the church."

As Lukas proceeded to explain that the altar was located inside the church, Julie felt a tug on her sleeve and saw Shane looking up at her. She was eager to make her escape to the kitchen, but she couldn't ignore the little boy's overture.

"Did you want something, sweetie?"

He shook his head. "We gots Legos."

She breathed a slow sigh of relief, confident this was a subject could handle. "I know. I saw you and Quinn playing with them earlier."

"When Caden gets big enuff, he can play Lego with us."

The offer, so unexpected and earnest, caused her throat to tighten. Or maybe it was regret that she knew they would be long gone from Pinehurst before her son was old enough to play anything with these adorable little boys.

"I know he would really like that," she said, because it was the truth.

"I like the blue blocks best," he told her.

"I like the yellow ones."

He offered her one of his shy smiles, and she made her escape with the handful of cutlery she held clutched tight in her fist and tears shimmering in her eyes.

Julie was quiet on the drive back to his house after dinner, and Luke didn't try to make conversation, either. He was thinking about the discussion Quinn and Shane had initiated, and wondering how it was that a couple of kids could so easily see what adults tried so hard to deny.

When they got home, Julie took Caden upstairs to feed and bathe him while Luke took care of feeding his pets.

Uncle Luke could be his daddy.

The words echoed in his head as he measured out food and filled bowls with water. They were words that, even a few weeks before, would have sent him into a panic. Because at that time, he hadn't been thinking about kids or a family.

But everything had changed when Julie and Caden came into his life. And now, instead of causing his chest to tighten with fear, those words filled his heart with hope.

He *could* be Caden's daddy. He *wanted* to be Caden's daddy. And he wanted Caden's mommy with a desperation that made him ache.

But over the past couple of weeks, he'd been careful to keep things light between them. He tried to remind himself that Julie was a guest in his home and he didn't want to make any overtures that might make her feel pressured or uncomfortable.

After the animals were fed, he went to the office to check his email. Then he played a few games of solitaire on the computer as he waited for Julie to come downstairs. Then he played a few more games and wondered if she'd fallen asleep with Caden or was avoiding him.

It was Einstein who alerted him to her arrival. The pup's keen sense of hearing always picked up the soft creak of the sixth step, and he raced out from under the desk to the bottom of the stairs.

"I thought maybe you'd fallen asleep," Luke said to her when she came into the family room.

She shook her head. "Unfortunately, Caden didn't want to, either. I think he was a little overstimulated today."

"Is this where I apologize for dragging you to the chaos that was Thanksgiving with the Garretts?"

"No. This is where I thank you for dragging us into the chaos." Then she touched her lips to his cheek. "Thank you."

"You really had a good time?"

"I really had a good time," she assured him. "Your family is wonderful."

He took her hand and led her over to the sofa, drawing her down beside him. "Even Quinn?"

"All of them," she confirmed with a smile.

"I wasn't sure if that was more awkward for you or for me," he admitted.

"I'd say for you—because I had an excuse to escape from the table."

And he suspected that she was thinking of making an escape now.

A suspicion that was confirmed when she said, "But his comment did make me wonder if we're giving people the wrong impression about us."

"What do you think is the wrong impression?"

"I think that the longer I stay the more awkward it's going to be when I go," she said, deliberately sidestepping his question.

"So what's your plan? Are you going to pack up now?"

"Do you want me to?"

He shook his head. "No. I don't want you to go," he said, and barely managed to hold back the word *ever*.

He let his fingertip follow the soft, full curve of her lower lip, felt it tremble in response to the slow caress, before he forced his hand to drop away.

The tip of her tongue swept along the same path as his finger, making her lip glisten temptingly. "Then we'll stay until December seventh, if you're sure it's okay."

December seventh was when her parents were due back from their cruise, and the date was now just a little more than two weeks away. It didn't seem like nearly enough time—but he would take whatever she was willing to give him.

"I'm sure. Besides, you promised to be my 'plus one' for the wedding," he reminded her.

"I know I did, but—"

"Ava's finished the seating plan," he said. "If you try to back out now, you'll have to face her wrath."

"I'm not backing out," she denied, though they both knew she'd been thinking about doing precisely that.

He tipped her chin up, forcing her to meet his gaze. "But you're still worried about 'people' getting the wrong impression."

She nodded.

"Then let's clarify the situation," he suggested, and covered her mouth with his.

It had been so long since he'd kissed her that Julie had forgotten how good he was at it. Of course, there didn't seem to be anything that Lukas Garrett wasn't good at, but kissing was definitely near the top of his list of talents.

He used just the right amount of pressure, so that his kiss was firm but not forceful. And he took his time. The man certainly knew how to draw out the pleasure until it seemed as if time was both endless and meaningless. His lips were masterful, his flavor potent, his kiss a leisurely and thorough seduction of all of her senses.

She was lost, drowning in sensation. He could have taken her anywhere, done anything, but he only continued to kiss her. In her admittedly limited experience, men raced around first base with their gaze already focused on second. Lukas didn't seem to be in a hurry to go anywhere.

And she didn't want to be anywhere but right where she was—in the moment with Lukas.

She lifted her arms to link them behind his neck, pressing closer to him. The soft curves of her body seemed to fit perfectly against the hard angles of his. He was so strong and solid, but when he was holding her, she didn't feel vulnerable, she felt…cherished.

His hands slid down her back, over her buttocks. He drew her closer, close enough that there was no doubt he was as thoroughly aroused as she was. Heat pulsed through her veins, pooled between her thighs. She wanted this man— she couldn't deny that any longer. But she couldn't afford to be reckless. She had a child to think about now—a four-week-old baby who had been fathered by another man. She had to be smart, rational, responsible. Unfortunately, that reprimand from her conscience did nothing to curb her desire.

Or was she just lonely? She'd been away from her family and her friends for so long, she wasn't sure how much of what she was feeling for Lukas was real and how much was simply a need for human contact. Except that being close to him now had her feeling all kinds of other things—none of which was lonely.

When he finally eased his mouth from hers, she touched her fingertips to lips still tingling from his kiss. "You're awfully good at that."

His lips curved in a slow, and undeniably smug, smile. "My father always told us that anything worth doing is worth doing right."

"Why do I think he probably wasn't expecting you would apply that advice to seducing women?"

"Do you think I could? Seduce you, I mean."

After that kiss, she didn't have the slightest doubt. "Just because you can doesn't mean you should."

"I realize that I'm probably a few steps ahead of you, that you probably haven't even thought about—"

"I've thought about it," she interrupted softly.

His gaze narrowed. "About what?"

"Making love with you."

He started to reach for her, then curled his fingers into his palms and thrust his hands into his pockets.

"You have?"

She nodded.

"So why are we talking instead of doing?"

"Because you scare me," she admitted.

He took an instinctive step back, his brow furrowed.

She immediately shook her head. "I'm not afraid that you'd

hurt me—not physically," she assured him. "But the way you make me feel—the intensity of it—absolutely terrifies me.

"When I'm with you, everything just seems right. But I don't understand how that's even possible. I've only known you a few weeks and there is nothing usual about the circumstances that brought us together. How can I trust that any of what I'm feeling is real?"

Luke didn't know how to respond, what to say to reassure her—or even if he should. She was right to be wary. He was wary, too. Neither of them could have anticipated what was happening between them. Neither could know where this path might lead. But he wanted to find out.

She'd been clear from the very beginning that she didn't plan on staying in Pinehurst beyond the short-term. Her family and her life were in Springfield. And even though he knew he could be setting himself up for heartbreak, he couldn't stop wanting to be with her, wanting to share every minute that she was in Pinehurst with her.

"I can't make you any promises or guarantees," he told her. "But I can tell you that the feelings you just described—I'm feeling them, too."

"You know I don't have a very good track record with men," she reminded him.

"It takes two people to make a relationship work."

"And I'm only going to be here another couple of weeks, so I can't let myself fall in love with you."

He wanted to smile at that. Though he was hardly an expert on the subject, he knew that falling in love wasn't a choice. He certainly hadn't chosen to fall in love with Julie, but he knew that he was more than halfway there.

Of course, admitting as much would only scare her more. So instead he said, "I'm not asking you to fall in love with me—just to let me make love with you."

She nibbled on her lower lip, something he'd realized that

she did when she was thinking. Unfortunately, the subconscious action deprived him of the ability to think. Instead, he wanted to cover her mouth with his own, to sink into the lush fullness of those lips again.

Then she drew in a deep breath and looked up at him, meeting his gaze evenly. "I guess those are terms I can live with."

His brows lifted. "You guess?"

She smiled. "Do you want to stand here and argue about my choice of words or do you want to take me upstairs?"

Before the words were completely out of her mouth, he swept her off her feet and into his arms.

Chapter Thirteen

Julie took a moment to glory in the thrill of being carried by a strong man. It was another new experience for her and a memory that she knew she would carry with her forever. As he made his way up the stairs, her heart pounded inside her chest and anticipation hummed in her veins. There wasn't any hesitation in her mind, no reservations in her heart.

But when he set her on her feet beside the bed, she felt the first subtle stirring of apprehension. When she realized that he'd already unfastened the buttons that ran down the front of her blouse—that he was undressing her—nerves jittered.

She hadn't thought about the "getting naked" part. It was a usual prerequisite to adult lovemaking, but it wasn't something that her lust-clouded mind had grasped when she'd suggested they come upstairs.

Then he pushed the blouse off of her shoulders and reached for the zipper at the back of her skirt. Except that there wasn't a zipper because it was a maternity skirt, complete with the stretchy panel in front because she wasn't yet able to squeeze into any of her pre-pregnancy clothes. But he quickly figured things out, and pushed the skirt over her hips until it pooled at her feet.

"My body isn't as toned or tight as it was a year ago," she said apologetically.

His hands skimmed from her shoulders to her knees, leisurely caressing her curves along the way. "You feel perfect to me."

She shook her head. "I'm not—"

"Shut up, Julie." The words were muttered against her mouth as he covered it with his own.

She wanted to make some sort of indignant reply, but she couldn't say anything while her lips were otherwise occupied kissing him back. And truthfully, kissing him was a much more pleasurable pastime than arguing with him. And when he kissed her and touched her, she couldn't think clearly enough to worry about the extra pounds. In fact, she couldn't think at all.

And when he pulled her closer, the turgid peaks of her nipples brushed against the hard wall of his chest, making her ache and yearn so that everything else was forgotten. His hands skimmed up her back, and down again. Lust surged through her veins, making her blood pound and her knees weak.

She slid her hands beneath the hem of his sweater, then upward, tracing over the ridges of his abdomen. His skin was warm and smooth, and his muscles quivered. The instinctive response emboldened her, and she let her hands explore further.

"Do you know what you're doing?" he asked, his voice strained.

"It's been a while," she admitted, with a small smile. "But I think I'm on the right track."

"You stay on that track and the train is going to start forging full-steam ahead."

She nibbled on his lower lip. "Is that a promise?"

"Yeah, it's a promise," he said. Then he captured her mouth, kissing her deeply, hungrily.

She pulled away from him to tug his sweater over his head, then reached for his belt. The rest of their clothes were dispensed with quickly, then he eased her back onto the bed. The press of his body against hers, the friction of bare skin against bare skin, was almost more than she could handle.

And then he cupped her breasts, his thumbs rubbing over the aching peaks, and she actually whimpered. When he replaced his hands with his mouth and laved her nipples with his tongue, she felt as if she might explode.

She arched beneath him, pressing closer so that his erection was nestled between her thighs.

"Somebody seems to be in a hurry," he mused.

"It's been a long time for me," she told him.

"Then let's not make you wait any longer."

"Condom?"

"Yeah, I'll take care of it," he assured her. "But first—I'm going to take care of you."

He kissed her then, deeply, hungrily and very thoroughly. Then his mouth moved across her jaw, down her throat. He nibbled her collarbone, licked the hollow between her breasts then kissed his way down to her navel, and lower. He nudged her thighs apart, and her breath backed up in her lungs.

Before she could decide if she wanted to say "Yes, please," or "No, thank you," his mouth was on her, stroking and sucking and licking, pushing her toward the highest pinnacle of pleasure. She fisted her hands in the sheets and bit down hard on her bottom lip as everything inside of her tightened, strained, and finally…shattered.

* * *

She was absolutely and stunningly beautiful.

Luke had meant it when he told her that he'd thought so from the very first, but never had Julie looked more beautiful than she did right now, with her cheeks flushed, her lips swollen from his kisses and those dreamy blue-gray eyes clouded with the aftereffects of passion.

But he wasn't nearly done with her yet.

He wanted to make love with her, slowly, patiently endlessly. And it would be making love. This wasn't sex—not on his part, anyway. Because he was in love with her. Not halfway in love or starting to fall, but one hundred percent head over heels. And for him, that changed everything.

Unfortunately, he knew it wasn't the same for her. She'd told him clearly and unequivocally that she wasn't going to fall in love with him. She was still intending to go back to Springfield on the seventh of December, with the expectation that he, of course, would stay in Pinehurst. Because this was where he lived, where his family, his career and his life were. But if she left—*when* she left—he knew that his heart would go with her.

And that was why this moment mattered so much. He wanted to touch her as no one had ever touched her before, so that when she was gone, she would always remember him. Their time together was already nearing its end, but he was determined to ensure that she enjoyed every minute of the two weeks that they had left together. Starting right now.

He worked his way back up her body, kissing and caressing every inch of her smooth, silky skin. He nipped her earlobe, nuzzled her throat, and his name slipped from her lips on a sigh. "Lukas."

He wanted to spend hours touching her, learning her pleasure points by listening to her soft gasps and throaty moans.

She had a lot of pleasure points, and discovering each and every one of them gave him an immense amount of pleasure.

But he was already rock-hard and aching for her. He sheathed himself with a condom and fought against the urge to lift up her hips and plunge into the sweet, wet heat at the apex of her thighs. Even if she hadn't warned him that it had been a long time for her, he knew it was her first time since giving birth, so he forced himself to go slow. He wasn't usually patient or restrained, but he focused his attention on both, easing into her a fraction of an inch at a time, giving her a chance to adjust and accept him.

Apparently he was taking too much time, because she suddenly planted her heels in the mattress and thrust her hips upward, taking him—all of him—fast and deep inside her. And that quickly, the last of his restraint snapped. She was so wet and tight around him, he feared for a minute that he would erupt like a teenager in the backseat at a drive-in.

But he drew in a deep breath and fisted his hands in the sheets, and when he had at least a semblance of control again, he began to move inside her. And she met him, stroke for stroke, in a synchronized rhythm that mated them together so perfectly he couldn't tell where he ended and she began.

Together they soared high and ever higher, until he captured her mouth and swallowed the cries that signaled her release even as his own rocketed through him.

Luke awoke alone in his bed. He'd heard Caden fussing in the night and then Julie had slipped out of his arms to attend to her child. He wasn't really surprised that she hadn't come back to his bed, but he was disappointed.

He grabbed a quick shower, shaved and headed down to the kitchen to make breakfast. To his surprise, Julie was already there, taking a pan of cinnamon buns out of the oven.

He crossed the room and nuzzled the back of her neck. "I'm not sure what smells better—you or breakfast."

"It's breakfast," she said, turning to face him. "And you have—"

"To kiss you," he said, and covered her mouth with his own.

Julie held herself immobile for the first three seconds, then her lips softened, and she responded to his kiss.

"Just because it's the morning after doesn't mean it has to be awkward," he said.

Her cheeks filled with color. "It's not the timing," she said quietly. "It's the fact that your brother's fiancée is sitting at the table."

He hadn't noticed Kelly when he walked in. He hadn't noticed anything but Julie. It didn't matter that they'd made love through the night—he only had to look at her to want her all over again.

"I brought over some leftovers from Thanksgiving dinner," Kelly said. "There's no way Jack and Ava and I will eat everything, and I'd hate to throw it out."

"Thanks," he said. "I'll think of you when I'm enjoying turkey sandwiches later. Now get out."

"Lukas!" Julie was shocked by his blunt—and undeniably rude—comment.

But his childhood friend simply pushed her chair away from the table and carried her empty coffee mug to the counter. "I'm going," she said. "I promised to take Ava shopping today, anyway."

But she looked worried as her gaze moved from Lukas to Julie and back again. Because he didn't want her expressing her concerns to Julie, who already had enough of her own, he kissed her cheek and steered her toward the door.

After he'd closed it behind Kelly, he turned to see Julie

spreading icing over the top of the warm pastry. "I kind of thought we would keep…this…between us," she said.

He went to the cupboard for a mug, poured himself a cup of the coffee she'd made. "I wasn't planning on any billboard advertising, but I don't keep secrets from my family."

She put two of the warm buns on a plate for him, took one for herself. She sat down beside Caden's carrier, tapped a fingertip to his nose, earning a wide, gummy smile.

"You're not worried that they'll disapprove?"

"No," he said simply. "I'm thirty-four years old—long past the age where I look to my big brothers for approval."

She poked at her cinnamon bun with a fork, peeling off layers of pastry. Luke had polished off one of the pastries and was halfway through the second before he realized that she hadn't taken a single bite.

"What else is on your mind?" he finally asked her.

She picked up her glass of juice, sipped. "Last night," she admitted. "It wasn't quite what I expected."

"Disappointed?" He didn't mind teasing her with the question because he knew very well that she had not been. "Because I promise you, I can do better."

"I wasn't disappointed," she said, and the color that flooded her cheeks confirmed it. "More like…overwhelmed."

"Why do you say that as if it's a bad thing?"

"Because I had no intention of getting involved with you. Because I thought—I'd hoped—the attraction was purely a hormonal thing."

"An itch that would go away once it was scratched?"

"I wouldn't have put it in such crude terms but, okay, yes."

"And now?"

She shook her head. "It's not just the way you made me feel last night. It's how you make me feel all the time. I've been happy here with you. Happier than I could have imagined."

He actually felt his heart swell inside his chest. "I'm glad," he said. "Because you make me happy, too. I care about you, Julie. You and Caden both."

Her eyes filled with tears. "I told you—I'm not going to let myself fall in love with you."

"I'm just asking you to give us a chance."

"A chance for what?"

He shrugged. "For whatever might happen."

"You make it sound so simple."

"I don't see any reason to complicate the situation unnecessarily."

"So you think we can keep this simple?" she asked hopefully.

"As simple as you want." He lied without compunction because he knew that the truth would send her back to Springfield before the words *I love you* were out of his mouth.

He couldn't have pinpointed when it happened. The revelation hadn't come to him like a bolt of lightning out of the sky, but he didn't doubt for a moment that it was true. What had started out as attraction had developed into affection that, over the past few weeks, had deepened and intensified. He loved her.

But he knew that even hinting at that would induce a panic. Instead, he gestured to her plate with his fork and said, "Are you going to eat that or dissect it?"

After breakfast, Lukas tidied up the kitchen while Julie nursed Caden and tried to convince herself that her relationship with the sexy veterinarian wasn't getting more complicated by the day.

When she'd put the baby down in the cradle, she checked her email and found a message from her parents. They'd been in regular contact over the past few weeks and their messages were always rich with details about excursions they'd taken, places they'd seen and people they'd met. In every word she read, Julie could tell that they were having a fabulous time, and she was happy for them. Because as much as she missed her family, she realized that she was happy, too. Being here with Lukas made her happy. Happier than she could ever remember being. So why did that scare her?

After things had gone so wrong with Elliott, she hadn't been able to imagine being with another man. How could she trust anyone when her judgment had been so wrong? Maybe she was confusing sex with love. Maybe her mind was still clouded from the incredible orgasms Lukas had given her the night before.

She wanted to believe that was the answer—that what she was feeling for him was lust and gratitude and nothing more. But she knew that what she was feeling was about so much more than the phenomenal lovemaking they'd shared. In fact, if she was being honest with herself, she would admit that she'd probably fallen in love with Lukas before he'd ever kissed her.

Yeah, she could tell him she wouldn't fall in love with him, but those words didn't actually give her power over her heart. And the fact was, she loved who he was and everything about him.

The past few weeks with him had been absolutely fabulous, but as much as she enjoyed being with him, she didn't belong here. She lived and worked in Springfield. And Evangeline was expecting her back at The Grayson Gallery at the beginning of February.

She didn't need to work, and she certainly wasn't working for the money. Being a part-time curator was never going to make her rich. True, there was a certain amount of prestige associated with her position, but that had never mattered to Julie. She'd taken the job because she'd needed the sense of purpose that it gave her, the independent identity. Something that separated her from Elliott, goals and ambitions that were entirely her own.

Except that, sometime during the past few months, those goals and ambitions had changed. Or maybe it was having Caden that changed everything. Now her career didn't matter to her nearly as much as being a good mother to her son. And she didn't want to go back to Springfield nearly as much as she wanted to stay with Lukas.

She'd never imagined herself living in a town like Pinehurst—but only because she'd never known that towns like it existed. She'd never thought of settling anywhere outside of Springfield because everything she needed and everyone she loved was there. Four years at college aside, she'd never lived anywhere else. She'd taken plenty of trips—educational jaunts to various destinations in Europe and Asia, vacations to sandy beaches in the Caribbean and exotic ports of call on the Mediterranean.

Her trip across the United States probably represented the most significant journey in her twenty-three years. Not just because she'd seen so much of the country and met so many interesting people, but because she'd learned so much about herself. And her favorite part of the journey was this unscheduled and extended layover in Pinehurst.

She felt as if she belonged here, in this town, with Lukas. She loved his house—the history and character of it; she adored Einstein—despite the prime rib incident; she was even starting to develop warm feelings toward Daphne—although she wasn't entirely sure the cat reciprocated. And she loved Lukas.

Her mind was still spinning with that realization when she walked into the bedroom and found him on her bed. He was lounging against a pile of pillows, reading a book. Or maybe just pretending to read while he waited for her, because as soon as she stepped through the doorway, he closed the cover and set the novel aside.

He rose to his feet and reached for her, drawing her into his arms and covering her lips in a slow, mind-numbing kiss.

"Are you okay? After last night, I mean."

Of course he would ask. And of course, the fact that he did made her heart go all soft and gooey. "Yes, I'm okay. Better than okay," she admitted.

"Good." He smiled and drew her closer.

"Lukas—" She tried to wriggle out of his embrace. "It's the middle of the day."

"And?"

"And I have to get dressed."

"Why would you bother putting clothes on when I'm just going to take them off of you again?" he asked logically.

Because she wasn't quite sure how to respond to that, she folded her arms over her chest. "Just because I let you seduce me last night, doesn't mean I'm going to get naked with you—"

With one quick tug, he had the belt of her robe unfastened. She sucked in a breath as the cool air caressed her bare skin, then released it on a sigh when he cupped her breasts in his palms.

"You were saying?" he prompted.

She didn't see any point in fighting with him when the truth was, she wanted the same thing he did. She reached for the hem of his sweatshirt. "I was saying that you have far too many clothes on."

"I can remedy that."

The night before Jack and Kelly's wedding, Matt and Luke decided to take their brother out for an impromptu bachelor party. In other words, wings and beer at DeMarco's.

"Tomorrow night's the big night," Matt said, pouring draught from the pitcher into three frosty mugs.

Jack's smile was wide as he accepted the first glass. "The biggest."

"Well, I guess I don't have to ask if you're having second thoughts."

"Not a one," his brother agreed.

"I'm glad," Lukas said. "Because I'm not sure whose side I'd be on if something went wrong."

"Nothing's going to go wrong," the groom-to-be said confidently. "In fact, for the first time in my life, I feel as if everything is exactly the way it should be."

"You're a lucky guy—she's an incredible woman."

"I know it."

"And though I wouldn't usually admit this, I think she's pretty lucky, too."

"Undoubtedly." Jack grinned again.

"It's a second trip down the aisle for Jack, and I've done it twice myself," Matt noted, turning to Luke. "When are you going to take your first?"

"When I find the woman who makes me believe that the first will also be the last," Lukas told them.

"You don't think you've already found her?" Jack prompted.

"Maybe I have."

"So why are you hesitating?"

"It's...complicated."

"It's always complicated," Jack noted.

"You mean because she has a child with another man?" Matt guessed.

"I don't want to go through what you went through," Lukas told him.

"It's not even close to being the same situation," his brother pointed out. "Lindsay lied to me. For three years, she let me believe that I was Liam's father. I don't think you're under any similar illusions about Caden."

He wasn't, of course. And the paternity of Julie's son wasn't an issue for him—except when he thought about what his brother had gone through. "And when Liam's father came back into the picture, you lost your wife and your child."

"Is that what you're afraid of?" Matt prompted. "That Julie will go back to Caden's father?"

"No. She's been clear about the fact that he's not part of her life anymore."

"But he could be part of Caden's," Jack reminded him.

Luke nodded.

"So what?" Matt challenged.

"So what?" he echoed.

"Maybe Caden's biological father will be part of his life," his brother acknowledged. "So what? I know it isn't an ideal situation, but at least you'd be with the woman you love."

"I never said I loved her," Luke said, just a little defensively.

"If you don't, then why are we even having this conversation?" Jack wanted to know.

"Okay—I do love Julie. And Caden. And the idea of being without either one of them…" He shook his head. "I don't even want to think about it."

Matt clapped a hand on his shoulder. "Then I guess you'd better convince her to stay."

Chapter Fourteen

While the Garrett brothers were drinking beer at DeMarco's, the women were eating chocolate fondue at Kelly's house. It was a girls' night in under the guise of a bachelorette party.

Ava hung out with them for a while, more for the chocolate than the conversation, and when she'd had her fill of both, she retreated to her room to study for a history test. Georgia had earlier sent the twins to the basement to play video games and since that was about as much privacy as they were going to get in a house full of kids, she took advantage of the moment to ask Julie, "So, how long have you been sleeping with Lukas?"

Julie paused with a chunk of chocolate-covered banana over her plate and glanced over at Jack's fiancée.

Kelly held up her hands. "I didn't tell her."

"She didn't tell me," Georgia confirmed, then turned to scowl at her soon-to-be sister-in-law. "You knew and didn't tell me?"

"Well, it's not as if I had a chance," Kelly admitted. "This is the first time I've seen you since Thanksgiving."

"So how did you know?" Julie asked Georgia.

"I'm not sure," the other woman admitted. "It wasn't anything obvious, but you seem...different. More relaxed and contented."

"One of the benefits of mind-blowing sex," Kelly agreed.

Georgia kept her gaze on Julie. "So...is it?"

She felt her cheeks flush, but she couldn't stop her lips from curving in a slow and very satisfied smile.

"That good, huh?"

"I don't know if it's hormones or Lukas," she admitted. "But I've never experienced anything like what I've experienced with him."

"So why are you not dancing on the ceiling?" Kelly asked.

"Because there are too many reasons why a relationship between us would never work."

"From where I'm sitting, I'd say that you already have a relationship," Georgia noted. "And it seems to be working just fine."

"I'm going back to Springfield after the wedding."

Kelly frowned. "Does Lukas know?"

"Of course he knows. We both knew, from the beginning, that this was only a temporary arrangement. My family, my job, my *life* are in Springfield." But the most important factor, from her perspective, was that Lukas hadn't asked her to stay.

"You're going back to work?" Georgia asked.

"I have to." Well, financially she didn't have to—she had a trust fund from her maternal grandmother and significant savings of her own that she didn't need to worry about where she'd find the money for rent, but she'd promised Evangeline that she would come back.

"When?" Kelly asked.

"In a couple of months."

"Who's going to look after Caden while you're working?"

"I haven't had a chance to make those arrangements just yet."

"When I was living in New York City, if you weren't on a waiting list before you were pregnant, you weren't going to get a spot in any reputable daycare before your child's third birthday," Georgia told her.

"Springfield isn't Manhattan."

"I did the single-working-mother thing," Kelly told her. "And I lucked out in finding an absolutely wonderful woman who looked after Ava while I was working. But I promise you, if I'd had any other choice, I would have done things differently, and I'd have spent every possible minute with my child."

"I don't have any other choice," Julie insisted.

The other woman's pithy one-word reply made her blink.

"If you think you don't have any other choice, it's because you don't want to see the opportunity that's right in front of you."

"Kelly," Georgia admonished. "Julie was always clear about her plans to go back to Springfield."

"Then she shouldn't have let Lukas fall in love with her."

"He's not in love with me," Julie denied.

Kelly scowled at her. "Do you really not see it?"

Julie refused to argue with the bride-to-be on the night before her wedding. "How did we get on this topic, anyway? Aren't we supposed to be celebrating one of your last nights as a single woman?"

Kelly stabbed a strawberry with her fondue fork, a little more viciously than necessary. "I just have one more question."

"Okay," Julie said cautiously.

"Do you feel *anything* for him?"

She couldn't lie, not to Kelly and Georgia, and not about this. "I feel *everything* for him."

Georgia's brows drew together. "Then why are you leaving?"

"Because he hasn't asked me to stay."

Kelly blew out a breath. "The man truly is an idiot."

"But even if he did," Julie said, "I wouldn't want to stay so that Lukas could take care of me and my son."

"No one's suggesting that," Georgia told her.

"You should stay here with Lukas because it's where you want to be," Kelly said. "Because he's who you want to be with."

Julie wondered if it could be that simple, because she had no doubt that it was true.

Later that night, when Julie and Lukas were snuggled together after lovemaking, he said, "I've been thinking about what Quinn said on Thanksgiving—about us getting married so that I can be Caden's father."

"He also said that Finn and Fred should marry Puss and Boots so that they could have 'pup-tens.'"

"I think the former idea is a little more valid and definitely worth considering," he insisted.

"I'm not surprised that you'd be thinking about marriage when your brother's getting married tomorrow. But to think about marrying a woman you've only known a few weeks is crazy."

"I am crazy about you, Julie."

Her heart felt as though it was going to leap right out of her chest. But someone needed to be rational, and it obviously wasn't going to be him. "This entire conversation is insane."

"I'm starting to get the hang of this daddy thing," he told her. "And if we got married, it would alleviate a lot of questions and speculation about Caden's paternity."

"Do you really think anyone would believe that story about the two of us having a torrid affair in the spring?"

He shrugged.

"And even if they did, that's hardly a valid reason to get married."

"Okay, how about the fact that I want to spend every day—and every night—for the rest of my life with you?"

Her heart leaped again, but she knew she couldn't accept his offer. He'd said that he was crazy about her, that he wanted to spend his life with her and be a father to her son, but he hadn't said anything about loving her.

"I'm flattered, Lukas," she said, because she was. "But when I gave Elliott back his ring, I promised myself that I wouldn't ever get married for the wrong reasons."

"And you don't think you could love me?" he guessed.

Julie didn't know how to answer that question. Because the truth was, it wasn't that she didn't think she could love him but that she already did.

Because Jackson had insisted on a short engagement and the church that Kelly wanted to get married in was booked for every Saturday into the following spring, they decided to have a midweek evening candlelight service. And when the bride and groom held hands and looked into one another's eyes to exchange their vows, it was one of the most beautiful and heartwarming ceremonies Julie had ever witnessed.

Of course, being at Jackson and Kelly's wedding got Julie thinking about her own aborted plans. She'd been so excited when Elliott proposed. As many young girls do, she'd dreamed about her wedding for a long time. She'd stockpiled bridal magazines, clipped out photos of dresses and flowers and cakes. Yet when Elliott put his ring on her finger, she'd never taken her planning to the next level. She hadn't gone dress shopping or visited floral shops or sampled wedding cakes.

And she had absolutely no regrets that the wedding had

never happened. Because even if Elliott had never raised a hand to her, he'd also never looked at her the way Jackson looked at Kelly. Or the way she looked right back at him.

Of course, Julie hadn't looked at Elliott that way, either. She'd loved who she thought he was and the life she'd envisioned for them together, but in the end, she'd had no difficulty walking away from him. There'd been no void in her life when she left him. In fact, she'd felt a sense of relief, a feeling of peace that she'd finally made the right choice. And that choice had, eventually, brought her to where she was today.

Glancing over at Lukas now, she saw that he was looking at her, and the warmth and affection in his gaze made her tingle all over. No one had ever looked at her the way he did; no one had ever made her feel the way he did.

But did he love her?

Despite Kelly's conviction that he did, Lukas had never said those words to Julie. And why would he put his heart on the line when she'd told him that she wasn't going to fall in love with him? Of course, she knew now that those words had been a lie even when she'd spoken them. But was she strong enough—brave enough—to trust in what they had together?

She thought about that question through the meal and the numerous toasts and speeches in honor of the happy couple. The first dance of the bride and groom was usually followed by the traditional father and bride dance. Instead, it was the groom who danced with his daughter. As they waltzed around the dance floor, Julie marveled at the fact that Jackson had only recently learned that he had a daughter—and now he was dancing with her at his wedding to her mother.

Her gaze shifted across the table to Lukas's other brother. Matt, always the doting father, was sitting beside Georgia with Pippa in his lap. Certainly no one would ever guess that he wasn't the biological father of the three kids he loved as if they were his own. Julie didn't have to wonder if Lukas could ever love Caden the same way—because she knew that he already did.

And it wasn't just Lukas—his whole family had accepted Julie and her son, easily and without question. Well, Kelly had had more than a few questions, but Julie understood that her inquiries were motivated by concern and affection. She was trying to protect Lukas, and Julie could appreciate and respect that kind of loyalty.

That was one of the reasons she could imagine herself living here, being part of this family, part of the community. Pinehurst would be a wonderful place to raise her son. In fact, Georgia had said one of the reasons she'd decided to move here with her family was to raise them in a smaller town with old-fashioned values. Looking at Georgia's adorable twins now, Julie remembered Shane's impulsive offer to share his building blocks with Caden, and she knew that she didn't want to take him away from here.

She wanted her son to know Quinn and Shane and Pippa. And although Ava was already mostly grown up, she absolutely adored Caden and Julie knew she wouldn't ever find a babysitter for him that she liked or trusted more. Maybe they wouldn't be related by blood, but spending time with Lukas's family had made her realize that family was about so much more than shared DNA. It was the bonds and connections that developed through mutual respect and affection, but the greatest connection was love.

Julie loved Lukas with her whole heart.

And that, she finally realized, was why she had to go back to Springfield.

When the dance floor was opened up to all of the other guests, Lukas came looking for her. The third song had barely begun when she saw him walking toward her, determination in every step. There was something incredibly sexy about a man with a purpose. Or maybe it was the glint in his eye that made everything inside her quiver.

He offered his hand to her. "Dance with me."

It was more of a demand than an invitation, but Julie didn't care. She just wanted to be in his arms. Ava, back at the table after her turn around the dance floor, willingly took Caden from her.

"Have I told you that you look absolutely spectacular tonight?" Lukas asked, as he drew her into his embrace.

She shook her head.

"Well, you do. When I saw you come down the stairs in that dress...you actually took my breath away."

She'd gone shopping for the occasion, because she knew she didn't have any appropriate wedding attire with her, and because she was always happy for an excuse to go shopping. The emerald-green wrap-style dress was both flattering and functional, with long, narrow sleeves and a full skirt that twirled above her knees.

He dipped his head and lowered his voice. "But as fabulous as you look in that dress, I can't wait to get you out of it."

The words sent a quick thrill through her veins. And as much as she wanted the same thing, she couldn't resist teasing, "You think you're going to get lucky tonight?"

He smiled, but his eyes were serious. "I think the luckiest day of my life was the day I met you."

"I feel the same way," she admitted.

"I realized something today, when Jack and Kelly exchanged their vows. For the first time in my life, I seriously envied my brother. And no—not because he was marrying Kelly, but because he was marrying the woman he loves. And because I know that they're going to be together forever, happily ever after.

"I want the same thing, Julie. I want to spend the rest of my life with you because you mean everything to me. But

I don't just want you—I want Caden, too. I want to be your husband and his father, and maybe, in the future, we could add another kid or two to the mix, but that doesn't matter to me nearly as much as being with you."

Her heart was pounding so hard inside her chest it actually ached. "Is that your idea of a proposal?"

"I've got the ring in my pocket," he told her. "And I'll get down on one knee right here and now if you want me to."

She shook her head. "No."

The last thing she wanted was the focus of all of Jack and Kelly's guests on them—especially when she couldn't give Lukas the answer he wanted.

"I'm hoping for a different response to the spending our lives together part," he prompted.

"I want to give you a different response," she admitted. "But I'm going back to Springfield. Tomorrow."

"What? Why?"

"To see Elliott."

Though the music continued, he stopped moving. "You're still in love with him."

"No." Her response was as vehement as it was immediate, because she didn't want Lukas to believe that for even half a second. "But I have to tell him about Caden. I've been putting it off, for reasons I'm not even sure I understand. But sometime during the past few days, I realized that I won't ever be able to move forward with my life until I know that the past is behind me." She held his gaze, not even trying to hide the depth of emotion she knew would be reflected in her eyes. "I want to move forward with my life—with you."

He took her hand and guided her off the dance floor. But instead of heading back toward their table, he turned in the opposite direction. He found a quiet corner, behind an enormous Christmas tree, and faced her. "So when are we leaving?"

She blinked. "What?"

"Do you really think I'm going to let you meet your former fiancé without backup?"

And that was just one of the reasons she loved him. But as much as she appreciated his protectiveness and willingness to rearrange his schedule to be there for her, she wasn't going to let him go all Neanderthal man on her.

"I'm meeting him for coffee at The Cobalt Room—a restaurant in the Courtland Hotel," she explained. "It's a public place, so there's no need to worry about backup."

"You don't want me to come with you?"

"I do want you to come to Springfield with me, but I need to meet with Elliott on my own. I need to stand up for myself. You don't have to like it," she told him. "But I hope you respect me enough to understand that this is something I have to do."

"I don't like it." He touched his lips to hers. "But I understand."

"Do you think you can clear your schedule so that we can stay in Springfield for the weekend?"

"Absolutely."

She took his hands, linked their fingers together. "Good. My parents will be home on Saturday and I'd really like them to meet the man I'm going to marry."

"Does that mean you accept my proposal?"

"It means that I'm hoping you'll ask me again after I've cleaned up the mess I've made of my life."

Julie was more worried about her meeting with her former fiancé than she'd been willing to admit to Lukas. Although she'd never loved Elliott with the same depth and intensity that she loved Lukas, she'd had genuine feelings for him. She didn't regret walking away. She would not be a victim and she would never forgive Elliott for what he'd done, but she still worried that seeing him again might stir up old feelings that she didn't want stirred.

"Mr. Winchester called to say that he would be a few minutes late, but his table is ready, if you'd like to be seated," the hostess told her.

"Yes, please."

She wished she'd accepted Lukas's offer to come with her. She'd wanted to do this on her own, to prove to herself that she could, but now she was regretting her decision. She wanted him there with her. She wanted the man she loved beside her, and she wanted the comforting weight of her baby in her arms. She felt so much braver and stronger when she was with Lukas, and she knew she was capable of doing anything to protect her son.

She ordered decaf coffee and was stirring cream into her cup when she spotted Elliott crossing the room.

She watched his approach, trying to view him through the eyes of an objective stranger. He moved with purpose and authority. He was a good-looking man, charming and charismatic, and he drew attention wherever he went.

She exhaled a grateful sigh at the realization that she honestly didn't feel anything for him anymore. Not even fear. And with that realization, a sense of peace settled over her, calming any residual nerves. He couldn't hurt her. She wouldn't let him. And she wouldn't let him hurt her son.

But could he hurt her father? That was the question that continued to nag at her.

He reached the table and leaned down to kiss her cheek, and though she stiffened, she didn't pull away. She'd wanted this meeting with Elliott to take place in a public venue for a number of reasons but causing a scene wasn't one of them. So she forced a smile and kept it on her face while he seated himself across from her.

"I'm so pleased you called," Elliott said.

"Are you?"

"Of course. I know the situation between us didn't exactly end on a positive note, but I hoped we could find our way back to being friends."

"Do you have a spin doctor on your political team now? Because 'didn't exactly end on a positive note' is an interesting interpretation of the fact that you slapped me around."

He winced at the bluntness of her assessment. "I'd had too much to drink. I lost my temper."

"That doesn't justify what you did."

"I'm not trying to justify it," he assured her. "I know the alcohol isn't an excuse, but it is part of the reason.

"When you left—when I realized what I'd done to make you leave—" he hastily amended "—I hit rock bottom. I finally accepted that I couldn't fix everything on my own. I went to an AA meeting, then I found a counselor who specializes in anger management, and I turned my life around."

"If that's true, I'm glad."

"It is true. But I couldn't have done any of it without Genevieve."

"Genevieve Durand?" She'd met the woman, whose family had been close friends of the Winchester family for years, on several occasions. But she'd never thought that Genevieve and Elliott were particularly friendly.

"Well, she's Genevieve Winchester now."

She just stared at him, still not comprehending.

Elliott's easy smile faded. "You didn't know?"

"Know what?"

"I got married. Four months ago."

"Oh. Well…congratulations."

"I'm sorry—I honestly thought you knew. The engagement announcement was in both the *Globe* and the *Herald*."

She shook her head. "I've been out of town. I didn't know."

If she had known, she might not have stressed for so long

about the possibility that he might want to reconcile for the sake of their child. The child who was, of course, the reason she'd needed to see him today.

"Does Genevieve know what happened between us?"

"I told her everything."

"Not quite everything," she countered.

Elliott's gaze narrowed. "What do you mean?"

She blew out a breath. "I had a child," she finally said. "He was born the first of November."

Chapter Fifteen

It went against every instinct Luke possessed to let Julie meet with her former fiancé by herself. He understood why she wanted to do so, but he didn't like it. And if she left that meeting with even one hair on her head out of place, the aspiring politician was going to be very sorry.

He'd been tempted to follow her, to lurk behind a potted plant in the restaurant or hover at the wine bar. And maybe she suspected that he would do something like that because she'd left Caden in his care. Or maybe she just didn't want the baby anywhere near his biological father.

Julie never referred to Elliott as Caden's father. As far as she was concerned, he might have contributed to her son's DNA but that didn't make him his father. Lukas agreed that biology was only part of the equation, because while there was absolutely no genetic link between him and the little boy, there was an undeniable connection. And there wasn't anything he wouldn't do for the child—or his mother.

Which was undoubtedly why he ended up babysitting while Julie went to meet with the man she'd once planned to marry. The man who had used physical strength and threats to intimidate her.

Thankfully, she'd been strong enough to break away from Elliott. And while he understood that she wanted to prove that she could stand on her own two feet, he suspected that she'd also wanted to keep Luke a safe distance from her ex. Because if he came face-to-face with the man who had dared laid a hand on Julie, Luke knew it was entirely possible that he'd end up in jail on an assault charge.

Which reminded him of one more thing that he wanted to take care of while they were in town.

He'd dropped her off at the restaurant where she was meeting Elliott, and it turned out that the Courtland Hotel was conveniently located across the street from the DA's office. And by the time she called for him to pick her up, he'd made the necessary calls and contacts.

He very nearly forgot the plan when she came down the steps from the hotel lobby, her cheeks flushed, her eyes glowing. Just looking at her took his breath away. And when she planted her lips on his and kissed him, long and hard, right in the middle of the sidewalk, she took his breath away all over again.

"You look...happy."

"I am." She took Caden from his arms and held him close for a minute. "Thank you."

"For what?"

"For coming with me—and for staying away."

"You're welcome," he said dryly.

She grinned. "I've got something to show you."

"Here?" He looked pointedly at the pedestrians moving around them.

"Right here, right now," she said, and pulled a manila envelope out of her purse.

His curiosity undeniably piqued, Luke opened the flap and took out the papers inside. It was a formal legal document prepared, he noted, by Jackson Garrett. As he skimmed through the legalese, certain key phrases caught his attention, most notably "acknowledgment of paternity" and "voluntary relinquishment of parental rights." And it was duly signed and dated by Elliott Davis Winchester III.

"Why are you frowning?" Julie asked him.

He hadn't realized that he was, but he couldn't deny that he was a little perturbed by this unexpected turn of events. "I can't believe that he signed away his legal rights without ever seeing his child."

"I knew he'd be worried about the potential scandal of having an out-of-wedlock child. It turns out, that's only half of it."

"What's the other half?"

"His wife is pregnant."

"He's married?"

She nodded, apparently unfazed by the news. "They had a small, intimate ceremony in Boston four months ago."

"I guess it didn't take him long to get over his broken heart," he mused.

"I never thought I was the great love of his life, but I did think our relationship was about more than politics. But Elliott had a precise plan mapped out for his road to the House of Representatives, and finding a devoted wife was an important part of that plan—almost as important as his carefully documented ancestry and Ivy League education."

"Are you saying that when you left, he simply found an alternate bride?"

"And without much difficulty," she said. "Genevieve Durand's family and his have been close for a lot of years."

"Then I guess she knew what she was getting into."

She nodded.

"How do you feel about all of this?" he asked cautiously.

"Relieved. And ecstatic. My biggest worry was that he would try to make a claim on Caden—now I know that isn't a concern."

"What about his accusation against your father?"

"I didn't even think about that," she admitted. "And really, it doesn't matter anymore, because Elliott has nothing to gain by going public with his claim."

He stopped beside a two-story red brick building. "Don't you want to know if there's any truth to it?"

She looked at the writing on the glass door, then at him. "What are we doing here?"

"I thought, if you really wanted to put the past behind you, we should know exactly what's in that past."

"This is almost scarier than facing Elliott," she admitted.

He held out his hand.

After the briefest hesitation, she took it. And they walked into the DA's office together.

Nerves tangled in Julie's belly as Lukas chatted with the receptionist. After a few minutes, she led them down a long hallway to the conference room where Mr. Chasan was seated at the end of a long, glossy table, reviewing a file folder that was open in front of him.

He closed the cover when they entered and rose to his feet. "Harry Chasan," he said. "Former District Attorney, mostly retired now, but I hang around occasionally and consult on cases. I was hanging around today." He offered his hand to Lukas first, then to Julie, then smiled at Caden.

He gestured for them to sit, which they did. Julie didn't know what to say—she wasn't sure how Lukas had arranged this meeting or what information he'd given, so she let him take the lead.

"I was told that you were the prosecutor in the State of Massachusetts vs. Cosgrove case."

"I can't say the name rang any bells," Harry admitted. "But I pulled the file when your brother called to inquire about it, and sure enough, I was."

Julie looked at Lukas. Apparently he had no qualms about his brother pulling strings to help him get what he wanted. On the other hand, there was nothing unethical about one attorney contacting another for information about an old case.

"Do you remember it?"

"I do now." His gaze shifted from the file to Julie, and he nodded. "You've grown up, Miss Marlowe. I almost didn't recognize you."

She managed a smile. "It's been six years."

"A drop in the bucket when you get to be my age," he told her. "Can you tell me why you're digging into this now?"

"I just had some questions," she hedged.

"What kind of questions?"

"Mainly I wondered why I wasn't prosecuted."

"Insufficient evidence," he said bluntly.

"Who—" She swallowed. "Who made that decision?"

"I did."

"Did you, uh, consult with anyone about it?"

"Yeah, the idiot cop who arrested you."

She blinked at that.

"There wasn't any evidence to justify charges. You should have been released into your parents' custody as soon as you were brought in, but the arresting officer had a real hard-on about the fact that he'd busted a judge's kid." He shrugged apologetically. "Sorry, but there's no other way to describe it."

"So my father didn't pull any strings to get me released?"

Harry laughed at that. "Judge 'Morality' Marlowe? Not a chance."

"You didn't talk to him about the case at all?" she pressed.

"Sure I did. And Reg told me that I wasn't to do him any favors. If there was evidence to charge you, I should charge you.

"Between us now," he confided, "I think he was a little concerned about the path he could see you going down and thought a few hours in lockup might have done you some good. But I reviewed the evidence in this case the same way I would have any other, and the undisputed facts were that you went for a ride in a car that you didn't know was stolen. You made a bad choice, but you didn't commit a crime."

They shook hands with Harry again, thanked him for his time, and left the DA's office.

"I guess I owe you another thank-you," Julie said.

"Does that mean I get another kiss?"

"You're going to get a lot more kisses after we get back to my parents' place and get Caden settled down," she promised.

"When are your parents coming back?"

"Their flight is scheduled to get in to Boston at six-oh-five tomorrow morning, and it's about an hour and a half from the airport to our place." She glanced at her watch. "So we'll have the place to ourselves for about sixteen hours."

"Lead the way."

By the time they got back to the car, Caden was seriously fussing, so Julie fed and changed him before they started the drive to her parents. Sleepy and satisfied, the baby fell asleep within a few minutes. Fifteen minutes later, Luke pulled into the driveway of her parents' home.

He took Caden in his carrier while she gathered the diaper bag and her purse. Inside the door, he set down the carrier beside an antique chest so that he could take his shoes off. But he didn't get a chance before Julie pushed him back against the wall and started kissing him. A deep openmouthed kiss with full body contact. She teased him with her teeth and her tongue as she gyrated against him. And then, just as abruptly as she'd started, she stopped.

"That's just a prelude," she said, and turned away.

He snaked his arm around her waist and hauled her back against him.

"Two can play that game," he warned, and kissed her again, slowly and deeply, using his tongue in a teasing imitation of lovemaking until she moaned and shuddered against him.

"Julie?"

She jolted, dropping her hands from his shoulders and pushing him away. "Mom."

Luke closed his eyes and softly banged his forehead against the wall, cursing silently.

"I, uh, didn't think you were coming back until tomorrow," Julie said, crossing the room to embrace her mother.

The older woman's arms came around her daughter, and she held her close for a long moment. "We caught an earlier flight," she said. "And I'm so glad we did. I'm so glad you're home."

"It's good to see you, Mom. I missed you—so much."

Her mother blinked away the tears that had filled her eyes and turned her attention to Luke, who was hoping like hell she wouldn't notice that he was still partially aroused. Apparently being caught in an erotic lip-lock by a woman's mother wasn't quite humiliating enough to cool his ardor.

"And who is this?" she said, her tone decidedly less warm. "Is this the surprise you mentioned?"

"What? Oh, no. This is Lukas Garrett. Lukas, meet my mom, Lucinda Marlowe."

"I apologize, ma'am, for the, uh, situation you walked in on."

"I'm glad I wasn't ten minutes later." She took a few steps toward the staircase that led to the upper level. "Reginald— Julie's home."

"About that surprise," Julie began, just as her father came into the foyer.

There were more hugs and kisses and tears as Luke tried to blend into the elegant satin-striped wallpaper.

And then Caden woke up.

Several hours later, Julie took her overnight bag up to her childhood bedroom while Lukas was escorted by her father to the guest room on the opposite side and at the far end of the hall. After nursing Caden and settling him to sleep in his portable crib, she tiptoed down the hall in search of Lukas.

"I'm really sorry about this…arrangement," she told him.

"I'm not. In fact, I'm grateful they're not digging a hole in the backyard right now to bury my body."

"Maybe if it was the spring," she teased. "But this time of year, the ground's too hard for digging."

"Well, your brothers are supposed to be here en masse tomorrow. I'm sure between the three of them and your father, they'll figure something out."

She linked her arms behind his neck. "They'll figure out that I'm finally with the right man for me."

"Yeah, that's likely." His words dripped with sarcasm, but he wrapped his arms around her waist and drew her into his embrace.

"Seriously, I don't think either of my parents was as scandalized as you were," she teased.

"It's just that I'd hoped you'd have my ring on your finger instead of my tongue in your mouth when I met your parents for the first time."

"Actually, my dad was still upstairs when your tongue was in my mouth."

"Because that makes a lot of difference."

She laughed softly.

"I wanted to make a good impression."

"There's no doubt you made an impression," she assured him. "Now, about that ring you mentioned."

"You mean the ring you didn't want me to give you a few days ago?"

"If that's the same ring that I couldn't accept until I got my life in order, then yes."

"Are you saying you want it now?"

"I want the ring." She brushed her lips against his. "I want you."

"The ring's in my pocket," he told her.

"Really?" She immediately dropped her arms and began searching the pockets of his jeans, then she looked up at him and rolled her eyes. "It's *not* in your pocket."

"It's not? I was sure I put it there… Oh, right. It's in the pocket of my jacket."

She fisted her hands on her hips. "Are you going to give it to me—or have you changed your mind?"

He crossed to the wing chair in the corner, where he'd tossed his jacket, and retrieved the ring box from the pocket. "I haven't changed my mind," he assured her. "But I thought you might have reconsidered."

"Why would you think that?"

"Because Elliott is out of your life now, completely and forever. You don't have to worry about him making any claims on your baby, so you don't need a stand-in father for Caden."

"I never wanted a stand-in father for my son," she told him. "I want a real father for him. But that has nothing to do with my response to your proposal.

"I love my son, more than anything in this world. More than I ever thought it was possible to love another human being," she continued. "But I'm an old-fashioned girl at heart, Lukas. And I never would have agreed to marry you if I wasn't in love with you."

He felt as if an enormous weight had been lifted off of his

chest. "You told me you wouldn't fall in love with me," he reminded her.

"I didn't want to," she admitted. "But my heart had other plans."

He took the ring—a square cut diamond with smaller channel-set diamonds around the band—out of the box. "You really do love me?"

"I really do love you."

"And you want to marry me?"

She offered her left hand. "Yes, I want to marry you."

He slid the ring onto her finger, then dipped his head to kiss her.

There was no hesitation in her response, but when he eased his lips from hers, her brows drew together.

He rubbed a finger over the furrow. "Is something wrong?"

"Is something wrong?" she echoed. "Is that all you're going to say?"

One side of his mouth turned up, just a little. "What do you want me to say?"

"I'd kind of like to hear that you love me, too."

He skimmed his knuckles down her cheek. "Do you doubt it?"

"No," she admitted. "But it would still be nice to hear the words."

"I love you, Julie Marlowe." He brushed his lips against hers. Once. "With my whole heart—" twice "—for now and forever." And again.

She sighed happily. "Wow—that sounded even better than I expected."

"You'll probably get sick of hearing it," he warned. "Because I'm going to tell you every single day, for the rest of our lives."

"I'm looking forward to it." She snuggled closer to him. "It's hard to believe that only five weeks ago, I was stuck in my car in a ditch and thinking that things couldn't possibly get any worse. And then you tapped on my window, and changed everything."

"*You* changed everything for me," he told her. "You and Caden. Which reminds me—there was one more thing I wanted to ask you."

"What's that?"

"After we're married, will you let me adopt Caden so that I can be his father in every sense?"

Her eyes filled with tears. "You already are," she told him. "But yes, I would be thrilled if you adopted Caden."

"And maybe someday we could give him a little brother or sister?" Luke prompted.

She smiled, nodded. "I'd like that."

"But when we do start thinking about another child, could we try to plan it so that he or she will be due in the spring or summer?" he suggested.

"Why?"

"Because I don't want to chance you going into labor in the middle of another blizzard."

"You mean *you* don't want to have to deliver another baby," she accused.

"I'd rather not," he admitted.

She laughed. "I'll keep that in mind."

Epilogue

Julie stood at the window, her arms folded across her chest, watching the snow fall. Behind her, flames were flickering in the fireplace.

"I'm experiencing the oddest sense of déjà vu," she admitted to Lukas when he entered the family room.

"You said you wanted a white Christmas," he reminded her.

"I was hoping for a light dusting, just enough to make everything sparkly and pretty."

"Obviously Mother Nature had a different idea."

"So much for our plan to attend Christmas Eve church service," Julie noted.

He took her hand and drew her over to the sofa. Of course, Einstein tried to climb up, too, but settled when Julie reached down to scratch between his ears.

"Are you disappointed?" Lukas asked her.

"A little," she admitted. "It's one of my favorite Christmas traditions, and I wanted to share it with you and Caden."

"Next year," he promised. "And the year after that, and every year for the rest of our lives together."

"I like the sound of that."

"Me, too."

She settled into his arms. "I was thinking about a June wedding."

"June? That's six months away."

"A wedding takes time to plan."

"Ava managed to plan Jack and Kelly's wedding in a few weeks," he reminded her.

"And it was a beautiful wedding," Julie agreed. "But it's going to take some time for my mother to forgive me for not telling her that she was going to be a grandmother. I don't think she would ever forgive me if I deprived her of a proper wedding on top of that."

"I don't care about proper as long as it's legal. And my brother has connections at the courthouse—"

"No," she said firmly.

He sighed. "June? Really?"

"Maybe May."

"How about February?"

She shook her head. "Too soon, and the weather's too unpredictable." She tipped her head up to look at him. "Speaking of weather, I'm a little worried about my parents traveling through all this snow tomorrow."

"Your dad has an SUV with snow tires," he reminded her. "And as he assured you, no less than a dozen times, there's no way he and your mom are going to miss their first grandchild's first Christmas."

"I know they wanted us to spend the holiday in Springfield with them, but I wanted Caden's first Christmas to be here."

"No doubt it will be a Christmas to remember, with your parents and my brothers and their families all underfoot."

"It will be chaos tomorrow." And she was already looking forward to it. "But tonight—" she lifted her arms to link them around his neck "—it's just you and me."

"And Caden," he reminded her.

"Who has a full belly, a clean diaper and visions of sugar plums dancing in his head."

He dipped his head to nibble on her lips, and Julie's eyes started to close when she felt a swipe of tongue between her toes.

"And Einstein," she added, giggling when he licked her toes again.

Lukas went over to the Christmas tree and found a package with the dog's name on the tag. "Look, Einstein. Santa brought something for you, too."

He tore the paper off of the conical-shaped rubber toy that he'd prefilled with treats and offered it to him. Einstein raced across the room, his attention immediately and completely focused on the toy.

"That should keep him busy for a long time," Lukas said, returning to the sofa.

"And Caden will sleep for at least a couple of hours," Julie told him.

"If we have a couple of hours—" he brushed his lips over hers "—I have an idea."

His hands were already under her shirt, skimming over her skin, making her tremble.

"Am I going to like this idea?"

"I think so."

A long time later, snuggled in the warmth of his embrace, Julie knew that she had never been more blessed. Because she didn't just have their first Christmas as a real family to look forward to, but the rest of their lives together—and she knew the future was going to be a merry one.

* * * * *

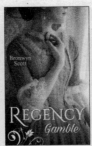

MILLS & BOON®

Why shop at millsandboon.co.uk?

Each year, thousands of romance readers find their perfect read at millsandboon.co.uk. That's because we're passionate about bringing you the very best romantic fiction. Here are some of the advantages of shopping at www.millsandboon.co.uk:

* **Get new books first**—you'll be able to buy your favourite books one month before they hit the shops

* **Get exclusive discounts**—you'll also be able to buy our specially created monthly collections, with up to 50% off the RRP

* **Find your favourite authors**—latest news, interviews and new releases for all your favourite authors and series on our website, plus ideas for what to try next

* **Join in**—once you've bought your favourite books, don't forget to register with us to rate, review and join in the discussions

Visit **www.millsandboon.co.uk**
for all this and more today!